Shelved Under Murder

Also available from Victoria Gilbert

A Murder for the Books

Shelved Under Murder

A BLUE RIDGE LIBRARY MYSTERY

Victoria Gilbert

CROOKED
LANE

NEW YORK

Published in the United States by Crooked Lane Books, an imprint of The Quick Brown Fox & Company LLC.

Crooked Lane Books and its logo are trademarks of The Quick Brown Fox & Company LLC.

Library of Congress Catalog-in-Publication data available upon request.

ISBN (hardcover): 978-1-68331-595-7
ISBN (ePub): 978-1-68331-596-4
ISBN (ePDF): 978-1-68331-597-1

Cover illustration by Cheryl Martucci.
Book design by Jennifer Canzone.

Printed in the United States.

www.crookedlanebooks.com

Crooked Lane Books
34 West 27th St., 10th Floor
New York, NY 10001

First Edition: July 2018

10 9 8 7 6 5 4 3 2 1

For My Husband

Kevin G. Weavil

Who thankfully loves books and
reading as much as I do.

"If you have a garden and a library, you have everything you need."

—Marcus Tullius Cicero

Chapter One

O ne thing every librarian learns is that people rarely ask the question they actually want answered.

"Do you have any books on art?" A high-pitched voice pierced the fog of my thoughts.

I looked up from the jumble of crocheted items donated for the library sale table at Taylorsford's annual Heritage Festival. Shelving my internal debate over whether bleaching would revive the dingy doilies, I crossed to the open door of the workroom. My assistant, Sunny, who was perched on a stool behind the built-in wooden circulation desk, glanced over at me, her golden eyebrows arching over her wide blue eyes. I shook my finger at her and mouthed, *Behave.*

Sunny turned away and focused on the patron, a young woman with dark hair highlighted with purple streaks. Not someone I'd seen in the Taylorsford library before, which meant she was either a new resident or a visitor.

Or perhaps she was a tourist. In October the streets of Taylorsford overflowed with visitors—many came simply to enjoy the autumn foliage, but most arrived for the Heritage Festival, which would be held the following weekend. A celebration of town history, the festival featured a wide variety of local artists and craftspeople as well as tours of old homes and nearby wineries.

"Art books? We have quite a few. Do you have a particular style or artist in mind?" Sunny's peacock-blue enameled bracelets jangled as she lifted her arm to shove a lock of her long blonde hair behind her ear.

"Well, yes." The patron eyed Sunny with a look I recognized—the suspicious stare of someone worried about being played. She was probably afraid narrowing her query would result in failure. "But I thought I'd just head to the general art section and poke around until I found what I wanted."

Sunny nodded. "You can do that. But if you have something specific in mind, I might be able to locate it quickly." She pointed at the Wonder Woman watch on her left wrist. "Might be helpful since you don't have much time today. It's four thirty and we close at five."

The young woman tugged on her large hoop earring. "It's probably too specific."

Aha, I'd been right. Miss Patron was convinced that her question was too obscure, when specific information was actually easier for an experienced researcher to find.

"Try me." Sunny flashed a bright smile.

"Well"—the patron toyed with the shoulder strap of her backpack—"it's this painter named Wynn. I can't remember his first name, and he's pretty recent, so I'm not sure you'll have anything . . ."

"So a younger artist? We should start with the periodicals then, but I'm sure we'll find something." Sunny slipped out from behind the desk. "This way." She headed for the stacks with one glance back over her shoulder. I gave her an encouraging smile. Of course she'd find something, if there was anything to be found. Having worked there several years before I became the library director, she knew our collections better than I did. She could often pluck requested materials from the shelves without even searching the online catalog.

I tapped my short fingernails against the oak circulation desk. Original to the 1919 library building, its grooved and pitted surface reflected its age. But the desk would not be replaced as long as I was in charge. Like the vaulted ceiling, deep-silled windows, and thick plaster walls, it exuded a well-worn elegance that could never be replicated.

After checking out some books and straightening the reshelving cart, I glanced at the wall clock. It was four forty-five, time to alert any remaining patrons that the library would close in fifteen minutes.

I walked through the main portion of the library, which was just one large room with a decorative mahogany arch dividing a reading area from the stacks. After straightening a display of library handouts, I cast a lingering glance at the NEW BOOKS rack. There were many recent books I longed to read, but I always forced myself to wait until they went into the general stacks, feeling it was more appropriate for our patrons to have first dibs on the newest materials. *Besides,* I chided myself, *you already have a stack of books threatening to topple off your nightstand.* I sighed as I contemplated the sad truth that in the years since I'd become a librarian, I'd actually read fewer books. My job required me to peruse tons of reviews to select items for the library, but it had become increasingly difficult to find time to read the books themselves. Despite what many people thought, librarians could rarely read at work. They were too busy helping patrons with research, acquiring and processing materials, and providing literacy tutoring and homework assistance.

As I circled around the shelves, I passed Sunny and the patron interested in art. "Find what you needed?" I asked.

"Yeah, great stuff." The girl clutched a sheaf of papers to her chest. "I had to make copies, though. Couldn't check anything out."

"There was nothing in the circulating collection anyway," Sunny said as she slid a copy of *Art in America* back into its slot in the current periodical rack.

"Sunny said the artist is too new to be listed in any books yet." The patron gave my assistant a grateful smile.

Sunny to the rescue once again. I made a mental note to remind the town council about her invaluable patron assistance. Maybe they'd finally see their way to giving her a raise. "Well, we open tomorrow morning at ten if you need to come back."

"Cool, but I think I've got what I need. Thanks, though." The girl stuffed the papers into her backpack. "Though I might want to come back later to look for something on that local artist, Rachel LeBlanc. I'm trying to complete several projects at once."

"You're at Clarion University?" I asked, then wondered if I'd misread her age. She looked too old to be in high school, but I'd guessed wrong before.

"Yeah. My roommate's family lives here and she comes home every weekend. It's only a thirty-minute drive, you know."

I knew that only too well, since I'd worked at Clarion until about a year and a half ago. But I just nodded.

"My roommate invited me for a visit just to get away from campus for a few days. Also, it's a chance to eat real food for a change." The girl's grin made her look instantly younger. "I guess I should've done the research at the campus library, but"—she hoisted her backpack straps over her shoulders—"I never got around to it."

"It happens," I said. "Anyway, you're always welcome here, although we don't have the resources the university library can provide."

"That's okay. It's just short reports, no big deal."

"By the way, I happen to know Rachel LeBlanc," Sunny volunteered. "Maybe I can snag you an interview."

The girl's kohl-rimmed eyes widened. "Really? That would be great."

"Can't promise, but I'll do my best." Sunny motioned toward the front doors. "Unfortunately, now we have to ask you to leave. It's closing time."

"Oh yeah, sure." The girl strode off, pausing to thank Sunny again before she pushed through the inner doors and into the foyer.

Sunny glanced back at me. "All clear in here. Did you check the children's room?"

"No, but I'll do that now. Richard's waiting for me in there anyway."

"In the children's room? What's he doing reading kids' books?"

"Research. Remember—he got that grant to create a new piece?"

"Oh, right, he's choreographing something to be performed at public schools." Sunny absently twirled her bracelets around her slender wrist. "I guess it's like that production of *Peter and the Wolf* they brought to my elementary school once. I was bored, to be honest. Now, if it had been a show with Richard dancing, I'd pay attention, believe me."

"Sadly, he's not going to perform. His teaching schedule at the university won't allow for that. But the piece is going to be danced by the seniors in his studio at Clarion, which is a great opportunity for them. He just wanted to look at picture books for inspiration. He claims illustrations sometimes spark ideas."

"Makes sense. Okay, you collect Richard and I'll shut down the circ computer." Sunny headed for the main desk as I made my way to the children's room.

Crossing into the annex meant stepping from early-twentieth-century elegance into late-1970s functionality. The children's room had been an addition to the original historic library, and its sheetrock walls and stained ceiling tiles betrayed the cost-cutting associated with its construction. Sunny and I had tried to enliven the space with posters and mobiles and other decorations, but I still always felt as if I were walking back into my public elementary school. The scent of chalk dust wafting from a blackboard that covered part of one wall only added to this impression.

Just inside the door I ran into one of our frequent patrons, Samantha Green, who often brought her young daughter, Shay, to the library.

"Sorry, it's closing time," I said, after a quick glance revealed no additional patrons. I frowned, wondering where Richard was.

Samantha laid her hand on my arm. "Just a little bit longer, please." Her voice broke on the last word.

I examined her face more closely and noticed the tears filling her brown eyes. "Anything wrong?"

"Yes and no. Not now. But if you could give them a minute." She gestured toward one of the chest-high sections of shelving.

I walked around the shelf, Samantha following on my heels. Richard was kneeling in the center of a geometric-patterned rug, talking quietly to the rather plump young girl who stood before him.

Samantha tapped my arm. "Shay was in here with some other girls," she whispered. "They were reading books about dancers and Shay said she wanted to be a ballerina and they said she couldn't. So she tried to do a little turn and fell and they . . . Well, they all laughed and she cried."

So, of course, Richard would try to comfort her. Of course he would.

Shay raised her voice to reply to something Richard had murmured. "But they said I was too fat."

I sucked in a sharp breath, knowing how this statement might affect him. One of his dearest friends had fled the dance world and disappeared from his life because she'd been told she was too large to succeed as a professional dancer.

"That's ridiculous." Richard's pleasant expression displayed none of the pain I suspected he felt. "Anyone can dance. Doesn't matter what size you are."

Shay rubbed her pudgy hand under her runny nose. "And they said ballerinas have to be white."

Anger flashed in Richard's clear gray eyes. "That's nonsense too. You shouldn't pay any attention to those girls—they're far too silly. Do you have a computer at home? With the Internet?"

Shay bobbed her head.

7

"Well then, you tell your mom"—Richard glanced over at Samantha, his face brightening when he made eye contact with me—"to look up videos featuring Misty Copeland, Yuan Yuan Tan, or Thaina Silva. You'll see you don't need to be white or tiny to be a ballerina."

Samantha gave him a thumbs-up gesture.

"Now"—Richard gracefully rose to his feet—"I think the real problem with the turn was that you didn't have a partner. Every ballerina needs her cavalier." He held out his hand.

When Shay shyly clasped his fingers, he lifted her arm above her head. "Try that pirouette again."

It was more of a shuffle around on two feet than a pirouette, but with Richard keeping her balanced, Shay was able to complete a full turn.

"There you go," he said, dropping her hand and executing a little bow.

I felt as if one of those heavy dodge balls from elementary school had just hit me in the chest. Every time I didn't think I could love Richard more . . .

Shay grinned and ran to her mother. "Did you see, Mama? Did you see?"

"I did," Samantha hugged her daughter. "But we have to go. They need to close up."

A smile lit up Shay's face. "Will you come back to the library again?" she asked Richard.

"I'm sure I will," he told her, his gaze fixed on me.

As mother and daughter left the room hand in hand, I crossed to Richard and flung my arms around him.

"Oof." He obviously hadn't anticipated the force of my hug.

But he recovered immediately and pulled me closer. "Now that's what I call a proper welcome."

"You just have to find ways to make me love you more, don't you?" I tipped back my head so I could look up into his face.

"One of my many talents," he replied with a grin, then gave me the kind of kiss I doubted had ever been seen in the children's room before.

A dramatic cough brought me back to my senses.

"Sorry to interrupt, but everything's shut down and the doors are locked, so I'm heading out."

Richard and I stepped away from each other and turned to the open doorway, where Sunny stood, a broad grin illuminating her face.

"Okay, sure." I tugged down my rumpled sweater.

Sunny tipped her head to one side and looked us over. "So, date night?"

"Just grabbing some dinner," I said.

"Then back to my place." Richard slid his arm around my waist.

"What about you?" I asked Sunny. "Meeting up with Brad or what?"

"No, he has to work. The sheriff's office is so short-staffed these days he's always pulling extra shifts. One of the problems with being the chief deputy, I guess. But anyway, I have to run an errand." Sunny slid her fingers through her silky hair. "Oh, yeah, I forgot to tell you—I scored a real coup. One that's sure to make Mel Riley happy."

"Something can actually do that?" I made a face. Melody

Riley, the new chair of the Taylorsford Friends of the Library, was notoriously hard to please.

"This can. You know how she goes on and on about wanting real, high-quality art and crafts for the library table at the festival? Well, I convinced Rachel LeBlanc to donate three paintings."

"Really?" Richard asked. "How'd you manage that?"

Like Richard, I was impressed. I had never met Rachel LeBlanc, but I knew about her international reputation as a painter. She'd moved back to Taylorsford from New York after inheriting her parents' farm ten years ago. Her studio and gallery, located in a converted barn on her property, was one of Taylorsford's popular tourist attractions.

"I just asked. She's very nice, you know. Not snooty or anything. Remember, Amy, when I took some painting lessons from her husband, Maurice? Well, Reese, as he likes to be called."

"Yeah, I remember. You said he's a great teacher, although he doesn't have Rachel's fame."

"I don't know why that is, exactly. I love his work," Sunny said. "But I guess he's more of a brilliant technician while Rachel has the unique vision. Reese can teach all kinds of styles, though, and I don't think Rachel could ever do that. She has her own signature style, and it's pretty distinctive. Anyway, one day after class, Reese introduced us, and Rachel and I hit it off. We've met up for lunch a few times since, so I thought, why not ask?"

"I'm sure if anyone could convince an artist to donate expensive paintings, it would be you," Richard said.

Sunny's bracelets jangled as she waved her hand. "Oh, it wasn't hard. Rachel's a real sweetheart and thinks supporting the library is important. My only worry at this point is whether three of her paintings will fit in the Bug."

"Yeah, aren't her paintings usually large?" I asked.

"Thus my dilemma."

"Easy enough to solve. We can follow you to the LeBlanc farm and transport one or two of the paintings in my car." Richard glanced down at me. "Is that okay?"

"Of course." I gave his waist a squeeze. "It's for the library sale, after all."

"I don't want to interfere with your plans," Sunny said, but her face visibly brightened.

"Not a problem. Maybe we'll just grab some takeout from that new Chinese place and head back home." Richard met my approving gaze. "We can even store a couple of the paintings at my house. I'll cart them over here before the sale."

"Well . . ." Sunny twirled a strand of her golden hair around one finger. "It would make things easier for me. But I hate to mess up your evening."

"Don't be silly. We're happy to help," I said.

Richard hugged me a little closer. "All for a good cause. Besides, I'll still be spending time with Amy and will have the added benefit of your company."

Sunny, heading for the back door, glanced over her shoulder. "You really must stop being so charming, Richard. It makes other men look bad."

Chapter Two

Although neither Richard nor I had ever visited the LeBlanc farm before, following Sunny's Volkswagen Beetle, with its canary-yellow paint job, was easy enough. Right outside of town we turned onto a side road that led up into the mountains.

"At least it's paved," Richard said as he sped up to keep pace with Sunny.

I nodded. "Yeah, I'm glad to be spared the bouncing." Many of the smaller roads near Taylorsford were dirt and gravel. Navigating their rutted surface felt like driving over an antique washboard.

"But narrow." Richard squinted and tightened his grip on the steering wheel. "Doesn't the county realize we've moved beyond the horse-and-buggy era? Two smaller cars could barely pass each other, so how the hell do those huge SUVs I see all around town manage it?"

"Okay, cool your jets, city boy." I shot him a grin. "I assume these roads were once just packed-dirt paths. Lucky for you that the county paved some of them."

"Lucky for my shocks."

"Uh-oh, looks like you spoke too soon," I said, as Sunny's Bug turned onto a gravel road.

Richard frowned but followed her. "I haven't met the LeBlancs yet. Have you?"

"No." The car hit a particularly deep rut, and I pressed my right hand against the locked passenger side door to steady myself. "I've actually spoken with the daughter, though. She's done some research in the library for her community college classes."

Richard glanced over at me. "Oh right, the daughter. Sunny mentioned her to me once when we were talking about issues I sometimes have with students at Clarion. I often refer students for help with addiction issues, so Sunny asked if I knew of any non-university programs for recovering drug addicts. Apparently the LeBlancs' daughter has had problems. Delilah, isn't it?"

"Yeah, but she goes by Lila." I looked over at him, admiring his rugged but handsome profile. "You keep helping out and you're going to develop quite a reputation."

Richard laughed. "Always my problem. Do-gooder for life. Hope you don't mind."

"Not at all. It's one of the many things I love about you. Like what you did for Shay. That was so sweet."

A faint blush tinted Richard's cheeks. "You know how I feel about that sort of thing. Children shouldn't be told they can't do something just because of the way they look. Nobody should, really."

"Yeah, but it was sweet anyway. You're good with kids. I've noticed that." As soon as the words left my mouth, I stared out my car window as if entranced by the vivid fall foliage. We'd never discussed the topic of children, and I was afraid I might be overstepping the bounds of our relationship.

"I like them. So much energy and potential. I wouldn't mind one or two of my own, to be honest. Hopefully more than one. Being an only child, I think it would be nice to have siblings. How about you?"

I turned my head slowly to meet his sidelong glance. "I have a sibling, if you recall."

"You know that's not what I meant. I'm asking if you'd like to have kids." He stared back at the road, his attention apparently fixed on the bumper of Sunny's car.

"Never really gave it a lot of thought."

"You're not one of those girls who's already planned out her future family and all that?"

"I've never even fantasized about a wedding," I said, surprising myself with the truth of this revelation. "I don't know why, exactly. I guess I was afraid if I fixated on such things, I'd be crushed if they didn't happen."

"Honest as always." Richard cast me a warm smile before turning his focus back to the road. "But I don't think you have to worry . . ."

Sunny's car turned onto a paved driveway. "Oh look, we're here." I motioned toward a wooden sign hanging from a cleverly designed frame that resembled an artist's easel. " 'LeBlanc Studio and Gallery,' " I read aloud.

Alternating stands of dogwood and sugar maples lined the paved driveway. *Spring blossoms and fall foliage*, I thought. *No doubt planted with an artist's eye for color.* Rain earlier in the day had washed away any dust, and the autumn leaves gleamed, a vibrant tapestry of crimson and gold. The long ribbon of blacktop curved picturesquely—just enough to give the sense of changing views without any hairpin turns. As we approached the end of the drive, the trees gave way to carefully composed beds of shrubs and flowers. We followed Sunny's car to a barn that looked too pristine to store hay or house livestock. Its freshly painted white trim glowed against blood-red siding.

"Good thing they don't pretend to be a working farm, 'cause this looks nothing like one."

"What gives that away?" Richard allowed the car to idle while Sunny parked her Bug and jumped out.

"No farm equipment anywhere, for one thing," I said. "And there's that lovely flagstone patio right outside the main barn doors—complete with vine-covered pergola. I'd bet money there are also twinkly lights threaded through those leaves. That sort of thing isn't typical for most working farms."

"As a city boy, I'll take your word for it." Richard shot me a grin before lowering his window to speak to Sunny. "Okay to park here?"

"Yeah, that's fine." Sunny stepped back and turned to look at the sliding barn doors, which were pushed back just far enough to allow one person to slip through. "Maybe I should run up to the house and see if Rachel's there." She frowned. "That half-shut thing worries me. They usually either open the doors completely or close them tight."

Richard turned off the engine and popped open his door. "Why don't Amy and I head into the barn to see if anyone's there while you check at the house? You know, double team it."

"Sure thing." Sunny turned away and headed for a flagstone path that disappeared into a stand of trees and shrubs hiding the house from view.

I climbed out of the car and crossed the small circle of pavement to join Richard at the barn doors.

"See—fancy." I pointed at the adjacent terrace. There *were* tiny clear Christmas lights entwined through the rain-washed clematis vines covering the pergola.

Richard's gaze followed my gesture. "I hear they use that area to serve the appetizers and wine at gallery events." He shrugged when I shot him a questioning look. "A friend of mine from Clarion got invited to one of the openings and told me about it. He said the LeBlancs also rent the barn out for events. Like receptions of one kind or another."

"And why did your friend think to mention that?"

Richard, pushing back one of the barn doors to widen the opening, didn't look at me. "I might have said something to them about wedding venues. You know, in passing."

"Uh-huh. Just happened to be talking about such things?"

He flashed me a wide grin. "Exactly. Now, shall we head inside? The sooner we collect the donations, the sooner we can grab dinner and get home." He slipped through the open doors.

"Where I expect you to explain a bit more about these random wedding reception comments," I said, following him into the barn.

In contrast to the dark, weathered wood of most working farm buildings, the cream-painted woodwork lent the space an airy feeling. But I was still thinking *barn* and blinked in surprise at the light spilling from the large windows that filled the top half of one of the long walls. *Northern light. Artists prefer that for their studios.* I remembered that tidbit from one of my college art history courses.

"Ms. LeBlanc?" I called out as Richard and I walked deeper

into the barn. "It's Amy Webber, the Taylorsford library director. I work with Sunshine Fields, and I'm here with Sunny and our friend, Richard Muir, to collect your donations for the festival."

There was no answer. "Seems Sunny was right to check the house." Richard wrinkled his nose. "What is that smell?"

"Rachel must've forgotten to cover her container of linseed oil," I said, as the pungent odor assailed my nose.

Richard made a face. "It sure stinks. Makes the place smell like old cooking oil. What's it used for?"

I rubbed my hand under my nose. "Thinning pigments and enhancing their gloss. It's commonly used with oil paints. But it's odd that Rachel didn't seal the container or cover it with something. Maybe she just stepped out?"

"Could be." Richard glanced up at the ceiling. "Look at that. Does she sculpt too?"

"No, that's probably her husband's work."

A gigantic mobile created from fencing wire and bits of old metal tools hung from the rafters. It resembled a lumbering sea monster moving underwater as it spun slowly among the dust motes floating in the light.

"Interesting," Richard said. "Look at that play of dancing shadows."

"Are you mentally making notes to use that idea in your choreography?"

Richard looked down at me with a smile. "Yeah, always thinking about that." He slid his arm around my shoulders. "It seems you can read my mind now. That could be scary."

I bumped his hip with mine. "Don't be silly—I didn't need to read your thoughts. Your fascination with any kind of unusual movement is pretty obvious."

Richard leaned in to kiss my temple before releasing me. "Fair enough." He scanned the barn. "I don't think anyone is here, so I guess we just wait for Sunny to bring Rachel from the house. But I think I'd like to take a look at those paintings first."

He gestured toward a circle of tall easels interspersed with small tables laden with art supplies. I assumed this was the area where Reese LeBlanc gave his art lessons. My gaze darted from the easels to the standing partitions lining one side of the barn. A collection of paintings and drawings covered the partitions, each piece as neatly labeled as works hung on museum walls.

One painting in particular caught my eye—a vibrant mosaic of color and dancing lines. As Richard walked around the circle of easels looking for an entry point, I took a detour to examine the work more closely.

As I suspected, it was signed by Rachel LeBlanc. I glanced at the label next to the painting, which simply read "Mountain Fall." I stepped back to get a better overall view of the painting and realized that this work somehow captured the essence of Taylorsford's autumn foliage better than a more realistic depiction ever could.

I stared at the painting for a few moments marveling, as I always did when studying works of this quality, at the magic of art. Someone—a human just like me—had used brushes and paint to create something from no more than what all other humans possessed—a brain, eyes, and hands. Yet the alchemy of their talent could take these tools and transform a blank canvas into something magnificent.

As I stepped closer to examine the brushstrokes, I felt a slight breeze, as if someone had stepped up beside me. A quick glance showed no one there, and I realized that it was just that feeling

I got sometimes when visiting art galleries. While contemplating paintings, I'd occasionally experienced moments of disorientation. I described it as a slippage of time—a feeling that the artist was standing beside me. I always explained this away by saying that it was simply me sensing their spirit in their work, as vivid as the day they'd signed the canvas.

I'd gotten used to this little peculiarity, writing it off as something arising from my overactive imagination. But this time I shivered. It *was* odd to feel that sensation in this instance. In the past it had only happened when the artist was deceased.

A string of expletives rang through the air. I spun on my heel and ran, shoving aside a table as I dashed into the circle to reach Richard's side.

He stared at the paint-spattered floor, his arms held stiffly at his sides and his fingers clenched into fists. Following his gaze, I spied a mug flipped over on its side on the small table placed beside one easel. Linseed oil—the obvious cause of the odor filling the barn—dripped down the legs of the table and pooled on the floor, lapping up against the fingers of a limp brown hand.

A strangled squeak escaped my lips. The body attached to the hand was hidden behind a large table draped in muslin.

"We shouldn't touch anything," I said, reaching for Richard's hand.

The rest of the body was revealed as we stepped around the table. Crumpled on her side, with her knees drawn up in a defensive posture, was a middle-aged woman. Her eyes were closed and her thin face partially veiled by locks of curly dark hair. I gripped Richard's fingers tighter. As my mind attempted to process the scene, I noticed that the fingertips of the artist's other hand brushed a palette knife that glistened as if it had been soaked in the oil and wiped clean.

The woman lay there so quietly, it was as if she were merely napping. For a moment I could imagine her grasping the knife and rising to her feet to resume work on the canvas sitting on the easel. But the crimson stains blossoming like roses against her white painter's smock told another story.

Rachel LeBlanc would not finish her latest work. In fact, she would never complete a painting again.

Chapter Three

Richard gently tugged me backward. "I'll call 911," he said, releasing his grip on my hand. "This is Rachel LeBlanc, I assume?"

I nodded. "Yes." Although I'd never met the woman, I recognized her face from online photos. I'd also seen her daughter often enough to catch the resemblance.

Lila. I bit the inside of my cheek. I hoped the girl wasn't at the house, or if she was, wouldn't accompany Sunny back to the barn.

"At the LeBlanc farm," Richard told the dispatcher. "And yes, this is Richard Muir. Again." He looked over at me, his eyebrows raised.

Again. No wonder they questioned that. Another murder, and you and Richard had to be the ones to find the body. Does sound peculiar.

My thoughts flew back several months, to the events of the past summer, when Richard and I had become entangled in another murder investigation. Stumbling over one dead body in a small town like Taylorsford was odd enough; now we'd found another? It was beginning to seem suspicious, even to me.

"They're sending out a team right away." Richard pocketed his phone. "They said we need to remain in place and do nothing until the authorities arrive."

"But we should warn Sunny not to come in. Especially if she has Lila with her."

"Right, the daughter." Richard ran his fingers through his dark hair, then pressed his palms against his temples as if attempting to hold his thoughts together. "All right, let's wait at the entrance so we can head them off."

Richard carefully stepped around one of the easels before striding to the open barn doors. I followed, jogging to keep up with his longer strides. When we reached the entrance, I turned to him.

"We must have some bad karma, stumbling over two dead bodies in less than six months."

"Or just a gift for trouble." He pulled me into a hug. "Don't start thinking this means we're cursed or something."

I tapped my finger against his chest. "I'm not superstitious like that. It's just a weird coincidence is all. Although Sunny might think there's some karmic reason . . ."

"Hmmmm, probably." Richard adjusted his hold on me so he could look down into my face. "How're you holding up? I'm feeling pretty awful myself."

"No one would know, with that brave front of yours." I stroked the side of his face with the back of my hand. "I'm okay. It's probably shock. But be prepared—I'll undoubtedly blubber like a baby later."

"I'll make sure to have lots of tissues handy." Richard's gaze moved up and over my shoulder. "Uh-oh, here comes Sunny. Alone, thank goodness."

I stepped outside to allow him to block the doorway with his body.

As Sunny stopped short in front of Richard, her smile looked a bit forced. I put this down to her being tired after a long day at work. "Rachel wasn't at the house. Just Lila, and I apparently woke her up. She was, as they say, dazed and confused."

Sunny attempted to slide past Richard, but he stopped her with his extended arm.

"What in the world?" Sunny looked us both up and down, wrinkling her brow.

I held up both hands, palms out. "Don't come in. I don't want you mixed up in another one of these things."

"Another one of what things?" Sunny's normally bright eyes were clouded with concern.

"Murder." Speaking that word broke something in me. I clenched my fingers and momentarily pressed my hands to my mouth to prevent a shriek of protest.

Sunny gasped. "What? Who?"

"Rachel LeBlanc. She's in there." I jerked my head to indicate the interior of the barn. "Stabbed, it looks like. With a palette knife, of all things."

Sunny didn't move, but the twitch in her hands betrayed her. Richard threw his arms around her shoulders as her knees buckled.

"Hang on," he said, holding her upright.

"Lila's at the house." Sunny's chattering teeth turned her words into staccato bursts. "And someone ran away . . ."

"What?" Richard slid his hands down her arms and loosely held her wrists.

Sunny pulled her hands free. "I saw someone." She stepped back and slumped against one of the pergola's supports.

I grabbed the hem of my sweater and twisted the soft wool between my fingers. "Saw who?"

"Someone running away. No one answered the front door, so I went around back and was almost knocked over by a guy fleeing into the woods."

"He came from the house?"

"Yeah, back door. I couldn't see him very clearly because he was wearing a hoodie, but I think it was Caden Kroft."

"The guitar kid?" I'd seen Caden busking around Taylorsford, something Mayor Bob Blackstone had unsuccessfully tried to stop. Apparently there was currently nothing in the town bylaws prohibiting street performers, although I was sure the mayor was working to change that.

"Was Lila . . ." Richard tented his fingers and pressed them to his lips for a moment before speaking again. "Did she look like she was on something? I know you told me she's had problems in the past."

Sunny lifted her chin and met Richard's intent gaze. "Yeah, I'm afraid she was. And Caden, well, he's kind of known to be a small-time dealer, so . . ."

"Oh God." I gripped the edge of the barn door. "They both could've been mixed up in this?"

"Maybe. No, I can't imagine . . ." Sunny dropped her head until her chin was pressed against her chest.

"We don't have to figure that out, thank goodness," Richard

said. "Although you'll have to tell the deputies about Lila's dazed appearance and Caden running off."

"I know." Sunny laced her fingers together so tightly her knuckles blanched.

Sirens wailed through the crisp autumn air. I gave Richard a quick glance before I crossed to Sunny. "Whatever happens, we're all in this together." I squeezed one of her shoulders. "We'll be right here with you."

"I know, thanks," she mumbled, before straightening and looking me in the eyes.

I sucked in a sharp breath. Shock and grief had altered Sunny's beautiful face. Her skin was pulled tight over her fine bones, and her blue eyes were glazed with tears.

A line of sheriff's department vehicles rounded the final corner of the driveway and screeched to a halt behind our cars.

"Here we go." I kept my hand on Sunny's shoulder as I focused on the tall, broad-shouldered, blond man who leapt from the lead car.

"Not you two again," said Chief Deputy Brad Tucker. "And Sunny?" He shoved his hat back from his forehead and expelled a gusty sigh.

"Sorry," I said. "But you don't need to interrogate Sunny extensively, as she hasn't been inside. Richard and I found the body."

Another deep sigh escaped Brad's lips as he motioned for several officers from the other cars to step forward. "Deputy Frye, come here. Coleman and I will question Mr. Muir and Ms. Webber, but you and Denton need to talk to Ms. Fields."

"Yes, sir." Alison Frye glanced up at Brad's face before she squared her shoulders and eyed Sunny with what looked like disapproval.

Oh, there's a wrinkle, I thought. That one glance had given the young deputy away. It was clear Alison had more than a collegial interest in her boss and wasn't impressed with his choice of girlfriend.

Sunny, whose confidence couldn't be shaken by such things, raised her voice. "Brad—I mean, Deputy Tucker—you should know that Lila LeBlanc is up at the house. Alone, at this point, although someone ran off when I approached the back door."

Brad strode over to her. "Where? And did you see who it was?"

"He disappeared into the woods behind the house. And, not really. He looked a little bit like Caden Kroft. I think Caden dated Lila in the past, although I'm pretty sure her parents never approved."

Brad spun around and shouted at the additional deputies who'd just pulled up and jumped out of their vehicles. He told several of them to search the woods and the perimeter of the property while ordering others to secure Lila at the house. "But don't interrogate the girl yet," he told them. "I want to be present for that. Don't ask any questions or tell her anything. Just keep her at the house."

He turned back to Sunny, his expression changing for a moment to one of concern. "Okay?" he asked softly.

She nodded. Brad's face hardened back into its professional mask as Alison Frye and the other young deputy reached him. While they led Sunny to a bench under one of the maple trees, Brad crossed to me.

"Now," Brad said, as he was joined by an older man in an

ill-fitting uniform. "Let's get your stories. Coleman, you take Mr. Muir's statement while I talk with Ms. Webber." He waved me toward one of the metal chairs under the pergola. "Coroner here yet?" he called out as another deputy approached the barn with an evidence case in one hand and a digital camera in the other.

"Right behind us."

"Well, don't do anything until he gets here. Take photos, of course, but don't touch anything."

"Sure thing, sir." The deputy with the camera disappeared into the barn, followed by another man in a suit. A plainclothes detective, no doubt.

"Okay, so let's start from the beginning," Brad said, fixing me with a piercing stare. "Why were you out here?"

I explained Sunny's errand and how Richard and I had offered to help. "It really was a last-minute thing. So definitely not premeditated." I twitched my lips into a smile, hoping my little quip would lighten the mood.

No such luck. Brad was a complete professional when he was on the job. I actually appreciated that, although I had to admit that his intense examination of my face was unnerving.

"So Sunny heads to the house, then you two go inside, find the body, and Richard calls 911. That's it?"

"Yeah. I did knock over a table, though. One of those small side tables. So that wasn't something the killer did." I frowned. "But we didn't touch anything else. That mug of linseed oil was already tipped over when we found the body. We even smelled it when we entered the barn."

"Okay." Brad tapped some information into his cell with a stylus. As he snapped the phone case shut, his expression softened. "Sorry you had to go through this again, Amy." He laid his hand over my wrist. "I really am."

I sniffled. His sympathy was actually more difficult to bear than his tough cop attitude. "You're going to think I'm bad luck or something."

"I don't believe in luck, bad or otherwise." Brad tugged his hat back down lower on his forehead. "We'll need you and Richard to come into the office for a more formal statement tomorrow, but I think I have enough for now."

Deputy Coleman had apparently finished questioning Richard too. As they both approached the terrace, the deputy paused at the edge while Richard stepped under the pergola and crossed to stand beside me.

"Can we let these two go home?" Coleman asked Brad. "It doesn't seem like they saw anything except the murder scene, and it might be easier to get more work done . . ."

"Yes, yes." Brad waved him off. "Send me your notes and then join the group searching the woods."

Coleman touched the rim of his hat and nodded sharply. "Will do, sir."

"So we can go?" I asked, rising to my feet and moving to Richard's side.

Brad looked us over. "Yes. Just come in tomorrow. Don't worry"—he cut me off as I opened my mouth again—"I'll make sure Sunny gets home safely. I won't let her drive alone."

"I know you'll take good care of her." My warm smile brought a slight flush to Brad's cheeks.

"And I'll take care of Amy." Richard slid his arm around my waist and guided me toward his car.

As he opened the passenger side door, the deputy with the

camera burst out of the barn, shouting for Brad. "Boss, you need to see this!"

Richard slammed the car door shut and grabbed my hand as we turned to stare at the flustered deputy.

"What is it?" Brad strode forward, his height making him loom over the man in the doorway. "Another body?"

"No, but maybe a motive. There's paintings in there. A whole slew of them."

"Well, of course there are. It's a gallery," Brad said.

The deputy shook his head. "Not those paintings. Others. Stashed in a hidden room. Detective Carver says they look like valuable stuff. Impressionists and that sort of thing. Well, according to Carver, anyway."

"What the hell?" Richard said under his breath.

Impressionists? I tightened my grip on Richard's fingers. That was impossible. As far as I knew, the LeBlancs did not deal in other artists' work and certainly not in expensive masterpieces. That sounded more like something that might involve local art dealer Kurt Kendrick.

Richard rubbed his chin with his free hand—a telltale sign that something was bothering him. "Why would any paintings owned by the LeBlancs be stashed in a secret room?"

"I can't imagine," I said. "Unless they were involved in some illegal activity no one knew about . . ."

Except perhaps Kurt Kendrick. My suspicions immediately fell upon the wealthy, extremely secretive art collector and dealer, who I knew was not above getting his hands dirty with some shady transactions. The fact that he owned an estate not far from this location unfurled several red flags in my brain.

"Amy, sorry, but could you do me a favor?" Brad asked.

I focused on him, noting how his tall, muscular figure filled the open barn doorway.

"I know I said you could go, but I wonder if you might take a look at this discovery." Brad jerked his head toward the interior of the barn. "You have a background in art history, right?"

"I majored in it as an undergrad, but I'm no real expert."

"I'm sure you know more than any of these guys. It'll be a few days before the state sends an official expert, so if you can just take a look and let me know if Carver is right in his assessment . . ."

"Okay," I said, although I had no desire to enter the barn again. I glanced up at Richard. "Come with me?"

He sighed. "I think dinner's going to be cold cuts back at the house at this point, but sure. If it's all right with Deputy Tucker, of course."

"That's fine." Brad waved us forward. "Just don't touch anything."

"Not really hungry now anyway," I said as we followed Brad into the barn.

We had to walk by the studio area, although fortunately we couldn't see Rachel's body. Any view of that was blocked by deputies, detectives, and the coroner.

"Prints?" I heard one of the detectives say. "Doubtful. Looks like our killer wiped down that palette knife with the spilled oil and a rag he or she probably took with them."

I shared a glance with Richard as we followed Brad and the camera-wielding deputy. *No prints*, I mouthed at him.

"Careful killer," he whispered back

Which got the wheels in my brain spinning. The use of the

palette knife made the murder appear not to be premeditated, but the wiping down of that knife indicated that the killer was not entirely thoughtless.

We reached the back of the barn and a large square column enclosing what looked like an old hay shaft—where bales would've once been tossed down from the hayloft above. But closer examination showed that the actual space was completely closed off, and the illusion of an open shaft had been achieved by a skillful trompe-l'oeil painting.

"Clever," Richard said, rapping his knuckles against the fake shaft.

Brad shot him a sharp glance. "Touch nothing, I said."

Richard clasped his hands behind his back.

"Right around the corner, sir," said a man in a severe navy suit. I assumed this was Detective Carver. He pointed to the side of the fake shaft with his latex-gloved hand. "Just seemed like regular boards at first, but when we saw that false front, we looked closer and found this." He slid his fingers over the rough surface until I heard a click and a hidden door popped open.

Brad held out his hand. "Light."

Carver slapped a flashlight into Brad's palm, then stepped back to allow me to stand next to the chief deputy.

The cool light of the LED flashlight flooded the small closet-sized space, illuminating rows of shelves filled with muslin-wrapped rectangles of various sizes. *Canvases*, I thought. Three or four had been placed on the floor, leaning against the lowest shelf. Their wraps had been thrown back, by Carver or the other deputy, I assumed, revealing vividly colored oil paintings.

I knelt down, ignoring the creak of the old floorboards.

"Morisot, Monet, de Chirico, Cézanne," I said, pointing at each canvas in turn. I sat back on my heels and gazed up at Brad's stern profile. "But these can't be real."

He frowned. "Because?"

"Because these are painters whose works are not going to be stuffed in a closet in a barn, even if it does function as an artist's studio and gallery. I mean, I don't know for sure, but I highly doubt it. Not all of them together like this, anyway."

Richard helped me to my feet. "So what do you think? Stolen and stashed before being sold on the black market? Or forgeries?"

"I don't know enough to say that. I can do some research to see if any of these match lost paintings from the artists' catalogs, but I suspect they're fakes. Really good fakes. But I'm not absolutely sure. You'll need someone who can verify their authenticity, one way or the other."

Brad fiddled with the gold badge on his uniform. "Could you do some research? I mean, before the art expert arrives? I would like to have a sense of what we might be dealing with before I move this stuff to another location. Or do anything else, for that matter."

"Sure, if you want." I glanced back into the small storeroom. "Someone had to know they were here. To have painted that fake front and all."

"One of the LeBlancs. Had to be." Richard stared at the paintings over my shoulder.

"Or Rachel's parents," I said. "They lived here before she and Reese did, and I know they had lots of connections in the community."

And were nearly broke at the end of their lives, I thought. *So perhaps someone like Kendrick offering them money to store stolen or forged goods . . .* I shook my head. Reese and Rachel had renovated the barn after they moved to Taylorsford. Surely they would have discovered a hidden closet then. Which just led back to one or both of them also being involved.

Brad narrowed his eyes "We can't jump to conclusions, but it seems more likely it was one of the LeBlancs. Speaking of which, we know where two of the family members are, but where's the husband?"

"Reese?" Sunny's voice sailed in from behind us. "Lila said he was off on some business trip. Not expected back until this afternoon."

Brad turned on her. "You shouldn't be in here, Sunny."

She slid past him to step into the secret room. "These aren't works by the LeBlancs, either one of them."

"No," I said. "They aren't. At least not something they would sign with their own names."

Sunny's blue eyes widened. "What are you saying? That they were involved in forgery?"

I shrugged. "Could be."

"I can't believe that," Sunny said, as Brad laid a hand on her shoulder.

"So if he was to return this afternoon, where is Maurice LeBlanc? The daughter claims she hasn't seen him?"

"No, but she told me she was sleeping." Sunny bit her lower lip. She was probably thinking the same thing I was—that Lila had been passed out in some sort of drug-induced stupor. "She said her dad often goes right to the studio to see her mom when he gets home from business trips, so she didn't think it was weird that he hadn't shown up at the house yet."

"Perhaps he did come here." Brad's gaze took in the entire interior of the barn.

"Strolled in, stabbed his wife, and then just blithely left again?" Sunny's tone conveyed her doubt over this theory.

"It's a ways to the house," Carver observed. "He could've driven up and had an altercation with the wife without the daughter hearing anything. Especially if she was asleep."

"Okay, enough speculation." Brad took a deep breath. "Carver, head to your vehicle and put out a BOLO on Maurice LeBlanc. We need to find him as soon as possible." He scratched at the back of his neck. "As well as that kid who ran into the woods. Could be Caden Kroft. Put out a lookout request on him too."

"Will do." Detective Carver strode off.

"Did you already document everything?" Brad asked the deputy with the camera.

"Yes, sir."

"Then join Carver. He can probably use some of the images for his report."

The deputy nodded and dashed off after the detective as Brad turned to me. "I'm going to send some photos to you as well. I assume Sunny has your cell phone number?"

"Of course. But it might be easier to send them to my email if they're large files, which I suspect they must be."

"Sure, sure. Just give the address to Deputy Coleman outside. And Sunny"—Brad turned to her and laid his hand on her arm—"tell Coleman he's to escort you home. No, don't argue. I don't want you driving yourself. Not after all this. I'll stop by the farm later to pick him up, since he won't have a car."

And then you can also check on Sunny, I thought. Which

didn't bother me in the least. I knew Brad, who loved her, would make sure my friend was properly comforted when the reality of the situation hit her.

"So *now* we can go?" Richard asked.

"Yes. Just show up at the sheriff's office tomorrow so we can make sure we have everything correct in your statements."

Sunny pressed her fingers over Brad's hand, which still rested on her arm. "What about you?"

"I"—Brad tugged his tie so hard it went askew—"have to go and tell a young woman that her mother is dead. And then question the girl unmercifully."

I cast him a sympathetic smile. Whatever I felt, it had to be nothing compared to the stress Brad was under.

"Can't say I envy you that," Richard said, gazing at Brad speculatively.

It had probably just dawned on him what Brad's job really entailed. I tapped his arm. "Come on, let's allow the experts to deal with this."

"Glad to." Richard bent his arms so that Sunny could slide her hand through one crooked elbow and I the other. With us flanking him, he headed out of the barn and into the deepening twilight of the autumn evening.

Chapter Four

I glanced toward my aunt's house as Richard parked in his driveway. *Your house too, Amy.* Yes, since I'd been living with my aunt for the past year and a half, her home was now mine as well.

After unbuckling my seat belt, I paused with my hand on the door latch. "Should we stop in and tell Aunt Lydia what's happened?"

Richard shot me a quick, raised-eyebrow glance. "Seriously? You know Zelda's probably already told her more about it than we could possibly know."

I couldn't restrain a chuckle. He was right—my aunt's best friend, Zelda Shoemaker, was the town's former postmaster and a font of local gossip.

"Besides, Lydia knows you were spending the evening with me, right? She won't expect you back early or worry if you don't show up."

"True."

"So let's just have this evening for ourselves." Richard got out and walked around to open my door. "After everything

36

that's happened today, we deserve it. We don't have enough alone time as it is."

"That's the jobs and stuff interfering," I said, climbing out of the car.

"Hmmmm . . . Is that all it is?" Richard gave me a searching look before leaning in to kiss me swiftly on the lips. "Come on, I'm starving."

As he headed for his front porch, I paused to look over the rose-vine-draped picket fence separating the two lawns. Aunt Lydia had promised I would eventually inherit her turn-of-the-century house, but I wasn't sure if I wanted to take on the three-story Victorian. Built of fieldstone, with white gingerbread trim, a wraparound front porch, and even a turret, it was the loveliest house in town. But it was also large—my aunt and I rattled around in it like seeds in a dried pea pod—and difficult to clean and maintain.

I switched my gaze to its neighbor—Richard's two-story 1923 farmhouse. Although equally charming, it was a more modest structure, with a covered porch that stretched across the front but didn't wrap around to the side. Its pale-yellow wood siding was set off by simple emerald green shutters and plain white trim. It wasn't as fancy, but perhaps it was the type of house I'd feel more comfortable living in long-term.

I shook my head to banish this train of thought. Richard and I had known each other for only five months. It was too soon to start thinking about living together. Or at least that's what my rational mind told my more impetuous heart on a regular basis.

"Coming?" Richard paused on his top porch step.

Studying him, I once again marveled at the unconscious

grace he projected with every movement. Of course, he was a professional dancer and had the perfectly toned body that went with his profession.

I walked around the car and onto the concrete sidewalk that bisected his small front yard. I'd hit the boyfriend jackpot and I knew it. Yes, Richard was handsome, but he was also one of the nicest men I'd ever met. As I approached his front porch, I realized I had twisted the bottom of my sweater around my hand. I released my clenched fingers, silently acknowledging the cause of my stress. It was true that I loved Richard and trusted him, but I'd been burnt before. I couldn't always banish that insidious, insecure voice in my head that whispered—*why did he choose you?*

Richard waited for me to join him before crossing to open the front door. "You have that look on your face again," he said as he stepped back to allow me to enter the house.

"What look is that?" I walked into a front room that encompassed the entire width of the house. Although there was a traditional seating area, most of the room was devoted to a dance floor, barre, and mirrors. It was Richard's home dance studio, the only part of the house that didn't respect its farmhouse origins.

"The uncertain one. Like you aren't quite sure of my intentions." Richard crossed to the sofa and sat down. He patted the seat cushion next to him. "So come here and let me reassure you."

"It's not that," I said, sitting beside him. "I'm a bit worried about the possibility of a local connection to art forgery or stolen paintings. Not to mention another murder. Pretty distressing."

I could tell by his skeptical expression that he didn't believe this was the entire story. Which, of course, it wasn't.

He placed his arm around my shoulders and pulled me close. "You and that overthinking again." His lips tickled my ear. "But yeah, stumbling over a dead body is never my idea of a good time."

"Poor Rachel. I wonder what in the world would make anyone want to kill her." I swallowed hard as the image of her bloodied body resurfaced in my mind.

"As you know from past experience, there doesn't have to be a rational reason." Richard's fingers stroked my shoulder. "It's not like your cousin's motivations really made much sense."

"So true." I pressed my body closer to Richard. There was no way I could forget the past summer and my frightening encounters with my murderous second-cousin-once-removed, Sylvia Baker. "Aunt Lydia visits her, you know. She says it's partially because Sylvia had the grace to take a plea and spare us all testifying at her trial."

"I'm glad she chose that route, but she did murder three people, so I can't say I'd be as forgiving as Lydia."

"I agree and keep telling her it isn't necessary, but she says Sylvia's still family, even if she's justifiably serving a couple of life sentences in the state pen."

"Lydia is one of a kind. As is her niece." Richard's fingers traced a line from my shoulder to just under my ear.

I shivered with delight. Despite my best intentions, when Richard touched me that way, I instantly melted. But . . . "You said you were hungry."

"I didn't say for what." He turned me toward him and kissed

me until the image of the horrible scene we'd witnessed earlier faded from my mind.

When he finally released me, he sat back and helped me readjust my rumpled sweater as his gray eyes studied my face. "But here I am, being a very bad host. I did promise you dinner. Any preference? I've got salad stuff and some sandwich makings."

"Um, I don't know. A salad would work, I guess."

Richard rose to his feet. "Help me chop?"

"Sure." I leapt up to follow him down the hall.

"I need to tell you something anyway," he called over his shoulder as he stepped into the farmhouse-style kitchen.

"Oh, is that why you were taking me out tonight? Wine and dine me and then drop the bad-news bomb?"

Richard paused at the tall oak table that served as his kitchen island and turned to face the double-door refrigerator. "No, I'd call it unfortunate news. Now"—he pulled open the fridge doors—"I'm going to rustle up some vegetation. Grab a couple of knives and two cutting boards. You know where they are."

"Are you certain you trust me with a knife when you're sharing bad news?" I joked as I collected the requested items.

"It's not *that* bad." He dumped leaf lettuce and other vegetables on the table. "Just disappointing. Besides"—he picked up the extra knife—"I'll be armed too."

"Ah, a duel is it?" I shook my knife at him. "*En garde.*"

I caught his swift grin as he bent his head to focus on tearing some leaf lettuce into bite-sized pieces. "I'm not into armed combat, but if it's hand-to-hand grappling you want, I'm certainly up for that later."

Which made me blush as red as the tomato I was dicing.

"Now you're just being provocative. So, for penance, spill your unfortunate information. Might as well—this day can't get much worse."

"I think it's already improving, but okay." Richard tossed the leaf lettuce into a large wooden bowl sitting on the table and reached for a stalk of celery. "Remember a few weeks back, when I had to go out of town to set one of my pieces on the Ad Astra Dance Company?"

"Yeah. You said they're performing it for some sort of benefit thing."

"It's a charity that provides money for dancers who've fallen on hard times. The organization gives out cash for things like rent and groceries when dancers are sick and injured. Insurance won't cover that stuff and, anyway, a lot of dancers don't even have coverage. I like to support the effort, especially because I've been in those particular shoes once or twice." Richard expertly sliced the celery into bite-sized pieces. "Well, in this piece the lead male part is very challenging . . ."

"Because you originally choreographed it for yourself?"

"Yep." Richard tipped his cutting board over the bowl, dumping the celery on top of the lettuce. "I thought it would be fine, as their lead dancer is great. The understudy has really struggled, but it's only three performances, so I didn't think he'd have to go on. Then I got a call last night from the artistic director. He said the lead has broken his foot and the understudy just can't handle the piece."

I looked up to meet Richard's apologetic gaze. "So now you have to fly up there and perform the part yourself."

"It's for charity," he said. "And only three nights, so I won't be gone that long."

41

I used my knife to sweep my bits of tomato into the bowl. "But it's *next* weekend, isn't it?"

"That's the unfortunate part. I know I promised to help you with the library table at the Heritage Festival, but . . ."

"It's okay." I grabbed a green pepper and forcefully sliced it in half.

"It isn't." Richard tapped his knife against the cutting board. "Hey, look at me. I really am sorry. I know how you hate manning that sales table."

I glanced up and noticed the worry lines creasing his forehead. "Don't give yourself wrinkles. It isn't that big of a thing. I mainly wanted you there as a buffer against Melody Riley. She's so bossy. It's her way or the highway. I was worried we might clash if we had to spend a whole day together."

"So you wanted me to run interference?"

I cast him a smile. "Something like that. I knew you could charm her much better than I ever could." I dumped the chopped green pepper into the bowl. "How about we just add some shredded cheese and call it a meal?"

"Sounds good. I think I may even have some hard-boiled eggs we can toss in for extra protein."

"Works for me," I said, as he turned back to the refrigerator. "And seriously, I really don't mind about the festival thing. I know you can't leave that company in the lurch, especially since the production benefits a charity. I'm actually more upset that I can't be there to support your performance, but you know I can't get away during the festival."

"Jobs always get in the way of life, don't they?" Richard tapped an egg against the side of the bowl and expertly peeled away the shell. "Anyway, I just want you to know that I hate letting you down. I like to keep my promises."

"But you're keeping one by dancing for the company, so I think that counts."

"Thanks, but I'm not sure it's enough. Disappointing you makes me feel lousy." Richard placed the peeled egg on the cutting board and examined it as if it held the answer to some existential question.

I circled around the table and threw my arms around his neck. "Let me see what I can do to change that."

Richard dropped the knife onto the table as I stood on tiptoe to kiss him.

"You do realize this means another delay with dinner," he said before his lips met mine.

* * *

After we finally finished our salads, Richard and I moved back to the sofa in the front room, supposedly to watch a movie, although I had to admit we saw very little of it.

"There is one more thing," Richard said as I sat up and stared at the end credits rolling over the large television screen mounted on the opposite wall.

"What's that?" I brushed back my mussed hair.

Richard rubbed at his jaw. *Uh-oh, this is not just a minor problem.* I sat up straighter.

He was staring at a point somewhere over my shoulder. "It's about the dance performance. I was told something else last night that I thought you should know. Just so you don't hear about it later and wonder. Anyway, apparently the lead female dancer they planned to feature is under the weather too, so they had to get a sub. And the only dancer available who knew the part well enough to step in at the last minute was Meredith."

"Wait—Meredith as in Meredith Fox, your former fiancée?"

"Yeah, that one." Richard's abashed expression would've been humorous if I hadn't been so taken by surprise.

"That could be tense." I bumped his knees with mine. "You never spoke to her again after she ran off and married someone else, did you?"

"No. So it might be an awkward reunion. But I don't want you to worry." Richard leaned in and clasped my hands. "It's not like I have any lingering romantic feelings for someone who ditched me without a word."

I blew a strand of tangled hair away from my face. "Oh, I'm not worried about that."

Strangely, I wasn't. I knew Richard well enough to trust that he wouldn't chase after someone who'd jilted him. Nor would he mess around with a married woman.

"She's married, and you've moved on, so I'm not going to get jealous, if that's what you're worried about."

"I'm not really worried." Richard caressed my fingers. "I just didn't want you to hear about it through a review or something and wonder why I didn't tell you."

"You won't have a problem dancing with her?"

"No. I've danced with plenty of people I've disliked without it affecting my performance. Anyway, I don't carry a grudge against Meredith. She actually did me a favor." He released my fingers to brush the recalcitrant lock of hair behind my ear.

"Can I ask a question, though? If it's too personal, just say so, but I've always been curious." I stroked the side of his face before dropping my hands back into my lap. "It's just a puzzle. You believe in love so much, yet I've never gotten the feeling that your relationship with Meredith was really that . . . substantial." I took a deep breath before continuing. This was something that had nagged at me for a while, but I'd never worked up the courage to broach the subject before. "Correct me if I'm wrong."

Richard leaned back against the arm of the sofa. "You aren't wrong. Our relationship was just this thing that happened. We liked some of the same things, had enough sexual attraction to enjoy each other, and were thrown together a lot. So I guess you could say we simply fell into a relationship. To be perfectly honest, even though we were engaged, I never actually proposed."

"What? You mean to tell me the world's greatest romantic didn't go down on one knee, surrounded by banks of flowers and strains of mood music, to present his beloved with a ring?"

A smile twitched Richard's lips. "Nope. Actually, I can't even remember how it happened. We'd moved in together, more as a convenience than anything else, and then people started asking when we were getting married and we said, 'Oh, someday,' and then it was like everyone just assumed we were engaged, so . . . we were." Richard shook his head. "But we would never have actually walked down the aisle. I know that now. Fortunately, Meredith saved me the trouble of breaking up with her, which was bound to happen eventually."

"You sound awfully sure of that."

"I am. Think about it, Amy. Even if Meredith hadn't left me and I hadn't moved here, I would've had to visit Taylorsford to oversee the maintenance on this house or check on my renters. And since you live next door, I would've met you, sooner or later. And then"—his bright gaze swept over me—"I would've felt compelled to immediately call off my engagement."

"You don't know that," I said, running my fingers over one of his well-muscled arms. "If you were still engaged, you might not have noticed me."

Richard laughed. "Silly girl." He pulled me into an embrace. "I would've noticed you no matter what. And fallen in love with you, because . . . because I was always going to love you. All we had to do was meet. Honestly, I'm grateful to Meredith. She spared me the pain of being the bad guy."

I rested my head against his shoulder. "Okay, if we're being totally honest, maybe I am a teensy bit worried about you working with her again. Just because she can really dance. So she can share something with you that I can't."

Richard stroked my hair. "Dancing is my profession, sweetheart, not my whole life. I love it, but at this point I'm realistic about stage-based relationships. They don't last, most of the time. Performing with other people is usually just that—performing. When we work together, Meredith and I will have a lot of physical contact, but trust me, that won't have any effect on how I feel about her."

"So long as she gets to dance with you and nothing else," I murmured, nestling closer to him.

"Not to worry," Richard whispered in my ear. "There's only one woman I want for everything else, and she's right here."

Chapter Five

Although we usually alternated Saturdays, Sunny and I had both agreed to work the next day. Our plan was to take turns covering the desk while the other person supervised any Friends of the Library who showed up. We had hoped for more than our usual contingent of volunteers, as the Heritage Festival was only a week away and there were stacks of donated books and other items that needed attention.

But after hearing about the murder and Sunny's friendship with the victim, Aunt Lydia volunteered to take Sunny's place so that my assistant could have the day off. She'd even recruited Zelda to help sort and price donations.

"I just hope Sunny can get some proper rest today," Aunt Lydia said as she pulled another pile of colorful paperbacks from a donation box. "I'm sure she's pretty shaken up."

"Poor thing. Not that it was any picnic for you either, Amy. But at least you weren't friends with the deceased." Zelda placed the cobweb-festooned carton she'd lifted down from a top shelf on the workroom table and brushed something from her dyed blonde curls. "Now tell me this—who brings in donations without wiping down the boxes? This looks like it was just dragged out of someone's attic."

Standing in the open workroom doorway, I glanced over at my aunt and her friend. Although the library was quiet that morning, I still had to keep an eye on the circulation desk. "That's my fault. Someone donated that box last year, right after the sale, and I just stuck it up there. Guess the spiders have been busier with their work than I've been with any cleaning."

Zelda plucked a bit of spider silk from her neon-pink blouse. "You should get some of those volunteers to dust in here." Her light brown eyes narrowed as she examined the stacks of books on the table. "Speaking of which, where are these so-called *Friends* this morning? I thought they were supposed to help with this project."

"Oh, they'll show up after lunch. That's when they usually wander in."

Zelda sniffed loudly. I bit back a smile, unsure if she was reacting to the dust or expressing her opinion of the Friends. She'd been an active member of the group until a few months ago, when she'd quit in protest of Melody Riley being voted in as the new chair.

"I'd think you'd be happy not to have some of them here. Especially Mel. I know you don't exactly get along."

Zelda and Aunt Lydia both looked as if they'd smelled something unpleasant. Intrigued by their obvious but mysterious dislike of the other woman, I decided I could rely on the bell to alert me to any patrons at the desk. I walked into the workroom, puzzling over why they reacted so strongly to any mention of Mel Riley. Aunt Lydia simply refused to talk about the woman, while Zelda made no secret of her disgust over the

Friends of the Library's recent election. Perhaps she was simply pissed because, as she said, "Mel just waltzed back into town and took over." Or maybe it was based on some history between the three women. Mel, like Zelda and Aunt Lydia, had been born and raised in Taylorsford. At sixty-eight she was a bit older than Zelda and my aunt, but it was likely that they had known each other, at least by reputation, when they were all young.

I examined my aunt and her friend with interest. I'd known Aunt Lydia to hold a grudge—she still refused all of Kurt Kendrick's friendly overtures—but not Zelda.

"So what's up with this animosity toward Mel Riley?" I asked.

Aunt Lydia didn't look up from the labels she was slapping on paperbacks. "Just not my kind of person."

"Too bossy by half. Always thinking her way is best, just because she's lived all over the world and is *so very cultured*." Zelda spoke the last few words in an exaggerated, and completely fake, British accent.

"She does know a lot about art."

Zelda snorted. "I guess when you're the wife of a high-ranking diplomat, you learn a few things. But as for her trotting back into Taylorsford after her husband died and assuming that she should be treated like she's lived here for years . . ."

"She has owned property here the entire time, though." I hoped playing devil's advocate might spur Zelda to spill the real reason she shunned Mel.

"Sure, she kept the family farm. But even though she paid someone to maintain it, she and that husband of hers only lived there for six months at a time, and only between assignments. It's not like they mingled with us lowly townspeople when they were here, either. Didn't even let that son of theirs mix with any kids in the area." Zelda wrinkled her nose. "They named that poor child Henry Lee Riley the Third, then called him Trey. I ask you, what kind of name is that?"

Aunt Lydia picked up one of the paperbacks and studied its lurid cover as if a half-naked man and woman in a clinch was something that actually interested her. "I never thought I'd see two murders in Taylorsford in less than a year."

My aunt's forceful tone signaled a change of subject. So much for me getting to the bottom of the Mel mystery. *Foiled again.* I shook my head. "Richard says people will think he's a bad-luck charm because it all started after he moved here."

Zelda's face brightened. "Nonsense. If anything, he's brought good fortune, not to mention he's provided the town with some much-needed eye candy." She picked up a crocheted doily and made a great show of fanning her face. "Must admit I tend to get a bit flushed around him. I may be old, but I still have eyes."

I met her sly smile with a lift of my chin. "Yeah, he's pretty hot, I guess."

"You guess?" Zelda chuckled. "I bet you know."

Aunt Lydia shot her friend a warning look. "Let's not get into Amy and Richard's business, Zelda. You know how she dislikes that sort of meddling."

Zelda flung up her hands. "Okay, okay. Just joking around." She looked over at me. "But I don't know what you're trying to hide, Amy. You're a bit guarded, but it's pretty darn obvious how Richard feels. The way he looks at you sometimes"—she shook her head until her curls bounced—"deserves an R-rating, at the very least."

Fingers of heat danced up the back of my neck. "Oh? Well . . ."

The bell at the desk jangled loudly. I hurried out of the room, thankful for the interruption, even though whoever was ringing the bell had slammed it hard. Which meant I might have to gird myself to deal with an irate patron. Considering this, I closed the workroom door behind me.

It wasn't a patron but someone who might be even more difficult to handle. "Hello, Mel," I said, bobbing my head to acknowledge the chair of the Friends.

Melody Riley was a striking woman, larger than life in every way. At least five foot eleven, she had a Rubenesque figure that was enhanced by the expert tailoring of her wool suit. Its jade color also perfectly complemented her sea-green eyes. Her high-lighted blonde hair was swept back into a smooth chignon, exposing an expensive pair of square-cut emerald earrings.

A perfect Valkyrie. Yes, I could easily picture her commanding the stage in a Wagnerian opera—tall, blonde, and ready for battle.

And, like a Wagnerian singer, loud. "Hello, Amy. Surprised to see you here after the events of yesterday, but I am glad that you didn't desert your post." Her gaze swept over me, a little line of disapproval creasing the area between her perfectly arched eyebrows.

Black slacks and a simple rust-colored sweater were probably not what she considered appropriate attire for a library director. I would have betted she'd have preferred me to wear a business suit, complete with stockings and tasteful pumps. But I always chose slacks over skirts or dresses in the cooler months, mainly because there was nothing I hated more than pantyhose.

51

I bit back a smile. Well, I disliked a few things more. Like a rich, domineering woman who looked down her nose at me. Besides, I had dressed to deal with the dusty donations, which she obviously had not. I narrowed my eyes and looked Mel up and down, silently calculating the cost of her elegant ensemble. She certainly knew how to make the best of her appearance. Her flawless makeup obscured many of her wrinkles, and the peacock-tail-patterned silk scarf she wore at her neck hid any hint of a sagging chin. She could easily have been mistaken for someone a decade younger.

"I'm here to assist with pricing the donations," Mel said. "Has anyone else shown up to help?"

"Yes, but . . ."

As Mel waved her hand in a dismissive gesture, the multicolored gems in her rings flashed. "So show me where you've stored everything. In the back, I suppose?"

She strolled to the open edge of the desk as if she owned the place. Which, despite her position as chair of the volunteer group that raised money for the library, she did not.

"No one from the Friends has shown up yet." I placed my hands on my hips and stood in the middle of the opening to prevent her from actually stepping behind the desk. "But my aunt and Zelda Shoemaker are here."

Mel stopped dead. "Lydia's here?"

"And Zelda," I said.

"Ah well, you have enough help for now then." She glanced up at the wall clock and toyed with her scarf, not meeting my gaze. "And look at the time. I had no idea it was this late. To be honest, I have a lunch appointment, and I doubt I could accomplish much before I had to leave to make that date. I'll try to pop back in later." Mel crossed back around to stand in front of the desk.

"Okay, whatever works for you." I studied Mel's averted face, wondering what could possibly have happened to make her so reluctant to spend time with my aunt or Zelda.

Curiouser and curiouser. Must have been something pretty significant. I tapped my fingers against the desk. I had to solve this mystery someday soon. It was just too intriguing to let go.

Mel, lost in thought for a moment, glanced back at me. "I do wonder if perhaps you could convince Lydia to donate a painting or two. I hear she has quite a collection of her husband's works."

"She does." I stared at Mel, whose green eyes were focused intently on my face.

"Tragically, we won't have anything from the LeBlancs, but a few paintings by Andrew Talbot might work as decent substitutes. Perhaps Lydia could spare one or two? Tell her"—Mel fiddled with the gold brooch pinned to her scarf—"yes, tell her I'd be more than happy to stop by the house and look over the paintings to see what might work best."

I couldn't help but notice the sudden tension tightening Mel's strong jaw. She was seriously interested in seeing Uncle Andrew's paintings, and I had to wonder why.

"I'll mention it to her," I said as Mel turned away, her attention apparently diverted by the new book rack, "but I can't promise she'll agree. She doesn't like to part with Andrew's paintings."

"Just do your best," Mel called over her shoulder before glancing at her watch and moving toward the front doors.

As Mel exited the library, a tall blond of a very different variety entered and approached the desk.

"Have a chance to check out those pictures?" Brad Tucker asked.

I slid over to the circulation desk computer. "I only just glanced at them, to be honest. Anyway, I need your help with something before I can really conduct a thorough search."

"Oh, what's that?" Brad laid his hat on the counter and ran his hand through his short hair. "By the way, we still need you and Richard to come in today. Can you get away?"

"Not until five. Will the office be open?" I clicked on the file Brad had sent to my email and peered at the computer screen.

"I'll make sure we have the proper personnel on hand to check over your statements. What do you think? Five thirty to six?"

"Probably. Richard's going to pick me up and we can drive right over." I looked up from the screen. "But before that, could you authorize me as an official sheriff's department consultant or something?"

"What for?"

"I need proper credentials to get into the Art Loss Register."

Brad picked up his hat and rubbed the brim between his thumb and forefinger. "Some sort of database?"

"Yeah, for art that's been lost or stolen. It's a great resource, but private individuals can't really search it independently. The organization will do moderated searches, but only if you're the owner of a piece or looking to buy something. So I can't just pop on and search for information on the paintings your deputy photographed. But law enforcement agencies can get permission to search the database without all the restrictions. So I thought . . ."

"Sure. In fact, we'll just deputize you. The sheriff can

authorize it, and then we can take care of the paperwork when you come in this evening. Will that work?"

"Perfectly." I stared at him, surprised at this offer. "I didn't know you could do that. I thought that sort of thing only happened in the Old West."

"No, we can still deputize people. We don't do it often, and it's only good for a designated period of time, but when we need specialized skills on a case it comes in handy." Brad smiled wryly. "Not like we have an overabundance of staff."

"I know." I closed the file and moved away from the computer. Once I could access the Art Loss Register, I felt confident I'd be able to actually help the sheriff's office. No use messing with any research before I gleaned the essential information from that source. "How's Sunny, by the way? I called her last night, but she didn't answer her phone."

"She's hanging in there." Brad frowned. "I'm not sure why it hit her so hard. She went through all that stuff with your cousin last summer without cracking, but now she's struggling."

"Maybe that's why. She stayed so tough through all that—being kidnapped and threatened with death and all—she could've just reached her limit. It was probably one shock too many."

Brad's thoughtful expression told me he was carefully considering this idea. That's one thing I'd recently learned about the chief deputy—he might resemble the high school football star he'd once been, but he was a much deeper thinker than many of his fellow jocks. "Could be. I'm sure she'd be glad to see you, if you want to stop by after coming into the office."

"I'll try. I'm sure Richard won't mind, as long as he doesn't have some other commitment. He has to do a lot of videoconferences and phone calls at weird hours for his choreography work."

"He keeps busy with that, it seems. Must be a challenge on top of teaching full-time."

"Not as hard as your job, I'm sure, but yeah." I gave Brad a smile. "Thanks for being there for Sunny, by the way. Last night, I mean. You must've been exhausted."

A faint tinge of color rose in Brad's face. "Aw, that's just . . . Well, you know I'll always be there for Sunny."

"I know," I said. "And so does she."

Which earned me a warm smile in return.

The door to the workroom opened and Aunt Lydia poked out her head. "Is she gone?"

She meant Mel, of course. I wondered how she knew whom I'd been talking to earlier, then realized that she and Zelda must've heard at least part of our conversation. Mel's voice was more than loud enough to carry through a closed door.

"Yeah, she headed out a few minutes ago," I said.

"Oh hi, Brad." Aunt Lydia stepped up behind the desk, followed by Zelda. "How are you?"

"Fine, Mrs. Talbot. Good to see you." Brad bobbed his head. "Mrs. Shoemaker, nice to see you as well."

"Another murder," Zelda said. "It hardly seems possible."

"Yes, it is unusual." Brad fiddled with the brim of his hat. "We've had to call in extra help from the state again, which is especially tough because of the upcoming festival. All the hotel rooms in the area are booked up, even the bed-and-breakfast places. That makes it hard to house anyone coming into town to help with the investigation." Brad stared down at his hat and sighed. "That's my unhappy task right now—trying to find housing for all the extra people. Especially the art expert, who needs to stick around for a while."

"You need a room or two?" Zelda asked. "I could probably put a couple of people up at my house. Call it my contribution to the effort."

Brad looked up, his eyes brightening. "Seriously? That would be great. They wouldn't have to stay long. Well, except for the art expert. He might need lodging for a few weeks."

"If Zelda can help out with some of the others, the art expert could stay with us," Aunt Lydia said.

I shot her a surprised glance. Unlike Zelda, my aunt's aristocratic profile betrayed no excitement over this prospect, but I noted her hands clasped tightly at her breast.

She wants someone to stay at our house? But she rarely entertains and never invites complete strangers into her home. What gives?

"Is that all right with you, Amy?" Aunt Lydia turned to me, her blue eyes shrouded beneath her golden lashes. "I would like to assist the sheriff's office, and I think an art expert might be an interesting guest."

There it was—the real reason for her offer. She'd fought for years to promote my late uncle's work. Perhaps she thought if she could interest the expert in Andrew's paintings, she could revive his legacy.

"Sure, fine by me," I said. "As long as he doesn't expect room service."

Brad's smile broadened. "Great. I wish I could solve all my problems so easily. Thanks, ladies." He raised his hand to his forehead in a little salute. "I'll be in touch with the details."

As he turned to go, Zelda called after him, "Please give Sunny our regards and let her know we're thinking of her."

Brad waved his hand in acknowledgment but left the building without saying anything else.

"Now that's one problem that will never be easy to solve," Zelda observed.

"What's that?" Aunt Lydia asked.

Zelda flicked a speck of dust from the shoulder of her blouse. "Sunny. The poor boy loves her dearly, but she's such a free spirit I don't know if she'll ever agree to be tied down."

"Maybe she won't have to be, even if they are together long-term," I said, causing both women to eye me skeptically. "I mean, marriage doesn't always mean being tied down, does it?"

"Of course not," Aunt Lydia said. "Andrew never tied me down. Well"—she flashed a wicked grin at Zelda—"not without my consent, anyway."

"Aunt Lydia!" My hands flew up to my open mouth.

But Zelda and my aunt just fell into each other's arms and dissolved into peals of laughter. Despite my efforts to quiet them by repeatedly pressing my finger to my lips, they fell silent only when one of our regular patrons marched up to the desk and shushed them.

Chapter Six

Brad had called ahead to talk to someone at the Art Loss Register, so when Richard and I showed up at the sheriff's office, he was able to give me preapproved access to the website.

"So, do I refer to you as Deputy Webber now?" Aunt Lydia asked the next day. She'd returned from church to find me huddled on the sofa in our sitting room, perusing the Register website.

I glanced up from the laptop with a smile. "No, you can still call me Amy. Now, I might ask Mel Riley to call me Deputy . . ."

"You do that." Aunt Lydia sat in the overstuffed chair that faced the sofa and kicked off her chestnut-brown leather pumps.

"You really don't like her, do you?"

My aunt wiggled her toes inside her stockings. "No, I'm afraid not."

I minimized the website and placed the laptop next to me. "Can I ask why?"

"You can ask." Aunt Lydia sank back into the suede cushions of the chair.

"Sorry if I'm being nosy, but I've noticed the animosity both you and Zelda feel toward her, and"—I slid forward until I was perched at the edge of the sofa cushion—"I must confess I'm curious. Also, since she's the new chair of the Friends, I have to work with her. If there's something I should be aware of . . ."

My aunt's bright blue gaze didn't falter, but her slender fingers entwined tightly in her lap. "Very well, if you must know—she was the reason Andrew died."

"What?" I opened and closed my mouth twice before I could form words again. "But Uncle Andrew died in a car crash."

"Yes, but do you know why he was out driving after dark in that storm?"

"Well, no. I just thought . . . I guess I never really questioned it, honestly."

Aunt Lydia turned her head, staring at a collection of photos on a nearby table. I knew the display included several pictures of Uncle Andrew and assumed that was her focus. "It was Mel Riley who demanded that he come to her house that night, with one of his paintings she'd purchased for a friend. She said it was a gift and that she needed it immediately, as her friend was coming into town a day early." When my aunt glanced back at me, her normally smooth brow was wrinkled and the lines bracketing her mouth had deepened. "Andrew begged her to let it wait until the next morning, since the weather was so foul. But she said no. She told him that unless he brought the painting to her house that night, the deal was off."

"There was an ice storm or something like that, right?"

"Yes. The kind of weather that no one should've been out in, especially since very few people owned four-wheel drive vehicles back then. But Mel didn't care, and Andrew would never have turned down such a deal. He didn't sell that many paintings, you see." Aunt Lydia lifted her chin and looked up and over my head. "It was a bad storm—freezing rain and sleet—so the highway patrol asked everyone to stay off the roads. But Mel only cared about what she wanted, when she wanted it."

"You told me the crash destroyed the car."

"Yes, and her damned painting. Little good it ever did her." Aunt Lydia clenched and unclenched her fingers. "A rock or something pierced the gas tank and the car exploded into flames. Andrew was thrown clear. He was very bad about not wearing his seat belt." She met my pained gaze and softened her tone. "That was one reason he was killed instantly, but honestly, he would've died anyway. At least he didn't burn."

"I'm so sorry. I shouldn't have brought this up."

Aunt Lydia tucked one white lock of her short hair behind her ear. "No, no, it's all right. I really should've told you sooner. I just hate talking about it, as you can imagine."

"Of course." I studied her face—still lovely for all its sixty-four years. "That explains why you hate Mel. Even though it was an accident, her selfishness was partially to blame."

"I don't hate her exactly. I just have no use for her. She wasn't a mean person, but she was always so self-centered. She couldn't see beyond her own desires. Never considered how her actions might affect someone else." Aunt Lydia closed her eyes for a moment and took a deep breath. "Now, tell me what you've discovered about those mysterious paintings."

"Not much yet." I lifted the computer back onto my lap. "So far, no mention of any works resembling them in the Art Loss Register."

"What is that, exactly? The Register, I mean."

"It's a website and database where people or organizations can list works they believe are lost or stolen. Or search for works that have been recovered in raids or that sort of thing. Essentially it's a great way to track art so that thieves and forgers can't pass off a piece with a fake provenance."

"Interesting. I had no idea such a thing existed. But you haven't found any of the pieces from the LeBlancs' barn?"

"Not yet. Of course, it's pretty tough to find something when there's no title and you aren't entirely sure about the artist. I'm just using my best guesses. It will be easier when that art expert gets here. When is he or she supposed to arrive, anyway?"

"Tomorrow, and it's a he. Someone named Hui Chen, although Brad Tucker said he goes by Hugh." Aunt Lydia plucked at the cuff of her crisp linen blouse. "Asian, I suppose."

"American, I imagine." I wagged my finger at her. "You know not everyone came over here in 1756, like our family."

"I realize that, Amy, and I could care less about someone's background, but I haven't had a lot of contact with people of Asian descent. I just hope we'll be able to provide the proper accommodations."

I shook my head. "I'm sure he won't be expecting anything different than anyone else. Bed, bathroom, a few meals—that sort of thing."

"You needn't get all high and mighty with me, young lady. It isn't out of line for me to feel concerned over being a proper hostess."

"Yeah, but I don't think you should worry because of his ethnic background." I looked down at my laptop screen, reminding myself that my aunt had lived in Taylorsford all her life. Although she was open-minded, a trace of provincialism lingered.

"Anyway, I sure hope he has some insights, because I haven't found anything useful yet. Interesting, yes." I maximized the website and stared at the image on my screen, which depicted an artist walking on a dappled gold path with open fields and two trees in the background. "Like this lost painting, which is a Van Gogh. I think it might have been connected to the Monuments Men. Remember that film?"

"Yes, they were protecting art from the Nazis." Aunt Lydia smiled. "And they weren't all men."

"True. Anyway, they've kept the organization going, mainly to find pieces that are still lost. Like this painting by Van Gogh that belonged to a museum in Magdeburg, Germany." I tapped my screen with my forefinger. "The title is *The Painter on His Way to Tarascon*, but it's really a self-portrait. It was moved to some salt mines near Magdeburg for protection during the war, but then it disappeared in 1945."

"Shame," my aunt said. "Art shouldn't be hoarded."

I glanced over at her. This was my opportunity to fulfill Mel's request, although I certainly wouldn't mention her name. "Speaking of which, would you mind donating one or two of Uncle Andrew's paintings to the library sale? I know you don't like to part with them, but since we've lost any chance of getting some from the LeBlancs . . ."

Aunt Lydia met my inquiring gaze with a lift of her eyebrows. "Clever segue. Using my own words against me, are you?"

I grinned. "Maybe."

"Let me think about that. I might be able to spare one or two. Meanwhile, I believe I'll go change out of these church clothes." Aunt Lydia pushed against the chair arms to help her rise to her feet. Although her injured leg had healed and she no longer needed a cane, she was more cautious with her balance than before her accident. "You did invite Richard to lunch as I requested, I hope?"

"Yeah, I'm sure he'll be over soon."

"And you're wearing *that*?" As my aunt walked past the sofa, she eyed my worn jeans and faded Pink Floyd T-shirt with obvious disapproval.

I turned my head and pulled a funny face at her. "No, I thought I'd throw a flannel shirt over the T-shirt. You know, for added color."

She just sighed deeply and left the room.

* * *

Sitting at the dining room table after lunch, I tilted my head and noticed the lacy spider webs festooning the silver-plated chandelier. I twisted my lips into a grimace. We rarely used the dining room, but that was no excuse for the cobwebs, or the film of dust dimming the polished surface of the cherry sideboard and china cupboard.

Richard leaned in and whispered in my ear. "Bored?"

I shook my head. I didn't mind that Walt and Zelda, who'd joined us for lunch, had repeated stories about the past that I'd heard several times before. I was more disgusted over my inadequate housekeeping. Keeping such a large house clean was difficult, and although Aunt Lydia did her best, she depended on me for the tasks that required heavy lifting or climbing stepladders. Like dusting chandeliers.

But I'd been lax lately. Partly due to the increased workload associated with preparing for the library's participation in the Heritage Festival.

Be honest, Amy, it's also because of the man sitting next to you. You're spending more and more time with him, which means less and less time helping Aunt Lydia with chores.

Guilt washed over me, especially when I considered we would soon be housing a guest. I'd made up my mind to tell Richard that I couldn't see him that evening because I needed to do some last-minute cleaning, but when I'd turned my head and gazed into his beautiful gray eyes, the words had shriveled on my tongue.

"I just hope this art expert isn't as much of a slob as the two forensic experts they stuck me with." Zelda absently swirled the iced tea in her glass. "One would think someone in such a profession would be tidier. I expect they have to be precise in their work, but heavens above, are they ever sloppy in their other habits."

"Maybe that's why." Richard scooted closer and draped his arm across the top of my ladder-back wooden chair. "It's like me with food. I have to be so careful most of the time that, when I do let go, I turn into a pig." He grinned and patted his flat stomach with his other hand. "I probably gained ten pounds from this meal, but I don't care. It was delicious, Lydia."

"Thank you." My aunt looked him over. "But I doubt you've destroyed that perfect physique with just one meal."

"That's the problem, though. It isn't just one meal. I eat here pretty often, you know." Richard dropped his arm down onto my shoulders. "But I guess, if that's the price to be paid for Amy's company, I must make the sacrifice."

Zelda elbowed Walt. "Listen to him, dear. As if he's really suffering, with Lydia feeding him and Amy . . . Well"—she winked at me—"doing whatever she does for him."

Walt cleared his throat. "Now, Zel, enough with the teasing. You've got the girl blushing again." He turned sideways in his chair to stretch out his long legs. Although our dining room chairs were sturdy enough, they couldn't comfortably accommodate his lanky height. "I'm definitely curious to meet this art expert, Lydia. I hear he's worked for the National Gallery of Art, among other prestigious places."

"Yes, so I'm told." Aunt Lydia pushed back her chair. "Is everyone finished? I thought I'd clear the table, but I don't want to rush you."

I dislodged Richard's arm and leapt to my feet. "You sit and relax. Let me clear up."

"Here now, I'll help too." Richard stood to join me. "You gather up the plates and silverware, sweetheart. I'll grab that tray for the glasses."

As we collected the dirty dishes, Aunt Lydia pleated her cloth napkin between her fingers. "But honestly, don't you all find this murder so bizarre? Who'd want to kill Rachel LeBlanc?"

"You never know," Walt said. "Think about your cousin Sylvia. Who'd have guessed she was capable of cold-blooded murder?"

Aunt Lydia dropped the napkin back onto the table. "Oh, I always thought her capable. I just never suspected she'd actually carry it out."

"Yes, dear Lord," Zelda said, "that woman was capable of anything. And, you know, there's probably a simple answer to this latest murder, although a very sad one."

Walt looked over at Zelda, his dark brown eyes puzzled. "So what's this obvious answer, my dear? Because I admit I'm with Lydia and can't imagine what happened."

"Well"—Zelda leaned into the table and spread her hands across the white tablecloth—"it's probably that boy Sunny saw running away."

"Caden Kroft?" I paused in the doorway to the hall, balancing my stack of plates as Richard headed for the kitchen with his tray full of glasses. "Why do you assume that? The husband is still missing, so isn't that more likely? The spouse is always the primary suspect, at least in books and on television."

Zelda lifted her hands. "But that's fiction, my dear. I know that's what people always think, but I can't picture Reese stabbing his wife. They always seemed so devoted."

The plates rattled as I shifted my weight from one foot to the other. "*Seemed* being the operative word. Like you said about Cousin Sylvia, things aren't always what they appear."

Zelda lifted her shoulders. "But Caden was there, according to Sunny, and we don't know that Reese was anywhere nearby. It *is* strange that he hasn't surfaced yet, but there could be a good reason. Maybe his car broke down or something. I haven't heard any updates from the sheriff's department as to his whereabouts, but I hate to condemn the man just because he's the husband." Zelda tapped her chin with one finger. "Anyway, Caden's struggled with a drug problem for several years, poor lamb. At least that's what I've heard. Had some run-ins with the authorities, although nothing serious enough to send him to jail."

Aunt Lydia tapped her buffed fingernails against the tablecloth. "But how does that connect to a murder? Just having an issue with drugs doesn't necessarily turn someone into a criminal."

I leaned against the door jam, studying her tense face. I

knew this subject hit a nerve with her, since she'd once confided to me that my late uncle had struggled with drug addiction. Something he'd fallen into because of his friendship with Kurt Kendrick, called Karl Klass back then. Now a respected, and wealthy, art dealer and collector, but once—according to my aunt—a dealer in other, less savory, things.

And maybe still involved in shady transactions. He practically admitted it the last time you had a real conversation with him.

Kendrick was in his early seventies now, but in my opinion he was still more than capable of being involved in criminal activities. "Why would Caden want to kill Rachel, though? What's the motive?"

Zelda swept her plump hands through the air. "Oldest reason in the book. He's in love with the daughter and the parents don't approve."

"That's no reason to kill someone," Walt said with a frown.

I studied his somber face. He was probably considering how some people in Taylorsford wouldn't approve of his relationship with Zelda. The fact that he was black and she white had kept them from being more open about their love affair for several years. Sunny had repeatedly told them to ignore such ignorant attitudes, but as I reminded my friend, we couldn't really understand his reluctance to go public because we hadn't experienced what he had as a black man growing up in a predominantly white community.

Richard reappeared in the hall and pointed at the plates I was still holding. "Can I take those?"

I noted his amused expression. "Oh, sure. Sorry."

"No worries," he said, sliding the stack of china out of my hands. "I can see you're preoccupied." He shifted the stack, balancing them in the crook of his arm, and tapped my forehead with one finger. "That detective brain of yours is going all Sherlock Holmes over another mystery, isn't it?"

I wrinkled my nose at him. "And if it is?"

"Okay by me." He nodded his head toward Zelda. "Better listen up. She's probably already amassed more information than the authorities."

"Probably," I said, while he headed toward the kitchen.

As I turned back to the dining room, it was clear that Aunt Lydia was not done questioning Zelda. "So, even though Reese LeBlanc had forbidden Caden to visit Lila, you don't think that was the motive? You think this young musician killed Rachel looking for money for drugs?"

"I do. It's the only thing that makes sense. Sunny said the girl looked like she'd just woken from a stupor. She was coming down off something, and the boy decided they needed another hit or whatever but didn't have the money. So he goes to Rachel, who he knows is in the studio, to beg for money. She refuses, and pow!"—Zelda made a stabbing motion with her hand—"the kid grabs the first thing he finds and attacks her. Probably didn't mean to kill her, of course."

"I don't know." As I crossed over to the sideboard, my thoughts circled around the wiped-down palette knife. Would an impetuous, drug-fueled killer take the time to do that? And then there were the forgeries . . . "It still seems odd to me that the authorities discovered that secret closet full of paintings at the murder scene. I doubt Caden Kroft had anything to do with that, or even knew it existed."

"True," Zelda said. "But it could be coincidental."

"Awfully strange coincidence, dear," Walt observed.

I leaned back against the sideboard and stared across the table at the opposite wall. Catching a glimpse of my reflection in the glass doors of the china cupboard, I noticed that my T-shirt had rumpled up around my waist and tugged it down. "It's just odd. I can't help but imagine there's some connection . . ."

My aunt shot me a sharp glance. "Are you thinking of Kurt Kendrick?"

"Yeah." I drew figure eights in the dust on the sideboard with one finger. "He does live fairly close to the LeBlancs, and we know he's involved in buying and selling art."

Zelda propped her elbows on the table and supported her chin with her tented fingers. "You just don't trust that man, do you, Amy?"

"No."

"Neither do I," Aunt Lydia said. "But I don't know that we can accuse him of anything. At least not yet." She looked hopeful, as if she'd be quite happy if Kendrick could be implicated in this case.

Of course she would. She'd probably believe justice had been served if Kendrick got arrested for some crime.

Richard appeared in the doorway. "Sorry to eat and run, but I'm afraid I have a Skype session scheduled with the Ad Astra Company this afternoon."

"Oh, the company that's also taking you out of town this week?" Aunt Lydia asked.

"Yeah. I guess Amy filled you in. I hate that I won't be here to volunteer at the festival, but I feel obligated to help them out of a jam."

"We all understand, dear. Work must come first, even if it is a pain sometimes." Zelda patted Walt's hand. "I know I'll be glad when we're both retired and Walt doesn't have that long commute almost every day."

"I keep telling Richard not to worry about not being here," I said. "I'll have plenty of help. Honestly, the worst part is that I can't go with him. I hate missing Richard's performance."

Aunt Lydia and Zelda shared a glance. *Uh-oh*, I thought. *Maybe I shouldn't have been quite so vehement in my last statement.* They were probably reading too much into it and thinking about how soon they could start planning a wedding.

"Can't be helped. You have your job just like I have mine. And speaking of that, I really must go. Thanks again, Lydia," Richard said, before he turned away. "Amy, come with me?"

"Sure." I caught another knowing look between my aunt and her friend before I walked out of the dining room.

Richard met me at the front door. "This Skype thing will only last an hour if you want to drop by later."

I opened the front door and stepped onto the porch before blurting out, "I'd love to, but with that art expert coming tomorrow, I really should clean the house." I knew I had to say it quickly, and without looking at him, or I'd change my mind.

Richard shut the door behind him. "All right, I suppose I must be understanding, since you're doing it to help Lydia. But"—he took hold of my arms and turned me to face him—"I have to leave tomorrow, since I decided to drive instead of flying. And I need to get on the road pretty early, which means that after today we won't see each other for a week."

I gazed up into his face. The lines bracketing his mouth clearly indicated his disappointment. "Sorry, but I think we'll have to manage. I've been so lax with the housework lately that I have to make up for it today."

71

"I guess I'll have to channel my frustration into some extra rehearsal, then."

I tapped his lips with my fingers. "See, I'm helping you with your performance after all."

"Hmmm, not sure about that, but we'll see." Richard caught hold of my fingers and pressed a kiss into my palm before releasing my hand. "Now, give me a proper good-bye."

"Out here on the front porch in full view of all the neighbors?"

"The hell with the neighbors," he replied, and kissed me in a way that made me regret my earlier decision.

The house got a thorough cleaning, though, as I had to work out my own frustrations somehow.

Chapter Seven

It was difficult to drag myself out of bed the next morning, but I resisted the urge to slam the snooze button on my alarm clock more than once. Aunt Lydia needed the car for a doctor's appointment, so I had to walk to work, which required an early start.

As I locked up the front door and stepped off the porch, I glanced over at Richard's driveway, confirming that his car was already gone. We had talked on the phone the night before, a call that went on for far too long. It was one reason I'd had trouble waking up, although I actually thought the hours of frantic cleaning were more to blame. I had worked until almost nine o'clock before flopping across my bed, exhausted and feeling as if dust and grime had sunk into every one of my pores.

It didn't help that I'd subsequently dragged out my laptop and fallen into a research black hole. I'd spent far too much time seeking information on the people involved in the case. Although most of my searches were dead ends, I had discovered one interesting fact. There was apparently a lien against the LeBlanc farm, which meant they were in financial difficulty despite Rachel's success as an artist. I'd sent Brad a text about this situation and he'd thanked me, although he'd admitted that the state investigators had already uncovered a substantial life insurance policy that would benefit Reese. And Lila, too, but only if her father was also deceased.

I'd then stayed awake even longer, considering the possibility that Lila could've killed both her parents for the insurance money. After some thought, I'd concluded that this was unlikely. From the way Sunny had described the girl's state, I doubted that she would've had the presence of mind to cover up such a crime. According to Brad, the killer had left Rachel lying where she was killed, so why would anyone have felt the need to hide Reese's corpse? No, I concluded, it was much more likely that Reese had killed his wife and fled. Perhaps he planned to show up in a day or so, claiming that he'd just returned from his business trip. If he could pull that off, he might be able to collect on the insurance. But he had to know that was a long shot . . .

Puzzling over all these scenarios had robbed me of sleep, so I wasn't exactly bright-eyed the next day. Fortunately, the autumn morning was perfect for a walk—the air was brisk but not biting, and the sky was as clear as a newly washed pane of glass. I shouldered my soft-sided briefcase and set off, inhaling the woodsy smoke that wafted up from some neighboring chimney. The honking of geese made me lift my head to watch their flock wing across the sky. As I lowered my eyes, my gaze was captured by the dance of flaming leaves on the sugar maple trees that lined the sidewalk.

Dazzled by the beauty of the morning, I didn't realize that someone had stepped up behind me until I heard his voice.

"Good morning, Amy. Heading to work?"

I spun around so fast my elbow banged into Kurt Kendrick's hip. "Are you following me?"

Kendrick didn't even flinch. "That wasn't my original plan. I just drove out to walk over the old Cooper farm this morning. Getting the lay of the land, so to speak. You know I'm providing funding for the new town park, I suppose?"

"Yeah, I heard that." I gazed up into his craggy face. His brilliant blue eyes were examining me in a way I found unnerving. Or maybe it was just his size. His large frame—all muscle and bone—dwarfed me.

Kendrick ran a hand through his thick white hair. "I'm supposed to meet with Mayor Blackstone later today to discuss the preliminary plans, and I wanted to have a better sense of the terrain. I didn't think I could get a real feel for it just perusing a map."

I looked past him and spied his black Jaguar parked on the side of the road beyond Richard's house. So far it seemed that the art dealer was telling the truth about why he was in the area, but I remained on my guard. "I'm surprised he's willing to talk to you. Having to scrap his development plans and donate the land to the town must sting."

"He could hardly do otherwise." Kendrick looked down at me with a wry smile. "Considering that he had to cut a deal with the authorities to stay out of prison for withholding evidence in the Sylvia Baker case, he should be happy that all he lost was some money."

"I suppose."

"And the park will honor Eleanora and Daniel Cooper, as Paul wished. Which is all I ever wanted for that property."

I schooled my expression to hide my disbelief over this

remark. I suspected that Kendrick's donation to the park had less to do with honoring the wishes of his late foster father, Paul Dassin, and more to do with a substantial tax write-off. I simply couldn't imagine Kendrick waxing that sentimental over anyone. It seemed unlikely that he'd be so devoted to Richard's great-uncle when he'd fled Paul Dassin's home at eighteen and hadn't returned until after Paul's death. "It *will* be nice to have the Cooper farm land converted into a park instead of a subdivision. So thanks for that."

Kendrick displayed the large white teeth that always reminded me of a storybook wolf. "I'm sure Lydia approves, since the houses would've been built so close to her own home. I actually thought my sponsorship of the park might earn me her goodwill, but she still refuses all my dinner invitations."

"If you understood her at all, you'd know it's difficult to change her mind about anything."

"Oh, I do realize that." Kurt Kendrick stepped back and studied me for a moment. "You two share that trait, I think."

I shoved a lock of my straight brown hair behind my ear. "I'm nowhere near as intractable. After all, I *am* talking with you."

"True enough," Kendrick said, with another grin.

I glanced at my watch. "But I'm going to be late for work if I don't get a move on." I turned away from him.

One of his large, knobby hands landed on my wrist. "Wait."

I gazed up into his face. There was no grin now, only a stare that bored straight into me. "Excuse me, but if you could remove your hand . . ."

"In a minute. First I must tell you something. It's the real reason I walked up the road to talk with you."

"Tell me what?" I twisted my wrist, dislodging his hand. "I don't have time for this, Mr. Kendrick."

"Kurt. And yes you do. Because you need to be warned. You and your boyfriend." He waved his hand toward Richard's house. "It's common knowledge that you and Richard Muir found Rachel LeBlanc's body and that your friend Sunny was also involved."

"So?" Swinging my briefcase in front of me like a shield, I took two steps back.

"So that places you in the middle of something that could prove quite dangerous for you all."

"Why? We didn't see anyone. We just stumbled over the body. It's not like we can identify the killer or anything."

"But you were present when the paintings were discovered."

The paintings . . . I narrowed my eyes as I examined the older man, whose childhood nickname had been "The Viking." "You know about those?"

"Of course. Once Zelda Shoemaker heard about it, the news was all over town." Kendrick crossed his arms over his broad chest. "And I have a special interest in such matters, as you can imagine."

Yes, I could. Wherever secrets tangled up the truth, I could picture Kurt Kendrick as the pale spider lurking in the center of the web.

"I can also imagine that you might have something to do with that suspicious stash of canvases. Maybe some secret even the LeBlancs didn't know?"

Kendrick shook his shaggy head. "My dear, I think you are assigning much more power to me than I possess. I have nothing to do with those paintings, trust me."

I swallowed a bubble of laughter. Trust him? I'd sooner trust my murderous Cousin Sylvia. "So why warn me? If you aren't aware of any connection between those particular paintings and art theft or forgery, what is there to worry about?"

Kendrick's bushy eyebrows rose to the thick fringe of white hair falling over his forehead. "I didn't say that."

"So there is a connection?"

"Possibly. I have no hard facts, you understand, but in my world one hears things. Rumors, of course, but one must assume that where there is smoke, there could be . . . a conflagration."

"So what are you saying? That Richard and Sunny and I might be in danger because some criminal organization offed poor Rachel LeBlanc? But why? Don't tell me she was a forger. Why would she do that? She had plenty of fame with her own work."

"True, but she wasn't the only painter in the family."

I stared at him. "Reese? You think he was the target, or"—I narrowed my eyes as I examined Kendrick—"maybe he was the killer, following orders from some criminal organization that had a hold over him?"

He shrugged his broad shoulders. "I only know that any connection to the case could put you in the cross hairs of some disreputable individuals."

"Unlike people with stainless reputations, like you?"

Kendrick flashed me another toothy grin. "This is why I like you so much, Amy. Despite your obvious distrust of me. But seriously, dear"—the grin faded as quickly as it had appeared—"I am concerned about you, Sunny, and Richard, who I also hold in high esteem, and not just because he's a descendent of Paul Dassin. And then there's your aunt . . ."

My fingers clutched the strap of my briefcase. "But Aunt Lydia wasn't involved in discovering the body."

"No, but she's housing the art expert sent in to examine the paintings. Someone who might also be considered a target." Kendrick lifted his hands. "Don't look so surprised. It's common knowledge around town, and even if it wasn't . . ."

"You'd know?"

"I would indeed."

I unclenched my fingers and swept one hand through the air. "What, you have spies or something?"

Kurt Kendrick did not reply, but the slight incline of his head made me think the answer was *yes*.

"I just want all of you to be on your guard. Keep your eyes open and use that suspicious mind of yours to good advantage. Now, having said that, how about I drive you to the library? I'd hate to think my impromptu conversation had made you late for work."

"Oh, no, that's not necessary," I said, although a glance at my watch informed me that it was. There was no way I could walk fast enough to reach the library and open the building on time.

"Nonsense, I insist. I've completed my survey and need to head in that direction anyway. Come along now." He turned and strode back toward his car.

I trailed him, considering the pros and cons of his offer. I didn't trust Kurt Kendrick. Not one little bit. But I knew he was too smart to harm me in full view of Mr. Dinterman, who was grabbing his newspaper from his driveway, and Mrs. Hollins, who was out walking her Yorkie.

But if you get in his car, Amy, he could drive you anywhere.

I studied the tall, white-haired man opening the passenger-side door of his luxury sports car. He was mysterious, secretive, and, perhaps, shady. But he wasn't stupid. He wouldn't harm someone witnesses had seen getting in his car.

I sank into the plush leather of the passenger seat as Kendrick closed my door and walked around to the driver's side.

No one as wealthy and wily as this man can afford to take such a chance, I thought as I buckled my seat belt. I glanced over at my companion, noting the set line of his strong jaw.

Or at least I hoped not.

Chapter Eight

Naturally, my fears were unfounded. Kurt Kendrick dropped me off at the library after asking some brief, innocuous comments about my university studies. After I mentioned the name of my undergraduate advisor, a scholar who specialized in nineteenth-century European art, Kendrick shared an amusing story about bidding against her at an auction.

I was so bemused by the Jaguar, whose elegant interior and ride far surpassed any other vehicle I'd ever experienced, that I didn't respond to this odd coincidence. And maybe it wasn't so strange. The man moved in the highest circles of the art world. He probably knew most of the major scholars in the field.

Exiting his car with just a "Bye, thanks" and a wave of my hand, I hurried into the library to find Sunny already preparing the building for opening.

"I thought you were coming in late today," I said as I dropped my briefcase behind the circulation desk.

"That was the plan, but my dental appointment got rescheduled, so here I am." Sunny slid a lilac hair tie off her wrist and swept back her silky blonde hair with both hands. "But I would like to take a longer lunch, if that's okay. I have an errand to run and can't do it after work, since I assume we're still staying late today to price more stuff for the sale. Isn't that the plan?" She whipped the tie around her hair to create a simple but elegant ponytail.

"Yeah, if that still works for you. And the longer lunch is fine." I fiddled with the mouse, making sure the circulation desk computer was set to the checkout screen.

"That's going to make it a long day for you." Sunny lifted a stack of books from the bin she'd rolled in from our exterior book drop and placed them on the counter. "I can check these in if you need to go over the monthly stats. I know you have to compile the report for the next town council meeting."

"Ugh, why did you remind me?" If there was one thing I truly disliked about my job, it was the endless number crunching required by the mayor and the town council. They were obsessed with proving whether the library was a good investment or not, based on nothing more than patron visits, checkouts, and other statistics. What they never saw was the intrinsic value of a place where anyone, rich or poor, could find a wealth of entertainment and information for free.

But it was part of my job, and there was no one else to do it. I headed into the workroom and took a seat at the corner desk that functioned as my office, resisting the urge to check my cell phone for any texts from Richard before I began compiling statistics from our integrated library system.

But I couldn't resist the lure of research. I hesitated for only a moment before pulling up the file containing the paintings that had been discovered in the LeBlanc barn. Statistics could wait.

As I examined the photographs one more time, the question

that had been lurking in the corner of my mind consolidated into a coherent thought. Most of the paintings resembled the work of artists from the Impressionist period or later, but there were one or two that looked as if they could have been painted during the Renaissance. Studying one of these more closely, I realized what had bothered me. It resembled the work of Michelangelo Caravaggio, yet it seemed too small to be the work of that artist given the subject matter, which was the Nativity. I'd written a paper on Caravaggio in college and recalled that most of his paintings—especially those that dealt with biblical scenes—were quite large. I expanded the size of the photograph and noticed that this work appeared unfinished and included only a few figures—Mary, Joseph, and the Christ Child. But there was something about a lost Caravaggio . . .

I opened a new tab on my computer and pulled up the Art Loss Register. Searching specifically for Caravaggio, I discovered the painting that I'd vaguely remembered—the *Nativity With San Lorenzo and San Francesco*, which had been stolen from the Oratorio di San Lorenzo in Palermo, Sicily, in 1969 and hadn't been seen since. But that painting had featured additional figures and it had been six feet by nine feet, considerably larger than the canvas discovered at the LeBlancs'.

Yet the figures and style of the painting recovered at the barn matched the lost Caravaggio. So either this was a study for the final painting, unknown to art historians, or it was a forgery of such a study.

Very clever, I thought, sitting back in my chair. If this was a forgery, reproducing something like a study—which could easily be hypothesized to exist, given common practices of artists—rather than trying to recreate a well-known painting was a smart move.

Even if the *Nativity* was lost, producing a large and famous stolen work might raise too many eyebrows among those in the know in the art world. Whereas a study sold on the black market . . .

Which meant I was going about my research all wrong. I toggled back to the other photographs and allowed myself to follow this new train of thought. What if these works had all been created based on some specific criteria? There were many paintings mentioned in artists' letters or other documents that had somehow disappeared or been assumed lost, some of them even before they were ever sold or exhibited.

It would be one way to provide better provenance for any forged works, if they were indeed forgeries and not simply stolen.

Or maybe it was a mix of the two—forgeries mixed in with actual stolen works. I sighed. It was probably best if I waited for more information from the art expert. But the lure of the mystery was so strong . . .

"Amy," Sunny called from the other room, "Mr. Washington needs your help. He claims you were assisting him with some research the other day."

"Yes, I'm coming," I replied, with another sigh. My sleuthing would have to wait. I closed down the sites and left my desk to head out of the workroom.

Mr. Washington needed assistance in compiling a list of all known wineries in the region, and that, like all patron requests, had to take precedence over my own research, no matter how intrigued I might be.

* * *

After closing the library, we priced several boxes of book donations before Sunny dashed to the break room and returned with a white paper bag. "Grabbed these from The Heapin' Plate while I was out," she said, handing me a waxed-paper bundle and two napkins.

I unfolded one of the napkins and covered a portion of the workroom table before unveiling an overstuffed sandwich of pimento cheese and leaf lettuce on a brioche bun nestled next to a large dill pickle.

Sunny tossed me a package of potato chips. "Figured we wouldn't get out of here in time for dinner."

"Thanks. What do I owe you?"

"Nothing. I've eaten at Lydia's plenty of times, so let's call it even. While I was at the diner getting lunch, I thought I might as well grab something for after work. I figured sustenance was required for this pricing project."

"Good thinking." I studied her as she took a large bite of her veggie sandwich. "What exactly was this errand anyway? You looked as pleased as a cat in the cream when you got back to work."

Sunny waved her hand through the air and swallowed before replying. "Oh, nothing. Just arranging a little surprise."

"For Brad?" Sunny had been dating the chief deputy for exactly five months, so I thought perhaps she was planning something to celebrate that anniversary.

"No. As you can imagine, knowing Brad, surprises are not his thing." Sunny dabbed at her lips with her napkin. "Anyway, it's a secret."

That just made me more curious. "For your grandparents, I bet. Do they have an anniversary coming up or something?"

"Secret, Miss Nosy Pants," Sunny said and took a sharp bite of her crisp pickle.

We finished our takeout in silence, although I did pull a couple of funny, raised-eyebrow faces at my friend, who just wrinkled her nose in return.

"Better wash our hands before we tackle any more labeling." I crumpled my sandwich wrapper and napkins into a ball that I clutched in one fist as I headed out the workroom door.

The break room was located in the annex, so we had to cross a darkened expanse of the main room to reach it. Thinking of the electric bill, I resisted the urge to flick on the lights. It really wasn't necessary, as Sunny and I could navigate this path in the dark, and anyway, an outdoor floodlight cast a beam of illumination through the library's tall windows.

Sunny led the way, humming some tune I couldn't place. Which wasn't surprising. Despite a love for music, Sunny couldn't carry a tune in a bucket.

Her pitch rose, then ended in a gasp.

A slender figure in a dark hoodie and jeans jumped out of the shadows and yanked Sunny forward.

Casting aside the ball of trash, I leapt toward them, but the light spilling through the windows glinted off an object that stopped me in my tracks.

A knife blade.

The intruder spun Sunny around and pulled her back, holding her against his chest with one arm. His other hand, the one holding the knife, swung up to her neck.

"What do you want?" Sunny's voice shook, but the rest of her body was still as a stone statue.

"I want you to tell the truth," said her captor.

Keeping an eye on the two figures, I took several steps back. As I pressed my hand against the plaster wall for support, my fingers encountered a metal switch plate. Hoping to startle the intruder into dropping the knife, I flicked on the lights.

The intruder blinked in the sudden flood of light but did not release his hold on Sunny—or his weapon. "That was stupid," he said. "I could've sliced her neck right then and there."

A squeak like a mouse caught in a trap escaped Sunny's taut lips.

"Caden, please don't hurt her," I said. I didn't know Caden Kroft well, but I'd seen him often enough, singing and strumming his guitar on the street corner outside Bethany Virts's diner. "There's no need to harm anyone. Just tell us what you want."

"Told you. I need this one"—he flipped his hand so that the knife point touched Sunny's chin—"to tell the authorities the truth about what she saw the day Rachel was killed."

"Already did." Sunny's wide-eyed gaze was fastened on me as if she were drowning and I were the only lifeguard on the beach.

"No, you said you thought you saw me. But there was someone else there. In the woods. I saw them from a distance. You must've too." Shadows played over Caden's gaunt face, lending it a macabre quality.

He was whippet-thin and not particularly tall. I calculated the odds that I could overmaster him. But the manic gleam in his brown eyes and the knife at Sunny's throat kept me frozen in place. "How did you get in here, anyway?"

Lank, shoulder-length auburn hair spilled to his shoulders as a jerk of his head tossed back the hood of his dark sweatshirt. "Through the front doors. Just mingled in with the other people till closing time, then hid in a closet in the kids' room." He sniffed, then coughed. "You guys aren't very careful when you close up."

"We don't generally expect people to crawl into closets," I said, my eyes focused on Sunny's waxy face.

"It was too easy." Caden rubbed his forefinger over his upper lip, just under his nose. "Not that I expected a bunch of library types to be very smart about such things."

"So you saw someone else near the barn that day?" I asked, hoping to placate Caden while I mentally measured the distance to the main circulation desk. I'd left my cell phone in my briefcase, but there was a landline phone on the wall. If I could reach the desk . . .

But that knife was far too close to Sunny's throat.

"Yeah. Couldn't see who it was, or even how big they were or anything, 'cause they were too far away and hidden by the trees, but there was someone there. I know there was. I heard twigs snapping and boots stomping and saw a shadow moving through the woods in front of me. But the deputies zoned in on me 'cause of what you told them." As Caden leaned over Sunny's shoulder, he twisted his neck to look at her. The hand gripping the knife trembled.

"I only told them what I saw," she replied in a soft voice. "I'm sorry, but I didn't notice anyone else. If I had, I would've told them so, I swear."

"But there was someone." Caden's voice rose to another register.

Like his hand, Caden's entire body was shaking slightly. *Drugs. He's coming down off of something. Which could mean he doesn't have the physical agility to actually use that blade.*

But it could also mean that he'd react to any movement from me with irrational rage. I slowed my pounding heart with deep breaths. "I believe you, Caden, I do." I held out my hands, palms up. "I don't think you killed Rachel. There must've been someone else there. It's just that Sunny didn't see them, that's all."

"But the authorities are after me." Caden's resonant singer's voice had thinned into a whine. "And I got no proof, not without someone backing up my story."

"I know, but we can tell them. Sunny and me—we can let them know what you saw and heard so they won't just focus on you." I slid one foot forward, and then the other, my hands still extended in supplication. "How about we let you leave and not call the sheriff's department or 911 or anything. Not for at least an hour. So you can get away. I promise that's what we'll do if you just release Sunny. I swear it."

Caden blinked rapidly. "I dunno. Not sure I can trust you. Can't trust many people. Just can't." He sniffed several times and swung the knife through the air, away from Sunny's throat.

"You don't want to hurt me, do you, Caden?" Sunny kept her tone meek, which I knew must have been a challenge. She probably longed to scream at him, but she was smart enough not to exacerbate the situation. "I'm sure you didn't harm Rachel, or anyone else, so please don't hurt me."

"I don't want to." Caden flexed his other arm, loosening his hold on Sunny. "I just want to be free. Not be tracked like some animal."

"No one will do that," I said. "You can get away right now and we won't alert the authorities for hours and hours if you want. I promise." That was a lie, but one I was happy to offer up for Sunny's sake.

"I dunno, I guess, if you promise to tell them what I said. Tell them the truth about that other person . . ." Caden slid his hand from Sunny's ribs to her left wrist and stepped to the side. "But just to be sure, I want you both to walk back into that room behind the desk. And no sudden moves, 'cause I still have this knife."

I nodded and cast a reassuring glance at Sunny before turning and heading toward the workroom. When we reached the circulation desk, I considered making a grab for my briefcase but decided I shouldn't antagonize Caden. He still gripped Sunny by the wrist.

"In there, both of you," he commanded, pushing Sunny in front of him and pressing the tip of the knife against my shoulder blade.

I stumbled into the workroom with Sunny at my side.

"On the floor," Caden said, grabbing a roll of duct tape from a nearby shelf. "Each of you choose a table leg and sit back against it."

He was obviously going to tie us up, which didn't bode well. I leaned back, my palms pressed against the wooden surface of the worktable to steady my shaking legs. My twitching fingers tapped something hard that I realized was a stapler. If I could hit him . . .

I clutched the stapler and tossed it, but Caden moved just in time to miss being struck. He yelled a string of obscenities as he leapt forward and thrust the knife in my face.

"Sit or I cut you," he said.

The look in his eyes convinced me. Following Sunny's lead, I slid down to the floor.

Chapter Nine

As Caden fiddled with freeing the end of the tape from the roll, I glanced over at Sunny. She mouthed something that looked like *distracted*, but I shook my head. True, Caden wasn't focused on us for a second, but he still had a weapon, and after his last action I didn't trust him not to use it.

I comforted myself with the thought that if he tied us up and escaped before we could alert the authorities, which seemed to be his goal, we'd eventually be able to break free. Or someone would find us soon enough. Aunt Lydia and Sunny's grandparents knew we were working late at the library. If we never came home, they'd certainly inform the sheriff's office.

It was a risk but felt like a better choice than fighting an irrational young man who was probably under the influence of drugs. Especially a guy who was holding a knife with a dangerous blade that could inflict damage in any type of struggle.

Caden knelt by Sunny, holding the knife in one hand while he ripped a piece of the tape off with his teeth. "Don't try anything," he said.

Just as he leaned in to tape Sunny's hands behind her back, a series of knocks rattled the workroom's exterior door.

Caden leapt to his feet, his eyes wide and his mouth twitching.

"Hello there," yelled a voice from outside. "Anybody inside? The lights are on, so I thought . . ."

Swearing, Caden tossed the roll of tape at the door, which just made the visitor bang on it again.

"You okay in there? I'm going to call 911 if you don't answer!" shouted the stranger.

Caden clutched the knife to his chest and fled the workroom. As I used the edge of the table to pull myself to my feet, the back door opened and slammed shut.

"I think he's gone," Sunny said, standing and brushing the dust from her purple maxi dress. "Should we get the door? I'm kind of spooked about that, to be honest."

"I know, but I doubt there's anyone else waiting to attack us, and they offered to help, so . . ." I crossed to the door, unlocked it, and cracked it open.

A tall, broad-shouldered man stood on the stoop. Although he looked vaguely familiar, I couldn't place him.

"We're closed." I kept my hand on the edge of the door, ready to slam it in his face.

"I know," the man replied. "I'm just making a delivery for my mom. She told me you might be working late this evening."

Sunny stepped up behind me as I opened the door wider. "What kind of delivery?"

"Donations for the festival. I was out this evening and they were stuffed in the trunk of my car, so I thought I'd go ahead and drop them off."

I studied the stranger for another moment before it dawned on me. Donations. His mom.

"You must be Trey Riley." That was why he looked familiar, although we'd never met.

"And one of you must be the library director." Trey's gaze examined Sunny's slender build before lingering over my more curvaceous figure.

"That's me." I crossed my arms over my bust. "I'm Amy Webber. This is Sunny Fields, my assistant. Sorry if we seem a bit rattled, but we just had a frightening experience with an intruder." Speaking those words highlighted the reality of the experience. I swallowed hard, fighting a wave of nausea.

"I thought I heard something." Trey looked up and over my head. "Are they still here? I can quickly usher you both outside and call the authorities if necessary."

"No, he fled out the back when you yelled and banged on the door."

"Wow. I'm thankful I had such good timing. So glad you're both okay."

"Yeah, I'm thankful you did too." I clasped my trembling hands together at my waist.

Sunny turned and headed for the circulation desk. "Amy, you chitchat with our guardian angel," she called over her shoulder. "I'm going to call the sheriff's office."

Trey looked me over with what appeared to be sincere concern. "May I come in? I know you must be shaken up. Perhaps I can be of some assistance?"

I nodded and waved him inside, then closed and locked the door. Turning to face him, I realized why I should've recognized him immediately. Although his hair was light brown instead of blond and his eyes more hazel than green, he bore a distinct resemblance to Mel Riley. He also possessed her height and large-boned frame, and his pressed khaki pants and expensive leather loafers exuded the same casual air of wealth.

I twitched my lips into a semblance of a smile. "Sorry to be so unwelcoming. I'm very happy to meet you. Just wish it was under better circumstances. Anyway, I can't thank you enough. You saved Sunny and me from a very uncomfortable night, if not something worse."

Trey tugged on the collar of the cobalt-blue shirt peeping out from the neck of his ivory cable-knit sweater. "Honestly, I don't deserve your thanks. I didn't exactly do anything. Of course, I'm happy to have thwarted an attack, even if by accident. But I don't deserve a medal. I'm just a stranger with good timing." He ran the back of his hand over his eyes as if rubbing away some unpleasant thought.

"Still—thank you," I replied fervently. "And honestly, I can't think of you as a stranger. I feel as if I know you already, since your mom talks about you all the time."

Trey smiled, displaying gleaming white teeth that I suspected were veneers. "You have to take some of that with a grain of salt. Only-child syndrome, you know." He looked me up and down again. "She did tell me the director was fairly young, but she didn't mention you were so pretty. I'll have to give her some grief for that oversight."

I cleared my throat. "You couldn't imagine she'd notice such things."

"Oh, I don't know. You expect your mom to play matchmaker when you're new in town and single. Well, divorced, but it comes down to the same thing."

I pursed my lips. Right, the divorce. Zelda had shared the gossip about Trey and the ex-wife who'd taken him for millions. If the stories were true, it was no wonder he'd moved in with Mel. He might need free lodging for a while.

"Your mom said you were living with her for a bit?"

Trey's pleasant expression slipped for a second, but he quickly recovered. "Yes, for now. I thought she could use some help around the place, and since I needed to stay in town to oversee my latest development project, it seemed like the best option."

Sunny walked back into the workroom. "Authorities are on their way," she said, waving her phone.

"And we get to be questioned yet again." I sighed heavily.

"I guess we should be used to it by now." Sunny pulled a comical face at me before turning to Trey. "I couldn't help overhearing. So you're establishing a business in Taylorsford, Mr. Riley?"

"Please call me Trey." He flashed her a brilliant smile. "And yes, I'm starting a winery. Well, restarting to be more precise. The grapes were planted by the previous owners. Fortunately, the vines aren't in terrible shape, but there's still a ton of work to do to turn the place into a going concern."

I sat on one of the workroom stools, figuring I might as well make myself comfortable. Thank goodness Sunny had supplied dinner, since we'd probably be stuck in the library for at least another hour, talking to the authorities. "I remember—your mom said you were rehabbing an old lumber mill or something."

"Doing a full renovation." Trey rolled back the cuffs of his sweater, exposing the blue sleeves of his shirt. The vivid color against the neutral cream of his sweater lent him a jaunty, nautical air.

That's it, I thought. *He's going for the sporty sailor look.* The strawlike texture of his thick hair and the high color in his cheeks reinforced this image. He looked as if he'd spent a lot of time in the sun and wind. I could easily picture him at the tiller of an expensive sailboat. He wasn't my type but was still a very attractive guy.

"The Calloway place, right?" I narrowed my eyes. Zelda had mentioned that the winery, founded by a wealthy couple as a lark, had fallen on hard times and had been sold to a successful entrepreneur in his early forties. But Zelda hadn't linked this gossip to Trey.

"Yes. I'm converting the old mill into a tasting room. I may possibly add a restaurant once we're more established." Trey brushed a thick lock of his sandy hair away from his broad fore-head and turned his gaze back on Sunny. "So you're a Fields. Do your grandparents happen to own the organic farm right outside of town?"

Sunny toyed with the hair tie on her ponytail, twisting it around and around. "Yeah, that's our farm."

"Good to know. I'd like to talk to them about supplying some fresh veg to my restaurant. I mean, once I get it up and running."

I leaned forward, resting my arms on the top of the work-table. "A tasting room and a restaurant? You've certainly set some ambitious goals." I studied Trey's handsome face. So per-haps the gossip wasn't entirely correct and he wasn't broke. Trey's plans sounded expensive, and I couldn't imagine Mel footing the bill for such a venture. She lived well, but reliable sources— as in Zelda—claimed that Mel Riley wasn't quite as wealthy as she liked people to believe.

"Oh, this is pretty minor stuff compared to some of my

previous projects." Trey grabbed a pencil from the bin on the table and rolled it between his fingers as he stared at us. "By the way, what was your intruder after, anyway? I doubt the library keeps a significant amount of cash on hand."

"I don't know if we should say . . ." I shot Sunny a warning glance, but her gaze was fixed on Trey.

Sunny swept the hair tie out of her hair and shoved it in her pocket while tossing the shining fall of her loose hair behind her shoulders. "It was that Caden Kroft kid. He wanted me to tell the authorities that I'd seen someone else fleeing the LeBlanc farm the day Rachel was murdered. Someone other than him, I mean."

"But you didn't?" The pencil clattered to the floor. Trey bent over to pick it up, hiding his face from my inquisitive gaze.

"No, I didn't. Caden swore he glimpsed someone else in the woods but said he couldn't identify them." Sunny shrugged. "I saw no one else."

Trey straightened and flashed Sunny a brilliant smile. "I wouldn't spare it much thought. The young man probably made up some lie to exonerate himself and wanted to threaten you into supporting his story."

"Could be," I said, although, strangely, I found this hard to believe. Even though Caden had come at Sunny with a knife, he hadn't used it and had actually seemed relieved to leave Sunny and me unharmed when he couldn't get what he wanted. And there had been that look in his eyes when he was talking about someone else being at the scene . . . I shook my head. "I guess the authorities will figure it out eventually."

Through the thick fieldstone walls, sirens wailed, faint but piercing as a muted brass section.

Trey threw the pencil back in the bin and strode toward the exterior door. "If you don't mind, I think I'll pop outside and get my questioning out of the way so I can head home." He turned at the door to give us a sympathetic smile. "I'm afraid you're both in for a more lengthy interrogation."

"Sure, go ahead," I said. "No use all of us getting stuck here half the night."

Trey fiddled with the dead bolt, which could be tricky to unlock. "I'd enjoy the company, but it has been a long day . . ."

"Not a problem. Here, let me get that." Sunny crossed over to the staff door and flipped back the dead bolt in one swift motion.

Trey looked down at her with an expression that made my lips tighten. "Thanks. And nice to meet you, Sunny. I hope we can spend some less stressful time together sometime soon."

Sunny slid her tongue across her lower lip and gazed up at him from beneath her golden eyelashes. "Sounds fun."

"And you too, Amy," Trey called out as he stepped outside.

"Nice guy." Sunny closed the door and slumped back against it.

"You'll have to open that again in a second," I said. "You know, when Brad and the others arrive."

"Did you notice those muscles? I mean, that sweater kind of hid his body, but you can tell he works out." Sunny stared over my head, her dreamy gaze fixed on the fluorescent light fixture hanging over the worktable.

I snapped my fingers at her. "Brad, remember? And how can you be thinking about men or whatever after being held at knifepoint?"

"It helps," she said, looking at me. "Block it out, you know."

"I guess." I softened my expression as I noted the pain lurking in her blue eyes. "And remember—Trey seems nice, but there's that mother of his. Do you really want to date someone who has Mel Riley for a mom?"

"Oh, I can handle Mel." Sunny waved her hand in a dismissive gesture.

I couldn't hold back a little grin. Yes, she probably could. But as Sunny opened the door to let in the chief deputy and his team, my expression sobered.

"Poor Trey. He made a special trip and then didn't even get a chance to drop off any donations," I said.

Sunny, already talking with Deputy Coleman, didn't appear to hear me.

Brad crossed to me and looked me up and down. "We really must stop meeting like this," he said.

Which made me laugh before I burst into tears.

Chapter Ten

I arrived home so late that I didn't bother to call Richard, figuring he might already be asleep. I simply answered his text about arriving in New York City safely with "That's great. Talk tomorrow. Love you."

He didn't reply, which confirmed my thought that he was probably sleeping. I tapped my cell phone against my palm before placing it on the kitchen table. "I'm not sure if I should even say anything to him about today's incident," I told Aunt Lydia as she took a seat across from me.

She swirled a teaspoon in her cup of chamomile tea. "Don't you think he'll be upset if he doesn't find out until he gets home?"

I ran my forefinger over the ridges created by the dinosaur skeleton picture on my mug. "Dinosaurs Didn't Read and Now They're Extinct," the caption said. Richard had discovered the mug when he was off on one of his other choreography gigs and presented it to me on his return. "Probably. But I don't want to distract him. You know he'll be torn about staying or coming home. And he can't really come back until Sunday, since the final rehearsals start tomorrow and the performances are Thursday through Saturday. It's hard enough that he's had to step in with such limited rehearsal time. I'd hate for him to be worrying about me too. I'll tell him when he gets back Sunday night."

Aunt Lydia's eyes were hooded beneath her lowered eyelids. She examined her tea as if she could read fortunes in the pale jade liquid. "If you think that's best."

"I do. Changing the subject, you haven't told me anything about our new lodger. I assume he arrived sometime today, since I spied a strange car in the driveway."

"Yes, he showed up around ten this morning. Said hello, dropped off his suitcase, then headed back out to meet with the sheriff and other investigators. They moved those suspicious paintings to a secure storage facility. It seems that's where Dr. Chen will be working. Anyway, he got in late tonight, claimed he'd already had dinner, and headed up to his room."

I eyed her as I drank some tea. "What's he like?"

"Too soon to tell. He seems nice enough. He is Asian, as you would expect, given his name. Around my age, I guess. Says he goes by Hugh because no one can get his actual name right. He's rather nice looking. Distinguished, I would say." Aunt Lydia sipped her tea, her eyes unfocused as if her gaze was turned inward. "Dark hair and eyes, of course, but taller than I expected. My height, actually."

"Not all Asian people are short," I said, before downing another swallow of tea.

"I know that." Aunt Lydia's tone was testy, but I really couldn't fault her. She was undoubtedly exhausted, and I knew she'd been worried about me even though I'd called her from the library as soon as the authorities allowed me to contact anyone.

"I'll introduce you tomorrow morning. Dr. Chen did say

he'd appreciate breakfast." Aunt Lydia finished her tea before she looked up and met my inquisitive gaze. "I know you've been through a lot today, and it's late, but if you could join us before you head to work . . ."

"Of course. I'd like to meet him." I drank my remaining tea in two gulps before standing. "Now I think I'll go on up to bed if you don't mind. I'm pretty beat."

"I can certainly understand that." Aunt Lydia pressed her palms against the table, using that leverage to help her rise to her feet. "Just leave that cup. I'll wash up."

"No, I can do it. You must be tired too."

"But I wasn't threatened at knifepoint by a deranged murderer."

"Possible murderer," I said, crossing to the sink to place my mug on the adjacent butcher-block countertop.

Aunt Lydia carried her cup to the sink. "Who else could it be?"

I almost said "Kurt Kendrick" but bit back the words. No use bringing up my suspicions to my aunt, who always looked for any reason to speak ill of the art dealer.

"You never know," I said instead, as I headed for the door to the hallway. "Maybe our houseguest will turn up some other evidence soon."

Aunt Lydia just harrumphed and turned on the faucet.

* * *

The next day I hurried through my shower and other morning tasks, allowing my hair to dry naturally instead of messing with the blow dryer. Throwing on a pair of beige slacks and a crimson silk blouse, I tossed my caramel-colored jacket over my arm and headed downstairs.

The scent of coffee wafted upward as I made way down the stairs. I followed my nose into the kitchen, where Aunt Lydia was stirring batter in a yellow ceramic bowl.

"What can I do?" I asked when I joined her at the counter.

"Take that to the table," she replied, with a jerk of her head toward a pressed-glass bowl filled with sliced strawberries and pineapple chunks. "And the coffee carafe and creamer. There's sugar out already."

"You should've woken me earlier," I said as I carried the items over to the table.

"It's fine. I have everything under control."

Which she did, of course. I examined the table, noticing that three places were already set. "So, pancakes?"

Aunt Lydia, her hands clutching the ceramic bowl, blew a strand of white hair out of her eyes. "Yes. Just waiting for our guest before I drop them on the griddle."

I looked at her—in a purple sweater over worn jeans, her feet bare, her normally well-coiffed hair a bit mussed, and a spot of flour dusting the end of her nose—and thought she'd never looked so beautiful.

"Good morning," said a cultured male voice.

I turned to the speaker—an older man wearing a simple but well-tailored navy suit. He didn't notice me at first, though. He was staring at my aunt, and with obvious admiration.

Aha, I thought. *Aunt Lydia has made a conquest, and in just one day.*

She seemed oblivious to this. "Good morning, Dr. Chen. Please, have a seat. I was just about to make some pancakes, but there's fruit and coffee on the table if you'd like to start with that."

"Thank you." He sat down and examined the china and

silverware, the short crystal glass filled with orange juice at each place setting, and the cloth napkins. "You've gone to too much trouble, Mrs. Talbot."

"She always does that," I said, sitting across from him. "Guests are treated with the utmost respect in this house, Dr. Chen." I held out my hand, then pulled it back when I realized he couldn't reach across the table to grasp it. "I'm Amy Webber, the niece."

"Ah." He unfolded the napkin and placed it in his lap. "The library director."

"Yes." I looked him over as he scooped some of the chopped fruit into a small china bowl. "So, what do you think of those strange paintings, Dr. Chen? Are they forgeries or what?"

"Amy." My aunt shot me a sharp glance over her shoulder. "Don't badger the man with shop talk at breakfast."

"Oh, it's all right. And please, I'd like both of you to call me Hugh. I don't think we need to stand on ceremony. On that note, if I may call you Lydia and Amy, I'd appreciate it very much." Hugh Chen waved his spoon, including both of us in his request, but his gaze was fixed on my aunt's slender back.

"Of course," Aunt Lydia said without turning around. She gracefully wielded a plastic spatula to flip the pancakes on the griddle.

"Dr. Chen—I'm sorry, Hugh. I don't want to disturb your breakfast, but I am very curious about those paintings. I was there when they were discovered, you know, and I have an art history background, so Chief Deputy Tucker asked me to look into them before you arrived. I searched the Art Loss Register, among other things, but didn't find much, although the one that looks like a Caravaggio seems to be a study based on some lost painting."

"The *Nativity?*" Hugh replied, holding a spoonful of the fruit aloft. "Yes, it does look like a study for that work, which was stolen back in 1969, as you've obviously realized from your research."

"It's a forgery, though?"

Hugh chewed and swallowed before replying. "I believe so. I need to conduct some more in-depth research, but I suspect they are all forgeries."

Looking at his expression, which displayed a genuine interest in my words, I decided to share my latest theory. "Is it possible that they are all based on lost or stolen works, or even paintings that were only referenced in letters or other documents?"

Aunt Lydia carried over a platter of pancakes and set it on the table. "What are you getting at, Amy?"

"It's just a thought, but when I examined that study that was supposed to be a Caravaggio, it made me suspicious. It would be clever to fake something that looked like a study rather than a well-known lost work. That would display a high level of sophistication about the art world and the black market."

"Indeed," Hugh said, giving me an appraising look.

"So I wondered about the other pieces, the Impressionist ones in particular. I thought maybe the forgers had created them based on pieces the artists talked about in letters or other documents. Paintings they might have been working on at some point but never actually finished."

"Or finished and then destroyed. Or sold to someone who subsequently lost the painting somehow. It happens." Hugh used his fork to spear a short stack of the pancakes and transfer them to his plate. "Sadly, many great works have been lost in fires or floods, or even wars. At the time they might not have been considered extremely valuable, so they weren't protected against such catastrophes." Hugh winked at me as he reached for the syrup bottle. "That's some clever thinking on your part, Amy. You might be in the wrong line of work."

Aunt Lydia sat beside me, daintily unfolded her napkin, and placed it in her lap. "Hugh, if you prefer jam or something else . . ."

"No, this is perfect." Hugh glanced at Aunt Lydia. "What do you think of your niece's theory?"

"It sounds reasonable, but wouldn't such forgeries be easily exposed when the paintings were sold?"

"Not necessarily." Hugh took another bite and appeared lost in thought as he chewed and swallowed. "There's a lot of misinformation floating around the art marketplace. You'd be surprised how easy it is to fool people, especially when they want to believe something is an actual masterpiece."

"Meanwhile, my late husband's work goes unappreciated," Aunt Lydia said, before filling her bowl with fruit.

"Yes, it is a shame. A lot of collectors are only interested in 'names' and would rather own a disputed work that's supposedly by a famous artist than a true original by someone unknown." Hugh shrugged. "And of course, works like those discovered at the LeBlanc studio are probably intended for the black market. Collectors who buy items from shady dealers aren't likely to publicly exhibit them. If they're convinced the pieces are real, they'll just keep them hidden away for their own enjoyment. No scholars or experts are likely to ever see them, much less dispute their authenticity."

I cut my stack of pancakes into quarters, then eighths, before pouring on syrup. "So you agree that these paintings could've been created in the style of certain artists based on information about their lost works?"

"Yes, that makes sense. They'd have to forge the signatures too, of course, but that's much simpler than faking the actual art." Hugh polished off another forkful of pancakes. "These are delicious, Lydia. So light and fluffy."

"It's Aunt Lydia's secret recipe," I said between bites. "She's shared it with me, but no one else."

Aunt Lydia raised her narrow shoulders in a slight shrug. "Oh, it's nothing, really. Simplest recipe in the world. But I'm glad you enjoy it."

"Don't listen to her. She's a great cook. Totally rocks out everything she makes." I lifted my fork, laden with pancakes and syrup, and pointed it toward my aunt, who frowned at me.

But Hugh's expression brightened, as if this information confirmed his dearest hopes. "If her other meals are anything like this one, I believe you."

"The authorities," Aunt Lydia said, lifting her chin, "believe a young man named Caden Kroft murdered Rachel LeBlanc. I suppose that's likely, but it is strange that those odd paintings turned up at the same time. I just don't see Caden being involved in some art theft or forgery ring. He's not that clever, for one thing."

"It could merely be a coincidence, and"—Hugh, having eaten all his pancakes, dabbed at his lips with his napkin—"I wouldn't rule out some other suspect at this point. Perhaps the young man was merely in the wrong place at the wrong time."

"You think it could've been someone connected to the forgeries?" I propped my elbows on the table, resting my chin in my cupped hands.

Aunt Lydia cast me a disapproving look. *Right. Elbows never belong on the table.* I sat back without taking my eyes off Hugh. "Possibly. Something this elaborate indicates the involvement of a well-run organization."

"A well-run *criminal* organization," I said.

"Unfortunately, yes." Hugh took a sip of coffee before speaking again. "I probably shouldn't go into too many details until I know more, but this type of activity is undoubtedly backed by international criminals working at the high end of the forgery game."

I tapped my teaspoon against my coffee cup. "Who could and might put a hit on someone?"

"If necessary, yes."

Aunt Lydia coughed. "Please forgive us, Hugh. We don't usually discuss such things at breakfast."

He cradled his coffee cup between his slender hands. "Nothing to apologize for. It's sometimes the sad reality of my job, and I assure you, Lydia, nothing you or Amy could say would ever shock me."

She stared at him as if seeing him for the first time. "I suppose you have experienced quite a few disturbing things connected to your line of work. So what's your hypothesis? That this shadowy criminal cabal had Rachel LeBlanc killed? But why?"

Hugh shrugged. "That's something I can't answer. Although . . ." He set down his cup and leaned back in the wooden kitchen chair. "It is possible that one or both of the LeBlancs were involved in the forgeries. They were trained artists."

"Yes, but Rachel was already so well-known and respected. Why would she need to get involved in such a scheme?" I thought about what Kurt Kendrick had said and frowned. "Of course, there is Reese LeBlanc."

Hugh nodded. "The husband."

"Not so famous," Aunt Lydia observed, narrowing her blue eyes.

"If Reese was the forger, and Rachel didn't know . . ."

Aunt Lydia completed my thought. "She could've recently found out and threatened to turn him in to the authorities." She pressed her hand to her temple. "Yet my friend Zelda swears they were a loving couple. Would a devoted husband kill his wife over such a thing?"

"I can't say what a husband might do, never having been married," Hugh said. "But in my experience, love doesn't always trump self-preservation."

"Well, I have been married, and I can't imagine it." Aunt Lydia rubbed the spot between her eyebrows as if trying to banish a headache.

"Your husband was Andrew Talbot?" Hugh asked.

Aunt Lydia lowered her hand and looked up, her face brightening. "Yes. You've heard of him?"

"No, but I noticed the paintings in the hall."

"He was a great artist. Never really made the name for himself that he should have."

Hugh inclined his head in acknowledgment. "He was obviously very talented. But fame, you know, comes to so few."

"True."

I could tell by Aunt Lydia's pensive expression that Hugh's statement had hit a nerve. I tapped my fork against the edge of my plate. "Of course, we can't rule out the possibility that Caden

Kroft killed Rachel because he wanted money for drugs and she refused. He was there at the house with the daughter."

Hugh didn't look surprised. He'd obviously done his homework. "Delilah LeBlanc."

"Yeah, although she goes by Lila. And honestly"—I cast a swift glance at my aunt—"I've heard the girl's had problems with drugs too. And her parents weren't too happy about her relationship with Caden. So there's the slightest chance that Lila and Caden were in on it together."

"Stranger things have happened," Aunt Lydia said, sharing a glance with me.

I was certain she was thinking of her second cousin Sylvia, who'd killed three people over nothing more than family secrets and some business deals. The memory of the past summer's events reminded me of the other person who might have a hand in dubious art transactions. "Yeah, they have. But just so you know, Hugh, there is another person in Taylorsford with a connection to the art world, strange as that may seem."

Resting his elbows on the arms of his chair, Hugh laced his fingers together and studied me with interest. "Oh? Who's that?"

"Kurt Kendrick," I said, while Aunt Lydia sniffed loudly.

Hugh dropped his arms to the table and leaned forward. "Kendrick lives here? I thought his main gallery was in Georgetown."

"It is, and he doesn't live here full-time. But he does have a home here. It's not far from the LeBlanc farm, too."

"Really?" Hugh's thin eyebrows arched higher over his dark eyes. "That is interesting."

"You know him?" Aunt Lydia leaned into the table as well, all pretense of disinterest gone.

"Not personally. I've seen him around—at auctions and the occasional art show. And I am well aware of his reputation."

"Good or bad?"

Hugh took a moment to reflect on this question. "I'm not sure I can answer that properly," he said at last, his gaze fixed on my aunt's eager face. "A mix of both, from what I've heard. To be honest, he's a bit of a mysterious character in the art world, for all his wealth and influence."

"Slippery and cagey," I said. "I mean, that's my impression, anyway."

"And not a bad one." Hugh glanced from Aunt Lydia to me and back again. "You have both met him, I take it."

"Oh, I know him from way back," Aunt Lydia said. "I'll have to fill you in when you have time."

"And I would be happy to hear it. I have long wanted . . ." Hugh snapped his mouth shut and cleared his throat before casting a smile at me and my aunt. "Well, that's just a little personal interest of mine. Certainly nothing I need to bore you with. Now—thanks again for breakfast, but I must leave. Duty calls." He pushed back his chair and stood. "More of my lab equipment is scheduled to be delivered this morning, and I want to be there when it arrives."

"Understandable," Aunt Lydia said, also rising to her feet. "Will you be back for dinner?"

"If you're cooking, I'll certainly try to make it. But don't make anything special. I never know my schedule on these jobs. I may or may not be able to return in time for dinner. I'll call later this afternoon and let you know more, if that's okay."

"Perfectly fine." Aunt Lydia reached for the platter, which now held one lone pancake. "I wish you a successful day, Hugh."

"Thank you," he said, bobbing his head. "Amy, would you like a lift? I have to take the main street to head out of town, so I'll pass right by the library."

"That would be great," I said. "Just let me run upstairs and brush my teeth and I'll be good to go."

"I must do the same," Hugh said with a smile. "So no hurry. I'll just meet you outside." He glanced at Aunt Lydia. "Sorry to leave you with the cleanup."

She waved him off with one hand. "Oh, don't worry about that. I don't have any big plans for the day. I can take my time."

Hugh cast her another warm smile before leaving the room.

"He's nice," I observed as I carried my plate and silverware to the sink.

"Yes, very polite." Aunt Lydia rolled up the sleeves of her sweater and placed the stopper in the sink drain. "Seems quite intelligent too."

"I should think so, given his degrees and reputation." I side-eyed my aunt as she turned on the faucet. "He's certainly quite impressed with you."

Aunt Lydia made a tutting noise and squirted some dish soap into the rising water in the sink. "Don't be silly. The man just met me."

"Sometimes that's all it takes, or so you've always told me."

Aunt Lydia vigorously stirred her hand through the water, creating a tower of soap bubbles. "You're going to be late for work if you don't get a move on."

I grinned and left the room humming *Some Enchanted Evening* while my aunt tried to drown out the song by tossing a fistful of clattering silverware into the soap-filled sink.

Chapter Eleven

Although Aunt Lydia offered her car, I didn't bother driving to work after Wednesday. The Heritage Festival officially opened on Friday, and I knew from experience that it would be impossible to find a parking space anywhere in town later in the week. Even the lot behind the library, which was supposed to be reserved for library staff and patrons, had begun to fill up with vehicles with out-of-state plates by Wednesday afternoon.

"Couldn't you request that the sheriff's office ticket or tow?" Richard asked when we spoke on the phone on Wednesday night.

Stretched across the width of my double bed, I gazed longingly at my pile of unread books before eyeing the dust bunnies congregating in one corner of my bedroom. "Yeah, but Sunny told me that Brad and his team are already overwhelmed with traffic enforcement and other stuff. So I hate to bother them. I'll just walk. The weather is supposed to be clear, so it shouldn't be a problem."

"Sounds reasonable. How goes the setup for the library sale?"

I couldn't help but wonder if those dust bunnies bred like

actual rabbits. I'd just cleaned everything on Sunday, but there they were again, in all their fluffy glory. "Okay. Finally got everything priced and ready to go. Aunt Lydia even donated two of Uncle Andrew's paintings to replace Rachel LeBlanc's, which mollified Mel a bit. Although she's still pissed that Aunt Lydia wouldn't allow her to pick out the paintings herself. I don't know why she was so determined to be the one to choose, but she sure as hell was. She even showed up at the house yesterday asking if she could look at all of Andrew's works, but Aunt Lydia put the kibosh on that."

"As only she can do." There was a smile evident in Richard's voice.

"Yeah." I rolled over on my back and stared at the cracks in the plaster ceiling, which, if I squinted, looked like a leafless tree. "How are things going with the show?"

"Fine." The brightness in his tone had vanished. "I mean, the rehearsals have been great, and I think the performances will be top-notch, but . . ."

"You're having difficulties with your costar?"

"Hmmm . . ." I heard the clink of ice cubes in a drink. "Not difficulties exactly. As I mentioned last night, our first meeting was a little tense, but once we started dancing, everything was fine. Only . . . well, she told me today that she left her husband."

"What?" I sat up so fast the mattress bounced. "But didn't they just get married?"

"Yeah, less than a year ago. But apparently it was one of those 'Marry in haste, repent at leisure' situations."

"Well, not too much leisure, it seems."

Richard chuckled. "True enough. Anyway, I was a little surprised, so I just mumbled 'Sorry' and left it at that."

"She was probably hoping you'd fall to your knees and beg her to resume your relationship."

"If she was, she hadn't heard a single thing I'd said before her announcement, since I did talk about you incessantly."

"Did you now?" I flopped back against the bed.

"I did." More ice cubes clinked. When Richard spoke again, it was in a very different tone. "I miss you."

"You'll see me Sunday."

"That doesn't solve the problem of me missing you now."

"Just put all that energy into your performances and you'll be fine."

"Dearest, dancing is wonderful, but it isn't the solution to everything."

"So you'll just have to fantasize like I do," I said, then slapped my hand over my mouth. I hadn't intended to let that slip, no matter how true it was.

There was a pause, filled with Richard obviously taking a long swallow of his drink. "Well now, there's an idea. Perhaps you can talk me through some scenarios?"

Heat sailed up my neck and spread over my face. "Um . . . I've never . . ."

"Always a first time." Amusement colored Richard's voice.

I cleared my throat. "I think maybe we should call it a night."

Richard laughed. "Okay, but you're going to make me regret not taking Meredith's suggestion that we go barhopping. You know, for old time's sake."

"What?" I sat up and took a breath before speaking again. "You really thought that might be a good idea?"

"Sorry." Richard did sound abashed. "I shouldn't say stuff

like that over the phone, when you can't see my face to know I'm just teasing you. Meredith did invite me out for a drink, but I made it very clear that I was retiring to my room to chat with you right after the dress rehearsal."

"A drink, huh?"

"Yep, but I just ordered room service, so not to worry. Now, good night. I'm sure you could use some sleep, and I certainly can. But if you want to send some of those fantasy thoughts my way, maybe I can employ a little telepathy and dream about you." The ice clinked again. "God, I must be tired—not making much sense, am I? Just keep me in your thoughts, okay?"

"I always do," I replied without hesitation. Because it was true.

*   *   *

We made a pact not to call each other before Saturday so that, as Richard put it, he wouldn't be *quite so distracted* during actual performance days. Which meant that Thursday evening after dinner I caught myself roaming aimlessly around the house.

I wandered to the door of the sitting room and found Aunt Lydia and Hugh deep in conversation about the contemporary art scene. I didn't want to intrude on them, especially not when Hugh was gazing at my oblivious aunt with a look that spoke volumes about his interest in her. Turning on my heel before they even noticed me, I decided I should take a walk.

It was a gorgeous autumn evening. There was a fresh bite to the air, and the sky over the blue mountains was threaded with coral and rust ribbons of sunset. I stuffed my hands into the pockets of my hooded Clarion University sweatshirt and strolled to where the sidewalk ended, just past Richard's house. The fields beyond his yard were now brown with the stubble of the orchard grass someone had baled into hay.

I continued hiking down the gravel road to the woods that separated the old Cooper farm acreage from the working farm owned by Brad Tucker's family. I knew there was a path through the woods—an unofficial trail created over time by townsfolk stalking game with either guns or cameras.

Fortunately for Richard, my aunt, and the Tuckers, the Cooper land—once slated for a housing development—would soon be converted into a park. It was all part of Mayor Bob Blackstone's efforts to make amends for keeping silent over Sylvia Baker's crimes. I tugged my hood over my loose, shoulder-length hair as I crossed the edge of the field to reach the woods. The loss of the money on the sale to developers must've seriously damaged the mayor financially. Although, as Kurt Kendrick had said, it was little enough for him to do. Blackstone's refusal to expose Sylvia Baker when she'd first blackmailed him had cost three people their lives.

Vibrant red and gold leaves still clung to some of the branches overhead, although there were sections where the trees had already shed their foliage, creating natural skylights. A carpet of brown leaves crackled under the soles of my sneakers.

Leaves rustled up ahead of me. I paused and peered into the undergrowth, now mostly a tangle of bare vines and shrubs.

"Hello. Anyone there?"

A tall, thin figure slipped out from behind the thick trunk of an oak tree. Dressed in tattered jeans and a quilted flannel shirt over a black T-shirt, the stranger had a slender face surrounded by a halo of curly black hair.

"Lila," I said, recognizing the girl from the times I'd assisted her at the library as well as her resemblance to her late mother. "Are you all right? What are you doing out here at this hour?"

"Could ask you the same thing," the girl replied. She was very still, except for her dark eyes, which kept darting from side to side as if she were looking for something.

Or someone. I clutched my upper arms with my hands. *What if she's meeting Caden out here? You should turn around and walk away.*

But Lila appeared so distressed I couldn't leave. Not without seeing if there was anything I could do to help.

"I'm taking a walk. I live close by, you know. But you . . . how did you get here? I didn't see any cars." I took a few cautious steps closer.

"I parked behind the woods, on the Tuckers' farm road." Lila cast a glance over her shoulder. "You really should go, Ms. Webber."

"Are you expecting anyone? I mean, is someone meeting you here?" I pushed back my hood and moved close enough to see the sweat beading on Lila's upper lip and brow.

"Yeah, my dad." Lila held up her hand, palm out. "No, don't you go grabbing for your phone. I'll be gone before any cops get here, and if I run, so will my dad." She looked me over, her mouth curling into a sneer. "Doubt you could catch me. I used to run track, and I don't think you're in any shape to chase me down."

My lips twitched at this jibe, but I kept my voice calm. "So you're meeting your father in secret? But why?"

"Because the authorities are searching for him, of course." Lila's ringlets bounced as she tossed her head. "Or had you forgotten he's a wanted man?"

"But if he's innocent . . ."

Lila made a disparaging noise. "Sure, like those deputies will care. He's been missing since the crime and he's the husband, so of course he's guilty."

I opened my arms in a conciliatory gesture. "He just needs to tell his side of the story. The evidence will back him up if he had nothing to do with your mom's murder." *If what he told his daughter was the truth*, I thought, my concern for Lila rising. There was the insurance policy, and Reese LeBlanc's debts . . .

Lila's gaze shifted again. She stared over my shoulder and narrowed her eyes. "Right, 'cause innocent people never get rail-roaded into confessions and stuff." She waved her hand, as if pushing something back.

I spun around in time to see another figure disappear into a thick stand of scrub pines. "Is he here, then?"

"Not for long." Lila yanked her cell phone from her pocket and tapped in a quick message. "Just told him to get the hell out of here and lose the phone he used to text me. So I don't think your deputy pal will be able to track him down so easily."

"But if he didn't kill your mom, which you obviously believe, wouldn't it be better for him to turn himself in and get cleared by the evidence?"

"Like I said, we don't trust the system." Lila rubbed her hand under nose and lowered her eyes. "Besides, who says the sheriff's department is our biggest problem?"

"What do you mean?" I took two steps forward. "Come on, Lila. Head back with me and let's clear up this mess."

As I spoke these words, Lila lifted her head and widened her eyes. "Someone's coming. What'd you do? Walk out here to trap us?"

That was so irrational, I just shook my head. "I didn't even know you were here . . ."

But Lila shot me a furious glance and swore at me, using words that turned my face red. As I stood there, open-mouthed, she ran off, disappearing around a bend in the narrow path.

Shoes crunched leaves behind me. Reese LeBlanc, ready to make sure I would tell no tales? I turned around, my hands raised and fingers curled into fists. But that was ridiculous—I couldn't fight anyone. I opened my hands, hoping I could at least do some damage with my nails.

"Hey!" Trey Riley jumped back as I came at him, fingers extended like claws.

I dropped my hands to my sides. "Trey! What are you doing out here?"

"I could ask you the same thing." He looked me up and down. "Expecting an attack or something?"

"I was taking a walk and, yes, I thought . . ." Clamping my lips, I shuffled my feet through the dusty leaves. I had no reason to protect Lila or Reese LeBlanc, but I also didn't think my encounter was any of Trey's business. Or, more importantly, any of his mother's business. Not knowing what he shared with her, I thought it best not to provide her with more gossip about the LeBlanc family. The authorities should be the first to know that Reese was still in the area, not Mel Riley.

"You thought I was some vagrant wandering through the woods, looking to rob any unsuspecting hiker?" Trey tipped his head to one side and examined me for a moment before flashing a bright smile. "But as you see, it's just me, also out for a walk."

"A little far from your usual haunts, isn't it?" I met Trey's amused glance and lifted my chin. "Or are you scouting more property? Although, just so you know, this is going to be a town park. It's not for sale."

"I'm aware of that." Trey brushed a twig from his chocolate-brown suede jacket. "Just thought I should check out the area." He grinned, displaying a glimpse of his brilliant teeth. "Eventually someone will have to be hired to build the facilities for this future park, you know."

"Looking for development contracts, then?"

"Maybe. Now"—Trey held out his arm—"may I escort you back to your aunt's house? You look a bit shaken up, to be honest."

I patted down the flyaway strands of my hair. "All right, but you don't need to hold my arm. I'm not that feeble."

"Never thought you were. The opposite, I expect." He flashed me a warm smile before he turned and strode toward the head of the path, slowing his pace at one point so I could walk along-side him.

"You're dressed a bit elegantly for a hike in the woods," I observed.

Trey glanced down at his light-brown wool slacks and leather loafers. "I just came from a business meeting." He unbuttoned his jacket, exposing a tan cashmere sweater layered over a crisp white shirt. "One of those meetings where you hear news that isn't quite what you want to hear. So I thought—time for a walk."

"To plot future development ventures?" I was genuinely curious. It seemed an odd thing to do, especially since the Riley home was on the other side of town. I also knew from Zelda that it was a large estate, boasting plenty of wooded land of its own. I frowned and quickened my pace to keep up with his longer strides.

"Okay, you caught me," Trey said after a moment of silence. "I also wanted to take a look at your aunt's house. I thought I'd grab a walk to clear my head, then see if maybe she'd give me a tour. I'm very interested in restoration projects, and her house is so well preserved . . ."

"Really?" As we left the woods, I slid my hands back into my sweatshirt pockets. "It actually needs a lot of work. We try to keep it up as best we can, but it's a pretty overwhelming task."

Trey gazed down at me, his brown eyes gleaming with interest. "I mean *preserved* because not much has been done to alter the original design and decorations. These days, so many of the old Victorians and Queen Annes have been made over drastically inside. You know, following the trend of the whole open-concept thing, and great rooms, and so on."

"Yeah, we haven't done anything like that."

"That's why I'd love to see the interior. Get some ideas for the local renovation projects I hope to take on once my winery is up and running. I'll probably have to start a new company to handle that, of course."

I paused on the sidewalk in front of my house and glanced up at Trey's face, which seemed alight with some secret passion. "Well, as I said the other evening—very ambitious." I smiled at him, admitting to myself that his enthusiasm was infectious.

In fact, maybe it wouldn't be such a bad thing if he dated Sunny. I knew that she was a bit ambivalent about her relationship with Brad. Perhaps a charming businessman would prove a more compatible companion in the long run. Undoubtedly, Trey, unlike Brad, was interested in literature and other cultural pursuits. He might be a better match for my well-read friend.

"I'm a go-getter." Trey looked down at me with an answering

smile before raising his eyes to study my family home's impressive facade.

"I'm sure. But I'm afraid I can't invite you in this evening. My aunt isn't much for people just dropping by uninvited, and we do have that art expert, Hugh Chen, staying with us at the moment. I'm not sure a tour right now would be appropriate."

"Of course." Trey spoke cheerfully, but I noticed the tightening of his jaw. "Another day then."

"Sure. Just let me arrange it ahead of time."

"That does remind me, though, of the other reason I'd like to see inside." Trey turned to face me. "Mom claims that Lydia has kept most of her late husband's paintings. Is that right?"

"Yes."

"Well, I had this idea . . ." Trey traced a circle on the sidewalk with the toe of his loafer. "Once I get my tasting room up and running, I thought it would add a nice touch to include some paintings by local artists. Purchased, or even on loan if that's all your aunt would be willing to do. My first thought was of your uncle because I know my mom admires his work. It seemed like a win-win for both families. It could generate more interest in Andrew Talbot's paintings as well as providing some upscale decorations for the winery."

"So you want to check out Uncle Andrew's paintings as well as the house?"

"Basically, yes." His jaw was set and his eyes focused on me like a laser. He appeared as determined to see Andrew's paintings as his mother. Although it seemed that Trey was more interested in promoting my late uncle's work than Mel had ever been.

As I pushed open the front gate, something washed over me. It was a warning, like the tingling I sometimes felt at an intersection when I just *knew* that a vehicle was going to run the light. A voice in my head told me to be careful. I shivered as I experienced a sensation as definite as a hand on my shoulder, pulling me back from the brink.

I rested my fingers on the gate latch and examined Trey. He was a good-looking guy, with an expensive wardrobe, and an easy manner. Yet something made me hesitate to allow him to set foot through the gate, much less the front door. I shrugged my shoulders to shake off this feeling. My encounter with Lila had unnerved me, but I shouldn't take that out on Trey. Although I'd felt he seemed a little pushy about examining the house and Uncle Andrew's paintings, I could easily chalk that up to a sincere interest in art in architecture. No doubt my passions had made me come across the same way to others sometimes.

"I'll have to see what I can arrange with Aunt Lydia," I said, closing the gate behind me. "But it won't be possible until Dr. Chen wraps up his investigation and leaves us, I'm afraid."

"Of course," Trey replied in a cheerful tone.

"And in the meantime, I guess I'll see you at the festival?"

"For sure. I'm helping Mom with the library sale for an hour or two, so we're bound to cross paths."

"But not in the woods," I said, giving him what I hoped was a charming smile.

"No. Good night, then, Amy." Trey raised one hand to the left side of his chest, as if pressing his fingers to his heart. "I'm glad I ran into you. See you again soon."

As I watched him walk away, I couldn't help but notice that he'd parked his car just beyond the entrance to our driveway.

So had he come to walk in the woods, or to examine my aunt's house? As I climbed the steps to the front porch, I considered this possibility. He could've been lurking in the area and watched me head out for my walk and followed me. Perhaps his chatter about contracts for the park development was just a way to work around to talking about Aunt Lydia's house.

Maybe that was the property he really desired.

Aunt Lydia had always suspected that her cousin Sylvia had wanted to buy the house to turn it into a bed-and-breakfast. Perhaps, with a town park soon to be built so close by, Trey Riley also considered it a worthy investment. Upscale lodging within a block of a town park might prove quite desirable.

Aunt Lydia and I had no plans to sell the family home, but Trey Riley didn't know that. He might think he could acquire it, along with some of my uncle's paintings, if he waved around enough cash. It wouldn't be the first time a Riley had assumed their wealth could get them anything they wanted. Mel had probably raised her son to think that way.

Which only means, I resolved, as I shoved my key into the lock on the front door, *that, nice guy or not, he has another thought coming.*

Chapter Twelve

I waited until Trey drove off before I pulled out my cell phone and debated how to inform the sheriff's department about my encounter with Lila LeBlanc. On the one hand, I knew the authorities had to be told that Reese was still in the area and might have even been in the woods to meet Lila. But I hated the thought of being questioned again. It was selfish, but I just couldn't face any more interrogations. So I searched for the number for the anonymous tip line and sent a text instead. It would alert the sheriff's office without involving me any deeper in the case.

With that duty out of the way, I walked inside, careful to lock the door behind me. I called out, "Good night, heading up to my room," to Aunt Lydia and Hugh as I crossed the hall and clattered up the stairs to the second floor.

But Hugh wasn't in the sitting room. On my way to my bedroom, I noticed light spilling from the door to one of the spare bedrooms.

It was the bedroom Aunt Lydia had given to Hugh, but it also included the closet where she stored all of Uncle Andrew's paintings not displayed throughout the rest of the house. Since the door stood ajar, I didn't hesitate to peer into the brightly lit room.

Hugh sat cross-legged on the hardwood floor in front of the open door to the storage closet. Several of Uncle Andrew's canvases were spread out around him.

"Hello," I said, pulling the door open wider and stepping over the threshold.

"Oh, hi, Amy." Hugh waved me into the room. "Lydia said I could look at the paintings that were stored in here. Hope you don't mind."

"No, of course not," I said, crossing to him. "That's totally Aunt Lydia's call anyway."

"It's fascinating to examine someone's output like this." Hugh gestured to the paintings. "You can trace the evolution of their style and see what inspired them." He looked up at me. "By the way, I must thank you for your insights about those LeBlanc forgeries. It was a clever deduction to consider that the forgers focused on studies or lost works."

"Oh, I just like to puzzle out mysteries," I replied, fanning the sudden heat in my face.

"Well, I was impressed. Which makes me wonder if you would be willing to help with the investigation a bit more?"

"Sure, but what else can I do?"

"Research letters and other documents related to the artists represented. I mean, assuming they are fakes, which I think likely, it would be helpful if we could discover some information linking the paintings to known descriptions of any lost or unfinished works. If an artist mentioned working on a piece but that painting either never materialized or has been lost or stolen, it could solidify your theory and give the investigators new avenues to explore. Assuming that this forgery ring is still active, which I suspect it is."

"I'll do what I can, although all I can access is stuff on the Internet. Or maybe the collected letters of various artists in some of the books in the library." I rubbed the tense muscles of my neck with one hand. "I can request other materials through interlibrary loan, but that will take some time."

"Whatever you can do will be helpful." Hugh gave me a smile before turning his attention back to Uncle Andrew's paintings. He lifted one of the smaller canvases. "He was a great technician."

"Yeah, but at the time he was painting, realistic art wasn't so popular." I sat on the floor in front of Hugh, paintings fanned out on the floor between us. "So he never sold much."

"Shame." Hugh turned around the canvas he was holding. It was a still life of oranges in a blue-and-white bowl decorated in the style of Chinese Ming porcelain. "I would've thought he could have made good money selling to interior design firms. This style is still popular with a lot of people who own hotels and office buildings. But Lydia told me he refused to turn his art into 'decoration.'"

"He was a bit of a snob about that sort of thing, from what I hear."

"Nothing wrong with that." Hugh flipped the painting over and studied it for a moment. "There *is* more here than just a pretty picture. Something in the brushstrokes, and the use of light. He was definitely striving for something more."

I examined another one of the paintings—a landscape

capturing the fields and woods of the old Cooper farm at dusk. Strangely, although I'd never felt such a thing when I'd glanced at Andrew's paintings that hung in our front hall, the sensation of my uncle being right at my elbow washed over me.

But that was the thing—I'd never really studied those paintings, simply accepted their existence. I'd looked past them, really. *Sorry,* I told my dead uncle as I touched the surface of one of the unframed canvases. "You should tell Aunt Lydia that. She'll appreciate it."

"I did. And she did." Hugh carefully placed the small still life on the floor and picked up an unframed canvas and unrolled it. "Now this one is interesting. Looks unfinished, almost a sketch, and it's in a very different style—like Andrew was copying the work of Monet in his later years. The water lily period, I mean." He stretched the canvas between his hands and turned the painting around so I could view it. "See what I mean? Much more Impressionist than most of his other work."

"Yes, that is different." I narrowed my eyes. I didn't recall ever seeing that particular piece before. It looked nothing like my uncle's typical style.

But what do I really know of you? I asked the imaginary spirit of my uncle. *Only what Aunt Lydia and others have told me. Perhaps I should've studied your paintings a bit more if I wanted to know you better. Maybe you would've spoken to me more clearly through your art.*

Hugh allowed the canvas to roll back up and tapped the loose cylinder against his palm, his eyes shadowed under his lowered eyelids. "It's probably just a study. You know how artists often copy the masters for practice." He rose to his feet, still holding the painting. "But I think I'm going to lay this on the dresser rather than putting it back in the closet, if that's all right with you."

"Sure." I studied his profile, my curiosity piqued by his apparent interest in a simple study.

"I just thought that it should be stored properly. I have a few leather map and print cases I carry around in the trunk of my car in case I need to transport unframed pieces. I don't mind donating one to Lydia." He glanced over at me. "It would protect the work."

"I'm sure my aunt would appreciate that."

"Good. I'll do that later," Hugh said, not meeting my gaze. He laid the rolled canvas on the dresser and rested his hand on it for a moment before turning to me. His sober expression brightened. "May I ask you a somewhat personal question, Amy?"

"I suppose so." Examining his earnest face, I could guess what it might be. "You like my aunt."

"I do. I know we just met, but she is so . . ." Hugh threw out his hands. "So unique. Intelligent and beautiful and deeply interested in so many things. I have not met many women like her."

"Few have, I think," I replied with a smile. "So what do you want to know? Why she's never remarried?"

"No, I believe I understand that." Hugh swept one hand through the air over Andrew Talbot's paintings. "She loved him very much, I think."

"Yeah, she did. And still does, I suppose."

"Ah, and you have answered my question already."

I sat back on my heels and tapped one finger against the frame of a canvas depicting Aunt Lydia's garden. "She hasn't ever given anyone else a chance. She says she had a once-in-a-lifetime love, and that's enough."

Hugh nodded. "I understand this. But it isn't true, you know."

"Isn't it?" I thought about Richard. If something happened to him, I wasn't sure I could ever love someone else. "Why do you say that?"

"Because I know this feeling. I too, lost a love. Many years ago, when I was young."

"I'm sorry. She died?"

"No." Hugh leaned back, pressing his palms against the dresser. "Although, like me, she was born in San Francisco, she came from a very different sort of family. Her parents had emigrated from Hong Kong not long before she was born, while my family had been in the U.S. for a couple of generations. She came from a wealthy, well-respected family, while my ancestors came over to work as laborers on the railroad."

"So they didn't approve of you?"

"Not at all. Despite the fact that we owned a prosperous business, we were still 'beneath' her family. At least in their opinion." Hugh gazed down at one of Andrew's landscapes thoughtfully. "When they forbade her to ever see me again, I believed my life was over. I was only twenty-two at the time," he added, looking at me with a wry smile.

"But you did survive, and thrive, it seems."

"Yes, but I turned this thwarted romance into something that it was never meant to be—a fantasy of perfection that prevented me from accepting the possibility of love with anyone else. Which is why I am alone today."

"You don't feel the same now?"

"No. It's funny. I eventually realized that I had given my heart to a dream. Something that would never have been, at least not in that form, if I had actually married my love and lived with her all my life. One day I woke up and understood that I had substituted a fantasy for any chance of a real love."

I pressed my hand to my heart, feeling a wave of certainty sweep through me. *Yes,* said the voice in my head. *This is the truth. This is what you must make her see, what she must admit.* I nodded. It was something that I'd always sensed in my aunt but could never put into words. "You believe Aunt Lydia has done the same thing."

"Yes. I see it in her eyes when she talks about your uncle. I know that look, that tone of voice. I have lived it."

I stared at him speculatively. "She is very stubborn."

Hugh's wry smile broadened. "I'm sure she is. As am I."

"She won't change her mind easily."

"No, I don't expect she will. But perhaps, someday . . ."

I offered him a warm smile. "I think that would be a good day."

His cell phone jangled before he could reply. "Sorry, I must get this," he said, after sliding the phone from his pocket and glancing at the screen. "Work."

He left the room, already lost in an animated conversation with the caller.

I sat in silence for a moment. As I mulled over his words, a dull thump made me glance over at the storage closet. I scooted across the floor and stared at the pile of canvases that had toppled forward to reveal one large canvas leaning against the back wall.

Pulling the exposed painting from the closet, I saw that it

was another landscape—or, actually, a seascape. That was unusual. My uncle rarely painted such scenes. It was also somewhat larger than most of his pieces. I estimated it was at least thirty-six inches wide and thirty inches tall. But even odder was the fact that the stretchers that held the canvas taut were much deeper than usual, as if two bars had been glued or nailed together.

It was also heavier than most of the canvases I'd handled, and unbalanced, with extra weight tipping down one side. I lifted my right hand from the stretcher bar and slid my fingers onto the back of the canvas. Instead of the taut, flat surface I expected, I encountered a thick roll of material.

It was another unframed painting, rolled tight in a piece of unpainted canvas and pressed up against the right stretcher bar. It was obviously intended to be hidden from view unless someone picked up this piece.

I laid the painting on the floor, face down, and gently pried the cylinder of canvas free. Unrolling it with great care, I dropped its wrap in my lap and held the painting up with both hands.

It was approximately the same size as its parent canvas, and painted in a fashion that once again mimicked the Impressionists. I squinted and sucked in a deep breath. In fact, it looked very much like a Van Gogh. There were two figures—a man in pale blue with a yellow hat, and a woman in a black skirt and a pink bodice—in a landscape of sand and thistles. Behind them, green cypress trees stood in a row against a rosy pink sky.

As I glanced down at the unpainted piece of canvas overwrap draped across my lap, searching for any type of label, my breath caught in my throat. There were markings, but they were simply repeated versions of a name, as if someone had used the material to practice a signature.

Vincent Van Gogh's signature.

Footsteps in the hall compelled me to roll up the loose canvas in its wrap and shove it behind the other painting. Driven by an unshakable feeling that I should protect this secret, I jumped up and thrust the seascape and its hidden cargo at the back of the closet, burying it behind other paintings as Hugh walked into the room.

"I'll get out of your way now," I said, brushing some canvas threads from my jeans. "You'd probably appreciate a little quiet time before bed."

"Thank you," Hugh said, examining me in a way that made me wonder if my expression had betrayed my shock over my latest discovery.

I forced a smile and scooted past him to slip into the hall.

Reaching my bedroom, I sank down onto my bed with only one thought racing around my brain, frantic as a squirrel stuck in a cage.

When I closed my eyes, I saw the images painted inside my eyelids—the sketch that looked like a Monet, that hidden completed canvas that resembled a Van Gogh, and the signature practiced with such diligence, as if the painter were attempting to mimic another's hand.

It wasn't possible, and yet, how could I escape the evidence? Or the little voice that whispered the truth in my ear.

My uncle, Andrew Talbot, had not only been a talented, if unrecognized, artist. It was quite likely he'd been a forger too.

Chapter Thirteen

I got another late start the next day, having spent far too much time the night before researching Trey Riley's business interests as well as information on the history and practice of forgery. From my survey of Trey's background—at least what was available online—I decided he was one of those people who started and abandoned businesses like some people changed socks. Not that he hadn't made money—it appeared that he had. But he had lost a great deal too, if his trail of less-than-successful ventures was any indication. There was also the very expensive divorce. I'd halted my research on Trey with the sense that he might not be in any position to buy more property, even if he would like to. Which meant I probably shouldn't worry too much about his interest in my aunt's house.

The forgery research was less reassuring. I was astounded by how much of it had actually occurred throughout history and how it continued to impact the art world. Even with modern methods of detection and attribution, it seemed that the market was flooded with works of questionable provenance. There were apparently large networks of thieves and forgers who had infiltrated the highest levels of the art world, duping even the most educated appraisers.

And Kurt Kendrick is mixed up with some of those criminals, I bet, I thought, although his name appeared nowhere in my cursory research, which was instead peppered with mentions of individual forgers who had either been exposed or had eventually outed themselves, such as Elmyr de Hory, Han van Meegeren, and Ken Perenyi. The most notorious forgery ring still in operation was apparently run by the Quinns—a family operation that had expanded into an international crime cabal. According to my research, despite being a high-value Interpol target, the Quinns' organization had yet to be cracked by the authorities.

Pondering this new information, I braved the crowds that filled the sidewalks as I walked to the library the next morning. The festival didn't officially open until nine o'clock, but many visitors arrived early to snag parking spaces on the side streets. Although the sheriff's department had set up temporary lots outside of town and several businesses had offered their vans as shuttles, it seemed people preferred to park on streets outside the cordoned-off downtown blocks.

I slid past a group of older women and men who were chatting about scooping up some of the antiques and crafts offered by the festival's vendors.

"You absolutely must get here on the first day, and early, to find the best items," one of them said, ignoring my apology as I bumped her elbow.

I shook my head. Although there were many talented craftspeople and artists who sold items at the festival, I couldn't imagine battling the crowds to buy anything. It was bad enough that

I had to supervise the library sales table all day. I had no desire to actually brave the festival crowds beyond the library lawn.

Shouldering the heavy tote bag that held my lunch as well as bottled water and snacks for the volunteers, I zigzagged around the groups of people clogging the sidewalk. I was anxious to reach the library before eight thirty, which was a challenge due to my late start.

I patted the pocket of my wool jacket, making sure I had my library keys handy. Sunny and the volunteers had probably already set up the library table, but I owned the only key to the lockbox that held the change money and the device needed to accept credit and debit card payments.

At least the weather was cooperative, making it the perfect day for a fall festival—not too cold but just crisp enough to provide the proper autumn atmosphere. I glanced up at the white clouds sailing through the clear sky.

Before I could lower my gaze, I stumbled into someone and squashed down the back of his black leather shoe with the toe of my sneaker. "Oh, so sorry," I said, as he shoved his heel back into his shoe and turned around.

I shrank back. The man had short, dark hair, broad shoulders, and a neck as thick as a tree trunk. Although of average height, his bulging arm muscles pressed against the fabric of his crisp white shirt as if they might split its seams at any moment.

"No problem," the man said, but I could tell this was a lie. Reflective sunglasses hid his eyes, but the set of his heavy jaw and the thin line of his mouth betrayed his annoyance.

"It's crowded," I replied with what I hoped was an apologetic smile.

The man just grunted and turned aside.

Strange, I thought as he strode away. *He doesn't really fit in with this crowd.* The button-down, long-sleeved shirt tucked into black pants screamed midmanagement worker at an office, not someone visiting an outdoor festival. And that tension in his jaw and his sharp movements betrayed him as a man on a mission, not a sightseer.

Curious, I kept my eyes on the man's broad back as we both headed for the center of town. Yes, he definitely looked like someone on assignment, not a tourist. Then it occurred to me that, *duh*, he was probably one of the plainclothes detectives brought in on the LeBlanc murder, or even an FBI agent involved in the forgery investigation. I exhaled a held breath. *No reason to feel nervous, Amy. He must be a detective or something, that's all.*

I elbowed my way past a cluster of moms and dads pushing strollers, earning a few dirty looks. "Sorry, I'm working the festival and I'm late," I called over my shoulder. Which, judging by the language one of the men hurled back at me, didn't mollify them.

By the time I reached the barricades that closed off the festival area, I'd lost sight of the white-shirted man, but—to my dismay—caught a glimpse of Mel Riley. She stood at the edge of the cordoned-off area, talking with one of Brad's deputies.

Great. If she made it to the library before me, I'd never hear the end of it.

Swinging down a side street that would provide me access to the narrow road beside the library, I turned my walk into a jog. If I could get to the parking lot and slip in the back door, I could emerge from the library, cashbox in hand, and neither Mel nor any of the other volunteers would know how long I'd been in the building. That could conveniently cover my tardiness.

Yes, it was duplicitous, but . . . I quickened my pace to reach the crossroad that ended at the library parking lot. Catching a flash of white out of the corner of my eye, I turned my head and spied the strange man I'd bumped into—crouched amid the glossy-leaved branches of a holly bush.

I slipped past him and ducked behind the trunk of a pin oak tree as quietly as I could. Fortunately, his attention was focused on a section of the main street framed by the sharp-edged holly leaves. He was obviously tailing someone. Following his line of sight, I noticed his quarry and bit my lower lip to stifle a gasp. The man was surveilling Mel Riley.

She'd turned from the deputy to chat with Mayor Bob Blackstone. Despite my concern over the man hidden in the shrub in front of me, I felt a tinge of amusement over her outfit. Her caramel-colored wool slacks and forest-green sweater were topped by a plaid jacket that captured all the hues of autumn leaves. A matching plaid tam-o'-shanter, perched precariously on her upswept blonde do, completed her ensemble.

She looked like an advertisement from a fall-themed fashion catalog and, somehow, more fragile than I'd ever seen her. Perhaps because I knew she was being watched.

I pressed the heel of my hand against my temple. *Get it together, Amy. You don't know the man's focused on Mel. Perhaps he has his eyes on the mayor, who's been mixed up in some questionable business in the past.*

But even after Bob strolled off, the man kept his eyes on Mel. That was odd. I couldn't imagine why a detective would be stalking Mel Riley, unless . . .

Perhaps this stranger was a private eye, not an FBI investigator. He could be one of those PIs who collected evidence for suspicious spouses contemplating divorce. I supposed it was possible that Mel, a widow, had jumped into a relationship with a married man.

Yeah, that had to be it. Mel might be almost seventy, but she was still attractive, and quite the social butterfly. It wasn't impossible to imagine her embroiled in some romantic affair.

I slipped out from behind the tree and jogged to the road that intersected the lane beside the library. Glancing over my shoulder to ensure that the man wasn't following me, I turned the corner and once again ran into someone.

"Well, Amy, fancy meeting you here. Sneaking in the back way, are you?" Kurt Kendrick grabbed my upper arms and steadied me as I stumbled over his feet.

I looked up into his lined but still handsome face. "I should ask what you're doing here."

"Taking the scenic route," he said, releasing his hold and stepping back. He flashed a smile before staring at something over my shoulder.

Following his gaze, I realized that he was peering through the shrubs—and at the man who'd been watching Mel.

"You know him?" I asked, brushing bits of bark from my navy sweater.

"Who?" Kendrick fixed his brilliant blue gaze on me.

"That man tailing Mel Riley. At least that's what I figured he was doing."

"I don't know what you mean, Amy. What man?" He motioned toward the holly with one of his large, knobby-knuckled hands.

There was no one hiding in the shrub now. "Guess he heard us and beat it before he could be caught."

"Couldn't say, as I didn't see anyone." Kendrick casually brushed a lock of white hair away from his forehead. "You're headed for the library, I assume? I'm happy to accompany you."

"No, that isn't necessary."

Humor lit up Kurt Kendrick's craggy face. "If you truly think someone was lurking in the bushes . . ."

"Oh, very well. But I did see someone," I called out as I jogged toward the parking lot behind the library.

Kendrick easily kept pace with me without breaking out of a walk. "I'm not accusing you of seeing things, my dear. I just didn't notice anyone. Changing the subject—I have a favor to ask."

I shot him a suspicious glance as we crossed the parking lot. "What's that?"

"I heard you are planning to sell a couple of Andrew's paintings."

"Yeah, Aunt Lydia gave them to the library sale after we couldn't get the LeBlanc donations." I paused at the back door to the library and fumbled through my tote bag. "Hold on, have to find my keys."

"I'd like to see them. Before they go on sale, I mean."

"Because?" I opened the door and stood with my hand on the knob, blocking Kendrick's entry into the building.

"Because I might like to buy them before they're offered up to the public." Kendrick spread out his hands. "Call me sentimental, but Andrew Talbot was my best friend and I actually don't own a single one of his paintings. I'd like to remedy that."

I studied the tall figure before me. *Call him sentimental? Never.* Of course, as always, it was impossible to discern whether he was lying by reading his expression. "I'm not sure that's what Aunt Lydia would want."

"I would pay top dollar. And"—Kendrick's wolfish grin was disarming but also slightly threatening—"why would she need to know? She's aware the paintings will be sold this weekend, probably to a stranger. And if the library makes good money off of them, so much the better, right?"

"Hmm . . ." I twisted my lips before blowing out a little puff of air. "All right, come in. The paintings are inside. We weren't going to put them on the sale table until later in the day, after we'd sold some other, less interesting, stuff."

I held the door open and Kendrick bounded through, his athletic grace belying his seventy-one years. "Flip on that switch for more light," I told him. "The paintings are on one of the tables in the reading area. You can take a look while I collect something from the workroom."

After dropping off my tote bag and grabbing the cashbox, I made my way over to the reading room, where Kendrick was intently examining my uncle's paintings.

"He was pretty good, wasn't he?" I lifted the larger of the two works—a landscape that captured the fields behind Richard's house while they were draped in snow. Behind the white-and-gray scene, the Blue Ridge Mountains rose like azure thunderclouds tipped with silver.

"He was very good." Kendrick tapped the back of the stretched canvas before holding up the other painting, a smaller piece enhanced by an elaborately carved gold-painted frame.

"That one's heavy, isn't it? Mostly the frame, though. Seems like he repurposed an antique frame from some other work."

"Apples and oranges." Kendrick carefully laid the painting back onto the table before meeting my questioning gaze. "The title of the still life, according to the tag on the back. It's a play on words too, you see."

I stared at the painting, which I judged to measure about eighteen inches by two feet. It was smaller than most of my uncle's other works, but I supposed that suited the subject, which was indeed a bowl of apples and oranges. The luscious, warm tones of the fruit, which played off the cool gray of the simple bowl, were picked up in the vivid paisley print of the scarf draped over a cherry table.

The sideboard, I thought with a smile. I recognized the bowl as well. Aunt Lydia still used it for decoration—although on a shelf in the sitting room, and filled with a dried flower arrangement instead of fruit.

"Well, I must get outside and make sure everything's ready," I said. "Could you let yourself out the back? The door will lock behind you."

"Afraid to be seen with me?"

I met his amused grin with a lift of my chin. "Yeah, because Aunt Lydia is one of the volunteers. We could waltz out there together, but you'd have to explain the situation to her."

"No, no." Kendrick lifted his hands in mock horror. "I'll just go out the back. But what about my offer to buy the paintings? We haven't settled that."

"Sorry, but I don't think so. Not right now, anyway. Come around to the library sale table later in the day and make an offer. Mel Riley is expecting me to put out those paintings this afternoon, and she may have told some friends, so . . ."

"Very well, I'll come back later." Kendrick cast one last look at the paintings. "But shouldn't you put these in the workroom until then? I thought the library was opening for business today as usual, despite the sale out front."

I slapped my forehead. "It is. I wasn't thinking. Could you grab the gold-framed one and help me carry them into the workroom? We can lay them on the table in there."

Kendrick complied with my request before wishing me a good day and heading out the back. I waited for him to leave the building before I exited through the front doors.

Aunt Lydia and Zelda, who were arranging items on the sale table, paused long enough to greet me. Sunny stood off to the side, instructing a few other volunteers who were unboxing stacks of donated books. I grinned when I saw what she was wearing—a bright-blue peasant top decorated with white embroidery over a cobalt dirndl skirt. She'd also plaited her golden hair into a single braid. She looked beautiful but also rather like an actress from a roadshow production of *The Sound of Music*.

"I see you got into the spirit. At least to celebrate the German heritage portion of the festival." I waved my hand, indicating my plain navy sweater and worn jeans. "Guess I should've put in a little more effort."

Sunny flipped the braid over her shoulder. "I just think it's fun to play around with different looks." She pointed at the sales table. "Everything's ready and the Friends have worked out a schedule for covering the table as well as the circulation desk, so we should be good to go."

"Thanks," I said, setting the cashbox on the table. "Sorry to be so late. I overslept."

Aunt Lydia shot me a concerned look. "Are you feeling okay, Amy?"

"I'm fine," I replied, forcing a neutral tone. "Just a lot on my mind, I guess."

There was no way I'd tell her what was really bothering me. I had no proof that my late uncle was a forger, and even if I did . . . I studied my aunt's fine-boned face and shook my head. No, I wasn't going to be the one to tell her such a thing.

Zelda and my aunt shared a conspiratorial look. "Of course, my dear. There's so much dreadful stuff happening lately, what with poor Rachel LeBlanc, and you and Sunny being held at knifepoint." Zelda patted my arm. "And I'm sure you must hate being stuck here and missing Richard's performances too."

I caught the lift of Sunny's golden eyebrows as she glanced at my aunt.

"Is there something going on that I should know about?" I asked, straightening a pile of crocheted doilies.

"No, of course not." Sunny fiddled with the end of her braid in a way that made me suspect she was lying.

But I couldn't pursue that thought because it was nine o'clock and Brad Tucker's deputies had opened up the barricades. After that it took the combined efforts of Sunny, me, and all the volunteers to handle the waves of visitors who engulfed our sales table.

Chapter Fourteen

Brad stopped by around noon, bringing Sunny something to eat from the stall Bethany Virts had set up outside her diner. Taking one look at Brad's weary face, I shooed them both off to the library break room to enjoy their lunch.

"Go on," I said, when Sunny protested. "It might be the only chance Brad gets to sit down today."

Aunt Lydia and Zelda left around the same time, after some additional Friends of the Library volunteers finally showed up. The two women argued with me, but I insisted they'd done enough. "You've been on your feet for at least five hours. Why don't you two go home? Everything's under control here."

They thanked me and headed off to Zelda's house for lunch and, I suspected, a few glasses of wine or sherry.

Which left me alone with the volunteers, and Mel.

"Time to bring out the Talbot paintings," she said after we sold a set of miniatures painted by a local folk artist.

I looked out to see if I could spot Kurt Kendrick's white hair among the crowd. If he was truly willing to pay top dollar for

Uncle Andrew's paintings, I wanted to give him that opportunity. The library could certainly use the money.

His towering figure was nowhere to be seen, but I did spot another man who made me do a double take. It was the dark-haired stranger from earlier, still wearing his mirror-lensed sunglasses. But from his posture and body language, I could tell that he was staring across the street, directly at the library.

No, at Mel. I tugged on the sleeve of her jacket. "Do you know that man?" I whispered to her when she looked down at me with annoyance.

She lifted her head and followed the trajectory of my surreptitiously pointed finger. "What?" Her face paled until her carefully blended blush stood out like the imprint from a slap. She grabbed the edge of the sales table with both hands. "No, I've never seen him before."

Obviously that was a lie, but seeing her discomfort, I didn't press her. "Do you want me to get Brad Tucker? He's just inside."

"No, no." Mel tightened her grip on the table until her knuckles blanched. "Just go get those paintings, please." When she glanced up at me, I was shocked by the look in her green eyes. "Please, Amy."

Fear, that's what it was. Absolute terror. I glanced out over the crowd again and glimpsed a tall figure. Not Kurt Kendrick, but someone far better, at least as far as Mel was concerned. "Hey, Trey!" I called out, waving him over.

He made his way to the table. "Hi, Amy. Mom, is everything all right?"

Mel released her hold on the table and straightened. "I just felt a little faint. Standing too long, I guess."

"You should rest for a minute. Let me take you inside. I'm sure they can spare you for a bit." Trey sent me a questioning look.

"Of course," I said. "We actually have enough volunteers to provide coverage until five if you want to go home, Mel."

"No," she replied. "Just take me inside for a minute, Trey."

I told the other volunteers I'd be back soon and followed Trey as he guided his mother into the library. "Glad you showed up when you did," I told him.

"I meant to get here earlier, but business interfered." Trey settled Mel in one of the reading room chairs.

"Feeling better now?" I asked Mel.

She just waved me aside. "Don't make such a fuss. You either, Trey. I'm perfectly fine. I just need to rest for a bit. Meanwhile, you two go and get those Talbot paintings and carry them out to the sale table. Hurry along now." She made a shooing motion with both hands.

"What really happened?" Trey asked as we walked around the circulation desk and entered the workroom.

I glanced at his concerned face. "I'm not sure. It was like she saw something in the crowd that startled her." I almost mentioned the strange man but decided it was probably best to say nothing about a possible PI tailing Mel. If she was embroiled in an affair, it wasn't my place to inform her son.

Although I would tell Brad. Just in case my theory was wrong. After all, there was a murderer possibly still lurking in the area. I couldn't imagine what might connect Rachel LeBlanc to Mel, but I needed to make sure the sheriff's office knew about this strange individual trailing the older woman. She might not be my favorite person, but I certainly didn't wish her harm.

I offered Trey a reassuring smile. "Like she said, it was

probably a spell of weakness brought on by being on her feet for too long. You know how older folks can be—they don't want to admit they can't do everything just like when they were young."

"Boy do I ever." Trey gave me a quick grin before turning his attention to the worktable. "So, I see one painting. Was the other carried out already?"

I looked down at the table, where the larger of the two paintings lay. Although Kendrick had placed it beside the landscape, the still life in its gold frame was nowhere to be seen.

As a few expletives burst from my lips, Trey added his own colorful words. I glanced up at him, surprised that he looked almost as distressed as I felt. Which was odd. It wasn't his head on the block.

But perhaps it was just the thought of having to explain the loss to his mother, which frankly also gave me the shivers. That was even more frightening than the idea of telling Aunt Lydia that someone had stolen one of her beloved husband's paintings.

"You're sure it was here?" Trey asked.

"I'm sure. I never moved it outside, and I haven't seen anyone else do so, which means"—I rubbed at my forehead with one hand—"someone has stolen it. Right out from under our noses. Not sure how they could have, but it isn't here . . ."

"You need to report that right away." Trey laid his hand on my arm, and I didn't pull away. The warmth of his fingers was comforting.

I nodded. "Fortunately, the chief deputy is sitting in the library break room at the moment."

When Trey offered to go get Brad, I weakly nodded my agreement.

Staring at the landscape painting, I racked my brains to

recall if I'd seen anyone suspicious enter the library earlier in the day. Someone carrying a satchel or other bag they could've used to stash the painting. *Of course,* I thought, *all it would've taken was a coat.* Someone could've wrapped the painting, tucked the coat under their arm, and just strolled out of the building.

But why that painting? The landscape was the more attractive work. Although, if I was honest, I had to admit that perhaps the thief hadn't cared about the painting at all and only wanted the antique, gold-painted frame.

I walked out to the circulation desk and quizzed the volunteer, who admitted that she'd had to leave the area for a few minutes to help patrons in the children's room.

"You should've come and gotten me," I snapped in exasperation, before I realized what I was saying. "Sorry, you would've had to leave the desk to do that too." I gave her an apologetic smile. "Not your fault. I should've locked those paintings up somewhere. It's on me. Sorry."

She shrugged. "Who'd have thought someone would steal from the library? Especially a donation? Losers."

"Yeah, they undoubtedly are." I stepped away from the desk to meet Brad and Sunny, who'd rushed out of the break room, followed more slowly by Trey.

I explained the situation to Brad, who told me to secure the landscape painting as evidence and said he'd send another deputy to take statements from me, Sunny, and all the volunteers. "But I have to be honest with you, Amy," he said, brushing some crumbs from his uniform jacket. "We can try to lift some prints from the remaining painting, since it's possible the thief touched that one too, but it's unlikely we'll find the perpetrator. You don't have cameras . . ."

"Town won't pay for them," Sunny said.

"Be that as it may, you don't have any surveillance equipment. And apparently no one saw anything, or at least no one who has spoken up yet. Then there's the crowd today and all the strangers in town . . ."

I groaned. "Impossible, is what you're saying?"

"Not impossible, but very difficult. Still, I'll put someone on it."

I thanked him and told Sunny we probably should lock the other painting in the tall metal cabinet where we stored billing information and other papers that included patrons' personal information. Although we always shredded that material at the end of every fiscal year, we had to keep it long enough to reconcile our books.

"Only you and I have a key to that," I reminded her.

"High security for papers?" Trey asked, widening his eyes.

I met his gaze squarely. "Libraries take the protection of patron information very seriously. A few librarians have actually gone to jail rather than turn over circulation records without a warrant. It's for the security of your reading habits as well as your personal information."

"We don't want discrimination leveled against anyone based on what they read or research," Sunny added when Trey continued to look puzzled.

"Ah, okay." Trey glanced over my shoulder. "Mom, you don't need to get mixed up in this."

Mel strode up to the desk, demanding to know what was going on. When I explained what had happened, her face changed color again, but this time she flushed red rather than blanching.

"Unbelievable! That someone could just march in here and steal a painting from the workroom, pretty as you please." She cast her glare over our little group but rested her angry gaze on me. "What kind of security do you have in this library anyway?"

"Very little," I admitted.

"Taylorsford won't give us cameras," Sunny said again, "even though Amy has asked for them numerous times. Maybe you should take that up with the town council, Mel. You might have more influence."

"Perhaps I will." Mel huffed and turned away, but not before she cast one glance at her son, who had made no move to join her.

A curious look—more questioning than angry. I wondered what that meant. Maybe Mel thought that her son was shifting his allegiance to me, or Sunny, rather than her?

I touched Trey's arm as he watched Mel leave the building. "Perhaps you should take her home? This latest shock might be the last straw, and since she basically passed out earlier . . ."

His stern expression softened. "You're probably right. Mom's so dynamic, I forget that she might not be able to handle bad news as easily as she once could."

Sunny stepped up beside him. "Yeah, I get that with the grands. They can still do everything like before, but unexpected events really throw them off their game."

Trey touched the back of her hand with the tips of his fingers. "A wise observation, Sunny. I think I will go and see if I can convince Mom to head home."

"That would be sweet of you." Sunny returned his warm smile with a dazzling one of her own.

A loud series of coughs erupted behind us. I glanced over my shoulder and caught Brad tugging at his collar while frowning darkly. "Better lock up that other painting," he told Sunny.

She wrinkled her nose and wished Trey a good afternoon before turning to Brad. "I'll get to it."

"See that you do. I don't want to have to chase down another lost artwork."

Trey frowned as he looked from Sunny to Brad and back again. "Well, let me go talk to Mom. And if she doesn't feel like coming back tomorrow, I promise to volunteer in her place." He turned his focus on me before he smiled again.

I had to give Trey credit for attempting to diffuse the situation. Judging from Brad's expression, he'd definitely caught wind of Sunny's interest in the other man. I lightly tapped Trey's arm. "Thank you. Now go take care of your mom. We have this under control, right, Brad?"

Brad muttered something that sounded like a *yes* before he raised his voice to address all of us. "I'll walk out with you. Need to get back on the job anyway." He glanced at me. "I'll send someone in for those statements as soon as I can find a deputy who can be spared from festival duty."

"Thanks," I said, and waved at both men as they headed for the front doors.

"Let's go lock up that painting," I told Sunny, ushering her back around the circulation desk. "Just make sure to handle it with gloves so we don't contaminate any fingerprints."

When we entered the workroom, I sat on one of the stools at the table as she carried the landscape to the storage cabinet. "You know you just pissed off your boyfriend, right?"

Her back was to me as she locked the painting in the cabinet. She lifted and dropped her slender shoulders before stripping off the pair of white cotton gloves. "Why do you say that?"

"Because it was pretty obvious you were flirting with Trey."

"Any reason why I can't?" Sunny turned and leaned back against the steel cabinet, slapping the gloves against her palm.

"Well, since you're dating Brad . . ."

"Not exclusively. Not like you and Richard."

"Okay, but it was pretty blatant, and I just think . . ."

"For goodness' sake, Amy, you're not my mother." Her blue eyes defiant, Sunny threw the gloves onto an adjacent shelf and tossed her braid over her shoulder. "And you know I am not into that 'only one guy in the world' thing." As she continued to stare at me, her gaze softened. "I'm not like you. I just can't see limiting myself to one person forever. Which is why—as I have told you before—I have no intention of ever getting married."

"Does Brad know that?"

"He should. I've told him often enough." Sunny crossed to the table and sat on the stool beside me. "You know I would. I'm an honest person—with myself as well as everyone else."

"I know," I said, as she hiked her full skirt up above her knees.

"No point in pretending to be something you're not." Sunny pushed off against the floor and then lifted her feet so that the top of the stool could spin freely. "I like my independence," she said, grabbing the edge of the table to stop the momentum of her spin. She lifted her head and faced me, her expression unexpectedly serious. "Sometimes I really do wish I could fall madly in love with just one person, but so far it hasn't happened."

I leaned forward and laid my hands on her exposed knees. "It still might. You never know."

"Doubtful, but I guess anything's possible." Sunny yanked the tie from her hair and began untwisting her braid. "It won't

154

be with Brad, though. I wish it could be, but I know it won't."
She ran her fingers through her silky hair and fanned it out over
her shoulders.

"Too bad. But I agree that you have to follow your own heart."

"Yeah, and"—Sunny's somber expression brightened—"so
do you. Which is why Lydia and Zelda and Walt and I have
planned a little surprise for you."

I stood up, pushing back my stool with one foot. "So you
have been keeping secrets, just like I thought."

"We have. And it's spectacular." Mischief sparkled in Sunny's
blue eyes.

"What are you talking about?"

Sunny leapt to her feet and dashed over to her backpack,
which she had stuffed into one of the workroom shelves. Digging through the bag, she extracted a large envelope and waved
it over her head. "Your ticket to happiness," she said.

I stared at her, totally bemused. "My what?"

"Or to Richard, which is really the same thing, isn't it?"
Sunny danced her way over to me and handed over the envelope
with a flourish. "Go on, look inside."

I opened the envelope and pulled out three documents. One
was a ticket for a nonstop flight from Dulles Airport to LaGuar-
dia in New York. For Saturday.

"But this is for tomorrow . . ." I squinted and examined the
ticket. "One way?"

"Yeah, 'cause Richard drove and we figured he wouldn't
mind giving you a ride back on Sunday."

I just stared at her for a moment. "But the festival . . ."

"Is all covered. We've got enough volunteers, especially
with Lydia and Zelda, and Walt offered to help out too. I can

supervise everything tomorrow and Sunday, so—believe it or not—you can actually be spared." Sunny pressed her palms together. "Now look at the other two things."

I laid the airline ticket on the table and examined the next piece of paper. "A hotel reservation for tomorrow night?"

"Yeah, and at the place where Richard is staying." There was no denying the glee in Sunny's voice. "I checked. Sneakily."

"I see. And this final thing . . ." I lifted the narrow rectangle of heavy card stock. "A ticket to the final night of the dance performance. Of course." I placed the other papers on the table, next to the airline ticket, and stepped forward. "You complete and utter romantic fools." My voice grew muffled as I wrapped my arms around my friend and buried my face in her shoulder. "You shouldn't have."

"But we wanted to." Sunny pushed me back, keeping a hold on my arms. "Because we all love you, and Richard too, and we thought it was just criminal that you couldn't be there at his performance, especially after what you guys have been through recently."

"I can't ever repay you for this."

"Yes, you can. You can have the best time imaginable"— Sunny slid one hand up my arm to wipe away the tears dripping from my chin—"and then tell me all about it." She gave me an arch look. "And I mean *all* about it."

When Deputy Coleman walked in to take our statements about the lost painting, he discovered me laughing and crying all at the same time and had to be reassured by Sunny that I was unharmed and, actually, *quite happy, thank you.*

Chapter Fifteen

I arrived at the hotel about an hour before the performance, which meant all I could do was check in, toss my carry-on suitcase on the bed, and hurriedly change my clothes before hailing a taxi to take me to the theater.

I huddled in the back of the taxi, chewing on my pinkie fingernail and debating whether the dress I'd chosen to wear was actually appropriate for the occasion. I hadn't visited New York often, much less attended many shows there, and wasn't entirely certain what one was supposed to wear to a dance performance at an off-Broadway venue.

I smoothed down the full skirt of my crimson silk dress and examined my kitten-heeled black pumps. I'd made the ultimate sacrifice of donning pantyhose but refused to wear the strappy, spiked heels Sunny had produced from somewhere deep in her closet.

"You've actually worn those?" I'd asked, raising my eyebrows.

"Well, not outside the bedroom," Sunny had replied, which made me groan and toss the shoes back into the closet.

I tugged up the bodice of my dress, which had a scooped neckline that tended to slip into a little too much décolleté. I'd even mentioned this to Sunny, who'd rolled her eyes and said something about that being *the point*.

"Right here," I told the taxi driver, and handed him what was probably too much cash. Jumping out of the taxi, I tucked my beaded purse tightly under my arm, gripped the front of my black coat together with one hand, and pushed through the glass-fronted entrance doors into the elegant marble lobby.

Richard's face smiled out at me from a lobby poster. I paused, noticing that the advertisement also featured photos of the other principals, including Meredith Fox. The vision of her beautiful, heart-shaped face surrounded by a nimbus of loose auburn waves brought me a momentary frisson of panic. *She's gorgeous, Amy, and she can dance. How can you ever compete with that?*

But Richard loved me. If I knew anything, I knew that. I squared my shoulders and marched into the theater, flashing my ticket at an usher, who handed me a program before waving me down front.

My seat, in the middle of the orchestra section, had excellent sight lines to the stage. I wondered how Sunny had managed to score such a great ticket.

It must've cost a mint, I thought, abashed by the generosity of my family and friends. But since they'd gone to so much trouble, I decided I should thoroughly enjoy myself. I slipped off my coat and laid it across my lap before opening the program to read up on the production.

I knew from the little that Richard had told me about this piece that it was an adaption of the Orpheus myth but was surprised to realize that it was a full-length work. The videos I'd seen of his choreography generally featured shorter dances, usually staged as part of programs featuring other works. However, this piece, titled *Return*, comprised the entire program for the evening.

Richard was credited as the choreographer as well as—via a special, obviously last-minute, insert—a lead dancer. Reading his biography in the program brought home how much he'd already accomplished in his career. *And yet*, I thought, *he's the same guy who'll climb a ladder to sweep dead leaves from Aunt Lydia's gutters.* I smiled to myself. *Getting drenched in leaf meal and muck while he's at it.*

The lights in the chandeliers twinkling overhead blinked and faded. I placed the program in my lap and settled back against the amber velvet upholstery of my seat as the maroon curtains parted to reveal a bare stage.

At the back of the stage, fabric screens lit up with images, creating scenery that didn't interfere with the open expanse of the floor. I clutched my hands in my lap. This was a new experience for me. Before this, I'd seen Richard dance only on video recordings or in his home studio.

Sound swelled from the small pit orchestra. I couldn't place the music and glanced at my program. Although it was difficult to read in the darkened theater, I was able to discern that this music had been written specifically for *Return* by a composer whose name I didn't recognize. It was beautiful, though—at times haunting and melodic, then strident or soaring when required by the story.

After a short section featuring dancers who I assumed

represented denizens of the underworld, the stage emptied and the music fell away, until all that remained was the reverberating ping of fingers plucking a harp.

Clapping filled the theater as a figure emerged from a haze of smoke at the back of the stage. I watched the dancer move downstage and realized that this stunning creature was the man I knew so well.

And didn't know at all. I sat through the rest of the evening with my mouth alternately dropped opened in silent wonder and clamped tight to prevent any gasps from escaping my lips.

He was perfection in motion—human and yet somehow more. A physical body that could convey so much more than the physical.

I also had to admit that Meredith, portraying Eurydice, was a superb partner—all gorgeous arms and incredible legs. She was somehow able to convey a graceful fragility despite the strength inherent in her lithe body. At one point, when Orpheus made the tragic error of glancing back at his beloved, the woman sitting next to me murmured to her companion that Richard and Meredith "had once been a thing, so maybe this is his way of expressing his loss."

But I knew better. As I watched the story unfold through music and movement, I knew exactly what Richard was attempting to convey.

It had nothing to do with the loss of Meredith or their less-than-ideal relationship. He was mourning his true muse—the woman who'd been his best friend and the dance partner of his youth. A talented dancer who, unlike Richard, had been rejected by every top-tier dance company.

I slid to the edge of my seat, certain that this piece had been created in honor of Karla, whom Richard had loved as a sister—and lost when she'd cut off all contact with him after fleeing the dance world.

At the end of the performance, when Orpheus expressed his pain in a solo that brought the audience to their feet, I silently wept. After dashing away tears with the back of my hand, I joined in the enthusiastic applause as the performers took their bows. When Meredith and Richard appeared, hand in hand, the audience also broke into cheers and *bravo*s, and several bouquets of flowers winged their way to the stage.

After the curtains closed again and the lights came up in the theater, I headed toward a door I hoped might lead backstage. It took some time—everyone was moving in the other direction, so I felt as if I were swimming against a strong current. When I finally reached the door, an usher stopped me, but I gave him my name and asked him to check with someone in the company to see if I could be admitted. The usher soon returned, smiling and directing me backstage, toward a cluster of dancers.

"Come on," said a young woman still arrayed in her costume and stage makeup. "I'll take you to Richard's dressing room." She looked me over as she guided me through a maze of black curtains and flats. "So you're Amy, huh?"

"Yeah, that's me," I said, clutching my wadded-up coat to my chest. The young dancer was half my size, making me uncomfortably aware of my more generous curves.

"Glad you could make it. Richard will be thrilled. He talks about you constantly, you know."

"Really?" I followed her down a flight of stairs to a short hall. The doors off the hall were marked with placards bearing the names of the lead dancers.

"Here you go." The young woman rapped on one of the doors and called out, "Approved visitor!"

"Come on in," said a familiar voice.

I shared a glance with the dancer, who winked at me and pushed the door open. "Go on. He'll be over the moon, trust me."

Walking into the small, windowless room, the first thing I noticed was an overwhelming smell of sweat, mingled with a chalky scent I assumed was connected to the container of loose powder on the cluttered dressing table.

The second thing I noticed was Richard, his face already devoid of makeup. He'd obviously taken a quick shower, since his skin glistened with water droplets and he was attired only in boxer briefs and a damp towel draped around his shoulders. Facing him, with her back to me, was Meredith Fox.

She was still wearing the short white tunic that had been her costume. Her hair, unpinned from the golden net that had confined it during the performance, fell in loose waves down her slender back.

As I stepped into the room, Richard glanced over Meredith's shoulder. His gray eyes opened wide and his lips curved into a broad smile. "Amy!" He stepped around Meredith and reached me in two swift strides.

Before I could even say hello, Richard wrapped his arms around me and pulled me close. "What are you doing here?"

"Blame it on Sunny and my aunt. And Zelda and Walt. They all conspired to get me a ticket to the show, as well as an airline ticket and a hotel room," I replied, lifting my chin so I could gaze up at his face.

"Hotel room? Now there's a waste of money. They should've

known better." Richard grinned and leaned in until his lips were only inches from mine. "I have a hotel room," he whispered.

"I think they didn't want to assume . . ." My words were cut off, quite delightfully, by Richard's kiss.

A cough finally brought us back to our senses. Meredith. I'd forgotten she was still in the room.

"Oh, forgive me," Richard said, although he didn't sound the least bit sorry. He stepped back but kept one arm around me as we turned to face his dance partner. "Meredith, as you may have guessed, this is Amy Webber."

"Hello." Meredith examined me with an intensity that made me shrink a little closer to Richard.

"And, of course, this is Meredith Fox." Richard waved his free hand in her direction. "She was just talking to me about an opportunity at Clarion," he added, glancing down at me with a lift of his eyebrows.

"Yes, Richard's been kind enough to agree to put in a good word for me with the dance department." Meredith gracefully swept one hand through her auburn locks before placing it on her hip. "I need a steady job for a while, and there's a position open at Clarion for a dance instructor next semester. Only temporary—covering for someone on maternity leave."

"I see." I slipped my arm around Richard's still-damp waist.

"Clarion seems interested, but I was told the administration was concerned that my presence might . . . disturb Richard." Meredith's perfect nose twitched. "Apparently they're terrified he might flee the department if I'm hired. They seem to think he's irreplaceable."

"As they should," I said, which earned me a kiss on the shoulder.

"Anyway"—Meredith flicked her hand like someone swatting away a fly—"I just dropped by to once again beg Richard to tell them that it won't really bother him to work with me again."

"And obviously it won't, since we've just performed together with no problem." Richard glanced down at me. "So I agreed."

"Which of course you should," I said, leaning my head against his shoulder.

Meredith's smile tightened. "I suppose I should go change. See you at the after party?" she called out to Richard as she sailed past us and headed out the door.

"Party?" I asked, after she'd left the room. I released my hold on Richard and stepped back. Catching sight of myself in his dressing room mirror, I pulled my travel brush from my small black purse.

Richard whipped the towel from his shoulders and rubbed at his damp hair. "Yeah, and unfortunately I must make an appearance. Schmooze the patrons and all that. This being a charity thing, I'm kind of stuck."

"I understand. I can just head back to the hotel, I guess." I gave my straight brown hair a couple of swipes with the brush. "I'm in room two fifty-four. Just stop by and let me know when you get back to the hotel." I tucked the brush back into my purse and tugged at the neckline of my dress, which had dipped alarmingly.

"Don't be silly. You're coming to the party with me. And leave that alone." Richard crossed to stand behind me. Reaching around, he took hold of my hand and lifted it away from my neckline. "It looks fine just as it is."

"A little too much exposure," I said, wrinkling my nose at him in the mirror.

"Not at all." He squeezed my fingers. "You are beautiful just as you are."

"Don't you have to get dressed? Or are you planning on showing off"—I slid my fingers from his grip and turned and looked him up and down—"everything? I know some of your admirers might appreciate that, but perhaps a little discretion . . ."

"Actually, the company might raise some additional funds that way," he replied with a smile. "But no, I think I'd better wear a few more clothes, since we need to walk a block or two, and it is chilly out tonight." He leaned in to kiss my shoulder again. "Just give me a minute."

"Are you sure you want me there? I don't know any of these people and I'm not very adept at schmoozing," I said as he changed into black jeans and a white linen shirt.

"You'll be fine. And just knowing you're there will make the whole experience bearable."

"Well, in that case . . ." I shrugged on my coat as I waited for him to throw on a gray wool jacket. After he slipped his feet into some well-worn loafers, I held out my arm. "You may escort me to the ball, kind sir."

"With pleasure, my lady." He offered me a graceful bow before taking my arm. "Although," he added, flashing me a wicked grin as we walked into the hall, "I expect things to turn much more pleasurable later."

Chapter Sixteen

As we walked arm in arm to the party, which was apparently being hosted at a nearby art gallery, I told Richard about meeting Trey, my encounter with Lila, the missing painting, and my suspicions concerning Uncle Andrew.

"So you're afraid your uncle might have been mixed up in some forgery work too?" Richard punched the elevator button.

After observing our surroundings, I wondered how and why the Ad Astra company had selected this venue. The glass-and-steel skyscraper felt eerily quiet, as all of its offices were closed for the day. If you didn't know the gallery was on the top floor, you wouldn't ever have guessed an event was taking place. *Although maybe*, I thought, *that was the point.*

"Yeah. Probably not with the same group, of course. But those paintings that resemble old masters are rather suspicious." I stepped into the hall, which was so plain I wouldn't have suspected that there was anything but a storeroom behind the wood-paneled double doors that faced the elevator.

"He may have just been copying their work as a sort of practice." Richard held one of the doors open for me.

"I might believe that, if he hadn't copied another painter's signature. That, linked with the painting that resembles a Van Gogh, is pretty damning evidence."

"Yeah, that does lead one to think he meant to forge a Van Gogh, at least." Richard glanced down at me, cutting his eyes toward the crowd. "We'd probably better discuss this later."

"Agreed," I said, as we walked into the gallery.

It was a loft that had been renovated to retain an industrial feel. The entire space was off-white except for the pipes and vents, which were painted a flat black so they would disappear into the dark ceiling.

Paintings were aligned along each of the four walls. There were also a few museum-style dividers set up to display more pieces. I glanced at the informational poster displayed near the entry doors and realized that these were all the works of a single artist. It was someone I had never heard of, although that wasn't surprising. Despite my background in art history, I'd been out of the loop of the modern art scene for several years.

The open space was filled with a hum of voices and occasional bursts of laughter. I looked over the milling crowd while Richard handed off my coat to a volunteer at the coat check table. It was easy to tell the dancers from the other guests, since they tended to be younger, fitter, and more casually attired, while those I assumed to be patrons of the charity were older and decked out in outfits that made me feel distinctly underdressed.

"Richard!" An elderly woman, her wrinkled neck draped in diamonds, bustled forward. She threw one rather dismissive glance at me before grabbing Richard's arm. "Darling, you must come chat with my friend, Agnes." She pronounced this name in the French fashion so that it sounded like "Ayn-yes." "She has inherited quite a fortune from her late lamented husband and needs someplace to spend it. And"—the woman cast Richard an arch look—"she has been dying to meet you ever since she saw you dance last winter."

Richard smiled brightly but didn't move. He motioned toward me with his free hand. "Leah, may I introduce Amy Webber? Amy, this is Leah Carlisle, one of the contemporary dance world's most generous supporters."

"Hello," I said, eyeing the older woman, whose petite figure was swallowed up by her billowing lavender chiffon gown.

"How do you do," Leah Carlisle said, sucking in her rouged cheeks. She surveyed me, her dark eyes opaque as those of some predatory bird. "This your new girlfriend, then, Richard dear? I did hear you'd found someone."

Richard tightened his grip on my arm. "Yes, although I didn't exactly *find* her. She wasn't for sale in a gift shop."

Leah tittered, obviously trying to fake amusement despite the lines that had formed between her penciled-in eyebrows. "Ah yes, I suppose you two met after Meredith left you . . . Well, these things happen, don't they? Now where is that darling girl? She was quite brilliant this evening too. I do so love watching the two of you dance together."

I'd already spotted Richard's former fiancée chatting up an attractive older gentleman, but apparently Leah had not. "They do make excellent partners," I said, causing Leah to snap her sharp gaze back to me. "As dancers, I mean." I looked up at Richard. "And that reminds me—I haven't told you how absolutely wonderful you were tonight. Sorry about that."

"Not a problem." He leaned in closer and whispered, "Will

you be okay on your own for a bit? I must do the rounds. For the charity, you understand."

"Sure. I want to take a closer look at the paintings anyway." His lips were close enough to mine that I gave him a swift kiss before stepping back. "And I think there's champagne. Perhaps I'll grab some of that first."

He winked at me, his gray eyes alight with mischief. "Just save me one glass." He turned and extended his arm to Leah, and raised his voice. "So, introduce me to this friend of yours and let's see if we can relieve her of some cash. All for a good cause, of course."

Leah tittered again and took hold of his arm. As they strolled off into the crowd, I caught her words—"Quite a change from Meredith, dear boy."

I made a face but smiled when I heard Richard's reply— "Yes, thank God."

The refreshment table sat at the back of the room, near a bank of floor-to-ceiling windows. I grabbed a glass of champagne and stared out at the view. The lights of the city sparkled beneath a dark sky, dimming the stars but creating their own web of glittering color.

"Hello, you must be Amy," said a voice behind me.

I spun around, sloshing the golden liquid in my glass. Thankfully I'd downed enough that nothing spilled over the fluted rim. "Oh, hello," I said to the silver-haired lady standing before me. "Yes, I'm Amy Webber. Nice to meet you."

"Delighted." The woman, whose posture and toned figure granted her simple black sheath more elegance than the more flamboyant outfits at the party, smiled warmly. "I'm Adele Tourneau." She extended one fine-boned hand.

I shifted my glass to my left hand and clasped her fingers for a second. "Are you a dancer? You have that look."

"I was," she replied, inclining her head slightly. "Then a teacher for many years. Now I'm primarily retired, although I occasionally still do some coaching."

"So you're here to support the charity?"

"Yes, and a few of the dancers." She tucked a strand of hair that had escaped her loose chignon behind her ear. "You probably aren't aware of this, but I've known Richard for many years."

"Oh?" I polished off my champagne and set the glass on a small pedestal side table. "Were you one of his teachers?"

"Indeed I was." Adele looked past me, into the crowd.

I turned and followed her gaze to Richard, who was chatting with a couple who were both dressed as if they'd just come from some royal court. Meredith was at Richard's side, leaning against him.

"I wouldn't worry about that if I were you." Adele touched my arm to draw my attention. "It's just business, dear. Anyway, the last time I talked to Richard, I could tell that he had fallen head over heels in love with someone, and it wasn't Meredith Fox."

Heat tingled the back of my neck. "He mentioned me?"

"Mentioned you? He couldn't stop gushing about you." Adele's smile was beatific. "Which I must say was delightful to hear. He's been lonely for far too long."

"Lonely?" I followed Adele's lead and grabbed another glass of champagne from one of the passing waiters. "What do you mean? Richard is such an open-hearted guy. I can't imagine why he'd ever be lonely."

"Can't you?" Adele took a sip of her drink and studied me intently. "You haven't met his parents, then?"

"No, not yet."

"I see. They are—how shall I put it?—not the most affectionate people on the planet. And you know they don't approve of his dance career."

"I'd heard that."

"Yes, if it hadn't been for his great-uncle Paul Dassin, Richard wouldn't have had the opportunity to dance." Adele raised her feathery eyebrows as she studied my face. "I see you know about that as well. It was so fortunate that his great-uncle left money in his will to support Richard's training. Otherwise the world would've been deprived of a great dancer and choreographer." She smiled, but I could tell by her expression that her thoughts had turned inward. "I met Richard when he was quite young, when he'd just started at the conservatory. He had so much promise, even then, but that caused problems. So many of the other dancers were jealous of him. They resented his looks, his athleticism, and his innate talent. So there was that. And I understood, from things he said, that he'd been ostracized in high school, since he was a guy who preferred dancing to other, more mainstream, sports." She shrugged. "It was a public school and you know how young people can be. Anyway, there was all that, and the cold and disapproving parents, and being an only child . . . So yes, he was very lonely. Such a warm-hearted boy, with no one, really, to love."

"Except Karla?" I met Adele's intense gaze and held it.

"Yes, except Karla Dunmore." Adele took a long swallow of her champagne. "They were magic, those two. Like twin souls. When they danced together . . . well, let's just say, take what you saw tonight with Meredith and Richard and multiply it times ten."

"This piece, *Return*, is really about losing Karla, isn't it?"

Adele's eyes were liquid with sorrow. "You saw that too? I believe so. She was his closest companion, and the sister he never had. When he lost her, he didn't just lose a friend and partner . . ."

I couldn't hold back a deep sigh. "He lost his family."

"Yes." Adele looked me over. "But now I think he's finally found another one. Which makes me very happy."

"Me too," I said, sharing a smile with the older woman.

"It's like I told Kurt . . ."

"What?" This time, champagne did slosh over the rim of my glass. "Kurt who?"

"Kendrick, of course." Adele's hazel eyes widened. "You did know that this is his gallery?"

I glanced around the room. "No. I thought his gallery was in Georgetown."

"One of them is. But for his New York shows, he uses this space." Adele clasped her fluted glass between her hands. "You know Kurt?"

"Yes, he lives in my town. Well, part-time, anyway. So we've met. And years ago, he was Paul Dassin's foster son, so that's another connection."

"Yes, and the reason he was so eager to host the party here tonight. He's followed Richard's career for years, you know."

"No, I didn't know that." I finished off the champagne. As I plunked down the glass, I grabbed the edge of the table to steady myself. I was feeling a little light-headed, which wasn't surprising, seeing as I'd had only a snack on the airplane and nothing since.

Except too much to drink, too fast.

"Anyway, Kurt heard about this charity production and decided to offer up this space, free of charge, to Ad Astra for the after party." Adele set down her glass and touched my arm. "Richard didn't ask him, from what I was told. Kurt approached the company on his own."

"You know him well? Kurt Kendrick, I mean."

Adele lifted and dropped her slender shoulders. "No. I doubt anyone knows him well. But we've had some dealings in the past. He's donated money to several dance charities I'm involved with."

"And you think he's a legitimate businessman? I mean, not a crook?" After I blurted this out, I lowered my head in embarrassment. *It's the champagne*, I told myself. Still—it wasn't outside the realm of probability that the murder of Rachel LeBlanc could be linked to Kendrick's business dealings. If Adele knew information that would clarify this mystery, I had to try to ferret it out.

"Dear child, I really don't know."

I met her expressionless gaze. "From things I've heard, it seems that he might have some shady connections."

"Yes, I've heard those rumors as well." Adele tugged down the long sleeves of her dress. "I suppose there's probably something to them, since they are rather widespread, but I make it a practice not to look gift horses in the mouth." She tapped the tips of her fingers together. "I did run into him once in a restaurant, and the people he was with were not exactly what I would call gentlemen. And last year he wanted to give me a small Degas as a gift but asked me not to report it on my property taxes. I found that odd and said no to the gift. But those instances don't prove anything, of course."

No, but they did show a pattern. I looked out over the city. A gallery on the top floor of a skyscraper in New York? That took lots of cash and connections.

Possibly questionable connections.

"Does Richard know?" I asked, turning my gaze back to Adele. "I mean, that Kurt Kendrick has been following his career, and maybe even assisting him from afar, over the years?'

"No, I don't think so. He's never mentioned it, anyway. Apparently he didn't even know about Kurt's connection to his great-uncle until recently."

"It's all very strange," I murmured, as Adele's face lit up.

"Ah, and look who's here," she said, as I felt a familiar pair of arms slide around my waist. "Hello, Richard. I was just chatting with your delightful girlfriend."

"I knew you'd approve." Richard pulled me back against his firm body, his lips at my ear. "Now confess. Has Adele been telling tales from my early days? She knows quite a few."

"Uh, no," I said, catching Adele's almost imperceptible shake of her head. "I should have wormed that out of her before you showed up, but I'm afraid I didn't."

"Just as well." Richard kissed my neck before lifting his head to gaze at Adele. "She's wonderful, just like I told you, isn't she?"

Adele cast him a beaming smile. "Well, I haven't had a chance to get to know her very well, but I can see how happy she makes you, so that's good enough for me."

Richard's fingers caressed my waist. "Speaking of feeling

happy, I'd certainly be more so if I could get out of here. Adele, please tell me I've spent enough time playing the dutiful artiste and allow me to leave."

She shook her finger at him. "Have you managed to sufficiently charm enough of these people?"

Richard released his hold on me and stepped around to stand at my side. "*Oui, madame*, and several have promised some rather significant donations."

"Then I think you have been a very good boy and may be excused." She examined Richard's face. "You do look exhausted, my dear. And no wonder. I suggest you take Amy and sneak out of here. I shall make your excuses if anyone asks."

"You are an angel." Richard moved forward and kissed Adele on the cheek.

She playfully waved him off. "You know better than that. Now go before another wealthy grande dame corners you."

Richard grasped my hand and led me through the crowd, tossing off "Hello," "Good to see you," and "Thanks for coming" at anyone who appeared poised to stop our progress toward the exit.

We grabbed my coat and made it to the hall without incident. In the elevator, Richard pushed the ground floor button before slumping against the wall.

He *was* exhausted. I eyed him with concern as we headed outside.

As Richard glanced up and down the busy street and said something about hailing a cab, I considered sharing Adele's comments about Kurt Kendrick. But gazing up at his tired face, I changed my mind. *A very lonely boy*, Adele had said, and in that moment, as his mask of good humor was washed away by the streetlights that hollowed out his face, I realized what she meant.

It was in his choreography, and his dancing. It was in his fierce loyalty to those he cared about, and his willingness to give love without measuring it against what others gave him.

I laid my fingers over his arm and stroked the soft wool of his jacket.

"Hey you," he said, glancing down at me with a smile.

No matter how tired he was, always that smile for me.

My fingers tightened on his arm as I looked him in the eyes. "I just want you to know that I will never leave you. Not voluntarily, anyway. You will not lose me. You won't."

He inhaled sharply before pulling me to him. He kissed me passionately then, in the middle of a sidewalk, with pedestrians walking around us, with a whole city watching, with no concern for what anyone else thought of such a spectacle.

We missed quite a few taxis before we finally nabbed one and headed back to the hotel, but neither of us cared.

Chapter Seventeen

The drive back to Virginia on Sunday took over four and a half hours, so Richard and I had plenty of time to toss around theories concerning recent events.

"Not really sure how Reese and Lila LeBlanc meeting up in the woods ties in with some guy surveilling Mel Riley," Richard said, after I finally remembered to call Brad and relay my information on the strange man at the festival.

"I don't think it does, actually," I replied, tucking my cell phone back into my purse. "Seems like it's two entirely separate instances of weirdness, if you ask me."

Richard shot me a smile. "A whole lot of weirdness, for sure. Oh, did Brad mention anything about locating Caden or Reese? They're both still suspects, so I assume the search for them is pretty intense."

"He said they hadn't found either of them yet. It seems like both guys have just vanished into thin air."

"Speaking of vanishing—no trace of your uncle's painting either?"

"Nope. Aunt Lydia is not happy about that, as you can imagine."

"Yeah, I can." Richard tapped the steering wheel with his fingers. "Glad I wasn't there when you told her, to be honest."

"She took it well, all things considered. But Brad said she's not thrilled with the lack of investigation into the theft. Although, with a murder and two suspects on the run, you can't really blame the sheriff's department for not focusing on a missing still life."

"True." Richard lifted one hand off the steering wheel and rubbed at his jaw.

I laid my left hand on his knee. "What is it? You look concerned."

He lowered his hand over mine. "Just thinking about what you told me this morning about Kurt Kendrick hosting the reception. I wasn't aware of that."

"Yeah, that's what Adele said."

"Honestly, I'm not thrilled with the idea that he's been following my career for years when he's never approached me until this past summer. And asking Adele to stay quiet about it . . ." Richard's fingers tightened around my hand. "That's a little disturbing."

"I thought so too." I gave his fingers a squeeze. "But you know how I distrust the man."

"Good call, I think." Richard slid his hand away and gripped the wheel again. He glanced over at me before focusing back on the road. "So do you actually believe he's entangled in this forgery business?"

"I think it's possible. He has the necessary connections in

the art world—and the black market, I suspect—to move paintings like that. With no one the wiser."

"Then there's your suspicion about your uncle, and their close friendship. It seems like they stayed in touch after high school too, although your aunt was kept in the dark. So perhaps . . ."

"Kendrick encouraged Uncle Andrew to dabble in forgery? Yeah, I've had that same thought. If that's true . . ." I stared out the car window as other vehicles zipped past us. Although Richard was driving over the speed limit, apparently it wasn't fast enough for most of the drivers on Highway 81. "That would set Aunt Lydia off like a grenade."

"Yep. So perhaps discretion is the better part of valor."

"Probably the best choice. There's really no reason to tell her. Uncle Andrew's been dead for over thirty-seven years, so I can't see how he would be connected with the current investigation."

Richard looked thoughtful. "Although, as we discovered this summer, sometimes things from the distant past can affect current events."

I gnawed on my pinkie fingernail. Richard had a point. Events from 1925 and 1958 had definitely tied into the murderous mayhem we'd experienced just a few months before. "But even if Uncle Andrew forged a few paintings, nothing he painted could be in the collection found at the LeBlancs', could it? They didn't move here until about ten years ago, and at that point the farm was in really bad shape. If those paintings were already stored in their barn, Reese or Rachel would've discovered them during their renovations, wouldn't they?" I dropped my hand into my lap and drummed my fingers against the worn knee of my jeans. "Unless one or both of them were in on the whole deal from the beginning and the canvases were moved from some other hiding place."

"That seems unlikely to me. I personally doubt the LeBlanc forgeries are connected to your uncle." Richard pointed at a highway sign. "Ah, getting closer. We should be home by four o'clock."

"I know we told Aunt Lydia around two, but we left a little later than you originally planned. I mean, you even had to pay a surcharge at the hotel." I fiddled with a button on my jacket as I remembered why.

Richard grinned. "Worth every penny."

"Well anyway, I was thinking we should stop and pick up something for dinner. Aunt Lydia covered for me at the festival today, so I know she must be dead tired. I don't want her to feel compelled to cook."

"How about trying that new gourmet kitchen outside of town? The one that caters but also sells premade casseroles and stuff."

"That sounds good. We can grab a variety of things so everyone can choose what they want." My lips twitched as an errant thought flashed through my mind. "Hugh Chen might not be thrilled with our plan. He loves my aunt's cooking."

"She is a fabulous cook. But I bet he'll understand. Dealing with the festival crowds all day would tire anyone out."

"Yeah." I gazed appreciatively at his handsome profile. "It was so good of her, and Sunny and the others, to arrange this trip. Not to mention taking over for me at the festival, the plane ticket, and all that. Not sure I can ever repay them."

"I must thank them profusely as well. Not just for your

company, which is much appreciated, but also for making it possible for you to see the show. I've always wanted you to actually see me perform. I mean, in a live production, not just on video."

"It was amazing." I placed my hand back on his right knee. "I know I've told you that a couple of times, but it can't be said often enough."

He cast me a warm smile. "Thank you. I'm glad I got to share it with you."

"That piece"—I twirled a lock of hair around one of the fingers of my free hand—"excuse me if I'm being intrusive, but it was really about Karla, wasn't it? I mean, in part."

Another quick glance, but this one was sharper, and lacking the smile. "So you figured that out, did you?"

"Not so difficult, when you know the story. You told me most people don't, so I doubt many would make the connection."

"No, I suppose not." Richard sighed. "It's in the past, and I should get over it. Or at least that's what Meredith always told me."

I bit back a swear word as I contemplated how satisfying it would be to slap Meredith's pretty face. "That's nonsense. If a person means the world to you, how can you just forget?"

Richard's hand landed on mine. "Thank you."

"You don't have to thank me for being a decent human being."

His fingers caressed the back of my hand. "Then thank you for being you. And for coming into my life."

A very lonely boy . . . I stroked his thigh absently. "That wasn't exactly under my control."

"Just my good luck." He lifted our joined hands and placed

my hand back in my lap. "Sorry, sweetheart, but that's too distracting while I'm driving. I want to get us home in one piece."

"Didn't know my mere touch held such power."

Richard shot me a look that made my stomach turn a flip. "Oh trust me, it does. Now, how about we discuss what we are and aren't going to tell Lydia? I mean, about Kurt Kendrick's gallery hosting the reception and"—he winked at me—"that extra hotel room."

"Nothing and nothing," I said firmly.

"Okay, that was a short discussion. Next topic?"

"You inviting Kurt Kendrick to your house for dinner."

Richard glanced over at me, eyebrows raised. "Am I doing that?"

"Yes, because I certainly can't. Not with Aunt Lydia refusing to even talk to him, except when it's unavoidable." I clasped my hands demurely in my lap. "I just have this feeling he's mixed up in this forgery scheme somehow. And maybe even the murder. It's time for some answers, and I want to be the one to grill him."

Lifting one hand off the steering wheel, Richard tapped his temple with one finger. "I don't know. Considering his size and all, maybe we should just grill some salmon instead."

I would've thrown something at him, but I had nothing at hand, and he *was* driving. "Wait until we get out of this car, mister. You're going to pay for that remark."

Richard just grinned. "I'll take my punishment. As long as it's at your hands."

* * *

When we pulled into Richard's driveway, I noticed that my aunt's front door was standing ajar, yet no one was on the porch or in the front yard.

I was instantly on alert. *Someone probably just opened the door for whatever reason and forgot to close it tightly and the wind caught it . . .*

But there was still the matter of an unsolved murder, as well as two fugitives unaccounted for, and an art forgery ring. I turned to Richard. "I think I'd better run over and check on Aunt Lydia. The door . . ."

"I saw." Richard jumped out and jogged around to meet me at the passenger side. "I'm coming with you," he said as I climbed out of the car.

"Not about to disagree." I followed him across his lawn to my aunt's front gate.

We climbed the steps and quietly crossed the porch. Approaching the open front door with caution, Richard peered inside before he allowed me to accompany him into the hall.

"I don't see anything," he said. "But voices are coming from the back."

Loud voices. I identified my aunt's and one other—Hugh Chen. It sounded as if they were arguing.

Richard motioned for me to head on down the hall while he closed and locked the front door.

"I don't know why you've concocted this preposterous theory, but I can assure you that you are mistaken." Aunt Lydia's normally clear voice was as gravelly as a backcountry road.

I blinked rapidly and took a deep breath before stepping onto the enclosed back porch. I'd never heard my aunt speak in such a tone before. "Hello, sorry to interrupt, but Richard and I just got back, and when we saw the door ajar . . ."

Aunt Lydia stood ramrod straight, her hands clenched at her sides and her blue eyes blazing. "I was headed outside, but then Dr. Chen stopped me with some unwelcome news and I suppose I forgot to close it."

"Okay, we wanted to let you know that we picked up some stuff for dinner. It's in the trunk . . ."

"Dr. Chen will not be staying," my aunt said.

"Yes, I'm afraid I've been asked to leave." Hugh's posture was just as stiff as my aunt's, but his hands were held before him, clasped at his chest.

Richard stepped up beside me. "What's going on here?" He eyed Hugh with narrowed eyes. "Do you need help, Lydia?"

I realized that Richard had never met the art expert and probably assumed the fault lay with him. "Hugh," I said, pressing my hand against Richard's forearm to prevent him from moving forward, "can you explain what's happened?"

Hugh opened his hands and held them out, as if in supplication. "I merely shared some information with Lydia. What I believe to be the truth." His dark eyes sought mine. Reading the pain in them, I knew what he must've said.

"You told her."

Beside me, Richard gulped. "Andrew's paintings," he said under his breath.

"He spewed a lot of nonsense is what he did." Aunt Lydia gave a defiant toss of her head. "Just lies and more damn lies."

Hugh glanced in my direction. "Trust me, Amy, it was not my intention to offend your aunt. But I've uncovered some information on one of the paintings we were looking at the other night. The Monet study, remember? I simply felt Lydia should hear the truth from me, before the authorities get involved."

Aunt Lydia turned on me. "You knew something of this?"

I couldn't meet her furious gaze. Looking down, I scuffed my sneaker sole against the wooden plank floor. "I saw the study that Hugh mentioned, yes." I swallowed back any additional words. No use bringing up the canvas hidden behind that seascape. Not when my aunt was already armed for bear.

"What are you saying?" Richard asked. "How does some study prove that Amy's uncle was a forger?"

"It doesn't, by itself." Hugh's words, punctuated by a surprising swear word from my aunt, made me look up.

I examined the art expert, noting the sharp lines bracketing his thinned lips. "So what's the connection, then?"

"A painting that shouldn't exist." Hugh took a deep breath as Aunt Lydia turned away to stare out the sunroom windows. "When I spied that Monet study, I immediately noticed its resemblance to a forgery case I'd worked on a few years ago. That case involved several pieces owned by a young man who'd inherited them from his parents. He wanted them appraised, and while most were originals, I had the unpleasant task of informing him that one painting attributed to Monet was a forgery. He didn't know where his parents had acquired the work, and at the time I had no idea who the forger might have been. I had my lab run some tests, and the fake Monet was dated to about forty years ago, give or take ten years." He fixed his dark gaze on Richard and me. "The sketch I found among Andrew Talbot's paintings was a match to the forged Monet I uncovered in that previous case. Right down to the unique element that we discovered through x-ray analysis. The element was painted over in the finished piece but visible in the sketch. It's not something I've seen in other Monets from the period." Hugh cleared his throat before continuing. "A rosebush at the water's edge, reflected in the pond."

As my aunt sucked in an audible breath, I recalled the rose finial that topped the weather vane on our house. So my uncle had added a symbol that referenced my aunt's family, although he'd obviously thought better of allowing that indulgence to remain in the completed painting.

"You believe Uncle Andrew painted that piece and it somehow ended up in the young man's collection?" I asked.

"Yes, judging by the correlation with the sketch. The lab dated the sketch to the same time period as the forgery, and there is that hidden element. Given those facts. I have to conclude that Andrew Talbot painted the fake Monet I discovered a few years ago. A work that I've been trying to match to a forger for a long time, with no success. Until now."

I slid my hand down Richard's arm and gripped his fingers as I gazed over at my aunt's rigid back. "I'm sorry, Aunt Lydia. Hugh showed me the water lily sketch the other night, but at the time I assumed it was just some type of practice work. I know a lot of artists do that—copy old masters to learn their techniques. So I really didn't give it much thought." I squeezed Richard's hand hard as he looked down at me with widened eyes.

Unlike my aunt, or even Hugh, he knew this was a lie, since I'd told him about the copy of a Van Gogh and those practice signatures I'd discovered stashed behind an innocuous seascape.

But I didn't want to bring that canvas to light. Not now. Not when my aunt's heart had been shattered by the revelation that her beloved husband—a man she'd always idolized—had been a forger. Besides, what harm could that painting do, buried in a closet? It wasn't as if Aunt Lydia or I would try to pass it off as an original to a buyer.

No one even needs to know it exists, I thought, and immediately resolved to drag it out of that closet and hide it in my room at the earliest opportunity. I could figure out what to do with it sometime later, after the LeBlanc forgery case was resolved.

"I find this all impossible to believe." Aunt Lydia leaned forward, pressing her palms against the wooden windowsill and her forehead against the glass.

"Perhaps there is a reasonable explanation," Hugh said. "It could be that your husband was forced into this situation somehow. Against his will."

While Hugh continued to focus on my aunt, Richard leaned down to whisper in my ear, "What about the other one?"

I touched my forefinger to my lips and shook my head just as Hugh turned back to us.

"As I mentioned earlier, Lydia has asked me to leave the house, which I totally understand. I've turned out to be a rather unfortunate messenger. But I wondered if you could suggest another place for me to stay? Now that the Heritage Festival has concluded, I thought perhaps there might be openings at some of the local motels or inns."

"Sure, we can help you find something." Richard released my hand and stepped forward. "By the way, we were never actually introduced. I'm Richard Muir."

"I assumed as much." Hugh moved closer and gave Richard's hand a firm shake. "Dr. Hugh Chen."

"How about we head upstairs and grab your suitcase and

whatever else while we discuss options?" Richard motioned with his head toward Aunt Lydia, who still had her back to us.

Hugh nodded. "A good plan. Thank you." He turned toward the windows. "I will go collect my things, Lydia, but I do wish to thank you again for your wonderful hospitality. I'm sorry our acquaintance has ended on such a sad note, but perhaps someday . . ."

"Just go," my aunt said, her tone now resigned rather than angry. When she glanced back over her shoulder, I spied the tension lining her forehead. "In fact, Amy, why don't you also help Hugh collect his things. I would like to be alone for a bit."

"Sure, okay," I said, sharing a concerned look with Richard.

Yes, I'd leave her to her thoughts, for a short time. But as soon as we grabbed Hugh's suitcase and Richard left to drive him to his new lodgings, I'd come back and we would talk, whether Aunt Lydia liked it or not. No way was I leaving her alone for long.

Casting one last glance at my aunt's hunched shoulders, I followed Hugh and Richard out of the sunroom. As we headed upstairs, Hugh asked Richard about his recent performances.

"Lydia was so excited to have sent Amy on that trip," he said, then tightened his lips. Obviously the new reality of their blasted relationship had hit him.

"It was a wonderful surprise." I paused at the door to Hugh's room and laid my fingers on his arm. "She'll come around, I think. It's just the shock."

Hugh shook his head as he pushed open the bedroom door. "I don't know if she'll ever forgive me. But I had to tell her. I couldn't bear her hearing about it from someone else. Which was bound to happen. Professionally, I have to reveal the truth about that forged Monet."

"A kind gesture, definitely," Richard said, following Hugh and me into the room. "Especially considering you had to know you'd bear the brunt of her anger."

"Better me than a stranger." Hugh crossed to the dresser. "Richard, if you'd retrieve the suitcase over there by the closet and put it on the bed, I'll grab my things and pack as quickly as possible."

I volunteered to pull Hugh's suits from the closet, not inclined to give either Richard or Hugh any opportunity to stumble over that other, hidden, canvas. After I tossed all the items on hangers onto the bed, I folded them while Hugh packed and Richard diverted our thoughts by bombarding the art expert with questions about his work.

"So you use infrared light for some of the testing?" Richard asked.

"We call it IR spectroscopic analysis. It's very useful in determining if the materials are compatible with the assumed age of the work. We can study many things, including pigments, binders, glues, and varnishes, to make sure they correlate with the presumed historic period of the painting."

Richard, who was standing by a window that looked out over the front lawn, absently ran his fingers across the sill. "Doesn't that damage the artworks?"

"No, most of the testing is no more harmful than a photograph. When we need more, very minimal sample quantities are used." Hugh took the last shirt from my hands and laid it on top of the pile of clothes filling the suitcase. "There, I think that's everything."

Just as he closed the suitcase and snapped the locks in place, the sound of a revving engine filled the room.

"What the . . ." Richard turned and stared out the window. "It's Lydia. She's taken her car and headed off like a bat out of hell."

"Oh no!" I couldn't imagine my aunt driving anywhere in her state of mind. "Where could she possibly be going?"

"Not good to drive when you're that upset," Hugh said, his face drawn.

"Come on, Richard, let's get your car and follow her." I sprinted for the door with Richard and Hugh on my heels.

We clattered down the stairs to find a white note card perched on the hall side table. Richard reached it first.

"Go ahead, read it," I said as I grabbed my jacket from the hall coat tree.

Richard glanced up from the unfolded note card. "She's gone to see Kurt Kendrick."

"What?" I shoved the wrong hand into the sleeve, whipped the jacket off again, and struggled to find the right armhole with my shaking hand.

"She says he must have been the one to involve Andrew in forgery, if anyone did." He ran his hand through his hair and waved the card at me and Hugh. "Grab my jacket too, would you? We do need to go after her."

"I'm coming with you," Hugh said, slinging his coat over his shoulder. "But what makes this so urgent, Richard?"

"Because she also says she's going to get some answers out of him, even if it kills her."

I met Richard's anxious gaze, my lips trembling. "And it might."

Chapter Eighteen

Richard drove fast, shifting Hugh from side to side despite his seat belt. I'd insisted Hugh take the front seat while I sat in the back but soon regretted my decision as we bounced over the gravel road that led to Kurt Kendrick's historic estate.

"What about the gate?" I clutched the back door handle, clinging tightly as Richard's car rounded the road's mountain curves.

"Gate?" Hugh, his face ashen, glanced back at me over the console that split the front seats.

"Kendrick has an automatic gate. You have to push a button and ask for entry," I said, recalling this fact from the one time I'd visited the art dealer's home.

"We'll handle that once we get there." Richard said, thankfully keeping his eyes on the road.

I sank into my seat, wondering how Aunt Lydia would manage to gain entry to the estate when she wasn't expected. But I slapped the knee of my jeans as I realized she'd have no problem. *If she gives her name, Kendrick will immediately open the gate.* He'd told me several times that he'd welcome a relationship with her. It was Aunt Lydia who wanted nothing to do with him.

We turned onto a blacktopped road. A short distance ahead, two fieldstone pillars flanked an automatic gate. A sign on one of the stone gateposts identified the estate as "Highview."

Richard leaned forward and peered through the front window. "That's odd. The gate doesn't appear to be completely closed."

"Let me go check." I unbuckled my seat belt and hopped out of the car before Richard could protest.

I jogged up to the gate. It was sitting slightly ajar, and I soon saw why—a large rock had been wedged between the gate and the posts. *Aunt Lydia, you sly fox*, I thought. She, who'd never trusted Kendrick, had been sensible enough to take precautions. She'd used the stone to prevent him from locking her car inside the estate.

"I'm going to hold the gate while you drive through," I called to Richard, who'd stuck his head out his open side window.

After the car passed through, I allowed the gate to swing back. It hit the rock and stopped, standing slightly ajar again. "Might as well follow Aunt Lydia's lead and ensure our getaway," I said as I climbed into the backseat.

"Such a clever woman." Hugh said this softly, as if speaking to himself, but I nodded.

"Always." I stared out my window. The last time I'd been here, it had been summer and everything had been a sea of emerald and jade. Now the hardwood trees that lined the driveway blazed with autumn color and only the leaves of the azaleas and rhododendrons gleamed green against the leaf-strewn brown mulch.

As we rounded the corner that revealed Kurt Kendrick's home, the beauty of the historic structure once again amazed me. A three-story central section of variegated fieldstone was set off by two-story wood-framed wings painted pale green. The home's many windows shone like crystal in the azure glow of twilight, and a coil of smoke rose from one of the ivy-draped stone chimneys.

"What a lovely place," Hugh said as Richard parked behind Aunt Lydia's car on the circle of blacktop that ended the driveway. "It's quite old, I imagine."

"Yeah, the central portion was built in the late 1700s, or so I'm told." Richard climbed out of the car. "Hold on, Amy—I'll get your door."

The minute he opened it, I leapt out and headed for the house, not giving the lovely cottage garden a second glance. Aunt Lydia was inside, and I didn't want to leave her alone with Kurt Kendrick too long.

When I reached the roofed porch, I leaned against one of its Grecian-style pillars and stared at the forest-green front door.

"Probably locked," Richard said as he and Hugh joined me on the porch.

"Doorbell?" Hugh suggested, but I'd already laid my hand on the old-fashioned metal latch and felt it move under my fingers.

"No, strangely, it isn't locked." I frowned. When I'd visited before, Kendrick had told me that the door locked automatically, but it seemed this time it hadn't closed tightly enough to engage the mechanism. I could picture a likely scenario for this—Aunt Lydia had probably barged in, furious, as soon as Kendrick had greeted her. If he was focused on her, it was possible he hadn't noticed that the door hadn't closed completely behind them.

"Shouldn't we ring the bell?" Hugh asked again, as I shoved the door open.

Voices from the back of the house, raised in anger, gave wings to my feet as I ran down the high-ceilinged front hall. The rare and beautiful artifacts in the hall didn't even distract me as they had on my previous visit.

Richard, with his longer stride, reached the door leading to Kendrick's living room before me. Holding up his hand, he tilted his head toward the back of the house. "Did you hear that?" he asked quietly.

Hugh also kept his voice low. "Sounded like someone running up the stairs."

"Yeah, but why?" Richard frowned. "Kurt told me that he doesn't have help living here—they just come in to clean and cook when needed. So who's here besides Lydia?"

"Could still be a maid or something. Might be cleaning day," I said.

"I don't like it. With the front door left ajar . . ." Richard glanced at the staircase again. "I think I'll go take a look. Just to be certain. You two go on into the living room and make sure that Lydia's okay, and I'll join you in a minute or two."

I touched his arm. "But if it's an intruder, you could be in danger."

He pulled his cell phone from his pocket. "Don't worry, I'll have this. I can dial in 911 in a second if necessary. Anyway, you're probably right and it's some worker wandering about. I just want to make sure." He patted my hand before striding off toward the back stairs.

"Should we go in?" Hugh slid past me and pushed open the door, his eyes widening as he gazed inside. Despite comfortable leather sofas and upholstered chairs anchored by worn Oriental rugs, Kendrick's amazing collection of paintings and objets d'art lent the space the air of a gallery rather than a living room.

As I followed Hugh into the room, my gaze flitted past the artworks to focus on the two people standing in front of the rustic stone fireplace. They both turned to face us—Kurt Kendrick's bushy eyebrows rising to meet the thick fall of his white hair while my aunt dabbed at her eyes with a lace-edged cotton handkerchief.

"What's going on?" I asked.

"Ah Lydia, I see your entourage has arrived." Kurt Kendrick flicked something from the sleeve of his cashmere sweater in a gesture that also seemed to cast Hugh and me aside. His eyes, the same ice-blue as his sweater, gazed at us with amused disdain.

"What are you doing here?" Aunt Lydia's own blue eyes— not as pale but no less frosty—surveyed us.

"We read your note and decided it would better if you had some backup." Hugh's gaze was fixed on my aunt. "In fact, I think you should join us over here, Lydia."

"Don't be ridiculous," she replied, wadding the handkerchief between her fingers. "Kurt was just about to confirm my suspicions about his criminal influence over Andrew, so if you don't mind . . ."

"I was not about to do anything of the sort," Kendrick said.

"You just admitted that you were the one who introduced him to drugs, as I always suspected."

Watching Aunt Lydia clench and unclench her hands, I

crossed over to stand beside her. She cast me a tight-lipped smile before staring back at Kurt Kendrick.

"Yes, to my eternal regret. Of course I had no idea that Andrew would be so susceptible to addiction. For me it was always just harmless fun, but Andrew . . ." He wiped his brow, as if erasing painful memories.

"He suffered greatly from your mistake. While it seems you went merrily on your way, without that regret you claim now."

Kendrick examined my aunt with narrowed eyes. "Still making excuses for him, Lydia? Even now? Yes, I did introduce him to a few substances, but let's be honest—what happened after that was his mistake as well as mine. Anyway, it was always his choice to partake. Whatever you may think of me, I didn't hold my best friend down and force-feed him drugs."

Aunt Lydia poked her finger at Kendrick. "You persuaded him. For some ungodly reason, he admired you. He looked up to you and wanted to follow your lead. You must've known that."

"Yes, I knew." Pain flickered in Kendrick's brilliant eyes. "I suppose it was because I was a couple of years older, and more experienced in . . . well, everything. But this is all ancient history. It has no bearing on his foray into forgery. That was not my doing. Something else drove him to it."

I tapped my foot against the marble hearth. "So explain, Mr. Kendrick. If you know why my uncle got involved in art forgery, you should tell us the truth. Right here and now."

Kendrick cast me a quick, pitying glance. "You won't like the answer, Amy."

"I want to know anyway."

"Very well." Kendrick's gaze slid over to the man standing a few feet away. "But are you sure you want me to speak about such things in front of this other gentleman?"

"It's fine with me," Aunt Lydia said. "Although we've only met recently, I consider Hugh a friend."

So she'd forgiven him for informing her about Andrew's forgeries. I toyed with a button on my jacket. Of course she had—Aunt Lydia was a sensible woman. Once she thought it through, she wouldn't blame the art expert for merely conveying the truth.

Hugh brightened at my aunt's words. But his smile faded as he stepped forward and thrust out his hand. "I should introduce myself properly. Dr. Hugh Chen, consultant for the state of Virginia."

Kendrick strolled closer to the art expert but did not grasp his hand. "I know who you are, Dr. Chen."

"Then you know that I specialize in art authentication. I'm called in for cases of forgery and similar illegal activities." Hugh dropped his hand to his side, his dark eyes hard as stones. "And, Mr. Kendrick, I know a great deal about you as well."

"Do you now?" Kendrick's height made him loom over the shorter man, but his expression remained amused rather than angry. "Well then, you know that I do not deal in forgeries. I love art too much to promote fakes."

"So you say." Aunt Lydia sniffed and crossed her arms over her chest. "And perhaps it is true now. But I still believe you dragged Andrew down into the muck. He would never have gotten entangled with a forgery scheme otherwise."

Kendrick lifted his hands in a "What can you do?" gesture before he walked back toward my aunt. "My dear, you've stated that opinion several times."

"Yet you have not denied it." Aunt Lydia's expression would've wilted a less confident man. As I glanced over at Hugh, I noticed the unadulterated admiration lighting up his face.

"No, because I have not wished to cause you additional pain." Kendrick examined my defiant aunt as if she were some rare artifact he couldn't quite identify. "I did know about Andrew's experiments with forgery, but I was not the reason he got involved in that nasty business. On the contrary, I warned him against it. Quite vehemently."

Aunt Lydia flinched but didn't lower her gaze. "If that's the truth, then explain why he'd do such a thing."

I laid my hand on her tensed shoulder. "Perhaps now is not the time . . ."

She shrugged off my hand and stepped forward until she was almost toe-to-toe with the tall, white-haired art dealer. "Speak. Although I expect you to lie, I do want to hear your version of the story. Just remember I know that every bad thing that happened to Andrew came from his involvement with you."

"You are mistaken." Kendrick held out his hands, as if in supplication. "I may have been a bad influence in other areas, but trust me, the forgery scheme was all Andrew's idea."

"Nonsense. Andrew was devoted to his craft. He was a true artist. He wouldn't even work for that interior design firm that wanted 'sofa-sized paintings.' He spurned such a crass use of his talent. So I can't imagine anything that would make him fake another artist's work." Aunt Lydia flicked her hand, as if she could brush Kendrick away like an annoying insect. "If you're going to accuse my husband of such a thing, you'd damn well better tell me why."

In that moment, Kurt Kendrick's face changed. Gone was

the sardonic mask of the amused courtier. In its place was pain, pure and simple. I swallowed hard and clasped my hands together as he began to speak.

"Lydia, there's one thing you should know—Andrew loved you. Whatever he did, he did for you."

My aunt's firm stance did not falter, but her lips trembled.

"You know he made very little off his paintings, despite his talent. He couldn't sell but a few of them." Kendrick sighed. "I tried to help him. I even took some of them into my gallery. Because, yes, he and I were in contact after I left Taylorsford. Not right away, but later, after your marriage. Which is something I don't believe he told you."

Aunt Lydia tightened her lips and said nothing.

"I couldn't sell his paintings either. No matter how hard I tried. So I suggested that he consider some other line of work. Keeping the painting as an avocation, of course. I thought he could still paint and sell a few pieces here and there without living under the weight of so much expectation. And, despite what you may think, he wanted to follow my advice."

"That's ridiculous."

"No, that's the truth." Kendrick's voice fell into a gentle cadence that made me clench my fingers tighter. "Andrew was actually willing to work for that design firm, my dear. He didn't turn them down because he thought such a job would be beneath him. He refused their offer because of you."

My hand shot out to grip my aunt's elbow as she wobbled slightly. "I can't believe that," I said. "Aunt Lydia's always told me . . ."

"That Andrew only wanted to be known as a professional artist? That he spurned any other use of his talent?" Kendrick tilted his head, studying me with what I was shocked to read as compassion. "Yes, I'm sure she has. But you see, that wasn't exactly true. It wasn't Andrew who was determined to limit his talent to fine art. It was Lydia who was obsessed with that notion."

My aunt cried out. I threw my arm around her shoulders as Hugh crossed the room and flanked her other side.

Kurt Kendrick didn't bat an eyelash at this activity. "Is the cavalry preparing to attack, or shall I continue?"

"Go on," my aunt said between gritted teeth. "It's time you told me what you really think."

Kendrick turned away, pressing both of his hands against the carved wood of the fireplace mantle. "Actually, it's what I know. That Andrew truly loved you, Lydia. More than art. More than honor. He wanted to please you in all ways, and he knew how important his status as an artist was to you." Kendrick stared into the soot-blackened interior of the fireplace. "In fact, he confessed to being afraid that it was what you loved most about him."

"He'd never have told you that," my aunt said, pulling away from me.

Kendrick glanced up at her. "Not in so many words, perhaps, but I knew what he meant. He guessed it from the start. Why else would you choose him? You were a beautiful and vibrant girl from a well-respected family. You could've had your pick of any single man in town. But they weren't what you wanted, were they, Lydia? You wanted different and slightly dangerous, and that's what Andrew could offer. He wasn't some boring banker or farmer or insurance agent. He was a free spirit, a dreamer, and an artist. Just a bit wild, but you liked that too,

I think." Kendrick shot another quick glance at my aunt's stony face.

"I loved him for everything he was," she replied stiffly.

"That's probably quite true, but Andrew was never really sure." Kendrick straightened and turned to face her. "You made such a big deal over his art career. He said that whenever he mentioned his guilt over living off your family's money, you demanded that he forget such nonsense and follow his vocation. You always told him that his talent was all that mattered."

"I never resented him for not making money. Even Grandma Rose didn't, and you know how she was."

"Indeed." Kendrick rolled his eyes at the mention of my great-grandmother. "But Andrew wanted out, Lydia. He longed to escape the constant rejection he experienced with his art. He sought a salaried job of some kind that would allow him to contribute to the household income. He wanted to feel that he was providing something to the family instead of being a burden. But he couldn't tell you that. You'd built your whole marriage around him being special. You'd created a fantasy where he was the struggling but brilliant artist and you were his loyal helpmate and muse."

Aunt Lydia stamped her foot against the marble hearth. "That's a lie!"

Kendrick shook his head. "No, it isn't. If you think about it honestly, you will see that it's the truth. You didn't want some ordinary Joe. Your head was stuffed full of romantic notions about finding, and nurturing, your very own artistic genius. You cast Andrew in that role, and he played along because he loved you so much."

Aunt Lydia lifted her trembling chin and held his fierce stare with her own.

"My dear Lydia, don't you see? He couldn't bear to disappoint you. He couldn't take another job when he thought doing so would break your heart. You'd placed him on a pedestal that left him little room to move. He didn't want to fall from your grace. So he turned to the only thing he thought would allow him to make money and still play the part you desired. He became a forger."

Aunt Lydia leaned forward, burying her face in her hands. While no sound escaped her lips, her shoulders heaved.

Feeling helpless, I lifted my hands and dropped them again as Hugh moved closer. He did not touch my aunt—he simply stood at her side and allowed her to cry.

"I am sorry," Kurt Kendrick said in a strained tone. "But it's the truth. I never planned to tell you. I thought once Andrew died, his forgery activities would die with him. I even searched out and destroyed any paintings I suspected he'd created, based on things he'd mentioned to me. But one or two slipped through my net."

I stared up at the art dealer's ruggedly handsome face. "You loved him too."

"Yes," he said. "Yes, I did."

I continued to stare at Kendrick, unsure how to read this declaration. But, as he'd said, it was ancient history. Unlike my aunt's current pain.

She lifted her head, heedless of the tears sliding down her cheeks. "So if it wasn't you, who did lure him into the forgery scheme? I know he wouldn't have come up with it on his own.

He wasn't duplicitous enough. And he didn't have the right, or I should say *wrong*, connections to make it work."

Kendrick lifted his hands. "I don't know. Honestly, I don't. I have my suspicions, but they are only that. Andrew would never tell me. I guess he feared I was too embedded in the art world to stay silent about something as significant as a forgery ring. But from time to time he let things slip. The way he talked, I assumed it was a well-organized operation."

"The money . . ." Aunt Lydia yanked the crumpled handkerchief from her pocket and dabbed at her eyes. "Not long before his accident, Andrew deposited a couple of large sums into our account. He told me he'd sold several of his paintings. I didn't question it. We even celebrated with champagne." She took the clean handkerchief that Hugh silently offered her and daintily blew her nose. "He must've thought it would be easy enough to deceive me, as I didn't keep track of everything he was painting. Especially then, when he was working in the garage rather than the sun-room. He told me he had some larger pieces he could only paint out there." She sniffed back another sob. "I guess I was thoroughly fooled, wasn't I?"

"He did it out of love," I said.

"Yes, but . . ." Aunt Lydia squared her shoulders before looking me in the eye. "Also out of fear. If Kurt is to be believed, Andrew apparently didn't trust me to love him enough. He was afraid I'd leave him if I knew the truth." She shoved the handkerchiefs in her pocket and tossed her head of white hair. "Which is a rather sobering thought, all in all. I believed we had a perfect rapport. That we had no secrets. Of course, I *was* very young, and I suppose far too idealistic. I was living in a dream world, it seems. But I did love him, truly and deeply. He was my whole world. I thought he knew that."

"I'm sure he did," Hugh said. "But it can be difficult to keep one's balance on a pedestal."

I thought Aunt Lydia might bristle at that remark, but she simply turned to Hugh and laid her fingers on his arm. "Yes, I suppose."

He covered her hand with his own. "And now that you know the truth, you can allow your husband to step down from that great height. He can live in your memory at your level—at your side. Isn't that better, in the end?"

"If only I had known sooner . . ." she murmured.

"I'm sorry, Lydia," Kurt Kendrick said. "Andrew swore me to secrecy."

"And your first loyalty was to him." Aunt Lydia pulled away from Hugh to face Kendrick. "Which . . . I can forgive, Kurt. There are other things I still hold against you, but not that."

He gave her a nod. "It's a start."

A clatter from the hall drew our gazes to the open doorway. Richard entered the room, but not alone.

Held forcibly in check by Richard's grip on one of his wiry, tattoo-sleeved arms was another man. A short, ginger-haired man with light brown eyes. Someone I'd seen only in photographs but recognized immediately.

Reese LeBlanc.

Chapter Nineteen

Aunt Lydia cast Kendrick a furious glare. "What's this?"

Reese squirmed in his tight grip, but Richard focused on Kurt Kendrick. "I found this guy hiding in one of the upstairs closets. Care to explain?"

"A thief?" Hugh studied the tattooed man with narrowed eyes.

Kendrick languidly brushed some imaginary speck from his sweater. "No, my guest."

Hugh's eyebrows shot up to the fall of his dark hair. "Your guests like to skulk about your house and hide in closets?"

I touched Hugh's arm. "It's Reese LeBlanc."

Hugh turned to me, his mouth dropping open. "The fugitive?" He thrust his hand into his jacket pocket.

His phone. He's going for his phone.

Hoping to draw Kendrick's eyes off of Hugh, I slid my arm through the crook of Aunt Lydia's elbow and pulled her toward the center of the room. "So you're harboring fugitives now, Mr. Kendrick?"

He made a disparaging noise and crossed to stand behind an

antique desk that sat in one corner of the room. "No, a man unfairly labeled and hounded by the authorities. If you will unhand him, Richard, I'll be happy to explain."

"Not sure I should do that," Richard said. "He is a wanted man, whether you believe in his guilt or not."

When Reese's eyes locked with Kendrick's icy gaze, I thought I glimpsed a flicker of something pass between them. Some type of signal.

Kendrick casually opened one of the desk drawers.

"I'm innocent," Reese declared. "If you'll just give me time to explain . . ."

"I'm not sure I can allow you that courtesy." Hugh held up his cell phone. "You're a wanted fugitive, Mr. LeBlanc, and as someone working with the sheriff's department, I feel compelled to report your presence here."

"Please don't." Kendrick's tone made Hugh lower the hand holding his phone.

"Let him go, Richard," I said, when I spied the object Kendrick had pulled from the drawer.

Aunt Lydia slipped free of my grip and gasped as Kendrick leveled a black revolver at Richard and Reese.

"I will ask one more time—please release my guest."

Richard immediately dropped his hold on the artist and stepped back. "Surely you don't intend to use that," he said, flexing his fingers.

"I don't want to," Kendrick said, "but I will if necessary. Oh, maybe not to kill. But I doubt a shattered kneecap would benefit your dance career. Now—sit." He waved the gun toward one of the leather sofas and Richard sat down, his eyes fixed on the weapon. "Amy and Dr. Chen, please toss your phones onto the floor and take a seat on either side of him. Lydia, do the same but take the chair next to the fireplace."

Aunt Lydia walked over to the wingback chair, her white head held high.

"Richard, please toss your phone on the floor too," Kendrick continued. He waited until Aunt Lydia sat down before he motioned to Reese LeBlanc. "Join me. We need to clear up some obvious confusion."

"I doubt you can hold us hostage forever," I said, settling beside Richard, who immediately put his arm around my shoulders. "There's only two of you and three of us. Well, four, counting my aunt."

Kendrick made a tutting noise. "But I think three of you can probably be discounted. Richard might be up to a fight, but two women and a smallish older man?"

"For your information, I have acquitted myself quite well in a few dangerous situations." Hugh glared at the two men behind the desk.

"Perhaps, but I still have a gun." As he brandished it, the revolver's sleek black surface glinted in the light from the Tiffany lamp behind him. After glancing at the cell phones piled on the patterned rug, he casually placed the gun on the desk. "Now, are you willing to listen to reason? Yes, Reese is hiding out, but it's not because he murdered his wife."

"I was nowhere near the studio that day, And I can prove it," Reese LeBlanc said, as he rounded the desk to stand beside Kendrick.

I studied the artist's thin face, noting the lines wrinkling his brow and bracketing his mouth. "So you say. I know your daughter thought you were on a business trip, but you could've lied to her easily enough, especially if you planned to murder Rachel for the insurance money . . ."

Reese raised his clenched hands to his waist, as if he would have liked to throw a punch at me. "Kill my wife for money? What do you think I am?"

"I can't say I know. Obviously your hands aren't entirely clean, whatever you say." Aunt Lydia's tone dripped with disdain. "Personally, I suspect that you and Kurt are both involved in some illegal art deals, and that's why you ran here to hide out after the murder."

Reese shook his head. "No, that's not it at all. I didn't kill Rachel, and Kurt isn't mixed up in this. Not in the way you think."

"But he's certainly been willing to help you out." Richard tightened his grip on my shoulder. "So how does that figure in?"

Reese pressed his palms against the surface of the desk and lowered his head. "I came to him because he already knew the trouble I was in. He'd approached me with . . . an offer of assistance a few months ago. I refused his help then, but he told me he'd keep the offer open and that I should come to him if things ever got really bad." Reese grimaced. "Sadly, they did."

"Because you've been painting forgeries?" Hugh asked.

"Yes," Reese muttered.

"You were in financial trouble before that, weren't you?" I asked.

Reese lifted his head and shot me a surprised glance. "Yes, but . . ."

"I found out about the lien on your property."

"Always the little researcher, aren't you, Amy?" Kendrick's sardonic grin vanished as quickly as it appeared. "But yes, poor

Reese got himself into some hot water. He has a bit of an issue with gambling, you see."

"Horses?" Richard asked. It wasn't a bad guess. A large race-track just over the river in West Virginia drew many people from our area.

"No, other sports."

"So, illegal gambling," Aunt Lydia said. "Football pools and such?"

"Something like that. Anyway, it doesn't matter what it was. And I stopped the betting about two years ago." Reese lifted his chin defiantly. "Cold turkey, if you must know."

"But you'd already lost a good deal of money, I expect," Hugh said thoughtfully. "So you decided to turn to forgery to make some quick cash."

"Yes." Reese's expression soured. "I couldn't make that kind of money off my own paintings. Not nearly."

"But your wife is a very successful artist," I said, then pressed my fingers to my lips as Reese's face crumpled like paper.

"I didn't want to involve Rachel." He buried his face in his hands. "Rachel . . ."

If it was an act, it was a good performance. But I wasn't entirely convinced. Reese LeBlanc appeared to have a rather his-trionic personality. It was possible that he could fake emotional outbursts as well as he could paintings.

Kendrick laid a hand on one of Reese's shaking shoulders. "Yes, poor Rachel got caught in the middle. She wasn't involved, of course. But apparently she discovered one of the fake paintings when Reese foolishly forgot to stash it properly after working on it."

"She threw me out on the spot." Reese's voice was thick with tears. "The forgery thing appalled her. So it wasn't a business trip," he added, looking at me. "We just told Lila that so she wouldn't worry."

"And you eventually came here." Aunt Lydia folded her hands in her lap and gazed speculatively at Kendrick. "But why take him in if you weren't involved, Kurt?"

"Because I knew who *was* involved." Kendrick glanced at Reese, who nodded. "Not a bunch of lightweights. It's a very well-established and ruthless criminal operation."

"The Quinns?" I asked, earning a smile from Kendrick and a surprised look from Hugh.

"I expect so," Hugh said. "If my information is accurate."

Kendrick tipped his head to the side and examined the art expert. "You're tracking them?"

"I've been following their operations for some time. As have many others. But no one can seem to get the drop on them."

"No, they are very clever." Kendrick tapped his chin with one finger. "They use go-betweens to contact artists they think may be interested in their scheme. People you'd never expect."

"Like you?" Aunt Lydia asked.

"No. Anyway, I believe I would not fit that role, since I'm on the radar of several investigators." Kendrick's gaze slid from my aunt to Hugh. "Isn't that right, Dr. Chen?"

"It is," he replied.

I shot him a sharp glance. "You've been looking into Mr. Kendrick's business affairs?"

Hugh shrugged. "I have, along with others. But I haven't found any irregularities. None I can prove, that is."

Kendrick flashed a wolfish grin. "I trust you'll keep looking. But that isn't relevant to the current situation."

"One thing that is relevant, at least to me," my aunt said, raising her voice as well as her chin, "is the identity of this go-between. I assume they're the liaison between you and the actual criminal organization, Mr. LeBlanc?"

Reese shuffled his feet. "Yes. They sought me out, you know. I didn't go looking for them."

Aunt Lydia examined Reese intently. "So this contact—they just walked into your studio one day and asked you if you'd like to forge paintings?"

"No, it was more subtle than that. The person got to know me first. It really seemed like they were interested in my work, and art in general, but who knows? That was probably knowledge that was fed to them, because they were also aware that I needed money. I guess the Quinns had collected that information on me . . ."

"As they do on many artists, especially those with great technical skill who are not quite famous," Kendrick said. "Or so I've heard."

"I suppose. Anyway, they must have sent my contact in to befriend me before we ever got to the subject of forgery. I trusted them by that point. I guess that was the plan." Reese wiped his brow with the back of his hand. "I was taken in, for sure. Used, then thrown to the wolves when I had to go on the run."

"But even so, it seems you won't disclose the name of this contact?" Hugh asked. "You'll have to eventually, you know."

"Yes, but not to you. It's one of my few bargaining chips, you see." Reese glanced at Kendrick. "I'll tell the feds, but only after I get my deal."

I leaned closer to Richard, but kept my gaze focused on the art dealer. "So you aren't tied in with the Quinn organization?"

"No, I'm not. I'm sure you'll dig into that later, Amy, but for now let's move on." Kendrick surveyed us, his blue eyes very bright. "The thing is, the Quinns are quite likely to murder people for any number of reasons. One of which is uncovering their operation."

"Which Rachel was about to do," I said, as the pieces clicked together in my mind. Perhaps Reese was telling the truth and he'd had no involvement in the murder of his wife. Maybe this Quinn organization had sent a hit man to kill Rachel without his knowledge.

I stared at the artist, unsuccessfully attempting to read guilt or innocence in his face. Or perhaps his criminal bosses had ordered Reese to murder his wife and he had complied. He could be a killer, despite his protestations. I knew from personal experience that not all murderers looked or acted the part.

"Unfortunately, yes," Kendrick said. "Not that she knew who was behind the ring, but simply exposing her husband as a forger could have eventually led back to the Quinns. Especially with people like our good Dr. Chen on their trail."

"I didn't kill her, but it was still partially my fault," Reese said, rubbing one fist over his right eye. "I wanted to keep her and Lila out of it and make sure they were safe, and all I did was . . . get Rachel killed."

Richard leapt to his feet. "Wait, you're saying this Quinn group had Rachel LeBlanc murdered? Then why haven't you told the authorities that?"

"Sit," Kendrick said, laying his fingers over the revolver. After Richard complied, the art dealer lifted his hand and continued talking. "Because we don't know anything for certain, and . . ." He took a deep breath. "Sorry, that's all I can share right now. But suffice it to say I took Reese in after Rachel's murder because I knew it was best for him to remain out of sight. At least until certain other measures were put into play."

"What about Lila?" I asked.

Reese banged his fist into his palm. "I've been trying to convince her to join me here, but she's been too concerned about that stupid boy . . ."

"We know she's possibly in danger," Kendrick said. "And as Reese mentioned, we have been in contact with her. Until recently, that is. Lately she hasn't responded to calls or texts."

"You don't know where she is?" I shared a worried glance with Richard. If some criminal organization had had Rachel killed with so little provocation, whether by using Reese or by hiring some hit man, Lila was in danger too.

"No, not for the last three days." Reese's tone shifted from agonized to angry. "And Kurt here won't allow me out of the house to look for her."

"Despite which, you did manage to slip out last night and go heaven knows where. A great mistake, although apparently no one followed you. But no more. It isn't safe." Kendrick shot the artist a look under lowered eyelids. We agreed," he added in a tone that seemed to convey a warning.

"I didn't agree to that." Reese's voice cracked on the last word.

Kendrick waved him aside with one hand. "Yes, you did."

"But Lila is still out there somewhere, and your efforts to find her don't seem to be accomplishing anything." Reese clenched and unclenched his fingers as he blinked rapidly.

He reminded me of someone. When I realized who, I sucked in a quick breath. He looked as wild-eyed as Caden when the young musician had held a knife to Sunny's throat. I swallowed the lump that had risen in my throat. I wasn't convinced that Reese was innocent at this point, and if he'd already killed his own wife, he'd probably have no compunction about murdering strangers. "Richard," I said in a low voice, "this might go off the rails."

Before he could respond, Hugh posed another question. "So you're saying that you're protecting Reese from the Quinns? But why not just turn him over to the authorities? Since you say you can prove his innocence, why not make your case with them?"

"It's more complicated than that," Kendrick said, just as Reese made a dive for the gun.

The shorter man grabbed the revolver and pointed it—not at us, but at Kendrick. "No more of this messing around. I have to find Lila."

"Please put that down," Kendrick said, his voice rock steady.

The artist shook his head and gripped the gun with both hands. "No. I've been listening to you and following your advice, and what's that gotten me? My wife's dead. I'm not gonna lose my little girl too."

Kendrick crossed his arms over his chest. "This is foolish, Reese. We had this under control."

"No, no"—Reese waved the gun about wildly—"you have everything set up to suit your purposes. That's fine for you, but it doesn't help Lila. I should've figured she wouldn't mean that much to you. She's acceptable collateral damage."

I blinked as I attempted to get a grip on my thoughts. Reese sounded sincere in his desire to find and protect his daughter, but there was still that life insurance policy . . .

Reese and Lila could've even been in on it together. I winced at this thought but had to admit the possibility. People had done far worse things for money.

"That is simply not true. I would never put Lila in jeopardy." Kendrick fixed Reese with his intimidating stare. "And our plans . . ."

"Mean nothing without Lila. I trusted you to find her and bring her here, and you failed. Now all this talk about Rachel has made me realize the danger my daughter is in. I can't allow Lila to be hurt too. I have to save her."

Aunt Lydia rose to her feet. "Look here, Mr. LeBlanc. I think perhaps you should put that gun down and do as Kurt says."

Reese glanced at her but kept the revolver trained on Kendrick. "Don't move, Mrs. Talbot. And the rest of you—stay where you are," he added, as Richard, Hugh, and I jumped to our feet. "I have no quarrel with any of you and don't want to see more innocent people hurt. But I'm quite willing to shoot Kurt if you don't follow my instructions."

We all froze in place, our eyes trained on the man holding the gun and his captive.

"Okay, so I'm going to ask Kurt to walk out of the room in front of me. And then we're leaving the house by the back door, and he's going to hand over his keys and climb into his fancy sports car with me. When you hear the car pull away and head down the drive, you can leave the house. Not before." Reese bumped Kendrick with the gun, forcing the older man to turn around. "If I see any of you outside before that black Jag is out the entrance gate, I blast him. Get it?"

A hysterical bubble of laughter trembled on my lips as the irony of the situation hit me. I'd never imagined I'd ever lift a finger to protect Kurt Kendrick. I met my aunt's determined gaze. No doubt she felt the same, but we both knew we had to do what Reese LeBlanc asked. It was quite possible that the artist was already a murderer, and whatever his faults or past misdeeds, Kendrick was a human being. He didn't deserve to die.

"All right," Richard said, reaching for my hand. "We'll just stand here. Right, Lydia?"

She nodded. "Of course."

Hugh lifted his left arm. "I'll even time it." He pointed to his watch. "We'll give you twenty minutes. That should allow you plenty of time to escape."

"But what will you do with him?" I asked, as Reese poked the gun into Kendrick's back and marched him across the room.

"I'll release him down the road. Somewhere off the beaten track. He can easily walk back," Reese said as he forced Kendrick into the hall.

Hugh waited until the back door slammed shut before darting forward. "He forgot about the phones."

"Right," I said, scooping up a couple of them. I tossed Richard his phone as Aunt Lydia picked up hers. "Who wants to call the authorities?"

"I'll do it," Hugh said, his phone at his ear. "I can make it official."

"I'm afraid Mr. LeBlanc wasn't thinking quite straight when he came up with this little plan," Aunt Lydia observed, as Hugh crossed to the doorway to place his call.

"He was frantic over his daughter." I pocketed my phone. "But you're right. He may think he can get away, but a black Jaguar is going to be easy to track."

"Abducting someone isn't going to help his case much either,"

Richard said. "But maybe it will get the authorities to focus on tracking down Lila. I hate to think of her out there with a possible target on her back."

I shuddered. "International criminals? What next?"

"Now we talk to the deputies again." Richard wrapped his arms around me and pulled me into a close embrace. "It almost feels like we've done this before," he whispered in my ear.

My hysterical laughter burst free at that point.

"Air," Richard said, guiding me to the door.

"Can't go out yet. Not twenty minutes," I muttered, but Richard just kept walking me toward the front door.

"Don't worry, I never planned to wait that long anyway." Hugh, who appeared at my other side, offered me an encouraging smile. "I assumed Mr. LeBlanc would reach the end of the lane in a few minutes and that no one could really see much looking back at the house. Especially if they were driving fast."

"Good thinking." Richard kept his arm around me as he pulled open the front door.

"Yes, very wise," Aunt Lydia said.

When I glanced at her, I couldn't help but notice how she was studying Hugh's calm face. Maybe there *was* one more man in the world that she could truly admire.

The sheriff's department arrived soon after we exited the house. Their sirens shattered the quiet less than ten minutes following Hugh's call.

"Seems like an excess of people," Aunt Lydia said as we huddled on the front porch, watching deputies and plainclothes detectives swarm the area. "I would've thought most of them would be off chasing Mr. LeBlanc."

"No, check it out." Richard pointed at a spot where some leafless shrubs allowed a view of the lower portion of the driveway. "There's the Jag. Looks like Reese didn't get too far."

I squinted and followed the line of his arm. "Yeah, there's the car. But I don't see any sign of Kendrick or Reese."

"Maybe they have Mr. LeBlanc in custody?" Hugh leaned against the balustrade and peered into the screen of foliage.

"Not exactly," said a familiar voice.

Brad Tucker approached the porch, his hand on the butt of the gun peeking from his holster. "Everyone all right?"

"We're fine," I replied. "But what do you mean by 'not exactly'?"

Resting one foot on the bottom porch step, Brad gazed up at us with weary eyes. "No one was in the car when we got here. I assume something happened that made LeBlanc take off with Mr. Kendrick. Maybe he heard our sirens in the distance or something."

"That's odd," Richard said. "They should've cleared the gate and been long gone before they heard you coming."

Brad shrugged. "Can't say why. I just know the car was empty, with both doors standing open. I've got people searching the woods, and I'm sure we'll locate them soon. In the meantime, I need to ask you to stay right here where my deputies can keep an eye on you."

"We can't go home?" Aunt Lydia moved closer to the steps.

Brad held up his hand. "Not with an armed fugitive still on the loose. Hell no." He shoved his hat back and rubbed his forehead. "Sorry for the language, but this has been a crap day already. First the Kroft kid, and now this."

"What do you mean?" I stepped down to face off with the

chief deputy as the memory of a knife-wielding, wild-eyed boy filled my mind. "Did Caden hurt someone?"

Brad sighed. "Okay, I guess you'll hear soon enough. We found Caden Kroft today in the woods near my family farm."

"He was hiding there, so close to our homes, all this time?" Aunt Lydia shared a concerned glance with Richard.

"No." Brad pulled off his hat and held it before his chest like a shield. "I guess I wasn't clear. We didn't locate Kroft hiding anywhere. We found his body."

Chapter Twenty

After being thoroughly questioned by two of Brad's deputies, we were allowed to leave the estate. Although I was so tired my legs felt like cooked noodles, I knew Aunt Lydia was even more exhausted and volunteered to drive her home, while Hugh rode with Richard.

I rolled down my window as I maneuvered my aunt's car around several official vehicles and the parked Jaguar, hoping to catch any news about Reese and Kendrick. But all I could discern from the deputies' chatter was that neither man had been located yet.

Later that evening, after Aunt Lydia and I had collapsed into two of the comfy upholstered chairs in the sitting room, I was startled from a light doze by the doorbell.

I motioned for Aunt Lydia to stay in her chair and ran to answer the bell. As soon as I opened the door, Zelda hurried past me.

Walt pulled off his golfing cap and clutched it in his hands. "Sorry, but Zel insisted."

"Oh, Amy knows I simply had to check on Lydia after the

horrid events of this day." Zelda waved one hand through the air like a conductor brandishing a baton.

"So you know everything already?" I followed her down the hall with Walt on my heels.

"Of course she does," he said, only loud enough for me to hear.

"Of course I do." Zelda sailed into the sitting room, the long tail of her purple-and-mauve tunic fluttering like a flag. "No, no, Lydia. Don't get up. Poor dear, I'm sure you're dead on your feet."

"But not actually dead, for which I am thankful," my aunt replied with a wry smile.

Zelda glanced around the room before she plopped down onto the suede cushions of the sofa. "Richard isn't here?"

I crossed over to my recently abandoned chair and sank back into it with a grateful sigh. "No, I sent him home to get some rest. He was exhausted from his trip and has a full day of teaching scheduled for tomorrow. He argued, of course, but he was up against both Aunt Lydia and me, so . . ." I shrugged.

"Didn't stand a chance, did he?" Walt grinned as he took a seat next to Zelda.

"Well, that's sensible." Zelda glanced over at Aunt Lydia. "And where's our resident art expert? Still on the case?"

"He's upstairs resting as well." Aunt Lydia shot me a warning look. Obviously she didn't want me to mention that he was also unpacking.

Walt stretched his long legs out over the multicolor rag rug that covered the hardwood floor. "I'm so sorry you all had to deal with this. Seems like you're always facing guns in the hands of twisted individuals."

"Yeah, but unlike my cousin Sylvia, Reese LeBlanc is sane. I think so, anyway." I snuggled deeper into the cushions of my overstuffed armchair. "My theory is that if Reese did kill his wife, his actions were based in greed or fear, not insanity. There was a substantial life insurance policy on Rachel. That's one strong motive. And if the murder was tangled up with his involvement with some criminal organization—well, maybe they threatened him or Lila if he didn't silence Rachel. Maybe Lila knows her dad is guilty and has been protecting him anyway. That happens sometimes, when kids don't want to lose both parents at once, even if they know one killed the other." I tightened my grip on the arms of the chair. "Or maybe Reese wants to locate Lila because he's afraid she'll eventually expose the truth. He has to know that could easily happen without her even intending it, considering her drug use."

"You think Reese LeBlanc would harm his own child?" Walt asked, raising his eyebrows. "As a father, I can't imagine such a thing."

I shook my head. "I don't think so, but who knows? He did seem genuinely concerned about her, but that could've been as much of an act as his tears over Rachel. Or not. I really couldn't tell. One thing that was clear was that Reese definitely seemed desperate to find Lila. In fact"—I drummed my fingers against the soft arm of the chair—"I heard Kurt Kendrick say that Reese left the house last night, even though he'd promised to stay put. Which makes me wonder . . ."

Aunt Lydia glanced at me. "I heard that as well. It does make me question whether Reese LeBlanc had any contact with Caden Kroft last night."

Zelda shifted on the sofa, bouncing her blonde curls. "You mean you think he might have killed the poor boy? But we don't actually know that Reese was responsible for his wife's death. It could've been someone from that criminal group. Anyway, even if Reese did murder Rachel for money or whatever, why kill someone else? Especially with the authorities looking for him? It doesn't seem worth the risk."

I swept my straggling hair behind my ears with both hands. "Because perhaps he thought Caden saw him that day? He might not know that Caden couldn't identify the person he claimed to see, or that the authorities didn't really believe him. And even if Reese is innocent of Rachel's murder, he could've been out for revenge. Maybe he believed that Caden killed Rachel, despite Mr. Kendrick's theories about some mysterious criminal cartel being involved."

Aunt Lydia absently stroked the upholstered arm of her chair. "That's possible, I suppose. Although I'd be more likely to agree with Kurt. If this group he calls the Quinns are as danger-ous as he claims, I'm sure they wouldn't hesitate to silence any whistle-blowers. It sounds like they could've sent someone in to kill Rachel with or without Reese LeBlanc's knowledge."

Walt snapped his legs back against the sofa and straightened in his seat. "Did you say the Quinns?"

"Yes." Aunt Lydia examined him with interest. "Don't tell me you've heard of them."

Zelda laid her hand on Walt's rigid forearm. "Is that true, dear? You know something about these criminals?"

"I've read some things . . ." Walt shook his head. "Can't really say much more, but that name has popped up in some

223

forensic accounting I've had to do for the government. There was this collection of paintings that someone tried to donate to the National Gallery of Art, and it all seemed a bit questionable . . ."

"So they really are a well-known criminal organization." I sat back in my chair and pondered this information. I was loath to credit Kendrick with speaking the truth, but it seemed he had, at least in this instance.

"Yes, but even if the Quinns had Rachel LeBlanc killed, why would they murder the Kroft boy?" Walt asked. "That isn't something a well-organized, secretive crime ring would do. It just draws more attention to the LeBlanc case, and I doubt they'd want that."

"Unless he saw something, or they thought he did." I remembered Caden's comments about a mysterious figure in the woods. "He told Sunny and me that he glimpsed someone else fleeing the scene, so maybe the murderer saw him too. They might've been afraid that Caden had seen too much."

Zelda fluttered a hand before her face. "Heavens above, that means we have three possible candidates for that poor lamb's killer—a ticked-off druggie, Reese LeBlanc, or some mercenary hired by these notorious Quinns."

Walt loosely clasped his long fingers together on one of his knees. "Well, Reese isn't doing himself any favors. Running away just makes him look guilty."

"Yes, and he's still on the lam, based on the latest updates from the sheriff's department," Zelda said.

I studied her sparkling eyes and the heightened color in her cheeks. She was obviously excited to share this information. I couldn't help but wonder if she had a police scanner at her house. It wouldn't surprise me.

"So he hasn't been captured yet?"

"No, although they did find Kurt Kendrick, and right there on his estate."

"Really?" Aunt Lydia sat up with jolt.

Zelda nodded vigorously, bouncing her crisp blonde curls. "He was tied up on the floor of one of his own sheds. It must have been quite traumatic for him. He isn't a spring chicken anymore, you know."

I made a face. "Seems awfully convenient to me."

Aunt Lydia's golden eyebrows arched over her blue eyes. "What are you saying, Amy?"

I tapped my foot against the floor. "I just don't trust Kurt Kendrick. He and Reese shared a couple of significant looks before Reese went for that gun. They could've been in on the forgery scheme together. Maybe that Quinn group had nothing to do with it. It could have been something Kurt Kendrick orchestrated on his own. Which means he might be protecting Reese just to keep his own involvement in the scheme a secret. Reese could've even bartered his silence about Kendrick's part in the crimes for Kendrick's protection. Come to think of it, the whole abduction thing could've been part of some contingency plan. Kendrick's smart enough to have worked out a few escape routes for Reese ahead of time. This could've been one of them. I bet that gun wasn't even loaded."

Walt's dark eyes narrowed. "That's a pretty sophisticated level of planning."

"But not outside the realm of possibility. Don't you think it's worth consideration, Aunt Lydia?"

"I believe Kurt's capable of such duplicity, but I don't know . . ." Aunt Lydia sat forward. "Something about the way he talked about that forgery ring made me think he truly believed they were behind the entire operation. Hugh was well aware of their activities too, so it wasn't something Kurt made up out of whole cloth."

"But as I recall, I mentioned their name first. So Mr. Kendrick could've just latched on to that. You know, agreeing that they were the group behind the forgery ring even if he previously knew nothing about them being involved."

Aunt Lydia tapped the tips of her fingers together as she considered this idea. "I suppose. But I sensed he was speaking the truth." She met my questioning look with a wry smile. "As you know, I usually take Kurt's words with a bucket of salt, but I felt he was being honest in this instance. He might be mistaken in his assumption, but I believe he is convinced that this Quinn group is tangled up in this case."

"You're saying this is tied to organized crime?" Zelda scooched around on her seat to look directly at Walt.

"Yes, at least it's a possibility." Walt hesitated for a moment, as if considering how much he could divulge. "Apparently the Quinn family started up their operation in Europe right after World War Two. It started as a family thing, but they've expanded over the years. Even though Interpol and other authorities have arrested a few of their low-level operatives, no one's been able to track down, much less bring in, the real brains of the outfit." He spread his hands wide. "Or so I've heard."

Zelda's light brown eyes widened. "But here, in Taylorsford?"

"I guess it doesn't really matter to them where the artists

live, as long as their 'go-betweens,' as Kurt called them, can keep in contact," Aunt Lydia said.

"That means there's someone in Taylorsford who works for these criminals?" Zelda looked both baffled and thrilled by this idea.

I bounced the leg I'd swung up over my other knee. "Not necessarily. It could be Kendrick, as I suggested, but I guess it could also be someone who just came to town whenever they needed to pick up a forged painting. Or maybe Reese shipped stuff to them? I don't know."

"Which brings us back to Kurt Kendrick." Zelda said. "Remember what I told you this summer, Amy? I mean, about him hiring my late husband's moving company to transport works of art? He could be moving forgeries too, for all we know."

I sat back, my head spinning from all these theories. Rachel LeBlanc and Caden Kroft had been murdered, and it was possible that some shadowy criminal organization had orchestrated their deaths. But it was also possible that Reese had stabbed his wife to obtain her life insurance, then murdered Caden to silence any possible witnesses. Of course, it wasn't outside the realm of possibility that Caden had killed Rachel in a drug-fueled rage, and Reese had then murdered him for revenge. Or the Quinns had ordered the hit on Rachel, but Reese—erroneously believing Caden was the murderer—had still been Caden's killer. Or Caden's death wasn't connected to Rachel at all. Maybe it *had* been a drug deal gone wrong, as Brad had suggested to us when we were waiting to be questioned earlier. I rubbed at my temples. The possibilities and permutations seemed endless.

"What makes the sheriff's office so sure Caden was killed

over drugs?" I asked, hoping Zelda had heard additional details about this part of the story.

Of course she had. "They found drugs on him, and he was stabbed. That apparently makes them think he knew his assailant, or trusted someone enough to allow them to get up close and personal. As you would in a drug deal, I suppose."

"But they left the drugs on his body?" I asked. "That seems odd."

"It does indeed," Walt agreed, looking thoughtful.

Aunt Lydia stirred in her chair. "What I want to know is who lured Reese LeBlanc into the forgery scheme. He had to have a contact, and that person is as culpable as he is, at least as far as the forgeries are concerned. They need to be found."

I studied her conflicted expression. Of course she wanted to know who it was. She was undoubtedly still obsessed with discovering who'd convinced Uncle Andrew to become a forger. Not that they were likely to be the same person, given the span of years between the events, but perhaps she thought arresting one of these liaisons could lead to answers about others. Even those from the past.

"If the authorities can track down Reese, they might get some answers out of him," Walt said.

"I don't understand how he just vanished into thin air." Zelda slumped back against the sofa cushions. "He supposedly ran into the woods on Kurt Kendrick's estate, and even though he could've hiked up into the mountains from there, it seems like search teams with dogs and such could track him down. How could he get very far on foot?"

"We don't know that he didn't have a car or something, though." I dropped both feet to the floor as a possible scenario occurred to me. "Sure, if he just took off without a plan, he'd probably be caught right away. But what if he had worked out various escape scenarios with Mr. Kendrick ahead of time? They could've stashed a vehicle somewhere. Maybe even a motorcycle. That would've been easy enough to hide somewhere on the estate, and Reese could've grabbed it and made his way to a back road before the authorities arrived."

"True." My aunt rubbed her right eye with her fist. Although she still sat straight as a spear in her chair, she was obviously exhausted from the day's events. "Anyway, I doubt we're going to solve all these mysteries tonight." She forced a smile as she looked over at Zelda and Walt. "Now, can I get you something? Coffee? Wine? A snack?"

"Oh no," Zelda said, "we don't want to put you out. We just stopped by to make sure you were okay."

"And deliver all the news." I flashed her a grin.

She smiled in return. "Just trying to keep you in the loop, my dear."

Walt stood up and held out his hand to Zelda. "We should be getting along, though," he said, helping her to her feet. "I bet you'd both like the chance to rest."

"I won't argue with you about that," Aunt Lydia said as she rose to her feet. "But thanks for coming over. We hadn't heard what had happened to Reese and Kurt after we left the estate."

Zelda paused in the doorway. "Oh—before I forget—I guess you did hear that Mr. Kendrick was taken in for questioning."

"No, we hadn't," I said.

Aunt Lydia grabbed the edge of a nearby bookshelf. "Really? After what happened to him?"

"Well, I think they did have a doctor or EMT or someone

check him out first. But maybe Deputy Tucker was thinking along the same lines as Amy. About Mr. Kendrick possibly being in on the escape, I mean."

"More likely the sheriff's office just wanted him to explain why he was hiding Reese LeBlanc all this time," I said.

"He was harboring a fugitive, so he could be charged with obstruction of justice at the very least." Walt placed his hand in the small of Zelda's back and pressed her to move forward. "Now let's go, Zel. Allow these ladies time to relax."

As I trailed them to the front door, I admitted that the idea of the authorities questioning Kendrick appealed to my sense of justice.

He may honestly believe in Reese's innocence and not be involved in the forgery ring, I thought, *but he's undoubtedly dabbled in some other shady deals.*

"Wouldn't it be ironic justice if his own questionable activities were uncovered as a result of him protecting another criminal?" I asked Aunt Lydia, after we'd said our good-byes to Zelda and Walt and locked the door behind them.

She headed for the kitchen without answering me, but after pouring a large glass of sherry, she leaned back against the counter and met my inquisitive gaze.

"Just remember that whatever comes out of this, Andrew's name is likely to be dragged through the mud," she said, before taking a long swallow of her drink.

"It was so long ago." I grabbed a wine glass from the rack and pulled an open bottle of Chardonnay from the refrigerator. "Don't you think people will just overlook that in the midst of all this other drama?"

Aunt Lydia shook her head. "In Taylorsford? Nobody

overlooks anything, not when there's a juicy story involved. In fact, I bet Mel Riley will be chomping at the bit to spread that gossip far and wide."

I frowned. The mention of Mel made me think of her son and our last encounter. "Oh, with everything that's happened, I forgot to tell you—when I ran into Trey Riley on my walk the other day, he followed me back here and displayed an interest in our house. I can't be sure, but I suspect he'd like to buy it for some future development project."

"That will happen when hell freezes over." Aunt Lydia took another sip of her drink. "And even then, I think I'd rather let the devil have it."

Chapter Twenty-One

The next week flew by in a blizzard of rumors. I dreaded heading into the library each day and spent my morning walks girding myself for the onslaught. My anxiety had nothing to do with typical library queries. It was fueled by the fact that our patrons spent more time clustered around the circulation desk, bombarding Sunny and me with questions about the LeBlanc case, than they did conducting research or checking out books.

Not that either of us had any news to add to what we'd already shared. Every day Sunny asked Brad for updates, and every day he told her the same thing—the authorities were still searching for Reese and Lila, who seemed to have evaporated like dew in the sun.

"I still say Kendrick had to have helped Reese escape," I told Richard when we chatted on the phone on Friday night. Stuck at Clarion for a dance recital technical rehearsal, he'd stolen a few minutes to give me a call.

"Possibly. But the authorities released him and claimed he was cleared of all suspicion," Richard said, before pausing to answer the stage manager's question about a follow spot.

I rolled over on my bed and stared at the cracks in the plaster ceiling. "Which makes no sense. You'd think they'd have charged him with obstruction of justice at the very least."

"Who knows? I have a feeling Kurt can talk himself out of most sticky situations."

"He's probably had a lot of practice," I said darkly.

"Could be. But listen, I have to go. We're about to start the run-through. You know I'm crashing at Deidre's place tonight, right? I have to be here bright and early, and I don't want to make that drive tonight and turn around and do it again tomorrow morning. I'll have to silence my cell for this rehearsal too. But you can always reach me by text."

"That's fine. But just so we're clear, please give me the details on this Deidre person again."

Richard laughed. "Another teacher. And almost seventy. And married to Vivian."

I chuckled. "Okay, I guess you're in no danger then, even if you are irresistibly desirable."

"Mmmm . . . saving all of that for you," Richard said. "So sleep in tomorrow if you can. I intend to keep you up late tomorrow night."

"You think so, do you? We'll see," I replied in teasing tone. "Anyway, I luckily don't have to work tomorrow. It's Sunny's Saturday."

"Good. You can rest all day."

"Not all day. I have to head out at some point. The cupboard's rather bare and Aunt Lydia asked me to pick up a few groceries. She has a lunch-and-movie date, you see."

"Aha, the plot thickens. This date is with Hugh?"

"It is. So of course I agreed to free her up."

"Of course. Anyway, I won't be home until around four or so. At least Deidre's taking over the dress rehearsal tomorrow night so I don't have to hang around for that."

"They don't need you?"

Richard sighed. "As I told you yesterday, this recital doesn't include anyone from my studio or my choreography. I'm just helping out with a few technical things. That's not Deidre's strong suit."

"Oh yes, you did mention that. Sorry—I've been so flaky today. The continued questions about the LeBlanc case and all that nonsense are destroying the few brain cells I have left."

"Still no word about your uncle's missing painting? The still life, I mean."

"No, and Aunt Lydia has given up. Too many other things for the authorities to deal with right now. She thinks it's gone for good."

"Too bad. Well, speaking of being gone, I'd better do that for real this time. Deidre is giving me the evil eye. And man, can she."

"Okay. See you tomorrow. Love you."

"Love you too," he said before he hung up.

I dropped the phone onto the bed and hugged my chest with my arms. Richard didn't seem concerned about Kendrick being cleared by the sheriff's office, but I still found it disturbing. Kurt Kendrick had hidden Reese, a wanted fugitive, from the authorities. Surely that deserved some sort of charge?

I chewed on a fingernail as I contemplated the implications of this outcome. Kendrick must've pulled some strings or called in favors to have escaped any repercussions for his actions. Which also meant that he possessed a powerful sphere of influence. I dropped my hand into my lap and sighed. Another mystery, and not one my research skills could solve.

* * *

I didn't manage to get to the grocery store until around noon the next day, after Aunt Lydia had left for her date.

"It's not a date," she'd told me for the umpteenth time as she slipped on her lavender raincoat.

"Hugh is driving back from his work at the lab to pick you up," I said. "And then bringing you home after. And no doubt paying for lunch and the movie. So it's a date."

She didn't reply, but I caught a glimpse of her lips curving into a smile before she turned her head and sailed out the door.

I frowned as I studied the threatening sky before hopping into the car. Aunt Lydia's preferred grocery store was located in a neighboring town about twenty minutes from Taylorsford. I didn't usually mind the longer trip, but it appeared that I might get caught in a bad storm, and I hated driving in heavy rain.

Oh well, there was nothing I could do but grit my teeth and deal with whatever the weather tossed my way. I knew I'd rather face a storm than Aunt Lydia's disappointment.

I reached the store just as the first drops splatted against the blacktop of the parking lot. Grabbing my umbrella, I dashed inside, hoping the rain would stop before I finished shopping.

As I pushed my cart down the produce aisle, I spotted a tall man hovering over a display of cheeses. "Hi, Trey, looking for anything in particular?"

He wheeled around so fast I had to yank back my cart so that he didn't bang his shins into the lower rack.

"Amy—hello." Rubbing at his temple with one hand, he looked me up and down. "Sorry, I'm just a bit confused by all these different varieties." He waved his hand over the piles of cheese wedges and wheels. "Mom wants something for a cock-tail party. Not sure whether I should stick with the classics like cheddar and brie or go for something more exotic."

"Knowing your mother, I'd say take the risk and choose a few things you've never bought before." I examined Trey, noticing how the harsh fluorescent lights seemed to have drained all the color from his face. Of course, no one looked good under those lights, but Trey appeared especially exhausted. *Staying up too late worrying over finances?* I wondered, and gave him a warm smile. I knew what it was like to worry over money.

"You feeling okay, Trey? You look a little pale."

"I'm fine, I'm fine," he said, offering an answering smile. "Just allergies."

He was dressed neatly as always, in khakis and an ivory cashmere sweater over a peach button-down shirt. I rubbed my right eye, clearing what felt like a film. Of course his wan appearance was simply an illusion caused by the lights. Unlike me, Trey Riley always looked calm and pulled together. "Oh, leaf mold? Yeah, that's bad this time of year. If we're lucky, the storm will wash some of it away and clear the air."

"Damn it to hell, there's a storm?" Trey snapped before casting me an apologetic look. "Sorry for the language. It wasn't raining when I came in."

"Yeah, I hope you have an umbrella," I said, wondering how he could've been so distracted he hadn't noticed the roiling dark clouds that had filled the sky all morning.

"I've got a raincoat in the car. Not that it will do me much good out there." Trey stared at the refrigerated dairy case as if he'd never seen cheese before.

I tugged on the ties of my hooded sweatshirt. "So your mom

sent you out to do the shopping, huh? Sounds like you're on a mission, like me. My aunt asked me to pick up a few things."

"It's just for the party," Trey said. "Cheese only. Mom hired a caterer, but she says their cheese selections aren't up to par."

Poor Trey, I thought. *Just like me, I bet he falls prey to Mel's whims.* "Seems like a waste, hiring someone and then having to do half the work yourself."

"That's just Mom, you know. Always the perfectionist." Trey grabbed a few random wedges of cheese and tossed them in his basket. "Anyway, glad I ran into you. I know things have been rather crazy lately, but I wondered if I might drop by sometime soon to see those paintings. For my tasting room, remember?"

I did remember but found this segue rather odd. Although perhaps seeing me had brought the idea of exhibiting the paintings back to his mind. "Right. You wanted to see if Aunt Lydia might sell or lend some of Uncle Andrew's works." *Those that aren't forgeries*, I thought, but of course I didn't say that aloud.

"Yes. Maybe even this afternoon? I have a window of time free. I just need to drop off this stuff at the house, and I could stop by."

"Um . . ." The rotting stench of Stilton rose from Trey's basket, which confirmed my suspicion that he'd grabbed the first cheeses his fingers had landed on. Of course, I'd probably have been tempted to do the same, given Mel's endless demands. "My aunt is out until late this afternoon, and I really don't want to let anyone rifle through Uncle Andrew's paintings without her there. Then this evening I have a date, so she'll be there alone, and anyway, I doubt she wants anyone dropping by at night. So not today, if you don't mind." I was hedging the truth—Hugh would also be at the house in the evening, but I wanted to allow him and my aunt a little more time alone. It didn't make sense to invite Trey to barge in just when they were getting better acquainted.

"All right," Trey said. His disappointed tone almost made me change my mind. "Another time, then." He turned away to peer into the cheese case.

"Have a good day," I said to his back.

He didn't respond. I shrugged and spun my cart around, heading for a display of seasonal fruits and vegetables.

As I collected the items on Aunt Lydia's list, I debated tracking down Trey and apologizing. *I should've told him he could stop by the house this afternoon, or at least offered an alternate time.* Although I had no interest in dating anyone but Richard, there was no reason I couldn't make more of an effort to befriend Trey. After all, I knew how difficult Mel could be. It couldn't be easy for Trey, living in his mom's house and being forced to dance attendance on her. Having dealt with a few of her imperious commands, I could certainly empathize with his desire to get his business up and running as soon as possible, if only to get out from under Mel's roof.

But when I searched the aisles and didn't see Trey, I finished my shopping and headed home, determined to rest for a bit before my date. Even if it meant locking my laptop in the closet so I couldn't delve into any more research about art forgery, the Quinns, or the LeBlanc case.

*   *   *

The rain had lightened by the time I got home, but I still had to juggle an umbrella as I unloaded the groceries from the car and carried them into the kitchen.

After I put away the food, I ran upstairs and changed out of my damp clothes and into sweat pants and a threadbare but comfy sweatshirt. I also whipped off my bra, as I was inclined to do when I was at home alone. I couldn't leave the house or receive company in that state, but when no one was around, there was no reason I couldn't make myself comfortable. Besides, I still planned to lie down for a brief nap . . .

But as I sat on my bed, my gaze fell upon my laptop. *Just one little search*, I thought, knowing I was lying to myself. Flopping across my bed, I once again perused the Art Loss Register and other websites that listed lost works of art. After an hour I stumbled across an entry for a painting I'd missed in my previous searches.

Even though it was represented only by a grainy black-and-white photo, something about the composition caught my eye. I looked closer, noting that it was a Van Gogh titled *The Lovers: The Poets Garden IV*. The accompanying article stated that the work had been missing since the late 1930s, when it was stolen by the Nazis to add to Hitler's collection of "degenerate art." It hadn't been seen since, and most scholars assumed it had been destroyed during the war. As I read on, I learned that the work had been documented in a letter Van Gogh had written to his brother Theo in 1888. The letter described the painting as comprising two figures—a man in a light-blue suit and yellow hat and a woman in a dress with a pink bodice and black skirt— standing in a rather vague landscape with a row of green cypresses and a rosy sky forming the background.

I shoved aside my computer and sat bolt upright. Green cypress trees and a pink sky? With two central figures? I leapt off the bed and ran to my closet, where I'd recently stashed Uncle Andrew's seascape and its hidden canvas behind an old suitcase and a pile of mismatched shoes.

Unrolling the canvas across the top of my dresser, I immediately realized I was holding a copy of the painting I'd just seen on my screen—only this was a full-size and full-color reproduction, obviously meant to be taken for the actual Van Gogh.

It fit the pattern of the other forgeries. Like them, it was a work based on a painting that had enough provenance to make its existence and recovery believable, yet so long lost that few living souls would've ever seen the original.

It also confirmed my suspicions about those practice signatures. So my uncle had definitely forged more than a Monet. I slid my fingers over the surface of the painting, admiring the attention to detail in the crackling and the obvious age of the canvas. Of course, an operation like the Quinns could probably get their hands on materials from the proper time period, one way or another. Or they would find a way to distress more contemporary materials to approximate the period of the original work. And I had to remember that this painting was older than the forgeries found at the LeBlanc barn, which were undoubtedly Reese's handiwork. If what Kendrick had said was true, this copy had probably been created almost forty years ago, not long before my uncle died.

I allowed the canvas to roll back into a loose cylinder and left it on my dresser, then shut down my computer. When Hugh and Aunt Lydia returned, I knew I would have to show it to them, no matter how difficult that might be. The painting would have to be added to Hugh's workload, despite the fact that its existence would undoubtedly thrust another knife into my aunt's wounded heart.

The doorbell chimed. That was odd. Aunt Lydia could simply

use her key, and I'd expected Richard to call when he got home, not just show up at the door.

The bell rang in a constant jangle, as if someone was leaning on the button.

"Okay, okay," I said, thrusting my bare feet into a pair of loafers and clattering down the stairs. "Hold your horses."

I crossed to the front door and cracked it open.

Trey Riley looked back at me.

"Oh, forgive me, Trey, but this isn't a good time. I did look for you again at the store to say you could stop by, but you'd already left. Now I'm not really dressed properly for visitors," I said, preparing to shut the door again.

"Sorry, but Mom said it was important . . ." Although the rain had finally stopped, Trey wore a knee-length charcoal-gray raincoat. Styled like a trench coat, it gave him the look of a slightly disreputable detective in an old noir film.

"What is it now?" I asked, not bothering to temper my impatient tone. Mel Riley had no business bothering me with work matters on my day off, even if she was the chair of the Friends. Of course, her son was only the messenger.

Trey lifted his hands. "I apologize. Mom called me while I was still out doing the shopping and asked me to pick up a check from Mrs. Andersen and drop it off with you. Some donation to the library, she said. Apparently you need to handle that?"

"Yeah, I have to sign it for deposit, but couldn't it wait? I mean, it's Saturday. It's not like the banks are open today."

"Yes, I know. But I thought it was best not to argue."

Trey looked so pitiful, standing on the porch in a coat that was still damp from the earlier rain, that I just sighed and opened the door. Hopefully my baggy sweatshirt offered enough coverage that my braless state wouldn't be too embarrassing. "Come on in. You can do your duty by handing over the check, and then I'm going to make you some coffee or tea or something. You look like you could use it."

"Thanks, that would be great. Mom's had me running around town all day and I've gotten soaked, as you can see."

I stepped aside as Trey walked into the front hall, but I paused long enough to lock the front door behind him. "Just drop the check on the side table and let me take your coat. You can't be comfortable. Maybe it will dry out better if I hang it on the hall tree and allow it to air out while you have your coffee."

Trey pulled off the coat and handed it to me, but he didn't produce the check immediately. Instead he strolled over to the wall that was covered with many of my uncle's artworks.

"These are Andrew Talbot's paintings?"

"Some of them," I said.

The damp raincoat thrown over my arm made me wrinkle my nose. It gave off an odd smell, especially when I lifted it to hang it on the hall tree. Of course, the rain might have raised some odors from the waterproof fabric, but this didn't smell like mildew or old sweat. No, it was a more distinctive odor—pungent and oily.

I froze with my hands still clutching the coat. Sliding my fingers into one of the pockets, I encountered a spot of slick goo. As I pulled my hand back and shook my fingers, a distinctive scent wafted through the air.

I recognized that smell. I had encountered it recently, at the scene of a grisly murder.

Linseed oil.

Chapter Twenty-Two

I blinked rapidly as a rush of thoughts flooded my mind.

It had rained the day Rachel LeBlanc had been murdered, which meant it wouldn't be surprising if her killer had worn a raincoat. Especially if the coat was dark and could cover someone's regular clothes. My fingers slid up to the collar, encountering the buttons that held the rolled-up hood. Yes, a murderer could have chosen to wear this coat to help disguise his appearance as well as to protect him from the rain.

Lifting one section of the coat, I confirmed what I had suspected—the scent of linseed oil was strongest around one of the pockets. That was probably where Trey had stashed the cloth he'd used to wipe down the palette knife.

The murder weapon. I allowed the coat fabric to slip from my hand and turned to stare at Trey Riley.

He'd killed Rachel LeBlanc. I didn't know why, but I knew for certain that he was her murderer. And now he was in my house.

"He was very talented," Trey observed. "I'm surprised he's not better known."

I stared at him, relieved that he was distracted by his study of the paintings. In fact, he was using his hands to measure them, as if he was searching for a canvas of a particular shape or size.

I took a couple of steps to the side, hoping I could unlock the door before Trey noticed my actions. But my foot banged into the metal plate on the bottom of the door with a loud thump.

Trey wheeled around to face me. "Move away from the door." He slid a dark object from the pocket of his jacket.

A pistol. Remembering the last time I'd stood in this hall with a gun pointed at me, I swallowed a shriek and forced a calm tone. "What's this all about, Trey?"

"You look like you want to slip out that door, and I'm not having that." Trey waved the pistol at me. "I want to search through the rest of Andrew Talbot's paintings. All of them. Now."

"I don't understand. What do you want with my uncle's paintings?" My cell phone jangled in my pocket.

"What's that noise?" Trey's gaze darted wildly from me to the staircase and back. "Anyone else here?"

"No," I said, pulling out the phone. "Just my cell. No need to point that gun at me. I'm turning it off now, see?"

"Throw that over here," Trey commanded, grabbing up my phone from the floor when I complied. "Now show me where your aunt stores those other paintings."

"Okay, but it might help if you told me more specifics, like if you have a particular work in mind . . ."

"I do, and it's something that actually belongs to me, if you must know. Or at least to Mom. But she shouldn't complain if I claim it as part of my inheritance. It's not like she's willing to give me much else." His chuckle sounded manic rather than amused.

"You can't be serious. None of my uncle's paintings belong to you or your mother."

"This isn't his work," Trey said, moving closer. "It's something my mom gave him to hold. For safekeeping. Only he died and she couldn't retrieve it without raising too much suspicion."

"What in the world are you talking about?" I felt it best to feign ignorance, even though I had a suspicion he was after one of my uncle's forgeries.

"A Van Gogh," he said, wiping a trail of spittle from the side of his mouth. "Stolen by the Nazis and supposedly lost forever. But it wasn't. Some officer must've carried it with him when he escaped Germany after the war. Anyway, it probably ended up in the hands of some fly-by-night dealer who didn't know its true worth, or didn't have the means to sell it without incriminating himself in its theft. I figure Mom bought it for a song and smuggled it out of Europe after one of my parents' diplomatic postings." He moved close enough that I could smell the acrid scent of his sweat. "She was afraid to store it at home so she gave it to your uncle to hold for her until she could arrange a discrete sale. It seems, from some other information I've uncovered, that this particular piece has been hidden among his things ever since. But now it must be returned to its rightful owner."

"Doubt that's you," I said, refusing to drop my gaze, despite the fire flashing in his eyes. If I could keep him talking long enough, maybe someone would show up. Richard or Hugh or someone.

"It's mine by right, and I will have it." He poked me with the barrel of the gun. "Now move."

"No need," I said. "I've looked through all of Uncle Andrew's paintings, and the only thing resembling a Van Gogh is a forgery."

Trey's lips twitched. "That can't be."

"It was a shock to us too, but Hugh Chen confirmed it." This lie tripped off my tongue so quickly I almost felt like someone else was speaking the words.

I straightened, feeling a surge of bravery, as if I had an army at my back, or at least one other person at my side. *Dive for his feet*, an inner voice whispered. *It's obvious he has little experience in handling guns. You can probably knock him off guard.*

But before I could take this action, a key turned in the front door lock.

"Hello," my aunt called out as she pushed the door open. "I'm back early. One of the investigators called Hugh into the lab, so we skipped the movie and he just dropped me off here . . . Oh." She stood motionless as she faced Trey and the gun.

"Say nothing, close the door, and lock it behind you," Trey commanded.

Casting me a concerned glance, my aunt did as she was told.

Trey motioned toward me with the pistol. "Now get over there beside Amy."

Aunt Lydia strolled toward me as casually as if she had guns pointed at her every day of the week. I swallowed a hysterical bubble of laughter. Considering our recent experience at Kendrick's home, she almost had.

"Okay, so now both of you lead me to that canvas," Trey said. "You might claim it's a fake, but I know what I overheard from my mom, and I'm not convinced you're telling the truth."

"I can show it to you, but it isn't going to solve your money wows." I offered my aunt an apologetic glance before continuing. "Because it isn't a real Van Gogh. It is most certainly a forgery. It was even wrapped in a piece of canvas Uncle Andrew used to practice faking Van Gogh's signature. Sorry, Aunt Lydia, but it seems he painted more than one."

Trey narrowed his eyes. "Why would your uncle keep it, then?"

"I'm sure he didn't mean to. My guess is that he planned to pass it along to his contact in whatever illegal scheme he was embroiled in. It's just that he died before he could do so. I guess we have to admit that he was a forger"—I glanced at my aunt, whose haughty gaze was fixed on Trey—"but I don't think he was a thief. If your mother gave him a painting to hide for her, maybe he did paint a copy, but I'm pretty sure he would've returned the original to her whenever she asked for it."

"She doesn't have it." Trey's hand holding the pistol was steady, but his other hand trembled like a leaf caught in an autumn wind. "If she did, she'd have sold it by now."

"So Mel just confessed all this to you?" Aunt Lydia asked. "That she'd given Andrew the painting to hold, I mean?"

"No. She isn't aware that I know anything. I had to find out on my own. Fortunately, you know how loud she is. It's not hard to overhear her." Trey's grin resembled a wild animal baring its teeth. "Anyway, not long ago I caught her talking to someone on the phone about a painting. It seemed like the person on the other end was pressing her to turn it over to them. Based on some of Mom's responses, I figured out the piece had been assumed lost, and the caller had just found out that the painting still existed. Anyway, Mom kept repeating that it had gone missing long ago, but I could tell by the raised voice blasting out of the phone that whoever she was talking to wasn't buying her story. Finally Mom said something about it being impossible and spilled the information about it still being in some artist's personal collection. I missed the rest of the conversation because Mom walked into another room, but I do recall she seemed terrified. So I was sure she was talking about an original painting, not some fake." Trey tightened his grip on the pistol. "An original I later discovered must have been hidden among Andrew Talbot's collection. A painting worth millions."

"More like zero minus zero," my aunt said. "Because Amy's right. Any so-called Van Gogh we own is a fake. I am sure of that because I saw Andrew working on it."

I knew this was a lie, but Aunt Lydia spoke so convincingly, Trey's eyes glazed over. "So now the question is—where is the original?" He pointed the gun at my aunt. "Did your husband sell it?"

Aunt Lydia lifted her chin and stared him down. "Do we look like we're worth millions? Honestly, I have no idea where the original painting might be. I assume if Andrew ever actually had it, he returned it to your mother. He may have been a forger, but as Amy said, he was no thief."

As she spoke these words, an idea popped into my head, as fully formed as if someone had just whispered in my ear. "Kurt Kendrick has it."

I didn't know why I blurted that out, but I did acknowledge it made sense as a stalling tactic. It wasn't irrational to suggest that Uncle Andrew had handed over an original Van Gogh to his art dealer friend, and planting that idea in Trey's head might send him off on a wild-goose chase. *A useless quest that would end at Kendrick's well-protected estate.*

I was tossing Kendrick into Trey's line of fire, but having seen the older man in action, I felt confident that he could handle Mel's son. And perhaps there would be a way to prevent Trey from reaching the estate. It was certainly worth a chance.

Anything was better than Aunt Lydia and I having to deal with an obsessed killer on our own.

To her credit, Aunt Lydia didn't bat an eyelash as she backed up my lie. "Yes, I remember now. Years ago, my husband mentioned something about giving Kurt a valuable piece of art to sell for him. I guess Andrew followed through on that plan before he died, but I doubt Kurt sold the painting. Or if he did, I never saw any of that money."

"So apparently Andrew was a thief, despite all your protests to the contrary. He probably planned to split the money with Kendrick and never give my mom a dime." Trey gripped his pistol with both hands and worked his mouth for a moment. "Well, that's in the past and can't be changed. But I can make up for my mother's misguided trust here and now. So this is what we're going to do—you two are going to take a little drive with me out to my winery property, and I'm going to call Kurt Kendrick from my car and tell him to bring me the original Van Gogh."

"Why would he do that?" Aunt Lydia smoothed down the front of her raincoat as if she didn't have a care in the world. "Kurt has no great love for either Amy or me."

"Well, maybe not, but I doubt he'd like to be the cause of your deaths. Because I'll tell him"—Trey aimed the gun at me—"that I'll kill you both unless I get that painting by five o'clock."

"He might not still have it. He could've sold it," I said, frantically thinking of a way to alert Kendrick to the actual situation. "And he could be out of the house right now."

"Well, too bad for you then, isn't it?" Trey grabbed his raincoat from the hall tree. "We're heading outside, nice and slow. Just like I was a family friend, escorting you to my car." He clutched Aunt Lydia's wrist and pulled her close, the gun hidden under the coat thrown over his arm. "Any yelling or bolting and I pull the trigger, Amy."

I swallowed and nodded. But as I opened the front door, I surreptitiously flicked the latch so that the door wouldn't automatically lock behind us. I hoped it would be a signal for Hugh or Richard that all was not well, since, after the events of the past summer, Aunt Lydia and I were diligent about locking exterior doors.

Trey guided my aunt to his cherry-red sports car. "You're going to drive," he told me as he thrust Aunt Lydia into the back seat, tossed the coat in after her, and slammed the car door. I complied, adjusting the seat slightly to accommodate my shorter legs as he climbed in the passenger side.

"Just remember—not only am I pointing this gun at you, but if you try anything clever, I can also swing my arm around quite easily to shoot your aunt." Trey tossed me the keys. "Same goes for you," he told Aunt Lydia, who'd leaned over as if searching for something on the floor.

Looking for an umbrella or ice scraper she could use as a weapon, no doubt. I glanced back at her in the rearview mirror and shook my head as she straightened and buckled her seat belt.

"I've never driven something like this before," I said, surveying the numerous dials and gadgets on the dashboard with dismay.

"It's a car. Put the keys in the ignition and let's go."

Gripping the leather-clad steering wheel with both hands, I pulled onto the road. "I don't know how to get to your property. You'll have to direct me."

"Take Main Street until you're out of town, then turn left on

Chestnut Hill. We'll be on that road for a while, so that's all you need to know for now. I'll tell you where to turn again later." Trey popped his cell phone into the Bluetooth attachment on his dash. "Call Kurt Kendrick," he instructed the device.

"You have it programmed?" I asked, shooting him a glance before focusing back on the road.

Trey shrugged. "I scout out possible investors everywhere I go, and he's a wealthy guy."

Kendrick picked up on the third ring, announcing his name cheerfully but falling silent as Trey blurted out his demands.

"So you understand—bring the original to my winery. You know where that is?"

"The old Calloway place, right?" Kendrick's voice was perfectly calm.

"Yes, and no alerting the authorities. I glimpse anyone other than you, and I shoot at least one of these women."

"I will come alone."

"See that you do. Now, you're clear what painting I mean? I hope you still have it, or things could go south very quickly."

"I have it," Kendrick said. "*The Lovers* by Van Gogh."

He might be a scoundrel, I thought, *but he's quite a clever one.* Not knowing all the details, he wasn't saying much, but he'd obviously guessed that Aunt Lydia or I had concocted this story for a reason.

"Yes. We're headed that way now, so get moving," Trey said.

"First"—Kendrick's polite tone was edged with steel—"have Amy and Lydia speak to me. I want to hear their voices before I do anything."

Trey grunted but waved the gun at us. "Say your names for the gentleman."

"Lydia Litton Talbot," my aunt said, her voice sharp and clear as an icicle.

Unable to maintain that level of calm, I squeaked, "Amy."

Kendrick cleared his throat before he spoke again. "Very well. I will meet you at the winery."

"With the painting," Trey said.

"With the painting," Kendrick replied, hanging up before Trey could say anything more.

Trey slumped in his high-backed leather seat, the gun in his lap.

If I could take a wrong turn and somehow end up where there were a lot of people, like the row of strip malls right outside of town . . . But Trey's hand was on the pistol and I didn't trust him not to use it. If it had been only me, I might have taken the risk, but I couldn't take that chance with my aunt as another target.

As I turned onto Chestnut Hill Road, I sneaked glances at Trey.

I marveled that I had ever considered him the least bit handsome. Now, sunk in his seat, his chin doubling as he pressed it to his neck and a tuft of thick hair sticking out from one side of his head, he certainly didn't look like any sort of prize. Of course, maybe it was just my new awareness of his true personality that had turned him from a charming frat boy into a fiend. Obviously desperate to acquire a painting he thought priceless, Trey had stepped over the line from duplicitous to deadly. His entire focus appeared to be the acquisition of that painting, and I didn't doubt he'd kill again if it brought him closer to his goal. Which meant his financial situation had to be dire, despite the smoke and mirrors of his various business interests. All of which he'd have to abandon now. Because even if he could've laid his hands on the original Van Gogh and sold it for millions, he'd still have had to disappear.

"So tell me," Aunt Lydia said, "why you really thought this painting was worth so much, and why you were so sure Andrew ever had the original, if all you heard was your mom talking to some unknown people on the phone."

Trey lifted the gun, weighing it in his hand. "I don't need chitchat."

"Just curious," my aunt said. I glanced at her in the mirror. Although her voice was perfectly calm, her drawn face betrayed her fear.

"I am capable of putting two and two together." Trey's declaration dripped with disdain. "I figured that no one would be hounding my mom for some painting unless it was worth a decent bit of money. And something I saw as a child . . . Well, never mind about that. When I connected what I overheard to a specific work of art, let's just say it rang a bell with me."

"And you assumed from what you heard that your mother smuggled it into the U.S.?"

"Yes. Like I told Amy, my guess is she got it off some less-than-reputable dealer in Europe, who got it from the Nazi who absconded with it while fleeing Germany after the war." Trey tapped the gun barrel against his palm. "It wouldn't have been difficult for her to smuggle artworks out of Europe, given Dad's diplomatic status."

"Well, I never," my aunt said, although she didn't sound that surprised. "And she mixed you up in this business? Her own son?"

Trey snorted. "She never told me a thing about it. I had to find out for myself. 'Her own son.'" He gave my aunt's words a sarcastic spin. "Like that mattered. She never intended for me to know anything about her little smuggling operation. It was only my accidental eavesdropping that clued me in. Mom didn't want to share the profits, I expect."

"You mean there were more paintings?" I asked, my knuckles blanching from my grip on the steering wheel.

"A few more, anyway. I'm not really sure how many." Trey's voice hardened. "In that phone call, Mom also mentioned some stuff stored at the LeBlanc farm. So I thought maybe she kept additional smuggled originals there, somewhere. I just had to figure out where. But when I went to look, I never got the chance to search . . ."

I bit my lip to stifle an exclamation. His thoughtless words confirmed my earlier theory that he was Rachel's killer, as well as the mysterious figure Caden had spied fleeing the area. Trey had undoubtedly confronted Rachel LeBlanc as he had me today, demanding to be shown the hidden collection of paintings. She hadn't complied—not because she had been defiant but because, despite throwing Reese out of the house over one forged painting, she'd known nothing about that hidden closet or the other fake works. So, thwarted and furious, Trey had grabbed Rachel's own palette knife and stabbed her.

I took a deep breath, swallowing back this accusation. To confront Trey now might simply ratchet his anger up another notch. I cast him a glance, noticing the bulging vein at his temple. He was obviously consumed with fury, although strangely, I didn't feel that it was directed at either my aunt or me.

His following words confirmed my suspicion. "Mom might talk me up to outsiders, but she never paid me much attention," he said. "Too busy with her friends and her parties and all that nonsense. I could sit in the same room with her and she'd never know I was there. So I overhear things. Like when those two FBI types stopped by the house not long ago. Mom talked to them in the music room, completely forgetting that I was working in the library, which has a connecting door."

"FBI types?" The hair rose on my arms as I recalled the man who'd tailed Mel at the festival. "You mean men in dark suits and white shirts and ties?"

"Yes. I figured maybe it had to do with a clearance review for someone she knew in the diplomatic corps, but no—they were questioning her about paintings. Just like in that phone call."

That wasn't the FBI, I thought. *Those were men sent by the Quinns.*

"One in particular," Trey continued. "It sounded like the same painting Mom was being hounded about over the phone. Turns out it was a long-lost Van Gogh, which the men fortunately described in detail." Trey glanced back at my aunt. "So a few days later, when Mom was talking about donations for the festival and seemed overly eager to look through Andrew Talbot's paintings, I casually asked her how she knew your husband. She said they were just acquaintances but he'd done her a couple of favors in the past. Then it dawned on me—she'd given him the Van Gogh to hold until she could find a buyer. I figured she offered him a cut of the sales or something. Probably the same arrangement she later set up with the LeBlancs."

"I don't think . . ." Aunt Lydia snapped her mouth shut when I shot her a sharp glance in the mirror.

But Trey was on a roll now. He continued as if she hadn't spoken. "As to your other question, Lydia—it really wasn't difficult to deduce that even though Mom might have used the

LeBlanc barn to store some stuff, she'd given Andrew Talbot the Van Gogh. Because my research on the clues I assembled from all those overheard conversations jogged a memory. Something from my childhood, long before Mom would've had any dealings with the LeBlancs. Once I realized what specific lost painting was being referenced, I knew it had to have been given to your husband to hold. It was the only thing that fit the timing. You see, I saw that canvas once."

"What do you mean?" I asked, scanning the back road for any sign of houses. Because if we could get away, we had to know where to run.

Trey expelled a huff of air. "I was only five or six at the time, but I could never forget that painting. It earned me the worst beating of my life. One day I walked in on Mom examining a canvas she'd unrolled on her bed. She went ballistic, gave me a thorough spanking, and threatened me with worse if I ever mentioned that painting to anyone." Trey leaned in and waved his free hand under my nose. "Left here."

I turned the car onto the rough gravel road. "But you can't know she gave it to my uncle after that."

"No, not absolutely for sure, but it disappeared from our house. I know that for certain because I searched diligently for it over the years and never found it. So when I heard her mention that the piece in question was in an artist's personal collection and put that clue together with the fact that she told me that your uncle had done her some favors"—he shrugged—"I figured out that your uncle's house was the only option. Of course, I wanted to search for any original paintings stored at the LeBlanc barn as well, but I once I couldn't go back there . . . I mean, once the authorities cordoned off the area, I figured I'd just cut my losses and focus on the Van Gogh."

"But . . ." I said before I stopped myself. Trey obviously didn't know anything about the connection between Reese, or my uncle, and an international forgery ring. He seemed to think his mother was mixed up in smuggling and selling artworks acquired through questionable dealers, but he hadn't yet indicated that he knew she was involved in any forgeries.

Which she was, I realized, as Trey barked at me to turn right onto a narrow lane. Driving past a heavily wooded area, we emerged into the bright sunlight of an autumn afternoon. On either side of the lane, gnarled grapevines covered row after row of rough trellises. I kept my eyes on the road, trying to skirt around the worst of the ruts, as I silently worked through the implications of my latest theory.

Mel Riley, town leader, wealthy patron of the arts, and widow of a diplomat, had to be the "go-between" Kurt Kendrick had mentioned—the connection between the Quinns' operation and local artists like Reese LeBlanc. Mel hadn't bought the Van Gogh off some disreputable dealer, as Trey thought. She'd probably been commissioned by the Quinns to smuggle it, and a few other paintings over the years, out of Europe. Her diplomatic status would have made her quite a desirable courier for any criminal organization.

And somehow she'd entangled my uncle in the scheme. I gnawed at my lower lip. The timing fit. But Trey was once again mistaken—Mel hadn't given my uncle the Van Gogh to hold it for her. No, she'd simply expected him to create the copy I'd found. I'd have bet the original would've been returned to Mel right after Uncle Andrew had examined it and taken a few reference photos. Surely Mel would've been required to return it to the Quinns as soon as possible. Why they were now ramping up the surveillance on Mel was puzzling, but perhaps it was connected to the forgeries discovered at the LeBlanc barn. Perhaps they suspected her of colluding with the authorities. After all, she could probably expose more about their operations than just Reese LeBlanc's forgeries.

Rounding a corner, we reentered a mountain forest, where deep-green pines reached for the sky, battling the bare-leafed hardwoods for light and air. I drove the car into a small circle of gravel in the middle of a clearing. Before us rose a rough-timbered, three-story structure that I recognized as an old sawmill.

Trey's future tasting room. I squinted and peered at the building. Apparently Trey's funds had run dry before he could do more than shore up some of the sagging timbers and replace a few broken windows on the badly weathered wooden structure.

"Park the car and hand me the keys," Trey commanded.

"I suppose you want us to get out?" I asked as I unbuckled my seat belt.

"Yes. And don't even think about running. You saw that there's nothing around here for miles. You'd wouldn't even reach the vines before I'd track you down."

I sighed and climbed out of the car. He was right. We couldn't possibly make a run for it, especially not with Aunt Lydia's bum leg. Walking didn't bother her too much anymore, but there was no way she could outrun Trey. "So where are we going?"

"Up there." Trey pointed at the open third-floor loft above one section of the old mill. "Always heard higher ground was an advantage," he added as he grabbed my aunt's arm and pulled her from the car.

"And once we're up there?" I followed Trey and my aunt, acutely aware that his gun was once again pressed against her slender body.

"We wait. And you hope, or pray if that's your thing. Because if Kurt Kendrick doesn't show up soon with that painting, you two are never leaving these woods alive."

Chapter Twenty-Three

Our progress was slowed by Aunt Lydia's difficulty in navigating the steep wooden staircase that led from the back of the building to the loft. As we climbed the creaking steps, I racked my brain to think of any way out of our dilemma.

Trey was a big man and, as Sunny had observed, well-muscled. I could never physically overpower him, even if he didn't have a gun. But based on his rash decision to kidnap two people who definitely would be missed, he obviously wasn't thinking clearly. Perhaps I could still reason with him. While it was true that he'd probably murdered Rachel LeBlanc in a fit of anger, surely he wasn't a cold-blooded killer . . .

Caden Kroft. Had Trey murdered him as well? Given the town rumor mill, he would've known about the young musician's claim to have seen someone else in the woods the day Rachel was killed. I grabbed the wooden rail so hard a splinter slid into my thumb. My subsequent exclamation made Trey release his hold on Aunt Lydia and spin around at the top of the stairs, pointing the gun at my forehead.

I held up my hands, palms out. "Sorry. Splinter."

"Just get up here," he said, stepping back so I could stumble past him to join my aunt.

The give of the weathered boards under my sneakers wasn't the only thing that made me clutch Aunt Lydia's arm. The opening in the far wall yawned before us. There was no barrier between that precipice and the edge of the sagging floor. We could gaze out and look into the crowns of many of the trees, a view that reinforced my terror. A fall from that height could be as deadly as any gunshot.

And easier to explain away as an accident, I thought. Such a scenario might not make a lot of sense to those that knew us, but if Trey believed he was getting his hands on a genuine Van Gogh, he might foolishly think he could flee the country with the painting—or the proceeds from its sale—without anyone connecting our deaths to him.

Except for Kurt Kendrick, of course. Trey would have to deal with him as well, and I doubted he had any idea how difficult that might prove to be.

"Over to the edge," Trey said, confirming my fear.

Aunt Lydia and I walked slowly to the opening, arm in arm. Trey urged us forward until we stood with the tips of our shoes touching the edge.

"Don't look down," I told Aunt Lydia as I stared out into the treetops.

"I've been in barn lofts before," my aunt replied. "Never fell out of one yet."

I had to keep Trey talking. Find a way to make him realize that killing us would only make it harder for him to escape.

"I get it," I said. "You need the genuine Van Gogh so you can get out from under some debts. Your mom should've recognized that and told you everything. She should've seen that it was the best way to help you."

Trey just muttered something that sounded like *too late now.*

"No, it isn't. Sure, you're in a bad situation at the moment. But if you get your hands on the painting, you can leave. I bet Kurt Kendrick could even help you sell it. You know, on the down-low. Nobody ever needs to know how you got the money."

"And why would Mr. Kendrick do such a thing?" Trey asked coldly, although I thought—I hoped—I detected a spark of interest in his tone.

"For a little cash on the side, of course." Aunt Lydia, true to form, played along with my fabricated story. "I'm sure he's not above a small commission, and if you can truly collect millions on the piece . . ."

"He'd turn me over to the sheriff," Trey said sullenly.

A hawk swept from the top of a spruce to the bare limb of an oak tree. "I doubt it. His own business practices are not above reproach. I don't think he'd want to have the sheriff's office or anyone else digging too deeply into his background." No sense in mentioning that several investigators, including Hugh Chen, were already looking into Kendrick's affairs.

"I'm in so deep." Trey's voice trailed into a whine.

"Not really. I mean, you haven't killed anyone yet," I said lightly.

Aunt Lydia side-eyed me, but I just squeezed her hand. To me, the better tactic was to give Trey an out rather than directly accusing him. After all, he wouldn't necessarily assume that I'd done enough research, and creative thinking, to suspect him of the murders.

But I'd underestimated the depth of his twisted pride.

"You think so, do you?" He tapped both of us on the shoulder with the barrel of the gun as he crossed behind us. "Well, for your information, I was the one who stabbed Rachel LeBlanc and that worthless Kroft kid as well."

"You killed Caden?" Aunt Lydia's voice trembled slightly, which wasn't surprising. Trey was confessing to two murders. She'd probably realized, as I had, that spilling the beans meant he had no intention of allowing us to live.

"I had to," Trey said. "I mean, I didn't plan it ahead of time. Just like with the LeBlanc woman, it wasn't premeditated." I grimaced at Trey's tone, which was cavalier enough to suggest he thought that this somehow excused his actions. "I just wanted to talk to the kid. I'd heard the rumors about him seeing someone else at the LeBlanc place that day, and I had to be sure I was in the clear. So I set up a little secret meeting, pretending I was looking to buy some drugs." Trey's sardonic smile betrayed his amusement over this ploy. "I guess Caden was pretty desperate for some cash, and I did offer to pay double, so he fell for it. Of course, at first he had no reason to suspect I was anything but some rich guy looking to score some pills to take the edge off. But once we met up and he saw me standing there, in the woods, with the light shadowed by the trees and all, he put two and two together. I could see the awareness dawning in his eyes. He realized it was me he saw fleeing the barn that day." Trey shrugged. "So I had to kill him too."

I gasped, which just made Trey's cold smile broaden. "Yeah, you can look shocked if you want. Nobody would believe that of me, would they? Everyone thinks I'm just the guy who's always had it all. A fine, upstanding scion of a distinguished family, raised in the lap of luxury. Ha!" He fondled the gun absently as he stared at us, his eyes wide and wild. "My parents were the stingiest pair of socialites who ever lived the high life in a diplomatic mansion. Oh, not when it came to themselves, of course. They'd splurge on their own desires whenever they wanted. But me—no, I had to be taught the value of a dollar. Had to learn to get by on my own. Make my own way."

"That must've been very frustrating," Aunt Lydia said softly.

"It was hell!" Trey slapped the gun against his palm. "There I was, stuck at all those expensive boarding schools with hardly a penny to spend. I couldn't reciprocate any of the other boys' generosity, so they labeled me unfriendly and mean and avoided me. But did my parents care? No. They just said if I wanted more money, I should get a job. Well, half the time I was living overseas and couldn't legally work, so how was I supposed to do that? In the end I had to resort to running little scams and making deals with the boys who were willing to be less than honest. Oh yeah, I learned to be an entrepreneur all right. Had to."

"With the painting, you'll have enough money to start over," I said, hoping to keep him talking.

"Yes, but I'll have to disappear." He shot me a twisted smile. "I do know I'll need a new identity. I'll have to leave everything behind. But at this point I don't really care. What do I have left, anyway? My business empire is in shambles and my ex took everything else, including any illusions I ever had about love. So now there's just my mom." He barked out a bitter laugh. "Like that matters. She barely notices me now. She's not likely to care if I fall off the face of the earth."

"I doubt that's true," Aunt Lydia said.

I cast her a surprised glance. My aunt putting in a good word for Mel Riley? It *was* the end of the world.

A cold wind whipped through the open loft. Maybe that last thought had been a little too on point. It could be the end of my world if help didn't arrive soon. I shivered, and blinked away the tears welling in my eyes. The helplessness of my situation was draining me to the point where I contemplated sinking to the floor, despite what Trey might do to me. Only the sound of tires on gravel brought me back to my senses.

"How about that, here comes your rescue," Trey said, pointing his gun at the clearing.

I had to look down then, and even though the drop to the ground made my head swim, I was happy to spy Kendrick's black Jaguar pull up in front of Trey's car.

I wasn't sure why Kendrick had parked nose-to-nose with the other car since that would seem to prevent his quick getaway, but perhaps it was so the driver's side was hidden under the overhang of the partial roof covering the extended first floor.

Well, if we fall, we hit that first. Which didn't really comfort me. It was still a long way down, and we'd simply roll off and hit the ground eventually.

But the overhang, and the position of his car, did allow Kendrick to remain hidden as he first stepped out of the Jag, which was a smart move on his part. He'd circled around to the other side of the car before Trey had a clear shot at him. Stepping back from the car, he held a large black portfolio in front of his chest like a shield.

"Hello," he called out. "I have your painting, Mr. Riley, so why don't you allow the ladies to step back from that rather precarious edge?"

"I want to see it first," Trey yelled down at him.

"Hardly practical." Kendrick shifted the portfolio so he could reach into his jacket pocket. "Hold on, no need to aim that pistol at me. I'm just getting out my phone."

"To call the authorities? You do and I shoot one of them." Trey cast us a wild-eyed glance. "Or shove one over the edge."

"No." Kendrick's voice took on a soothing cadence. "To show you it's turned off. And I've brought no one with me, as you can see. So how about we discuss terms in a civilized manner?"

As Trey peered down at Kendrick's darkened phone, I noticed a slight movement off to the side of the Jag. A figure in dark clothing slipped out of the back seat of the car and disappeared around the side of the sawmill. I shot a quick glance at Trey, but it seemed he was so focused on Kendrick and the portfolio, he'd missed this hidden passenger.

Richard. I clamped my lips to prevent the exclamation rising in my throat from escaping my mouth. So Kendrick *had* called someone. Not the authorities, but his former foster father's great-nephew. Or perhaps Richard had called him when he discovered the door to Aunt Lydia's house unlocked while our car sat in the driveway and my aunt and I were nowhere to be seen.

I squeezed Aunt Lydia's hand again, and she glanced at me with a question in her eyes. Noticing Trey's gaze was still fixed on Kendrick, I mouthed, *Richard, heading up the stairs.*

She blinked but made no move to look over her shoulder.

"May I climb up there, then?" Kendrick asked. "I can bring the portfolio and you can hold your weapon on me while I show you the painting. I think you know I'll play square. You have the ladies as hostages, after all."

"Damn straight. All right, come up." Trey turned to us. "You two—back to the center of the room. But don't make any sudden moves. I can still shoot one or both of you in a heartbeat, or even Mr. Kendrick before he reaches the top of the stairs."

I nodded and kept my grip on Aunt Lydia's hand as we backed away from the edge. Turning to face the stairs, I caught a glimpse of Richard slipping behind one of the rough timber pillars holding up the roof. I shot a quick glance at Trey, but he had crossed to the head of the stairs and was peering down, obviously awaiting Kendrick and the portfolio.

Kendrick huffed loudly as he reached the top of the stairs. "Just a minute, I need to catch my breath," he said, the portfolio dangling from his loose grip as he pressed a hand to his side. "Not as young as I used to be."

It was a good performance, but I knew this was a bluff. Despite his age, Kurt Kendrick could probably run rings around any of us.

"Slide that over here," Trey said, backing away to allow Kendrick to cross to the center of the loft.

"Just a minute. Those stairs . . ." Kendrick bent over, his fingers still clutching the portfolio handle.

Trey approached him, waving the gun. "Give that to me and back off."

He stared at the portfolio, his gaze so laser-focused that he didn't notice the figure slipping from the shadows. I shoved my fist to my mouth as Aunt Lydia released my other hand and widened her stance as if preparing for what might come.

Trained to be light on his feet, Richard moved soundlessly toward Trey, while Kendrick straightened and flung up his arm, swinging the portfolio in an arc that should have caught Trey under the chin.

Should have, but didn't. At that moment a cluster of barn

swallows dove from the rafters in a flurry of feathers. The whoosh of their wings sent Trey spinning on his heel, just in time to miss Kendrick's aim.

And spy Richard, standing exposed and defenseless a few feet away.

"Richard!" I screamed, diving toward Trey. But I just hit the floor with a thud that echoed the sharp crack of Trey's pistol.

Chapter
Twenty-Four

Ignoring the burn arising from scraped skin, I pressed my palms against the rough floorboards and lifted my head.

Across the loft, Richard was slumped back against one of the pillars. Kendrick knelt beside him, the portfolio cast off to the side.

Richard . . . I bit the inside of my cheek to prevent a scream. As he stirred and his eyelids fluttered, a wave of relief swept over me, leaving me limp with gratitude.

In that moment I knew my love for him was greater than any fear I'd ever felt. All I wanted to do was hold him and tell him that I'd stay with him forever.

But Trey and his gun stood in the way. "Is he all right?" I asked, rolling over so that I could sit up. Pain blazed through my right wrist, which had been injured during Cousin Sylvia's murderous assault in the summer. I flexed my fingers, relieved that it hadn't broken again.

Richard clutched his upper left arm with his right hand. A sheen of sweat covered his face and blood oozed around his fingers, darkening the sleeve of his sweatshirt.

I scooted closer until Trey swung the gun in my direction. "Stay," he said. As if I were a dog.

"I just want to know how he is, you bastard," I spat out.

Trey's hand shook, his finger twitching on the trigger.

"Just grazed his arm," Kendrick called out, drawing Trey's attention off of me. "Need to stop the bleeding though." The art dealer looked up, focusing his steely gaze on Trey. "Allow me to help him, or I'll set fire to your precious painting." He reached back and grabbed the handle of the portfolio and pulled it closer.

Trey made a dismissive noise. "With what? Your hot air?"

"No, with the lighter I have tucked in my pocket." Kendrick patted the left breast of his jacket. "I don't smoke, but many of my clients do, so I always carry a lighter. As a courtesy."

Trey gnawed at his lower lip. "All right. Help him if you want. But kick that portfolio over here."

Kendrick helped Richard slide off his dark sweatshirt. "I don't think so."

"You want me to shoot him again? Or you?"

"I doubt you will. That was a wild shot, wasn't it? It seems you aren't much of a marksman." Kendrick calmly wadded up the sweatshirt and pressed it against Richard's bare arm, which was slick with blood.

As I rose unsteadily to my feet, Aunt Lydia moved close enough to clutch my arm. "Let me go to him," I said.

Trey waved the gun at us. "No. I told you before—you stay where you are. Unless you want another bullet in your precious boyfriend."

Aunt Lydia and I froze in place.

"Not *in* him, fortunately," Kendrick said. "Ripped up the skin but didn't penetrate, thank God." He placed Richard's right hand over the material pressed against his arm. "Can you hold this tight?"

Richard gritted his teeth but nodded. "Yeah, think so."

"Good. Now"—Kendrick stood up and faced off with Trey—"let's discuss a little trade, shall we?"

"You forget I'm the one in control here," Trey said.

"Are you now?" Kendrick slipped a gold lighter from his jacket pocket and casually popped it open.

"I know about you, Mr. Wheeler-Dealer. You have a reputation as someone who truly loves art. You wouldn't torch a masterpiece."

Kendrick shrugged and flicked the lighter, igniting the flame. "Maybe. Maybe not. Do you want to take that chance?"

Aunt Lydia leaned into me as we stared at the two men, who were equally matched in size but not in demeanor. Trey, all twitching limbs, had the gun, although he obviously didn't know how to use it properly. Kurt Kendrick had the lighter, a calm countenance, and a portfolio containing something that Trey thought was worth millions.

Of course, there was no Van Gogh stuffed in that portfolio, and the moment Trey peered inside he would know the truth. Which was why Kendrick was stalling. I studied the white-haired older man's stoic expression. What was his end game? Keeping Trey off-balance long enough to attempt another attack?

My gaze slid over to Richard. *I love you*, I mouthed at him, and was rewarded with the faintest hint of a smile.

Footfalls rattled the steps. Trey gripped his pistol with both hands and spun around to face the top of the stairwell.

"Who's there?" he shouted, casting a sharp glance at Kendrick. "I said no cops."

271

"It isn't the authorities. It's your mother." The blue-hearted flame danced as Kendrick held the lighter higher. "So put down your gun."

"My mom? You called her?"

"I thought she might be able to talk some sense into you."

Trey let fly a string of swear words that would've done credit to a drunken sailor. He lowered the gun but didn't loosen his grip on the weapon.

"Trey." Mel Riley crossed the loft to stand before her son. "What's all this now?"

I had to give her credit—despite what had to be a heart-breaking situation, she managed to remain calm. Her voice, although loud, was chiding rather than angry.

"You have no business here." Trey shuffled his feet and stared down at the pistol in his hands.

"But I do. This all happened because you eavesdropped on some of my conversations, didn't it?"

Trey lifted his head and stared his mother in the eye. "What if I did? You can't exactly claim the high moral ground, Mom. Not when you've obviously been embroiled in smuggling art and who knows what else over the years."

"Yes, I've made some very bad mistakes." Mel clutched the amber silk scarf knotted at the neck of her cranberry wool sweater. "But I never meant for you to be involved. I couldn't climb out once I'd fallen into that pit. That was bad enough, but believe me, son, I never wanted you to tumble in after me."

Trey snorted and circled around her. "Such pretty words. But I know the truth. You just didn't want me to take a cut of your profits."

"That is untrue." Mel strolled over to the edge of the loft and stared out at the swaying treetops.

"You didn't understand what you were getting into, did you?" Kurt Kendrick, eyeing Trey's back, slipped the lighter into his pocket.

"No." Mel turned to face us. "I was bored, you see. Being a diplomat's wife seems glamorous from the outside, but it was stifling . . ." She tucked a loose strand of her honey-colored hair behind her ear. "There were so many rules and regulations. I longed to travel and experience other cultures, but all I ended up doing was hosting tea parties and extravagant dinners. I was forced to say all the right things, smile no matter how I felt, and make small talk with some excruciatingly boring people."

A surprisingly sympathetic expression flickered over Aunt Lydia's face as she studied her old nemesis. "You wanted adventure."

"Yes," Mel said, after taking a deep breath. "And I thought I found it when I met a very charming man with an English accent who tossed around far too much money."

Trey's lips twitched. "So you took a lover on top of everything else?"

Mel shook her head. "No, it was never like that. We mostly talked about art. I thought he was simply an aficionado like me, but after a few meetings he finally confessed that he was in the business of collecting and selling art—some of it with questionable provenance. But the way he described his business"—Mel's face brightened at this memory—"it sounded so exciting, like a game. He talked about secret meetings and coded messages until I felt like I was living in a Cary Grant movie. It didn't seem like a crime; it felt like a caper that simply put one over on the stuffy collectors and art experts who'd never take a chance on a work without a perfect pedigree."

"I take it he worked for the Quinns?" As Kendrick moved closer to Aunt Lydia and me, he pointed at Trey's back and motioned for me to move toward Richard.

I crept backward as Mel met Kendrick's icy stare without flinching. "Yes. I knew nothing of their organization, of course. I was simply told to use my diplomatic immunity to smuggle a painting into the U.S." Her green eyes sparkled at this memory. "I can't tell you how thrilling it was, standing in customs and knowing that I had a priceless masterpiece rolled up and tucked in amongst my suits and lingerie. Such an incredible rush."

Trey's eyes narrowed as he took two steps forward. "Who are you talking about? The Quinns? Who the hell are they?"

"An international art theft and forgery ring," Kendrick said.

Trey stabbed the air with his gun. "For God's sake, Mom. You weren't even doing this on your own? You were, or are, mixed up with criminals?"

"It would've been criminal either way," Mel said. "But yes."

Trey glared at his mother. "So it was more than one painting?"

"Not at first. My original task was simply to bring the Van Gogh into the country. I really thought that was all I had to do. One and done."

"But the Quinns had other ideas," Kendrick said.

I knelt beside Richard as Aunt Lydia shockingly allowed Kendrick to take her arm.

I leaned into Richard, careful not to jostle his injury. "Are you really okay?" I whispered.

"Yeah. Help me stand, would you?" he murmured.

We both staggered to our feet while the others focused on Mel. If Richard had been in any condition to back me up, I would've suggested an attempt to rush Trey from behind. But I couldn't take that risk. Not with Richard bleeding and Trey holding that gun. Despite his poor aim, even a random shot might hit one of us.

"They blackmailed you?" my aunt asked Mel.

The elegant diplomat's wife closed her eyes for a second before replying. "They did indeed. Threatened to expose my actions and perhaps even harm my husband, or Trey"—she cast him a quick glance—"if I didn't comply with their demands."

Trey raised his gun and moved closer to his mother. "Which was what? Force some artists to paint fakes? Tell me the truth for a change—were most of these paintings I overheard you discussing forgeries?"

Mel backed away from him, making me catch my breath. She was standing far too close to the edge of the loft. "Yes. That was my role, once I was back in the U.S. I had to entrap talented but unknown artists into painting forgeries based on specifications delivered to me by the Quinns. Sometimes the forgeries were based on descriptions of lost works from letters or other documents. Occasionally I was given a photograph, and even more rarely, an original work, like that Van Gogh. In those cases I was ordered to demand that the artist copy it and then return the actual painting as soon as possible." She returned Trey's angry glare with a sad smile. "I wasn't cutting you out of the profits, Trey. It wasn't like I could keep the originals for myself, and the amount I was paid for acting as a go-between for the forgeries was negligible."

Trey ran his free hand through his thick hair, causing it to stand up in tufts. "But the Van Gogh painting was authentic, wasn't it? At least that's the impression I got from your conversations. Your masters wanted it back, but you'd given it to Andrew Talbot and couldn't retrieve it before he died."

"Yes, that was different. The timing, with the accident . . ." Mel tightened her lips.

"So that's why you were so determined to sort through his paintings," Aunt Lydia said. "Both of you."

Mel and her son, focused on each other, ignored her.

Trey tapped the barrel of his pistol against his palm. "Explain, Mom—was the Van Gogh those men hounded you about an authentic painting or a copy? Because if I've done all this for some damned forgery . . ."

"There *was* an original. As I said, it was the first painting I smuggled into the country."

"And you asked Andrew to paint a copy." Aunt Lydia, leaning against Kendrick's strong arm, did not phrase this as a question.

Mel looked down at her clenched hands. "Yes, for some collector who supposedly didn't care much for provenance. The Quinns had arranged to sell the collector the fake and keep the original for themselves. Maybe they planned to sell the original to someone else at a later date. I don't know."

"But wouldn't that look suspicious?" Richard grimaced as I took over the task of applying pressure to his arm. "I mean, if the first collector heard about another sale of the same work?"

Kendrick stroked his chin thoughtfully. "Maybe. But someone who bought a painting on the black market, knowing it was likely stolen, would not be inclined to complain if another copy showed up later. Even if they did suspect they'd been duped. Clever ruse, that."

Mel nodded. "That was part of their game. They were clever, and extremely dangerous. It's why I never told you anything about my involvement, Trey. I knew they were capable of killing anyone who got in their way or took any action that might expose them."

Trey worked his mouth for a moment, as if struggling to put his thoughts into words. "But why don't you have the original, if Andrew Talbot was supposed to return it to you as soon as the copy was completed?"

"Things happened. Things I couldn't control," Mel said, not meeting her son's fierce gaze.

"Was it the copy you needed so urgently, then?" Aunt Lydia's voice was icy.

Mel glanced at my aunt before dropping her gaze again. "Well . . ."

Trey jumped in before his mother could say anything more. "Okay, so if Andrew Talbot painted a copy that was destroyed in his accident, then where is the original? I assume you don't have it, Kendrick?" Trey waved his pistol toward the art dealer, who shrugged.

"Sadly, no. I have no idea what happened to it."

Trey turned on me, gun raised. "What was that painting you mentioned, then?"

Richard moved to shield me from Trey's aim, but I shoved him back, eliciting a grunt as I pressed against his arm. "A forgery, as I said. I don't know how or why Uncle Andrew had it. The only thing I can imagine is that he painted two copies, hoping to sell the second one himself. Because I'm pretty sure your mother actually did get the original back, despite what she claims."

Mel expelled a loud breath of air before meeting my gaze. "You're right about one thing. The painting Amy found *was* the copy."

Trey wheeled around to face his mother. "This makes no sense. Why would this Quinn group be harassing you if they got their original painting back? I can't imagine they'd have much interest in Andrew Talbot's other paintings. And if Talbot returned the original to you, what happened to it?"

"It was destroyed," Mel said, casting an apologetic glance at my aunt. "Burnt to ashes in a fiery car crash."

"No." Trey's voice echoed as hollow as the ocean within a shell. "No, no."

Mel clenched and unclenched her hands. "I'm afraid so. The collector the Quinns hoped to swindle turned out to be more perceptive than they expected. After looking into his background, they were hesitant to sell him the forgery. They thought he might uncover their scam. Once they realized he had the ability to expose their entire criminal organization, the Quinns couldn't take that chance. So late one night they ordered me to collect the actual painting from the artist creating the forgery. They'd decided to sell that particular collector the original."

Aunt Lydia lifted her chin and leveled Mel with a frosty glare. "And you demanded that Andrew bring it to you. In an ice storm."

"Yes, and for that I am eternally sorry."

Trey blinked rapidly. "But no. No, that can't be. That means the original Van Gogh was burnt to cinders over thirty-seven years ago?"

Mel lifted her hands as if offering up an apology. "It was."

"But those people calling and visiting you . . ."

"Wanted the copy," Mel said, facing down Trey with a lift of her chin. "The first collector died, and enough time has passed that they felt they could pass it off as the original. Especially since someone new approached them, willing to pay any price for a Van Gogh. Someone who wasn't too picky about provenance. One of the older men who'd been involved in the first deal remembered Andrew's copy and decided they could finally make up their previous loss. They knew Andrew's work was good enough to pass this new collector's scrutiny." Mel shrugged. "The copy was worth as much to the Quinns as the original at that point."

"Is that why you were so determined to search through Andrew Talbot's paintings? I know you wanted to sort through Lydia's collection almost as badly as I did." Trey's grip on the pistol tightened until his knuckles blanched.

Mel bit her perfectly tinted lower lip. "Yes, but also because that wasn't the only original I smuggled out of Europe on that first trip. It was just the only one the Quinns knew about. I found another valuable piece in the shop where the Quinns had arranged for me to pick up the Van Gogh. I bought the second painting with my own money—it was more than the Quinns were willing to pay that dealer, so he kept his mouth shut. I never told my contact about that little transaction, so the Quinns never knew. I thought I'd just keep it for myself, but then it seemed wiser to have Andrew create a copy of that one too and sell both of them. Andrew didn't know this. He thought both forgeries would be turned over to the Quinns, along with the originals. I allowed him to think that, not planning to cut him in on the extra profit from the painting the Quinns didn't know about."

Mel blinked as a particularly strong swear flew from my aunt's lips. "But Andrew hadn't had time to paint that copy yet," she continued, her voice trembling slightly, "and after he died the original was lost to me. I thought perhaps he'd hidden it among his own paintings, but I never had the chance to look for it without arousing too much suspicion." She sent my aunt an abashed glance. "I had to wait until I was back in the country for good, when I could establish myself in the community and find some reason to ask you to see Andrew's paintings. It's why I fought so hard to become the chair of the Friends. I knew demanding fine art for the festival might provide an acceptable reason for me to search through your husband's works." She lifted her hands. "I'm truly sorry, but it *was* another masterpiece. I felt it was worth a little subterfuge."

"More conniving? More secrets?" Spittle flew from Trey's lips as he aimed the pistol at his mother's heart. "You still couldn't share, even if it meant saving me from financial ruin, could you? You knew there was another valuable work of art hidden at Lydia's home, but you weren't having any success even setting foot in the house. I was the one with the perfect scheme to gain access to Talbot's paintings. I was getting close to Amy . . ."

I snorted at this, but Trey continued as if he hadn't heard me. Which he probably hadn't. He was too focused on his mother.

"Working together, you and I might have quickly retrieved both the copy, which would've gotten your dangerous partners off your back, and the other original. Then we could've sold that one and shared millions. But no, you had to go and screw everything up, just so you could keep all the profits for yourself. You selfish cow!" Trey lunged at Mel.

She was far too close to the edge. I shouted "Careful!" just as Kendrick leapt forward.

But our words and actions were too late. Catching the heel of her suede boot on a loose plank, Mel tripped and stumbled backward.

Her high-pitched wail mingled with our shouts and screams as she tumbled from the loft.

Chapter
Twenty-Five

While the rest of us ran to the edge of the loft, Trey dashed down the stairs. I assumed he was rushing to aid his mom, but when he didn't immediately appear beside her crumpled form, I realized he'd chosen to flee.

I patted my pocket, feeling the lump of the keys. That was one more error on Trey's part. He couldn't take his car to make his escape, which meant he'd probably dashed into the woods on foot.

"Amy or Lydia, call 911!" Kendrick yelled as he sprinted for the stairs.

"I'll do it," Aunt Lydia said. "Amy, you help Richard down those steps."

We made our descent slowly, Richard gripping the handrail with his good hand as I hovered close to his injured side.

"You probably shouldn't be moving so much," I said. "It'll make the bleeding worse."

"Not staying up there, and I can still walk," he replied, gritting his teeth after each footfall.

When we reached the ground and stepped outside, we

paused at a small patch of grass in front of the sawmill. Mel's prone body was a few feet away. She'd obviously hit the lower roof and rolled onto the grass instead of the gravel, which was a blessing, although I could tell that she'd suffered severe injuries. She lay on her back, with both arms bent at unnatural angles and blood pooling under one leg.

Kendrick had stripped off his jacket and used it to elevate her legs slightly. "She's likely in shock," he said. "I checked her airways but don't want to move her again before the ambulance arrives. I'm worried about her spine."

Aunt Lydia stepped out of the sawmill and crossed to stand beside Kendrick. "Help's on its way." As she looked down at Mel, she sucked in a sharp breath. "Anything I can do?"

Kurt Kendrick rose to his feet. "Stay with her while I go after that worthless son of hers," he said, brushing the dust from his wool slacks.

"You should wait for the authorities. He still has the gun." Richard lifted his injured arm, then groaned and leaned against me so heavily my knees almost buckled.

"Here, sit on the grass," I told him, dismayed by the blood seeping under the makeshift compress. I helped him sink to the ground and sat down beside him.

Kendrick shook his shaggy head of white hair. "Trey will be long gone before they get here, and they need to focus on Mel and Richard." He met my concerned gaze with a sardonic smile. "I can handle myself. I don't intend to let that bastard escape."

"Just be careful," Richard said, as I slid my right arm around his waist.

Aunt Lydia, who'd knelt down by Mel's head, looked up at Kendrick. "Yes, take care, Kurt."

His eyebrows disappeared up under the fall of his rumpled hair before he gave her a smile and headed for the woods at a brisk jog.

After he disappeared into the trees, I glanced at Aunt Lydia, but she was focused on Mel and I couldn't catch her eye. *My aunt worried about Kendrick's safety? Will wonders never cease?* I thought, as I flipped over the wadded sweatshirt and pressed a slightly drier section against Richard's wound. "How're you holding up?" I asked after a soft moan escaped his tightened lips.

"Fine," he said, although the beads of sweat on his upper lip and brow told another story. He allowed his body to sink against mine. "Sorry. I'm going to get blood all over your clothes."

I caressed his uninjured side with my fingers. "Don't be silly. I don't give a rat's rear about that. I'm just worried about you."

"Your turn." He shot me a wry smile. "To sit by my bedside and fret, like I had to do for you a couple of times last summer, remember?"

"Fair enough, but let's not make a habit of this, okay?"

"I'll try not to," he replied, capturing my fingers with his right hand and giving them a squeeze.

Mel whimpered before some garbled words escaped her lips.

Aunt Lydia brushed Mel's forehead with her fingers. "Don't try to speak. Help is on the way."

But Mel continued to mutter agitatedly. The only word I could make out was *Lydia*.

"I'm sorry, I don't understand." My aunt cast me a pleading glance. "Amy, could you leave Richard for a moment? She's desperate to tell me something. I can't figure it out, and I'm afraid she won't rest until I do."

Richard released his hold on my hand. "Go on. I'll be okay."

I pulled back my arm and rose to my feet, but only after pressing a swift kiss against his lips. "All right, what do you want me to do?" I asked my aunt as I moved close to Mel.

Aunt Lydia shifted until she was seated instead of kneeling. She rubbed her bad leg as she met my concerned gaze. "See if you can understand what she's trying to say. Maybe between the two of us we can figure it out."

"Lydia," Mel muttered.

"Yes, she's here," I said, sitting down. "What is it you want to tell her?"

"Sorry, so sorry."

I slipped my fingers around Mel's hand as her damaged arm twitched. "For Andrew?"

A little sob escaped Aunt Lydia's lips but she said nothing.

"Yes. Never should have involved him. But he had the skills . . ." Mel's face convulsed with pain.

"It's all right, it's all right." Aunt Lydia gently took hold of Mel's other hand. "It was his choice, in the end."

"Never should have. Not that night. Not in that storm. But they threatened me. Said they'd kill my husband, or Trey." Mel's golden lashes fluttered against her paper-white skin. "Oh, Trey," she whispered.

Her voice was as broken as her body. I looked over at Aunt Lydia and spied tears trickling from her clouded blue eyes.

My cheeks were damp as well. I rubbed away the tears with my free hand and refocused on Mel's face. "You couldn't have known what would happen."

"Too dangerous," she murmured. "I knew it was. And then the painting was destroyed anyway." Her fingers tightened on mine. "The Quinns almost killed me over that, but I convinced them it was too risky. Diplomat's wife and all."

"That man watching you at the festival," I said, ignoring my aunt's exclamation of surprise. "He was employed by the Quinns?"

As Mel coughed, a bubble of blood rose at her lips. "Yes. Always watching me. Always."

I lifted my eyes and met Aunt Lydia's pitying gaze.

"Don't think of that now." My aunt pulled a tissue from her pocket and wiped the blood from Mel's lips. "Listen—there are the sirens. The ambulance will be here soon. They'll help you."

"Too late," Mel muttered. "Too late."

But whether she meant for her or Andrew or Trey, I didn't know.

Two ambulances and several sheriff's department vehicles roared into the parking circle, spewing dirt and gravel. EMTs leapt out and reached Mel's side before I spied Brad Tucker striding toward us.

Aunt Lydia and I stood and backed away to allow the first responders to care for Mel.

"Where's Trey Riley?" Brad asked.

"In the woods, we think. Kurt Kendrick went after him," Richard said.

Brad swore under his breath, but when he spoke his voice was calm. "Woods," he told the men and women clustered behind him. "Check the entire perimeter. Trey Riley is our suspect. Tall, brown-haired. Don't shoot the older, white-haired man, whatever you do."

I walked back to Richard. "He needs help too. Bullet grazed his arm."

Brad shoved his hat away from his forehead as he surveyed Richard. "God, can't you people stay out of trouble?' He motioned for one of the EMTs. "Apparently we have another patient."

Richard waved his good arm. "No, I'm okay. Stay with Mrs. Riley."

"Don't be silly," I said, as one of the medics approached Richard. "Gunshot graze and a hero complex," I told them while Richard made disparaging noises.

I moved aside to allow the EMT to work on Richard, who kept repeating that his wound was minor and they really should be focused on Mrs. Riley. Which the medic wisely ignored.

The other EMTs had Mel on a backboard and stretcher faster than I would've thought possible. As they wheeled her toward the ambulance, Aunt Lydia surprised me by asking to accompany Mel.

"She doesn't have anyone else," Aunt Lydia said, casting me a glance.

I nodded. Of course my aunt would make that gesture. She might hold a grudge, but she had a big heart. She wouldn't allow Mel to travel to a strange hospital on her own.

As soon as Mel's stretcher was loaded, the ambulance carrying her and Aunt Lydia roared off with its sirens blaring.

"Okay, so that ambulance is going to hightail it to a trauma center," said the older female EMT bandaging Richard's arm. "Best one is a ways off, in the city, so they needed to go on ahead. We'll take you down to the local hospital in a bit, if that's okay."

"Not a problem," he said. "Amy, maybe you can get one of the deputies to drive you home."

"You mean to the hospital. It's not like I'm going to go home and kick back and watch TV or something."

The EMT looked up at me. "You aren't hurt?"

"No, not at all. So I'll just meet up with you at the emergency room," I said.

Richard shook his head. "You've been through a traumatic situation. You might want to run home and rest first. You know it will take forever at the hospital. You can just meet me there later."

"No way." I met his stubborn gaze with my own recalcitrant stare. "I'll ask one of the deputies to follow the ambulance. End of story."

The EMT looked from Richard to me and back again. "Seems the matter is decided," she said.

Richard sighed gustily. "And this is my life now. Overruled by a determined woman."

"Absolutely." I shared a grin with the EMT, who motioned at two men standing behind the second ambulance.

"Bring the stretcher and let's get Mr. Muir off to the hospital as well."

"I can walk," Richard said, attempting to stand.

The EMT placed her hand on his good shoulder. "No, that's against protocol. You've been moving around too much as it is. One never knows about bullet fragments and such in these cases. Best to take precautions and keep that arm perfectly still."

"Well, there go my plans for the evening." Richard cast me a roguish glance.

"He really is pretty adorable," the EMT told me, her lined face brightening. "But I also see he can be a bit stubborn. We'll take care of him for now, but when they discharge him from the hospital, you'll need to make sure he behaves."

"I will," I said, as Richard sputtered in the background.

"Although"—the woman looked Richard over before winking at me—"I understand the temptation to let him have his way."

"I'm sitting right here," Richard muttered as the EMT and I laughed. A slightly hysterical laugh on my part, but it relieved the tension.

I waited off to the side as the ambulance personnel lifted Richard and secured him on the rolling stretcher. Following them to the back door of the ambulance, I called out to Richard, "I'll be right behind you, and I will stay at the hospital until you can go home."

Richard, who couldn't really move anything else, wagged one foot at me before the EMTs shut the doors and the ambulance drove off.

I immediately headed for two deputies standing by a patrol car, but Brad stepped in front of me before I could reach them.

"Hold up," he said. "I know they had to take Richard off, and your aunt needed to ride with Mel Riley, but I have to know what happened here. And why"—he fixed me with a stern gaze—"no one contacted us before all this went down."

I lifted my shoulders. "I'm not entirely sure. Aunt Lydia and I couldn't call anyone because Trey took my phone, and then he held a gun on us. I don't know why Kurt Kendrick didn't alert your office when he got that call from Trey, but maybe he was afraid Trey really *would* kill Aunt Lydia or me if he showed up with anyone from the sheriff's department."

"What call?" Brad fiddled with his badge as if he wished he could remove it and avoid this entire conversation. "What was Kendrick supposed to do?"

"Bring some painting to trade for our safety. Only he didn't actually have the painting because I made that part up to buy us some time . . ."

"Okay, now I'm lost. Never mind that for now; just tell me how Richard got mixed up in this."

"I think maybe he called Kendrick when he found our front door unlocked and nobody home."

Brad stared at me as if I'd grown an extra ear. "Trey Riley left the door unlocked?"

"No, I did. So Richard would know something was wrong. Which he obviously did. I don't know why he called Kendrick instead of you, but maybe it's because of that last visit to his house or something. I mean, maybe Richard thought we'd gone back there." I wrinkled my nose as I realized how crazy it all sounded. "Anyway, Kendrick apparently brought Richard along but had him hide in the back seat of the car. I guess they thought they could get the jump on Trey if he didn't know Richard had tagged along. That might have worked, except for some birds."

Brad rubbed at his forehead with the back of his hand. "Birds? What the hell do you mean?"

As I explained the sequence of events that led to Trey firing off his gun, Brad's face grew increasingly flushed. "Okay, hold on. This is too confusing for me to process right now. I think I have the basics, but I'm going to need written statements from all of you." He examined me, obviously noticing that I was bouncing on my heels, anxious to find a ride and get to the hospital. "Eventually."

"Sure," I said. "It all ties back to this forgery ring, you see. I think Kurt Kendrick really knows more about that than any of the rest of us."

"And he's now chasing down Trey Riley?"

"Yeah. I'll say one thing for the old man—he isn't afraid of a challenge." That was putting it mildly. I met Brad's intense gaze and shrugged my shoulders. "I think Mr. Kendrick's not quite what he appears."

"So I've heard," Brad said. "All right—you head to the hospital. I'll have someone drive you there, then send a couple of deputies to take statements from you and Richard later."

As I jogged toward one of the deputies Brad called on to give me a ride, a commotion arose from the edge of the woods.

I stopped in my tracks as Kurt Kendrick materialized from the trees, Trey Riley in tow.

Kendrick had the gun, as well as a tight grip on Trey's arm. "I think this is the man you're looking for."

There was a bruise blooming under Trey's left eye. I stared at the art dealer, who looked as calm as if he apprehended fugitives on a regular basis.

Well maybe he does, I thought, shoving my fist to my mouth to stifle a burst of nervous laughter. What did I know about Kurt Kendrick, really?

The team of deputies swarmed Trey and took him into custody while Kendrick simply handed over the gun, wiped his hands on his jacket, and stepped out of the way.

Brad strode up to the older man and shook his finger in his face. "What the hell were you thinking? You should've notified us as soon as Riley contacted you with a ransom demand."

"Sorry, but I felt that Trey was too unstable to send in the authorities right away." Kendrick was just a bit taller than Brad, which allowed him to look down into the chief deputy's angry face.

I realized this wasn't something Brad was accustomed to, and he took a step back. "You're not authorized to make such decisions."

Kendrick lifted his hands in a *mea culpa* gesture. "So sue me. Or arrest me. Or whatever. I simply did what I knew would save Amy and Lydia."

"You need to come in to the office with me." Brad said, refusing to wilt under Kendrick's icy glare.

"But what about my car?" Kendrick motioned toward the black Jag. "I'd rather not leave it out here in the wilderness, as you can surely understand."

Brad shuffled his feet. "All right. I'll drive it back, and you can ride with me." As he motioned to the deputy he'd already asked to escort me, he called over a petite female deputy. "Denton, go ahead and take Ms. Webber to the hospital. Meanwhile, Frye, you'll need to take my cruiser back to the station. I'll meet you there."

"Yes, sir," Alison Frye replied with enthusiasm.

Looking to score a few brownie points, I thought, remembering her—and her obvious crush on Brad—from the LeBlanc murder scene.

"Sure you can handle a Jag?" Kendrick's blue eyes were as clear as rain.

Brad snorted. "If it has wheels and an engine, I can drive it. Take it apart and put it back together too," he added, giving Kendrick a defiant look.

"Well, let's not try that." Kurt Kendrick motioned toward his vehicle. "After you, Deputy Tucker."

"Chief Deputy," Brad muttered as he headed for the black sports car. He paused for a second as he passed me. "You get to the hospital. I'm sure Richard will want to know where you are."

"Yes, sir," I said, snapping my hand to my forehead in a mock salute.

Brad muttered something that sounded like *women* as Kurt Kendrick winked at me and laughed.

Chapter
Twenty-Six

Richard had certainly hit the target when he claimed it would be my turn to wait. Wrinkling my nose at the acrid scent of disinfectant, I slouched in an uncomfortable wooden-framed chair with cushions worn thin as paper. A digital clock clicked off the minutes, then hours. According to the attendant at the desk, Richard had been rolled into an examination cubicle as soon as his ambulance arrived, but I wasn't allowed to see him, so all I could do was wait. And wait. And wait.

I didn't blame the doctors, though. One of the nurses informed me that they planned to be especially thorough with their scans and other tests to ensure that there were no bullet fragments lodged in his arm and no damage to his nerves or muscles. The nurse told me they always tried to take extra pre-cautions with dancers and athletes, since minor damage that wouldn't affect a typical patient could be catastrophic for some-one whose career required physical exertion. I was grateful for their efforts, but the nurse's words just amplified my concern over Richard's condition. His body was his canvas, and I knew he'd hate anything that would limit his ability to dance.

"You look concerned," said a familiar voice. "Everything going all right?"

I looked up into Kurt Kendrick's lined face. "Yeah, it's fine. It's just that, with Richard being a dancer, any damage to his limbs is problematic."

"Ah yes, I understand." Kendrick motioned toward the chair next to me. "Mind if I sit down?"

"No, although I must warn you that the cushions are thin and the frame hard." I frowned as he took a seat. "I thought Brad Tucker wanted to question you at the station."

"He did. I answered all his queries and came straight from there." Kendrick sat back in the chair and stretched his long legs out in front to him. "You're right—this chair is about as ergonomic as a seat in a rowboat."

"Just wait until you sit in it for an hour or more." I tapped the wooden arm of the chair with my short fingernails. "So not that many questions, then? I thought they'd keep you longer."

Kendrick waved one hand through the air. "Oh, they would have. But they received a phone call from . . . well, let's just say a higher authority. They released me immediately thereafter."

"Higher authority, huh?" I studied his rugged profile. "The feds?"

He glanced over at me, his ice-blue eyes very bright. "Could be."

I drummed my fingers against the chair arm. "You protected Reese LeBlanc because you absolutely knew for certain that the Quinns were involved, didn't you? Where is he, by the way?"

"In witness protection, along with Lila." Kendrick's knuckles cracked as he entwined his fingers and stretched out his arms.

"Your doing?"

"In part. I truly believed that the Quinns had arranged Rachel's murder and thought Reese and Lila were in danger as well."

"You seem to know a great deal about this Quinn gang." I scooted to the edge of my chair. "Were you once mixed up with them or something?"

"No, not in the way you think." Kendrick sat back and stroked his chin. "I was approached by some of their representatives over the years, but as poor, misguided Trey Riley said, I love art too much. I never wanted to be involved in their forgery schemes. In fact, my dearest hope has been to bring them down, one way or the other."

"So that's the fed connection? You've been trying to help them destroy the forgery ring?"

"Could be."

"Did you know Mel Riley was involved? I mean, as a go-between?"

"No." Kendrick tugged down the sleeves of his wool jacket. "I knew there had to be someone in the area, but I didn't suspect her."

"She was involved with them for over thirty years, it seems."

"Yes, quite astonishing, really. Few of their liaisons lived that long." Kendrick looked over at me with a lift of his bushy eyebrows. "I suppose that speaks well of Mel's cleverness."

"And her status. She was a diplomat's wife. If she disappeared or died mysteriously . . ."

"Yes, there is that. The very thing the Quinns thought useful also made her untouchable. But unfortunately, as often happens, it seems Mel's greed drove her to do some rather stupid things.

As greed often does. That second painting she hid from the Quinns could've cost her life if her duplicity had been discovered, diplomat's wife or not. But I can't feel much pity for her. Even if she was under threat as well, she used both Andrew and Reese for her own financial gain and placed them and their families in grave danger."

I sank back against the worn chair cushions and considered Kendrick's words. "I'm not so sure you should cast stones. You didn't turn in Reese, but not because you have such a big heart. Admit it—you were using him."

"In a way." Kendrick laid his knobby hand over my arm. "It was for the greater good."

"Oh, the greater good? That's a little odd, coming from you."

"I have my standards." Kendrick tightened his grip on my arm, forcing me to look at him. "When all was said and done, the Quinns were responsible for Andrew's death. I have never forgotten that."

"Or forgiven them, it seems."

"Should I?"

"No, I suppose not. So you decided to take them down. Is this something new, or has this revenge plot been brewing for some time?"

Kendrick studied me intently. "Always thinking, aren't you, Amy? To be honest, I've been working on this plan for many years. I wasn't certain that it could be accomplished, but these recent murders opened up a new angle. It was Reese LeBlanc's willingness to turn state's evidence that gave me my big break."

"But the Quinns didn't kill Rachel."

"No, but Reese is still willing to testify. I think he'd finally had enough when he came to me for help. At that point it didn't even matter who'd murdered his wife. He'd been living under constant threats to his family for several years."

I frowned. "I guess Uncle Andrew might've had that fear too. About someone harming my aunt, I mean."

"It's possible. If Mel Riley pulls through, she can probably tell us more."

"She will, at least according to the text I received from Aunt Lydia earlier. The trauma center seems to think she'll make it."

"That's good. Even though she's sure to face a lot of questioning, and possible charges, I'm glad she won't die over this."

"She said there was another original painting. Another masterpiece. I wonder what became of that one?"

"Hard to say. Perhaps Andrew hid it too well?" Kendrick stared at the wall clock. "Or sold it on his own."

I pulled my arm from under his hand as I remembered my aunt's words. "I doubt it. He was a forger, not a thief."

"I'm sorry, I didn't mean to suggest anything of the kind." Kendrick crossed his arms over his chest. "Andrew was a good man. He made mistakes, but don't we all? Anyway, I'm sure that he would never have done anything truly criminal."

"Forgery isn't exactly legal."

"No, but it doesn't hurt other people. Oh, I know it cheats buyers"—Kendrick lifted one hand and examined his neatly manicured fingernails—"but in this case, they had to know they were purchasing stolen goods, at the very least. So I can't feel too sorry for them."

"Of course you've never dealt in stolen goods," I said, not bothering to temper my sarcastic tone.

"Would I admit it if I had?" Kendrick glanced over at me, his face an unreadable mask.

"Probably not." I nibbled on my pinkie nail for a moment before looking back at him. "You said you loved Uncle Andrew. How exactly?"

Kendrick's expression shifted from stern to amused. "I think I'll take the fifth on that one."

"I see." I chewed on my nail again for a moment. "Did he know?"

"I'm not sure. I never told him, if that's what you're asking. There was a time . . ." Kendrick lifted his chin and took a deep breath. "But that passed, and then there was Lydia. He really did adore her, you know."

"So I've heard."

"It was true. I could tell the first time he spoke about her after they started dating. I thought it an odd match at first, but when you love someone, you want them to be happy." Kendrick bowed his head for a moment. "Andrew was happy with Lydia. So I resolved to be satisfied with that."

"You should be friends." I blundered on before I could think twice. "I mean, you and Aunt Lydia. You both loved my uncle, after all."

He gave me a broad smile. "That's one reason I've tried so hard to win her over."

"Keep trying. It might be working."

"From your lips to her very stubborn ears," he said, patting my hand. "Now—here comes a very official looking person. Perhaps they have news about Richard?"

I leapt to my feet as the white-coated stranger approached.

"Ms. Webber?" she asked.

"Yes, that's me." I smoothed down my rumpled sweatshirt.

"Mr. Muir is asking for you. He said you were his fiancée?"

I caught Kendrick's grin out of the corner of my eye. "Well, um . . . Sure. Yes."

"Then you can come back and sit with him." The doctor turned away. "He's doing quite well, by the way. I think we can release him soon."

I cast one last look at Kendrick, who gave me a thumbs-up gesture, before following the doctor down the hall.

"No permanent damage," she said as she pulled back the curtain on one of the emergency room cubicles. "Which I'm sure is a relief."

"Oh yes, definitely," I said.

"Just be aware that he's a bit out of it. We gave him an injection for the pain." The doctor grabbed a few slips of paper from the counter and pressed them into my palm. "But that will only last until morning. You'll have to pick up some prescriptions for him as soon as you can. One for antibiotics and one for pain pills. The pain might be bad for a few days, I'm afraid."

"Okay." I tucked the papers into my pocket.

"I'll leave you now. A nurse will be in shortly with some information about ongoing care and his discharge papers," the doctor said before disappearing through the curtain.

I approached Richard, who was lying on a narrow bed, staring up at the ceiling with his eyes half-closed. "I understand that you may be somewhat loopy. Which explains the strange fiancée comment, I suppose." I laid my fingers over his right hand.

Richard's fingers clutched mine. "It's not strange, not at all," he replied in a dreamy tone. His dark eyelashes fluttered, and he opened his eyes to look directly at me. "Bound to happen, eventually."

"Is it?" I took a seat on the hard metal stool pulled up next to the bed.

"Hope so," he murmured.

"Hmmm . . . well, how about for now we just say it was a clever ploy to allow me to stay with you?"

He blinked his gray eyes. "That too."

I caressed his fingers. "Are you feeling better?"

"Yeah, but it's the drugs, I think. So spacey. Can't focus."

"No need to right now. I'll drive you home once they release you and put you to bed."

"And stay with me?"

"Of course."

"Good." Richard pulled our clasped hands up to his lips and kissed my fingers. "Love you. So glad you're safe."

I sniffed back a sudden urge to blubber uncontrollably. He was the one who'd been shot, yet he was more concerned about me than his own injury.

"I love you too," I said, releasing his hand as I leaned in to kiss his forehead.

He threw his good arm around me and pulled me close.

"Good," he said. "That feels good."

Resting my cheek against his, I didn't reply. Because he was right, of course. After everything that had happened, this finally felt like something good.

Chapter
Twenty-Seven

After a week passed, Aunt Lydia finally felt up to inviting a few people over for Sunday dinner. The guest list included Zelda, Walt, Brad, Sunny, Richard, and—to my surprise—Kurt Kendrick.

"Don't say anything," she told me as we tag-teamed cleaning the house in preparation for this event.

So I didn't, although I'm sure my grin was enough evidence of my opinion on the subject.

We served the full Taylorsford feast—baked brown-sugar-coated ham with scalloped potatoes and green beans alongside grilled salmon for those who didn't eat pork, and even a vegetarian dish to please Sunny. Of course, those were only the main dishes. Aunt Lydia also provided a tossed salad, several varieties of pickles, homemade yeast rolls, and a fruit compote. Because heaven forbid anyone leave my aunt's table hungry. There were few sins worse in a town with Taylorsford's rural traditions. As Aunt Lydia often said—back in the day, local farm families might not have had two pennies to rub together, but they always had food. And they were always happy to share it.

"So who wants pie?" Aunt Lydia asked as our guests pushed back their chairs from the table after the meal.

"Oh goodness, I've already eaten so much I just might pop." Zelda fanned her flushed face with her napkin and cast my aunt a wide-eyed look. "What kind of pie?"

"Apple, of course." Aunt Lydia dropped her napkin beside her plate.

"And lemon meringue. And pecan," I said as I stood up. "Stay seated, Aunt Lydia. You made most of the food. I can certainly cut the pies and bring a selection to the table."

Richard jumped to his feet. "I'll help. I need to move around after that meal anyway."

"Make some coffee too, would you?" Aunt Lydia looked around the table. "Unless anyone prefers tea? Or more wine?"

"I think perhaps that bottle of brandy I brought would go well with coffee and pie." Kendrick stood and tucked his chair under the table. "And seeing that Richard's arm will limit him from lifting too much, why don't I help with carrying in the glasses and plates."

"Very kind of you." Aunt Lydia toyed with her napkin instead of making eye contact with him.

"Not at all." Kendrick paused in the doorway to survey the assembled guests, blocking Richard and me from leaving the room. "It's been such a pleasure to spend time with you all."

"If you need more help, just let us know," Zelda called out. "Although I'm not sure I can lift myself from this chair just yet."

Walt patted her hand. "I'd help you, dear, but it looks like Amy and the others have it under control."

"Seems like it," Brad said, turning his chair sideways so he could stretch out his legs. "I certainly appreciate the meal, Lydia. Don't tell my mom this, but your rolls are even better than hers."

Sunny giggled and waved her forefinger at him. "Ooooo, now there's some good blackmail. Better than your mom's, indeed. Boy would Jane be pissed if she heard that. You know that she and Lydia have been fierce competitors at county fair food contests for years."

Aunt Lydia made a tutting noise, but Zelda said, "It's true," with a knowing look at Walt.

"Yes, that's some dangerous information to share so openly, son," Walt said.

"It's a veritable grenade. One word to your mom about such a thing and boom!" Sunny grinned broadly as she leaned in to tap Brad's chest. "So now all I have to do is hold that little tidbit of info over your head and I can make you do whatever I want."

"It doesn't take blackmail for you to be able to do that," Brad said, with no trace of rancor in his tone.

Walt smiled and draped his sinewy arm around Zelda's plump shoulders. "I'm sure that's the truth."

"Oh man, is it," said Brad with a rueful grin.

"On that note, I think it's time for pie," Richard said.

As Aunt Lydia and Zelda joined in on Sunny's merry peals of laughter, I followed Richard and Kendrick to the kitchen.

"That young lady is quite something." Kendrick looked over at me and winked as he lifted a bottle of Courvoisier from the counter. "Almost as dynamic as you, my dear."

"Oh"—I waved a knife at him, scattering a few crust crumbs—"Sunny is much more vivacious than I am. More prone to get into trouble, too."

Richard, who was standing beside me at the kitchen table,

removed the plastic wrap covering the pecan pie before looking up at Kendrick with a grin. "Opinions differ on that point."

"Hey." I pointed the knife at him. "No comments from the peanut gallery."

Richard just grinned and continued unwrapping the pies. "I guess Lydia wants to use the china rather than paper plates?"

"Paper plates?" I said in a mock tone of horror. "The very idea."

Kendrick uncorked the brandy and set the bottle on a decorative metal tray. "I'm surprised Dr. Chen isn't here today," he said, crossing to the wine rack. "I hadn't heard that he'd left town."

"No, not until tomorrow." I crossed to the counter that held the coffee maker as Kendrick lifted some glasses from the rack. Apparently his spies were still reporting all the comings and goings in town.

"Pity that he has to leave so soon." Kendrick met my speculative gaze with a smile. "If my eyes weren't deceiving me, I believe he took quite a liking to your aunt."

"He did, and she likes him back. Which is great," I said, as I started the coffee.

"I agree, but with him leaving . . ."

"Yeah, but he lives in Maryland, near DC, which isn't that far away. I have a suspicion that he'll be a frequent visitor in the future. And Aunt Lydia can catch the Metro into DC without that much trouble."

"Hugh's a pretty determined guy," Richard observed as he deftly wielded a pie server to slide slices onto plates. "I have a feeling he'll make things work, one way or the other."

"I'm just surprised he's not here today," Kendrick said. "I thought his work on the forgeries was done."

"It is, but he wanted to check one more thing . . ."

"The fake Van Gogh you found?"

"Yeah." I wasn't keen about telling Kendrick too much concerning my uncle's painting. Forgery or not, it still involved something that belonged to my aunt.

Richard apparently had no such qualms. "It was the most amazing thing—Hugh found a hair embedded in the paint." He waved a handful of dessert forks through the air before setting them on the table. "So he took that sample and some strands from an old hairbrush that had belonged to Andrew and had a DNA analysis done. Just to prove beyond a shadow of a doubt that Andrew painted that particular forgery."

"What did he find out?"

I eyed Kendrick, not thrown off by his casual tone. Judging by the intensity of his gaze, he was extremely interested in this information.

"Nothing yet. Still waiting for the results." Richard helped me load a tray with the filled plates. "Think that's enough pie?"

"If it isn't, we can always come back for more. We'll have to get the coffee anyway." I surveyed the full tray while Richard placed forks caty-corner across each plate. "Anyway, that's partially why Hugh went into work today at his temporary lab. He was also going to oversee the packing up of some equipment, but he hoped he could check on those DNA results and also do some type of ultraviolet light test on Andrew's painting."

"Probably UVF," Kendrick said. "Ultraviolet photography to display fluorescence," he added when Richard raised his eyebrows at the acronym. "Authentication experts use it to date paintings as well as to show if works have been retouched. Varnishes and paints can fluoresce quite differently depending on their age or composition."

"So a forgery could be spotted because the pigment or the varnish is shown to be too recent, even if the artist has been clever about aging their materials to look like they're a match with the original work's time period?"

"Yes. It's all quite scientific. Forgers can acquire paints and canvas from the proper time period, of course, especially if they have an organization like the Quinns backing them. But a detailed analysis can still prove that the work is not as old as it appears."

"It's strange that a lot of collectors don't seem to bother with that, if what I've read about the number of fakes floating about the marketplace is true," I said. "You'd think you'd want to know for sure that something is genuine before you shelled out millions for it."

Kendrick shrugged. "Some people just need to believe. They want that piece by Monet, even if they aren't entirely certain he painted it. But if they can tell their friends it's real . . ."

"In other words, they want to be fooled." Richard wiped his fingers with a paper napkin as he gazed thoughtfully at the art dealer. "They prefer the illusion to reality."

"Yes, and it's something many exploit, I'm afraid."

"You as well?" I asked, wiping my sticky fingers with a damp dish towel.

"From time to time." Kendrick lifted the tray holding the brandy and glasses. "As I've told you before, Amy, my hands are not completely clean. But then, I've never claimed to be a Boy Scout."

"You assisted the feds with their investigation into the Quinns. That counts for something." Richard grabbed a pile of napkins in his good hand as I picked up the tray with the pie slices. "Hugh told us that Interpol busted several of the leaders and now they think they have enough to bring down the entire organization. You helped with that."

"For my own reasons. Trust me, if I could've gotten my hands on any original Van Gogh paintings, I would never have surrendered them to the authorities. Not even if it did help dismantle the Quinns' operation." Kendrick moved toward the hall. "Now let's carry this in to the other guests, shall we? I'm looking forward to a piece of pie myself."

As Richard and I followed him to the dining room, the doorbell rang.

"I'll get that," Richard said, dropping the napkins onto a clear corner of my tray. "Might not be able to carry trays yet, but I can open a door." He bounded down the hall as Kendrick and I entered the dining room.

Oohs and *ahs* erupted over the pie slices, which did look quite delectable. I'd made the pecan pie but allowed everyone to assume that Aunt Lydia had done all the baking. It was only fair. She had cooked most of the meal.

But she was having none of that. "Don't just thank me; Amy made the pecan pie," she announced. Looking toward the hall, she narrowed her eyes as I passed the tray to Walt. "Did I hear the doorbell?"

"Yeah, Richard went to get it."

"I wonder who that could be," she murmured, but her question was immediately answered when Hugh appeared, followed by Richard.

"Sorry, Lydia, I forgot my key," Hugh said. "It's up in the bedroom. Come to think of it, I suppose I should just leave it there on the dresser, since I'm leaving tomorrow."

"We can discuss that later," my aunt said, which spurred Zelda to share a knowing look with Walt. "But what do you have there? Is that my painting?"

Hugh held up the cylindrical black leather case. "I'm afraid not. That is to say, it is the painting you had me examine. But it is no longer yours."

Aunt Lydia rose to her feet. "What do you mean?"

"The truth is, I cannot return it to you." Hugh crossed to my aunt and shifted her plate and silverware so he could place the case on the table. "It appears that we were quite mistaken about this painting, and perhaps your husband as well. May I?" He motioned toward the other dinnerware cluttering the area. When Aunt Lydia nodded, he began collecting the plates and utensils on that side of the table.

"Here, let me help with that," I said, moving to his side. I carried the stacked items to the other side of the table while Richard picked up a few glasses and set them on the sideboard.

"I wanted all of you to see this one more time," Hugh said as he rolled back a section of the tablecloth.

Aunt Lydia tapped her foot against the hardwood floor. "You're being very mysterious, Hugh."

"I just feel that something like this deserves a little ceremony. It's a great surprise." Hugh slid a cylinder of canvas from the leather case and unrolled it across the cleared area of the table.

As Hugh's fingers gently slid over the forged copy of *The Lovers: The Poet's Garden IV*, I marveled again at my uncle's skill.

309

If I didn't know better, I would have sworn that Van Gogh had painted this work.

"Please"—Hugh motioned for everyone to move around to his side of the table—"come and look at this. Because it is the last time you will see it up close."

I slid closer to Richard as Sunny, Brad, Walt, and Zelda clustered behind Hugh.

Aunt Lydia stood shoulder to shoulder with Hugh as she leaned in to peer at the painting. "I know it's a forgery, but I'd still like to have it back."

"But that's just it," Hugh said, meeting her determined gaze with excitement dancing in his brown eyes. "This is not a forgery. This is the original."

"What?" My aunt stepped back, almost tripping over Walt's toes. He thrust out a hand to steady her as she wobbled slightly. "Are you sure?"

"Yes. The DNA results did not match Andrew, but they did correlate with information on file about Van Gogh. And the UVF analysis and other tests proved the painting authentic without a doubt."

"Well I'll be damned." Kurt Kendrick leaned over the table from the other side and stared at the unrolled canvas. "Andrew, you sly fox."

"He switched them," I said, with a swift glance up into Richard's amazed face. "He decided not to give Mel the original after all."

"He switched them," repeated my aunt.

As I glanced over at her, she lifted her chin and squared her shoulders and met Kendrick's delighted gaze with a smile.

"You see, he was more like the man you thought him to be

than a scoundrel, in the end," the art dealer said. "He must've had second thoughts about handing over such a masterpiece to those who only meant to exploit it, and him."

"Yes, I suppose when it came to actually relinquishing a work like this to thieves, he couldn't do it," Aunt Lydia said. "And he was willing to face their wrath if they discovered his subterfuge."

"Although from what I've heard, that might've put you in jeopardy too," Zelda said, her normally bright voice subdued.

"Perhaps. I think he would have talked it over with me, had he lived. There was that other original painting that Mel mentioned. I wonder what became of that?"

"We only have her word that it even existed," Kendrick said, uncorking the brandy. "And you know what that's worth. Maybe she simply said that to throw Trey off track. She probably took it back from Andrew before he even had time to paint a copy. I can imagine her reconsidering and deciding to sell it without having to share any profits with anyone else."

"That's possible, I suppose." Aunt Lydia gazed down at the Van Gogh once more before pressing two fingers against the back of Hugh's hand. "You'd better roll that up and store it away. I assume you plan to hand it over to the authorities?"

"Yes, although they've agreed to allow the National Gallery to take charge of it while all the ownership details are ironed out." Hugh slid the rolled canvas back into the protective leather case.

"So Andrew had it all the time." Kendrick shook his head. "That was one thing he never told me."

"Or me." My aunt leaned into Hugh.

The art expert held the case against his chest as he placed his other arm around her shoulders. "He was probably trying to protect you, Lydia. Hoping to figure out a way to return the original painting without placing you in danger."

"All this time, it was here in the house." Aunt Lydia glanced over at me. "Where did you find it again, Amy?"

"In that closet with all his other stored works. He hid it behind one of his own canvases. You wouldn't have noticed it unless you happened to pick up that one painting," I said, tightening my lips as I considered the coincidence that had led me to that seascape.

Or perhaps, like some of the occurrences from the past summer, it hadn't been entirely a coincidence. Those other paintings tumbling over to reveal the one Uncle Andrew had hidden so long ago, as if a hand had pushed them aside . . . I swallowed before speaking again. "Maybe he planned to return it to a museum, or the Monuments Men, or something later. But then . . ."

"There was no later." Richard wrapped his good arm around my waist.

"I would like to think that was his plan," Aunt Lydia said. "So I shall."

Kendrick leaned forward and filled nine snifters with brandy. "Everyone, please take a glass."

When we were all holding the snifters, Kendrick lifted his high. "To Andrew," he said, his gaze fixed on Aunt Lydia.

"To Andrew!" we all called out in unison, before taking a drink.

Sunny sputtered after downing hers, and Brad had to pat her on the back, but Kendrick just smiled and held out his glass again. "Now I would like to propose something, and I hope Lydia will agree."

"What? That she turn over all of Andrew's paintings to you?"

"Not exactly." Kendrick studied me, his blue eyes very bright. "But I would like to borrow them for a special show. I will have everything framed, at my expense, and have them professionally hung in my home."

"A special gallery exhibit?" Aunt Lydia leaned her head against Hugh's shoulder. "I think Andrew would've liked that. So yes. I agree."

"Good. And I shall give an obnoxiously lavish party and invite the glitterati of the art world. Everything will be disgustingly ostentatious, just the way they like it. Of course, all of you will be my special guests. Including you, Dr. Chen, if you are free."

"I will make a point to clear my calendar for that," Hugh said.

"So Uncle Andrew will get his due at last." I leaned back against Richard's warm chest. "I think it's about time."

"Past time," Kendrick said. "But always better late than never. Now—more brandy, anyone?"

Sunny waved him off with her hand. "No more for me, thanks."

Brad shook his head. "And I have to drive her home, so I'll pass."

"Well"—Aunt Lydia lifted her head and held out her glass—"I don't have to go anywhere but bed, so hit me up again, Kurt."

I shot her a sly grin. "As long as you can make it up to your room."

She cast her gaze from Hugh to Richard and then Walt and Brad before settling on Kendrick's elderly but still vigorous figure. "I believe there are enough strong arms between the lot of you to manage to get me up the stairs and into my bed."

"Now that," Kendrick said, arching his bushy eyebrows as

he looked over the other men before settling his gaze on my aunt, "sounds like a very intriguing prospect."

Which just made Sunny and me smile, Brad blush, Richard and Walt grin, and Aunt Lydia and Zelda break into bright peals of laughter.

Chapter
Twenty-Eight

In the end, Kurt Kendrick scheduled his party for early December. He claimed it would take that long to properly frame and hang Andrew's paintings, and he wanted to make sure the most influential art critics, gallery owners, and collectors could attend.

"It *is* much better timing. At least for me," Richard said as we took a walk through the woods on the day of the party. "I have the flexibility and strength back in my arm now, so I can properly partner you. Kurt told me he hired a band and had his people clear the room to create a proper dance floor. We can waltz the night away."

I shivered as the December wind bit through my sweatshirt. I knew I should've worn a jacket, but when Richard had asked me to accompany him on a walk, I'd simply grabbed the first thing off the hall tree and thrown it on. "You can sashay around all you want. But you'll need a better partner. Maybe Aunt Lydia or Sunny can do justice to your moves, but I'm certainly not in your league."

"Nonsense. It's just social dancing. You follow my lead and you'll be fine."

I sniffed and shoved my windblown hair behind my ears. "Right. More like I'd break your foot and then you'd be out of commission again just when your arm has healed."

Richard narrowed his eyes. "I'm going to dance one waltz with you, come hell or high water."

I brushed at the shoulder of my sweatshirt, sweeping away a dried leaf that had finally lost its tenuous grip on an overhead branch. "Get out your waders then, because the water is going to rise quite high."

Richard laughed. "After a hell mouth yawns?"

"For sure." I shoved my hands into my pockets and kicked at a pile of dead leaves littering the path. "But seriously, I don't feel comfortable dancing with you. Not in public. I'm just so intimidated. You must know that."

Richard slipped his hand through my crooked elbow and pulled me closer to his side. "I know, but I don't quite understand. Everyone knows that dancing isn't your profession. They aren't going to judge you so harshly."

"Ha! You need to live in Taylorsford a bit longer before you can say that."

Richard took hold of my other arm as he turned to face me. "Now listen, sweetheart—I know the whole point of this party is to celebrate Andrew Talbot and perhaps get some of his paintings into the hands of collectors and dealers. I support that wholeheartedly, especially if it benefits Lydia and maybe even Kurt. But there's only one thing *I* want from this evening, and that's at least one dance with you."

I stared up into his handsome face, noting the brilliance of his clear gray eyes. He had that stubborn look that told me he wouldn't give up without a fight.

Like it matters a bit more than you think, Amy. Maybe it does. You always think of him as so self-assured, but remember what Adele Tourneau said . . .

"All right, maybe one." I stood on tiptoe to kiss his lips. "But only later in the evening, when everyone is a little plastered. They might not notice my clumsiness then."

He leaned in, causing me to drop back on my heels. "Foolish girl, they'll only see how beautiful you are." He tightened his arms around me and whispered in my ear, "Especially if you wear that red dress you had on in New York. Promise me you will."

"That's the plan," I said, before his lips slid to my mouth and we stopped talking for quite some time.

* * *

I couldn't restrain a gasp as we stepped into the front hall of Kurt Kendrick's beautiful home. In keeping with the house's historic status, he'd limited the decorations on the outside to simple wreaths in the windows and a garland around the front door, but he'd obviously thrown away such scruples inside.

"It's like walking into a snow globe," Richard said as we handed our coats to a young woman dressed in a classic black-and-white maid's outfit.

My gaze darted around the hall, taking in the transformation. The fresh garlands that hung from the wide white moldings were festooned with red berries and pinecones and dripping with tiny white lights. More greenery and crystals draped each archway, and every hall doorway was flanked by small pine trees in silver-and-white containers. Tiny white lights twinkled amid the shaped branches of the pines.

We slipped past a couple of tuxedo-clad waiters bearing trays

317

of hors d'oeuvres and champagne as we walked toward the end of the hall. Although a quick peek into the other rooms showed that the entire main floor had been given over to the party, I knew from Aunt Lydia that Kendrick had staged the display of Uncle Andrew's paintings in the living room.

"Must be where they've set up the dancing too," Richard said, as jazzy strains from some musical ensemble wafted through the open door.

I gasped again when we walked into the living room. The furniture and Oriental rugs had been removed to display a wide expanse of buffed hardwood floor. Clustered in groupings near the edges of the room, white linen-draped pedestal tables and emerald velvet chairs and sofas offered vantage points to admire the paintings that lined the walls.

Studying my uncle's paintings, I had to admit that the new museum-quality frames displayed them to their best advantage. Many of the guests appeared to agree as they paused in front of each work and chatted enthusiastically.

"Going to grab some drinks," Richard said, heading for one of the waiters.

I nodded and moved toward the closest landscape as if pulled to it by an invisible string. Studying it intently, I spoke silently to my long dead uncle. *They finally see it. They recognize your genius now. At last.* Immediately after this thought faded, I felt the back of my neck tingle and the hairs rise on my arms. Glancing to my right, I caught a flash of movement, as if a tall man wearing a loose white coat—*or a painter's smock, Amy*—had just walked into the crowd.

But that was just my fancy—the strange affinity I felt for artists when standing before their works. The half-glimpsed figure was simply someone from the crowd, moving away. Of course it was. I didn't believe in ghosts. My fingers automatically flew up to my gold hair comb but I pulled them back and hugged my arms to my chest. No, I didn't.

Breathing rapidly, I searched the perimeter of the room for Aunt Lydia, certain she'd be stationed in front of the paintings all evening. But I was wrong. When I finally caught sight of her, she was moving elegantly across the floor in the arms of a slender dark-haired man.

"Lydia and Hugh seem to be getting into the spirit of things," Richard said as he approached me with two crystal flutes bubbling with golden liquid. "It really is some party. And this room has been converted into quite a gallery," he added as he handed me a glass.

I took a sip of champagne before replying. "When Kurt said ostentatious, I guess he meant it." Glancing over at Richard appreciatively, I smoothed the bodice of my crimson silk dress with my free hand. "Good thing you wore your tux, but now I feel a bit underdressed. Maybe I should've worn a full-length gown or something."

Richard leaned in and kissed my shoulder. "I disagree. I prefer this. A longer dress would mean I couldn't appreciate those lovely legs of yours. Now drink up and let's imitate Lydia and Hugh and dance." He pointed at the small musical ensemble set up before the one wall that included windows. "I bet I could get them to play a waltz. We've practiced that once or twice."

"I told you, later," I said, chugging down the rest of my champagne. "No one's drunk enough yet for that, least of all me."

"There you are!" Sunny's merry voice rang out behind us.

Richard and I turned around to face her and shared a

raised-eyebrow glance after we took in her slinky turquoise satin gown. Her only ornament was a blue-and-white cameo fastened to a silver velvet choker, and she'd allowed her golden hair to fall loosely about her shoulders.

"Wow, you look spectacular," I said, as Richard made approving noises.

"Not so bad yourself. I like the hair ornament. Doesn't she look lovely, Brad?"

I touched the Art Nouveau gold-plated comb I'd used to sweep back a section of my dark hair. It had once belonged to my great-grandmother Rose. Although I'd inherited her looks and coloring and her jewelry flattered me, I'd only recently felt inclined to wear any of it.

Brad tugged at the lapel of his navy-blue suit. "Very nice," he said, shuffling his feet.

Poor thing, he looked as if he'd like to be anywhere else. "So I heard that Trey's trial's been set for next month and he was denied bail," I said, hoping shoptalk might ease some of Brad's obvious anxiety.

Brad straightened as his official mask slid into place. "Yes. And although Mel's still recovering, she's technically out on bail. But then, her charges weren't so severe."

Sunny sighed. "I guess we'll all be called to testify. Not something I'm looking forward to."

"Me either," I replied, grabbing another glass of champagne before the waiter could move away. Richard shot me a questioning look, but I just took a drink and then waved my glass at him. "Told you I had to be a bit tipsy before I'd attempt that waltz."

He grinned. "Okay. Just warn me if I'll need to carry you out."

"Have you seen Walt and Zelda?" I asked Sunny after scanning the crowd.

Sunny brushed her hair behind her bare shoulders. "They were in the dining room the last time I spied them. I think Zelda was trying to wheedle the recipe for the chocolate tarts from one of the caterers."

"Sounds about right," Richard said. "But what about the Quinn organization, Brad? Any more news on that?"

Brad toyed with his gold tie bar. "Not really. No details anyway. Of course, that's way above my pay grade. The feds and international authorities are dealing with it now."

"I'm sure we'll hear all about it eventually." Sunny rolled her eyes and tugged on Brad's arm. "Come on, enough work stuff. Let's dance."

He grunted but followed her out into the swirling crowd of dancers.

"Deep waters," Richard observed as he sipped his champagne and watched Brad lead Sunny in a very respectable foxtrot.

"He's always surprising me," I agreed as I noticed Richard tapping his foot in time to the music. "Listen, I must run to the ladies' room, so why don't you go and ask Aunt Lydia for a spin around the floor? Or even steal Sunny from Brad? I know you're itching to dance."

He looked down at me with a warm smile. "I wouldn't mind."

"Then go. Here, give me your glass and I'll drop it off on one of those tables they've set up in the hall."

Richard gave me his champagne flute and a kiss before dancing his way into the crowd. I watched him tap Hugh on the back and take Aunt Lydia into his arms before I left the room.

As I exited the bathroom at the end of the main hall, I noticed a light fixture flicker on at the top of the back stairs. Looking up, I spied Kurt Kendrick standing with his back against the balustrade. He appeared to be staring at a painting on the wall of the upper hall.

I squinted as I examined the painting. I couldn't make out any details, but something about the frame sparked a memory.

Climbing the stairs, I kept my gaze focused on the painting. There was something so familiar about it . . .

I gripped the handrail and swayed for a second before taking another step. *That frame—doesn't it match the one on Uncle Andrew's missing still life?*

Except that this frame was dark wood, not gold. I sprinted up the remainder of the stairs to reach Kendrick's side.

"Hello, Amy," he said without looking at me. "Beautiful, isn't it?"

I stared at the painting for a moment, noticing a few flecks of gold paint still clinging to one of the deeper grooves in the frame. Then my eyes focused on the canvas itself and I gasped and grabbed the arm of Kendrick's white tuxedo jacket.

"It's another lost Van Gogh," I said in a whisper.

"Yes. Hidden under one of Andrew's canvases. I guessed that something else was in that frame when I held it at the library and remembered a visit Andrew had made to my Georgetown gallery not long before he died. Neither one of us ended up totally sober that evening, so at the time I dismissed his ramblings. But later, when I found out about the forgeries, I remembered him blurting out something about hiding two paintings that were worth a fortune." Kendrick covered my hand with his gnarled fingers. "I didn't know one was this painting, of course, but I was sure he'd hidden something valuable, especially after recalling he'd also babbled about the possibility of making money off of forgery."

"So you took it." I stared at the image of a man in a straw hat striding down a golden-yellow path with two trees in the background. *The Painter on His Way to Tarascon*, which had been stored in some German salt mine for protection during the war but lost in 1945. I shot a sharp glance up at Kendrick from beneath my lowered lashes. "You stole it."

"I did." There wasn't an ounce of remorse in his smooth voice.

"How?"

He stroked the frame with his thumb. "I simply shoved a small folded handkerchief in the library's back door so that the lock didn't quite catch. Then, when you'd gone back out front, I reentered the building, and when your volunteer left the desk to help some patrons, I took it. Easy as pie," he added with a grin. "Although pie really isn't that easy to make, is it?"

"Why?"

"Because I wanted it, of course." Kendrick released my arm and turned to face me. "Never fear—I didn't trash Andrew's painting. It's been carefully preserved and reframed and now hangs in my bedroom."

"You can't just keep this," I said, waving my hand at the lost masterpiece. "It isn't yours."

"It is now."

"But . . ." I met Kendrick's unflinching, icy, gaze. "I don't see how you think you can get away with this."

"It won't be hard. The world believes this work is lost forever, and I will allow everyone to continue to think so. Oh, perhaps some expert may see it one day and question me, but I can always claim it is a forgery created by my dear, departed friend Andrew

Talbot, and I doubt they will press me further. And perhaps"—
he lifted his broad shoulders and dropped them again—"someday
I will change my mind and return it to the world, claiming it
mysteriously turned up in a collection of paintings I discovered
in some dusty Parisian garret. One never knows."

"You really are the most twisted individual."

"Am I?" Kendrick tilted his head and studied me with interest. "Now the question is—will Amy Webber keep my secret or
will she turn me over to the authorities?"

"I should."

"Of course."

We locked gazes. There was something in his eyes—a flicker
of despair that caught me off guard. "Why do you want this one
painting so much? Because it's a Van Gogh?"

"My dear, I own other Van Goghs." Kendrick looked away,
staring back at the painting. "No, that isn't the reason. The thing
is, I know that Andrew looked at this painting. Studied it. Held
it. So when I stand here and gaze at it, it's like . . ."

"He's standing beside you," I said softly.

Kendrick simply bowed his head.

I touched his arm. "You really did love him."

"I still do," he said, touching the edge of the frame with his
fingertips.

Footsteps on the stairs made us both turn.

"There you are," Richard said, pausing at the top of the staircase. "I've been looking all over for you. Oh hello, Kurt. Everything okay?"

"Just fine," Kendrick said, shooting me a significant look. "I
think."

"Yes, everything's good," I replied, catching Kendrick's eye and giving him a little smile before I turned to Richard. "We were just chatting about our love of . . . art."

"Sounds great, but you still owe me that dance." Richard held up his hand.

I walked over to him and clasped his outstretched fingers. "I said later."

Richard grinned and pulled me close. "I must say, Kurt, you certainly have surrounded yourself with masterpieces. And I'm including Andrew Talbot's paintings in that comment."

"As you should," Kendrick replied, his brilliant blue eyes fixed on me. "But I think you possess the most priceless object in this house."

Richard, following the older man's gaze, grinned and tightened his hold on me. "I agree, but I would never claim that I possess her. She has chosen to be with me of her own free will, which is the way I want it. I don't want to own her—I just want to share my life with her. As long as she'll let me," he added, lifting one of my hands to his lips.

I pulled my hand free and flung my arms around his neck and kissed him with all the passion that had welled up in me. "So that's forever, then?" I asked when I pulled away.

His gray eyes sparkled with delight. "If you wish." He glanced over my shoulder at Kendrick. "Now if you will excuse us, we have a date with a waltz. Right, Amy?"

"Right." I clutched his hand, casting a smile over my shoulder as we made our way down the stairs.

Kurt Kendrick didn't see my smile. He was gazing back at the Van Gogh. His treasure. A rare thing, once thought lost forever.

Now found, perhaps, I thought, as Richard and I weaved

through the crowd at the edge of the living room and walked onto the dance floor.

Richard swept me into his arms as the last note of a jazz riff faded away and the strains of a waltz mysteriously materialized.

And we danced.

Acknowledgments

Once again, I must offer thanks where thanks are most certainly due:

To my amazing and dedicated agent at Literary Counsel, Frances Black. I'm grateful that I have her as a partner on my writing journey.

To my talented editor, Faith Black Ross, with great appreciation for her skill and support.

To everyone at Crooked Lane Books who helped to bring this book into being, including those who ensure that the world knows of its existence.

To my always understanding (and talented) critique partners, Lindsey Duga and Richard Taylor Pearson. (Look them up! Read their books!)

To my wonderful husband, Kevin Weavil, who puts up with my long writerly "absences" from his life with such grace.

To my lovely family and friends. I am thankful for the blessing of your presence in my life.

And finally, to the author community—those I know and those I don't (yet), in real life and online. Thank you so much for making the world a better place, one story at a time.